'LUCKY' MONTANA

Sean Rafferty wanted money to buy back the ruins of his family's estate in Ireland. He didn't care how he got that money or how many lives he ruined in the process . . . A man called 'Lucky' Montana found that fate threw him into the deal. With a bounty hunter already stalking him, Montana now had to contend with Rafferty's murderous crew as well . . . Now he must stride into battle, knowing that there is always a bullet waiting for him.

Books by Clayton Nash
in the Linford Western Library:

DAKOTA WOLF
LONG-RIDING MAN
THE MUSTANG STRIP
BRAZOS STATION
DIE LIKE A MAN
MISSOURI AVENGER
KILLER INSTINCT
MAN FROM BLOOD CREEK
RUN FOR THE MONEY

CLAYTON NASH

'LUCKY' MONTANA

Complete and Unabridged

LINFORD
Leicester

First published in Great Britain in 2005 by
Robert Hale Limited
London

First Linford Edition
published 2006
by arrangement with
Robert Hale Limited
London

British Library CIP Data

Nash, Clayton
'Lucky' Montana.—Large print ed.—
Linford western library
1. Western stories
2. Large type books
I. Title
823.9′14 [F]

ISBN 1–84617–355–8

Published by
F. A. Thorpe (Publishing)
Anstey, Leicestershire

Set by Words & Graphics Ltd.
Anstey, Leicestershire
Printed and bound in Great Britain by
T. J. International Ltd., Padstow, Cornwall

This book is printed on acid-free paper

1

All Kinds of Luck

He had often thought that the fool who had tagged him with the nickname of 'Lucky' — a tinhorn named Cash O'Brien — ought to be damn well shot.

This was another of those times.

O'Brien hadn't been shot but someone had slipped a knife between his ribs in a steamy rat-hole of a southern prison. That day he had almost wept — not because O'Brien had died, but because he hadn't been the one to send him to that big Poker Game in the sky.

Now none of it mattered.

'Lucky' was once again about to be proved a misnomer . . .

He could hear them on the stairs, coming up like treacle leaking from a cracked jug. There had been a muffled thud on the balcony outside the room, too. He swore softly: he had come in here too damn fast after he had recognized Dawson down on Main, picked the wrong room. The room he really wanted was next door. It had a balcony, but a short private one, separate to the long one that ran alongside the north-eastern wall of the hotel. Now it was too late to change.

Or was it?

If he stayed here he was a goner. They'd get him in a crossfire, blasting in the door while others poured hot lead in from the balcony window. *OK!*

That left only one thing to do: make a run for the room next door and hope like hell it wasn't occupied.

But first he had to get out of his door and make a run along the hallway to the room he wanted. He had noticed earlier it was entirely separate to this part of the hallway, the door a little more ornate, twenty feet away at least.

Jesus, it might be a suite of rooms, full of people!

Only one way to find out, and

without hesitation he unshipped his six-gun, took the spare from his warbag — he'd have to abandon that — and went to the door. An ear against the cold wood of the panel told him they were halfway up the stairs already — he had taken note of that creaky step when he had arrived. So he couldn't delay any longer.

And he didn't.

He wrenched open the door and went out shooting, left-hand gun blazing for the wild shots that would scatter the armed men on the stairs — *he hoped!* — keeping the right-hand Colt for the more serious business of bringing down the most dangerous of the posse.

His gunfire caused chaos on the stairs. Bullets whistled and splintered the wall and banister rails. Men yelled, the foremost trying to turn back, running into those behind who were still swarming upwards. There was a tangle and much cussing, a couple of men slipping and others falling over them. One man tumbled over the rail and landed on the floor like a spread crucifix, his back obviously damaged.

A lanky man broke through the mess, stumbling as he walked over the writhing bodies of his companions as he brought up his Greener and loosed off a charge of double-o buckshot. It chewed a good portion out of the rails edging the landing as the fugitive made his crouching run down the hallway, left hand thrust behind, firing his last shots in that six-gun. He ducked, slipped, skidded on the polished linoleum. He travelled faster this way and was down low so that the second charge of buckshot punched a large ragged hole in the wall three feet above his head.

He rolled and lunged for the ornate doorway, turning his left shoulder into the carved panel. The door trembled, but held, shrugged off his efforts. He sucked in a ragged breath as he found his balance and placed a boot violently over the lock area. Wood splintered and the nicely polished brass plate buckled as it tore out of the woodwork.

He was moving in a stumbling run when he entered, heard someone scream and glimpsed four people standing wide-eyed by a candle-lit table obviously set for supper, half-eaten food on the hotel's best plates.

Damn! It was a suite of rooms!

But the well-dressed, well-fed folk were too stunned or afraid to make any kind of a move to stop him. There were roars of vengeance out in the passage, the thud of booted feet coming. He rammed his empty gun into his belt, waved the other Colt vaguely at the group, then scooped up an occasional table that held a tall vase of flowers and decorative prairie grass. But not for long. It toppled and shattered and by that time he was moving like a log in a waterslide, table lowered at the french doors with their drawn drapes.

They yielded to the power of his charge, the table almost jarring from his grip as it smashed the doors open, glass tinkling. He had time to groan once when he saw he was on the small balcony but then he hit the rail and the table splintered in his hand.

So did the rail.

His yell made a brief fading wail as he sailed out into the night high above Main and its traffic of wagons and riders and people.

But it was only a fleeting glimpse as he dropped like a stone off a cliff. Something high and black and looking as solid as a mountain rushed to meet him and he thought, *Lucky? Hell, I wish I'd killed that son of a . . .*

He hit. It was hard, but not as hard as he expected. Breath slammed from his lungs and every bone and joint in him jarred agonizingly. He tasted salt and his eyes stung, there was a crackling of something — and then he *bounced*!

His yell was tremulous as his body lifted a couple of feet in the air and he was flung, tumbling, down the high side of a slab-bodied wagon and a foul stench filled his nostrils, constricted his throat. Even as he floundered onto the muddy street he realized he had fallen onto a buffalo-runner's hide wagon. It was packed with tightly rolled, salted hides with a couple of unsalted, partly fleshed skins on top to keep off the dirt and the frost that had laid a thin layer of ice on them.

That had made the crackling sound as he hit. Then he splashed into the mud again and lost some more breath that he couldn't afford, skidding and rolling. A couple of riders flanking the wagon cursed him and hauled their mounts aside. He ploughed through the slush, found he was sliding between the wheels of a second wagon, ducked his head and slid on through. By that time he had some kind of control and managed to slow, slew around on his belly, spitting mud, gagging.

Blinking his vision clear, he coughed up some muck and thrust to hands and knees, surprised to find he still held his six-gun.

'Man, you got the luck of the devil

hisself!' opined a rider, hauling rein and leaning from the saddle to offer his hand.

Then there were shouts from the hotel balcony, men calling for riders and wagon drivers to clear the street, to get the hell out of the way. Someone fired into the air to give weight to the warning and the fugitive took the hand of the helpful rider, hauled to his feet — and promptly yanked the man out of the saddle.

The cowboy yelled and splashed into the mud.

Guns hammered above as the armed men saw what their quarry was about. Men scattered, drivers tried to whip their ponderous wagons out of the way, a woman screamed, horses whinnied and whirled and reared, cannoned into one another.

Through the middle of all this unscheduled entertainment on Main, the lucky fugitive lay along the neck of his newly acquired mount and spurred into the cold night.

Lucky? Hell, maybe Cash O'Brien knew what he was talking about after all.

* * *

They got him on the very first day of spring, riding casually into a town called Murphy Creek at the base of the Rockies where they spurred eastward south of Cheyenne.

He was heading south, going to meet the warmer weather, his bones still aching from the long winter up north. Strangely enough, he was still riding the horse he had taken off the helpful cowboy back in Rapid City in the Black Hills of Dakota.

It was a good, range-bred smoke with a distinctive dark, saddle-patch under the left eye. He had rubbed light-coloured clay into this often, gradually covering it, although a shadow was still noticeable. *Just in case . . .*

And the thing was, this keen-eyed lawman just stopping over in Murphy

Creek after checking out a bunch of rustlers to the west, spotted the damn horse! Turned out he was a range detective, employed by a Cattlemen's Association in Casper, Wyoming, on his way home, decided to visit with his son and his family in Murphy before heading west.

And he had been in the livery, passing the time of day with the liveryman, who turned out to be the detective's son. As the smoke had been backed into a stall and unsaddled, the lawman sauntered in, leaned a shoulder against a post and lit his pipe, which he smoked left-handed. He gestured to the horse's head with the charred bowl.

'Fine-looking bronc — don't see many like him this far north.'

He earned a grunt from the rider as he swung the saddle across the stall partition. The man's son, apparently recognizing something in his father's voice, paused as he made to move away, casually picked a long-handled pitch-fork off the wall — and waited.

'What happened to his eye?'

'Nothing . . . that's just dirt. I'll get rid of it when I curry-comb him.'

The newcomer frowned as the lawman — he suspected he was *some* kind of sticky-nosed law — walked slowly around the smoke, gentling it with a lightly placed hand, pipe now clenched between his teeth.

'This here hoss belongs to the Casper Creek Cattlemen's Association that I work for. Name's Enright. I got a list of riders that work for 'em. Now, your name'd be . . . ?'

What was the use? His luck had held all through winter. Well, almost. There was that second run-in with Dawson but that could yet turn out to be good luck. Still, it was time for it to run bad again and he was too damn weary and hungry to care.

'I bought this gelding up in Dakota.'

'Rapid City by any chance?'

The son of a bitch knew! His luck had turned all right, turned right around and spat in his eye!

'No — Deadwood.'

Enright smiled thinly. 'I think Rapid City. That's as far as I trailed a rustler I was chasin', feller name of Brady. Still ain't heard your name, son.'

'Montana,' the trapped rider said with a heavy sigh.

'Got a monicker to go with that?'

He hesitated, then, 'They call me 'Lucky' — God knows why!'

Enright and his son both grinned. 'Someone had a sense of humour!' allowed the son, chuckling.

'A real first name,' insisted the detective and Montana shrugged.

'Got lost somewhere in between 'Lucky' and 'Montana', long time ago . . .'

'Uh-huh. Well, I reckon I could find a dodger out on you, all right. But don't matter really — I got you for hoss-stealin' and the Association'll want a piece of your hide.'

He protested, of course, got nowhere, not with the twin, shiny tines of a pitchfork up against his chest and

Enright's Colt pressed into his side as the man lifted his gun from his holster and rammed it into his own belt. The range detective was a hickory-lean man of about fifty, weathered and grey-haired with a close-clipped moustache framing his thin lips. He had a satisfied look about him, a man used to success, and Montana's heart sank.

'Another one to chalk up for you, Pa,' said the liveryman. 'You must be sockin' away a decent pile of cash with all them bonuses the Association pay you.'

'Retire in two more years — I'll go into partnership with you and we'll have the best livery-cum-black-smith's-and-saddlery this side of the Rockies.'

The son's eyes gleamed: obviously this was one of his dreams.

'Lucky' Montana didn't give a spit in hell. All he knew he was caught, *manacled*, and headed in a direction he didn't want to go — back into Wyoming.

* * *

There was no chance of escape from Enright. Montana knew of the man's reputation. He'd never seen the man before but just mention the name and most folk this far north knew who you were talking about. A relentless man who ran down his prey until he either brought him in or shot it out and carried just the ears back to his Association bosses.

The detective got the notion into his head that Montana was a member of this highly organized rustler gang he had been pursuing. So he treated him mighty roughly, actually beat him once. Then took it into his head that other members of the gang might try to bust Montana loose.

'You're crazy! I'm not a member of any gang! I'm a loner, a drifter, just heading south for some warmth and a riding job with any ranch that'll have me.'

'Wrong — you're headin' west, and the only ridin' you'll be doin' is through the air at the end of a rope with a hangman's noose under your left ear — after I collect my bounty on you.'

'Like I said, plumb loco!'

That earned him a kidney punch and Enright made arrangements for their passage on a nine-car freight headed in the direction of Casper.

It was a long, slow climb over the range and Montana had no sooner had the idle thought that the loco was going slow enough for anyone who felt like it to step on board and shove a gun in the engineer's face than the whole train suddenly shuddered to a halt, cars banging and clanging on the couplings, transferring the sudden cessation of movement clear down to the caboose where Enright and his prisoner travelled.

The train guard leaned far out, holding to a brass rail, looking along the still shuddering line of cars to where the locomotive had stopped, steam hissing, but not loud enough to drown the sound of gunshots from up there.

'Judas priest! It's a goddamn hold-up!' exclaimed the guard, pale-faced as he hauled himself back into the caboose.

Enright had his gun out, glanced from Montana to the guard. 'You carryin' . . . ?'

The guard swallowed, looked uneasy, then nodded. 'Payroll for the mines — but no one coulda known! It's been — '

Enright rounded on Montana, prodded him hard with the six-gun in the ribs, causing the prisoner to double up. 'Not a member of any gang, huh! They dunno about the payroll, but they know about *you*!'

'No one knows about me,' Montana gritted, his ribs sore. 'Because I'm a loner — I told you . . . '

By then Enright had his shirt collar bunched up and he dragged the prisoner past the frightened guard who was trying to unlock a chained shotgun on the wall. Montana staggered out onto the platform and started to yell as he was pushed violently over the rail. It hit him at hip level and he jack-knifed and crashed to the cinders on the side away from the bandits who were making their way down to the caboose. *They knew about the payroll all right!*

But it would be no use pointing that out to Enright.

The detective was beside him now, dragging him to his feet, shoving him roughly through the brush. Behind, a shotgun roared and then six-guns crackled and Montana turned in time to see two men swarming into the caboose, another down on the ground with an arm blown off at the shoulder.

One of the robbers on the steps saw Enright shoving Montana into the brush and fired a couple of shots. The detective fired back and the man swayed, clutching his shoulder, and hurled himself into the caboose for cover.

Enright pushed and dragged the manacled Montana through the brush and suddenly they were on the edge of a cliff above a boiling green river, frothing white where it surged between and over rocks. Montana balked, almost falling, held by Enright.

'Christ! That must be seventy feet down!' He gasped as he turned to Enright. 'Now that you've managed to wound one of them, they'll come after us! Thanks a lot, you goddamned idiot!'

Enright hit him across the jaw with the gun barrel, whirled as guns cracked and bullets tore through the brush. Three men were coming, wearing bandannas over their lower faces, guns smoking in their hands. Enright swore and shook the dazed Montana.

'Your damn cronies! Well, let's see how 'lucky' you are — Lucky Montana!'

Then he grabbed the prisoner's arm and jumped into space, dragging a shouting Montana after him.

2

Who's Lucky?

Gavin Leach cut through the narrow draw he knew about, the one that would take him to the top of a ridge that looked out across the shallow basin that eventually became the Carnaby Desert. It was fierce and had claimed many lives, and was named after the first man to cross it and live — though Sergeant Carnaby hadn't lived for long, not even long enough to know they had named a geographical feature after him.

Leach wasn't sure what brought him up here to the ridge, only that it was a good place to sit and think — and wonder at the extremities of this wild country. A desert out there that would boil a man's brains in his skull. Yet, over his shoulder, beyond the brush-smeared ridge, lay the rich and green Viper River Valley.

He was supposed to be just riding line for Angie but it was not only boring, he didn't care for the chore because he was afraid he might run into some of Rafferty's men.

Gavin Leach was only just twenty and he was a comparative newcomer to the frontier lands. Angie Bancroft was his sister, his widowed sister, and when he had heard of her tragedy, the death of her husband, Walt, after losing her two children to the plague that had swept this part of the country, he ran away from the boarding-school in Denver and came to help her on the ranch.

She was a stubborn woman was Angie, and she refused to consider selling — even though Rafferty made a handsome offer — dug in her heels and said she aimed to make a go of the A-Bar-W spread, just as Walt had planned.

Gavin sensed there was something

more behind it but she didn't elaborate, in fact, berated him for quitting school.

'Walt and I worked hard to give you a chance at a good education, Gav,' she told him with that fire in her eye he had known all his life — she had reared him after their parents had died in a Comanche attack back in north-west Texas. 'You owe us something. You go back to school. I can manage here.'

'How?' he had flared, stung by her reaction to his sudden appearance: he'd had visions of being greeted like a hero. 'You've only got Link and old Horseshoe, and he's not even a good cook!'

'I'll manage.'

Gavin threw up his hands. 'Stubborn as always! Sis, I've learned all I want to — I can talk properly, know my manners, can quote from the Bible and do sums that'd make an ordinary man's head spin. But I'm just not an indoor type, not interested in living in a city or even a big town. I *like* it out here and I *want* to help you. And I'm going to.'

It didn't end there, of course. There

were plenty of arguments over the next couple of weeks. But one evening, after her usual visit to the little graveyard atop the low knoll facing north where Walt lay between Bessie and little Joel, she came to him with a softer look on her work-worn though mighty handsome face and placed a hand on his arm, gentle as a butterfly landing on a prairie flower. Her clear hazel eyes moved slowly across his face, which was slightly tight, expecting another argument.

'Gav, I appreciate you coming here. You're right, I guess. Walt and I wanted you to have an education and then for you to use it whatever way you wished. If helping me out is what you want to do — and that's something I admit I need — then it's OK with me.' She smiled. 'I'm kind of — desperate, see . . . ?'

There was a little more to it than that, more explanations, more hugs and so on — they embarrassed him some, but he endured them because it was now going his way and, anyhow, he really did want to help. He owed Angie plenty.

He'd been here three weeks now and he had to admit that it was becoming a bit boring. Still, he would stick it out. He knew she had little money, couldn't understand why she didn't take Rafferty's offer and move closer to civilization.

He knew *why* she wanted to stay on, but damned if he understood it, not when she was struggling so hard. Link was virtually useless, a ranny a bit older than Gavin but hard-muscled and tight-lipped. He resented Gavin's presence and Gavin figured Link might've had some notion of gradually moving in on Angie and taking over, making a nice little safe and profitable niche for himself with the widow woman.

Gavin had put paid to any such ideas: leastways, he thought he had. He found Link in the back of the barn one day, stretched out on a bale of hay, smoking.

'Ought to go outside if you're gonna

smoke. A spark's all it'll take to send this place up.'

Link turned his head slowly, his wedge-shaped face impassive, eyes hard as he deliberately drew in deep on his cigarette and flicked some ash off the end.

'Word of an expert, huh?'

'Word of a partner in A-Bar-W,' Gavin gritted.

Link sat up, eyes slitted so that he had an almost Oriental look for a few moments. 'That the way it's goin' to be, huh? Figured you were just here for a holiday.'

'You're the one taking the holiday, looks like to me. Now, why don't you put out that cigarette and get to mending that loft ladder before you stack the hay up there?'

Link stood, three inches taller than Gavin's five-ten, broader, gun-hung, a man of the West, facing this greenhorn just in from having his diapers changed at some sissy damn Eastern school. He dragged on the cigarette again

— jumped when Gavin slapped it from his hand, his fingertips making Link snap his head back as the nails stung his mouth. Gavin ground the cigarette into the floor with a boot, looking coldly at Link all the time.

'The ladder needs repairs — Angie told you to get it done, not lie around risking fire in the barn.'

There was a slight tremor in Gavin's voice but he kept his mouth shut tight and his gaze steady. Link gave him a raking look, a cold study, assessing the situation. It was plain Link wanted to smash a fist into Gavin's face and he was a little surprised that he didn't try.

Then Link's shoulders relaxed some and, still looking mighty dangerous — *deadly* was a better word — he nodded.

'OK. But you ain't gonna bother me none, greenhorn. You might think you're king of the dungheap, but maybe that'll change sooner than you think.' He picked up the broken loft ladder and stood it against the wall, seeing the two broken rungs, glanced over his shoulder at Gavin. 'You think about that . . . '

Gavin did and it bothered him because he couldn't figure out what Link meant. But he said nothing to Angie — she had enough to worry about, what with mounting bills and broken fences and stock wandering all over the range.

Now, looking out over the heat-shimmer of the basin, Gavin wondered why she was having so much trouble with the ranch. Not that there hadn't been trouble before Walt had died but it seemed to be getting worse, more of it, and . . .

He stood in the stirrups suddenly, squinting, holding a hand above his eyes to reduce the glare. He took his field-glasses from his saddle-bag and focused them on the blurred movement out there in the shimmer. Some animal, hurt, looked like, crawling and floundering.

'Judas priest! It's a man!'

He rammed the glasses back into the bags and lifted the reins, heels touching his chestnut's flanks. The horse didn't want to go down the slope, knowing what the desolate basin was like — hard on the hoofs, dust that scoured eyes and nostrils, worked irritatingly into the genital pouch, and parched the throat.

But it had been trained to obey and it did so and in ten minutes Gavin was kneeling beside the hurt man. He was a rawboned type, muscles hard and long and powerful. He had a big lump with a short gash in the middle of it on his left temple. Dried blood, caked with alkali and sand had trickled in snaky patterns across his high-cheekboned face. Gavin turned him onto his back and a moan escaped the cracked lips.

The man's shirt was ripped and Gavin saw the body bruises and raw scrapes. The left arm was purple from shoulder to mid-forearm with massive bruising. The corduroy trousers were torn, showing one cut and swollen knee.

'God knows what's happened to you, feller,' Gavin said, unscrewing the cap of his canteen and lifting the man's head. 'You look like a survivor from a buffalo stampede.'

Gavin splashed water over the man's face, washing it free of alkali and grit and dried blood. A swollen tongue licked at the tepid liquid as it trickled over his lips. He made soft, unintelligible sounds deep in his throat.

He opened his mouth and Gavin let a little water trickle in. 'Not too much all at once,' he said pushing away the battered hand that tried to hold the canteen against his mouth.

That was when Gavin noticed the bruising on the man's wide wrist. The skin was torn and raw and blue-black, encircling the wrist completely. When he looked, Gavin found the swollen left wrist was the same.

He sat back as the man coughed up a little of the water.

He might be a greenhorn, but he had worked part-time deputy for the sheriff in Denver one trail-drive season during his college vacation, and he recognized the marks of handcuffs when he saw them.

'Mister,' he murmured, 'just what the hell have you been up to?'

* * *

By the time he rode back to the ridge, the stranger had slipped from the horse twice before Gavin could grab him.

The youngster winced each time as the man sprawled limply, jarred by his impact with the ground, adding to his already extensive injuries.

Gavin stopped on a rock ledge that looked back towards the ranch and, if he turned left, to the north-west, he could see part of Rafferty's big spread, too. He lifted the inert stranger one more time, dragged him up to a patch of grass and stretched him out. He covered him with a blanket as the man was starting to shiver despite the heat of the day. *Shock*, Gavin guessed.

Leach decided to camp here overnight. Angie wouldn't be expecting him back, although he had planned to cut corners and return to the ranch house instead of following the A-Bar-W line completely. No, he would camp here, he had enough grub, and a warm jacket. The stranger could have his blankets. Then he would make a *travois* like the Indians who worked on the ranch one time before they'd sent him south to school and college, had taught him. Angie would take care of him: she knew about treating injured rannies way out here.

He built a shelter with piñon branches over the stranger, made his camp-fire near its entrance so the man could get some of the warmth, and cooked a meal.

Gavin smiled as he took a sip of the hot, aromatic coffee, allowed his mind to drift while he chewed on the tough beefsteak he had brought from the ranch. It was cooked indifferently but filled a man's belly and gave him strength. Angie's cold biscuits tasted fine after he fried them up in the meat's grease.

The stranger moved under the blanket, rolling his head, muttering. Once, just after Gavin had turned in and the stars were blazing in a moonless sky, he had sat up and said clearly, '*I've never been lucky at cards — nor anything else.*'

Then he fell back and snored for most of the hours for the rest of the night . . .

Gavin woke after sun-up, the glare stirring him, for he wasn't naturally an early riser. He rolled out of his blanket, emptied his bladder over the edge of the rock and stoked up his fire.

He had coffee bubbling in the battered trail pot when he heard a sound behind him. Thinking it was the stranger, maybe coming round, he turned casually . . .

Gavin tasted bile and his belly lurched as he saw three men standing to one side of the pine-bough shelter where the injured man still slept. They held rifles, not pointed at him — yet — but he knew they would be soon.

'You're camped on Rafferty land here, kid,' said the man who stood slightly forward of the other two. He was solid as a mesa, shirt stretched tightly across heavy shoulders, the carbine like a toy in his large hands. He had a moon face, thick-lipped, heavy-browed, with tight-set eyes of a blue that reminded Leach of ice on a mountain stream.

'I'm not — this is Bancroft land!' Gavin knew he protested too loudly and his voice wasn't as steady as he wanted but his heart was hammering and he hoped his knees wouldn't shake noticeably.

'Sure of that, are you?' asked the big man. Gavin had never seen him before but he knew from Angie's description that he must be Claiborne, Rafferty's hardcase ramrod. The other two were Rafferty riders, McColl and Lindsey: he'd seen them in town once or twice and Angie had pointed them out to him.

'Yes — I'm sure!'

Claiborne smiled thinly, squinting. 'You'd be Angie's kid brother, huh? Come to protect her, I hear.'

Gavin swallowed, eyes flicking to where his own rifle rested beside his scattered bedroll, half-covered by the canvas outer layer.

'I-I came to lend my assistance on the ranch after Walt died. I — didn't expect she might need — protecting.'

Claiborne, clearly amused, looked around at the other two. 'Speaks fancy, don't he? Well, kid, I dunno whether Angie needs protectin' or not but I do know, if she does, you ain't the one to do it.' He jerked his head at the bough shelter. 'Nor that drifter you drug in from the edge of the desert.'

Gavin blinked. 'He's nothing to do with it! I just found him hurt. I was taking him in to get — looked after.'

'Yeah, he looked poorly when we seen him yest'y.'

The kid frowned. 'You *saw* him?

Yesterday? And you didn't even try to help him?'

Claiborne shrugged. 'Just watched him through the glasses. Didn't look as if he'd make it. Wasn't no sense in wastin' time or messin' up our hosses' hoofs ridin' out to see.'

'But — but that — that's unforgivable! I thought you westerners were supposed to help *anyone* in trouble!'

'Ah, you been readin' too many dime novels, kid. Look, tell you what, you seem to be outa your depth here. This ain't really your style, ridin' range, is it?'

The man expected an answer so Gavin murmured, no, it wasn't, but he owed his sister and he wanted to help her . . .

'Yeah, fine. You got a heart. Right — well, the best way you can help her is to tell her to take Mr Rafferty's offer. It's a damn good one and was me, I'd take it quick as I could snap my fingers.'

Gavin Leach was sure his knees were shaking now and they surely must see them, but he swallowed, licked his dry lips and had to clear his throat before he said, 'She doesn't want to sell.'

Claiborne sighed, leaned forward, thrusting his heavy face towards the kid. 'Hell, we know that, for Chris'sake! What the hell is wrong with her? She wouldn't get another offer to top Mr Rafferty's!' He reached out suddenly and grabbed the front of Gavin's shirt and shook the startled youngster. 'I asked you a question! *What the hell is wrong with her?*'

'I-I don't know!' Gavin tried to open the big hand that gripped his clothes but the fingers were like steel clamps. 'It's her business. Let — me — go!'

'Aw, you hear that, boys? He wants me to let him go.' Claiborne started to drag the struggling kid towards the edge of the rock. 'Mebbe I'll do just that — but just a *leetle* closer to the edge, eh?'

'Hope he can fly, Clay!' chuckled McColl and Lindsey laughed out loud.

Gavin kicked at Claiborne's shins, startling the man and hurting him.

The ramrod swore and shook Leach violently, backhanded him across the face.

'You little snake! I'm gonna beat your ribs around your goddamn backbone for that!' Without turning, he spoke to the advancing cowboys. 'Mac, you and Lin take hold this sonuver's arms while I give him a message for his sister. That's if she ain't too dumb to savvy it . . .'

Gavin reacted instinctively, just as Claiborne wanted him to. He tried to struggle free of the grip of McColl and Lindsey and, when he couldn't, spat at the ramrod, fouling the man's shirt.

'Ooh, now you gone an' done it, kid!' Lindsey said, winking at McColl. 'Bucktooth Bonnie give him that shirt for his birthday.'

Claiborne's fist was already working, slamming into Gavin's face, then his chest and his belly. He jack-knifed and Claiborne yelled to hold him up, set his boots solidly, shoulders spreading, preparing to give Gavin Leach the biggest hammering of his life.

Then there was a grunting sound and a *swish!* and suddenly a length of sapling that Gavin had cut last night to use on the *travois* smashed across Claiborne's head and knocked his hat spinning, driving the man to his knees. The sapling thudded again just where his neck joined his shoulders and he sprawled face down, one arm dangling over the edge of the rock. McColl and Lindsey let Gavin fall to his knees and reached for their six-guns.

The stranger stepped forward on unsteady feet and swung the sapling into Lindsey's midriff. The man gagged and retched as he collapsed, writhing. The sapling swung backhanded as McColl freed his six-gun from his holster and took him squarely across the face, smashing his nose, mouth and several teeth. McColl dropped, squirming and choking.

Breathing hard, the stranger leaned heavily on the sapling, blinking at Gavin, who, pale and startled, looked up at him from his hands and knees.

'You — you've killed them!' he gasped.

'No — not their — kind . . . Big drop off here?'

Gavin blinked again and shook his head. 'Six feet or so down to the next ledge.'

The stranger hobbled forward, kicked all three injured men over the edge of the rock. They hit awkwardly and sprawled amongst the brush and tufty grass and rocks six feet below.

'Find their hosses and run 'em off — they can walk back. If they're able.'

The stranger seemed to have exerted himself enough. The sapling fell from his hands and rolled over the edge, too. He sat down heavily, upper body heaving as he fought for breath.

'My God!' Gavin was horrified at the cold way the Rafferty men had been pushed off the ledge. 'I-I've never seen anything like this! It — it's barbaric! Just who are you?'

The stranger's face suddenly straightened and he stared long and silently at Gavin before finally whispering hoarsely, 'I-I dunno who I . . . am . . . or what I'm doin' here.'

3

Take Care

Sean Rafferty was in his mid-fifties and he had a head of black, silver-streaked hair that would have made any lion on the African plains mighty proud.

His face was rugged, yet wasn't as weathered as you might expect for a man his age who had worked outdoors in the West: the lines more clearly defined, not so wrinkled. And the eyes were a piercing brown with clear lenses, like those of a hunting eagle.

Average height but with a barrel chest, his voice was deep and easy-on-the ear with a faint Irish lilt that would never fade. But that voice could take on the cutting edge of an executioner's sword when he was riled.

Right now his clear eyes were narrowed as he stood on the porch of his large riverstone-and-log ranch house set atop a hogback rise commanding a fine view up the twisting length of the Viper River Valley. It was a view that reminded him daily of the emerald green fields of Ireland that he had left so long ago — and that he hoped to see again in the not-too-distant future — providing his plans went as they should. Now he tore his eyes from the valley, standing at the top of the short stone steps, hand-made leather riding boots spread, and looked down at the three battered men waiting there.

'And aren't you a sorry-looking lot,' he said calmly, studying them without any trace of sympathy. 'Clay, you're nominated as spokesman.'

McColl and Lindsey wanted to speak, too, but they had learned long since that that was the wrong way to go about staying in Rafferty's good books. Claiborne shuffled forward so he could reach out an arm and steady himself against the porch upright. His face was bruised and cut, his clothes torn, his boots filthy with both mud and dust and traces of alkali: telling their own story about where he had been.

In thick, halting words, he told his boss about his meeting with Gavin Leach and the mysterious stranger they had watched Leach haul in from the edge of the desert.

'Blind-sided us, chief,' Claiborne finished. 'Hit me with some kind a tree according to Mac.'

'Saplin',' McColl murmured, not looking at Rafferty.

'And . . . ?' Rafferty's bushy white eybrows lifted in a query.

Claiborne sniffed and spat to one side. 'Musta kicked us off the ledge. Lucky it was only a six-foot drop to the next one down.'

Rafferty said nothing, stood staring a moment longer, then turned and went to a high-backed rattan chair. He sat down, prepared a cigar leisurely, leaving the injured and near-exhausted men standing in the hot sun.

'Out at Midget Mountain, you say?' Claiborne nodded dully, wishing he could go stretch out on his bunk — or grab a shotgun and go blast that goddamn stranger to hell. 'Then they *were* on our land but I guess that kid wouldn't know. He's only been with Angie for a few weeks. Still, you did right to challenge him. But this stranger.' Rafferty's eyes narrowed again as he bored his gaze into Claiborne. 'Pretty tough, eh?'

'He blind-sided me!' Claiborne reiterated, straightening and you could tell it wasn't anything he was going to forget in a long while, what that stranger had done to him.

Sean Rafferty waved it away with one clean, long-fingered hand. He puffed on his thick cigar. 'You know for sure the kid brought him in from the desert? He wasn't shamming? I mean definitely an accidental arrival? You'd say that . . . ?'

Claiborne was uneasy. He had had past experience of committing himself and later having it go wrong. Rafferty's wrath was nothing to toy with.

'I can only tell you what I seen, chief,' he answered lamely. 'We seen him earlier in the desert, waited to see what the kid'd do.'

'Hmmm. And he took him back to A-Bar-W?'

'I — dunno. They was gone when we come round — and they'd run off our broncs so we had to walk goddamn miles!'

Rafferty merely stood and started for the door of the house. 'Saddle my palomino and get yourself cleaned up.'

'Aw, Judas, chief! I need rest and a wash and . . . '

Claiborne let the words trail off — the rancher had taken absolutely no notice of his protest.

* * *

'D'you think he really has lost his memory?'

Angie Bancroft rubbed her hands down her apron-fronted dress and worry lines etched between her eyes as she asked her young brother about the stranger who was now resting on one of the beds in what had once been the children's room at the back of the house.

Gavin sipped his coffee and shrugged. 'He could've, sis. You saw that bump and cut on his head.'

Angie nodded, pushed stray strands of deep brown hair back from her hazel eyes. 'Yes — I'd believe he has some degree of concussion and that could bring on memory loss — temporary or longterm, but — I have to be careful, Gay. Sean Rafferty is a devious man. I wouldn't put it past him to try something like this just to plant his man close to me.'

Leach scoffed. 'Drawing rather a long bow, aren't you, Sis?'

Her eyes glinted. 'Dammit, Gavin! You don't know! You've been away all the time Rafferty's been here, hounding not just me, but the whole valley! He's bought out a lot of settlers and now he wants my land — and I don't want to sell. At any price. He's going to crowd me till I do! And I have to fight him off by any means I can come up with!'

'OK, sis, OK! Calm down. You don't have to sell if you don't want to, so why get worked-up?'

Angie made an effort and forced a smile, reached out to touch his arm. 'I'm sorry. It's very — worrying — and it killed Walt.'

'*Killed* Walt? I thought he had a riding accident?'

She sat down opposite him at the deal table. 'Gav, it's one reason why I didn't keep at you to go back to school. I-I'm worried. All right, *scared*, at times. Walt was worried, too, and very edgy. You know what he was like. He'd stand up to anything that threatened his family, but he admitted to me that Rafferty had him really worried with his persistence and that hardcase crew of his.'

'Well, why does Rafferty want this place so badly? It's nothing special, is it?'

'Something to do with the valley as a whole — I'm not sure. He spoke once about bringing the desert back to life, which, of course, would take a massive amount of water.' Then she added quietly, 'Walt said he thought Rafferty wants to flood the valley, build a damn across from Midget Mountain to Isolation Peak . . . '

'Good God! That'd be a massive undertaking!'

'Yes. Walt was checking with some of his contacts amongst the engineers back east to see if Rafferty has backing we know nothing about. The day after he sent his telegraph, he had his — accident . . . '

'But that's what it was, Sis, wasn't it? An accident?' Gavin looked very worried now, felt his belly knot.

'Sheriff Nichols was supposed to be investigating, but — well, they call him 'Windy' Nichols and he is mostly talk — and also a good friend of Sean Rafferty's.'

Gavin finished his coffee, stood and

came round to stand beside his sister, slipping an arm across her shoulders. 'Sis, you've had a helluva lot of worry this last year or so, what with losing the children and then Walt. You've done what you always do: bottle up your troubles, try to solve them yourself.'

'It's my way, Gavin. Always has been. I can't help it.'

'Yes! And it's a wonder you haven't got a headful of grey hair! But you don't have to do that this time. Walt's gone, but I'm here. Oh, sure, I'm a green-horn, but I remember something of ranch work when I was a kid before you sent me away to school — I can help, I want to and I *will*. If I have to learn how to handle a gun, I'll do that, too.'

She stood, turned to him and put her arms around him, kissing his cheek, standing on tiptoe to do it. 'Thank you, Gav. I-I guess I need *someone*.'

'And it's me, I'm — ' He broke off, looking past her out of the window. He stepped back and she frowned, turning quickly. 'Well, we can soon find out just what Rafferty's plans are. Here he comes down the trail now.'

Angie pulled aside the curtain a little and said, with maybe a slight tremor in her voice, 'Yes — and he's got Claiborne with him!'

* * *

Rafferty doffed his fine-looking hat, a Western hat hand-made back East, as he sat his big palomino with easy grace and nodded courteously to Angie where she waited on her porch, Gavin beside her.

'Fine day, Mrs Bancroft.'

'It was shaping-up that way till I saw you and your tame coyote riding in.'

Claiborne scowled, his bruised face and swollen neck hurting with the effort. Angie looked vaguely amused.

'Why, I think you've somehow improved your looks, Claiborne. Whatever did you do to your face?'

The big man bared his teeth, thick

lips peeling back, but Rafferty chuckled and spoke, cutting off Clay's reply. 'He does look rather different. Thanks to your new hand, I believe.'

That startled Angie and she blinked. It was Gavin who replied, 'We don't have any new hands, Rafferty.'

'Oh? I heard you went to meet someone out in the basin and brought him back here.'

'He was hurt! Claiborne and his friends saw him *yesterday* in trouble and didn't lift a finger to help him.'

Rafferty shook his head, lips pursed. 'Well, that's not like Clay — or this legendary 'Code Of The West' you hear so much about — '

'I didn't think you'd even heard of it,' Angie cut in suddenly and Rafferty sobered, looking briefly annoyed.

He made the smile come back. 'I won't take up much of your time, Mrs Bancroft, I just wanted you to understand that I don't intend to make any trouble about your brother's trespass on — '

'Trespass?'

'On my land near Midget Mountain. Clay was trying to explain the boundaries to him when your man — er — this *stranger* he had befriended, attacked my men with a club.' He shook his head slowly. 'I don't want any kind of trouble — you've certainly had your share, lately. I don't intend to add to it.'

'You've wasted your time coming here, Mr Rafferty,' Angie told him coolly. 'You know as well as I do what really happened at Midget Mountain, so, I won't keep you any longer.'

She turned abruptly to the house door but Rafferty said sharply, 'Just one moment!' His voice was crisp, peremptory, but when she turned slowly, he brought back the smile. 'One more time, Mrs Bancroft, will you consider my offer for your ranch? Please? Surely you must admit it's more than generous.'

Angie stared down at him and his smile slowly faded. 'It is, as you say, Mr Rafferty, *more* than generous, which makes me wonder just why you want my land so badly.'

The smile returned but there was a stiffness around the edges now. 'Mrs Bancroft, I'm not sure that I can explain but — well, my grandfather founded a coach-making business in Dublin, built it up and sold out to competition, then migrated to America. But my father, the eldest son, stayed behind with my stepmother. The Estate was to be sold but somehow that bitch of a stepmother cheated us out of our heritage.' He paused to settle his breathing. 'While she destroyed our estate with her excesses, in America, my grandfather and uncles built a business empire in Boston and New York, invested in a railroad in which they eventually owned the majority of shares. A true land of opportunity, eh?'

Gavin whistled softly, but Rafferty waited in vain for the woman to express any interest. 'My cousins are partners in that railroad but because of — well, an unjust family decision, I, and my father were not admitted. So, after his death, I set out on my own to prove that I, too, had inherited the Rafferty business acumen, drive and ambition.'

'Buying my ranch will help you achieve this?' Angie asked sceptically and Rafferty flushed slightly at her tone.

'You may be surprised, but yes! It will. You see, it is my intention to show my family I, too, can leave something enduring and worthwhile for this great country.' His eyes sparkled and he lowered his voice. 'I am now in my fifties and I have — accrued — a considerable amount of money so profit is not the major interest here. I intend to revive the Carnaby Desert! Turn it into lush pastures for herds of fine beef cattle, forests of usable timber, land families will be proud to settle and perhaps, even reminiscent of my homeland, that green Ireland of my childhood — '

'A fantasy,' cut in Gavin.

Rafferty, eyes narrowed, looked at him coldly, unsmiling.

'So most people think, young man,

but it can be done. *I* can do it! And I will do it! I have investors back East, just waiting in the wings for me to give the go-ahead.' He turned back to Angie. 'Only you and the Pritchards are holding out, but I think Tate Pritchard is finally starting to see good sense — so you can see why I need your land, now, Mrs Bancroft — Angie, if I may call you that?'

''Mrs Bancroft' will do. I think I do see why you want my land — you're going to flood the valley, aren't you? Just as Walt predicted.'

Rafferty didn't like her being that much of a jump ahead of him but he finally raised a finger and wagged it at her, smiling again.

'I knew you were a smart woman, Mrs Bancroft! Yes, it will be necessary to flood the Viper River Valley in its entirety, turn it into a huge man-made lake and dam.'

'Which is why you built your place so high up, no doubt?'

'Yes, I admit to that. This has been a

long-term project for me — and I should mention that there is a good deal of government backing available, providing we meet certain criteria and deadlines.' He suddenly spread his arms. 'Well, I have been candid. If you still refuse to consider my offer, will you do me the courtesy of being candid with me as to your reasons for refusal?'

'Certainly — there are only two, Mr Rafferty. First, my husband sweated long and hard to build this ranch for me and his family. We were his life — '

'And you feel an obligation to carry on and see that his — vision — is realized.' Rafferty nodded several times. 'Yes, I can understand that. Very commendable indeed. And the second reason?'

Angie's face was very tight and a little pale as she said, 'My husband and children are buried here on this land.'

It took Rafferty a little time to understand and then his face registered shock and he frowned and he tried twice before he could speak.

'You — are you saying . . . ? Good God, woman! Is that why you've held us up for months, put us well behind schedule, because of a few *graves*?'

'My husband and children's graves! Not just any graves, damn you!' Angie snapped, and he waved irritably, failing in his rising anger, to see the cold, stubborn look turning her features to stone.

'My dear woman, I am quite willing to see that your family is disinterred with all propriety and moved to a safer, more suitable place, well above water level. If this is your major objection — well, I only wish you had mentioned it earlier! It could've been overcome in a few minutes!'

'*No!*' Angie's single word was said with such force and hostility that Rafferty actually reared back in his saddle, startled at her vehemence. She leaned over the porch rail. 'My family are resting where they should be and their peace will not be disturbed under any circumstances!'

'Good grief, woman, I've assured you it will be done in the best of tastes. I'll arrange for a preacher of your choice, for re-interrment. I'll even supply suitable new caskets — '

'*Get off my land!*'

Gavin stepped forward and took his sister's arm as she leaned far over the rail to hurl the words in Rafferty's face. This time he didn't rear back, but his frown deepened and Claiborne said quietly, 'I can handle this, chief, just say the word.'

Rafferty lifted a cautionary hand without looking at his foreman. 'Mrs Bancroft, if you would calm down a moment or two, we can sit down and discuss this reasonably — '

'My sister told you to get off our land, Rafferty!' Gavin said, cursing as that nervous tremor rattled his voice. He wished he was wearing a gun or had a rifle handy. His heart was hammering and Claiborne curled a lip.

'You'd best stay outa this, kid.' He dropped a hand to his gun butt, then stiffened and Angie heard a cold, rasping voice behind her say, 'Best do what the lady wants, mister!'

The words were followed by a cold metallic snapping sound that meant only one thing — a gun hammer had been cocked

She spun, as did Gavin, and they stared at the battered stranger swaying in the doorway, one shoulder pressed against the frame, holding a double-barrelled shotgun in his scarred hands, the bruised wrists showing plainly.

He was watching Claiborne and Rafferty, jerked the gun barrels a couple of inches. 'Trail's over yonder — I'll give you a slow count of three to get moving.'

Rafferty's face was cold and vicious. 'So you're the desert stranger I've been hearing about.'

'He's got the luck of the devil, chief! The desert should've finished him and if he hadn't blind-sided me I . . . '

Claiborne's words trailed off and the others, too, saw the way the man had tensed at Claiborne's words.

'You have a name, friend?' queried Rafferty tautly.

The man looked at him bleakly. 'Your sidekick said I'm 'lucky' — that's good enough. Call me 'Lucky'. Now, one — two — thr — '

By then Rafferty and Claiborne were wheeling their horses and riding across the yard towards the hills and the trail back to Rafferty's ranch.

The man slumped, the gun pointing floorwards, and Gavin stepped forward to support him. 'That gun's not even loaded, you know that?'

The man called 'Lucky' nodded wearily.

'Heard voices — sounded unfriendly. Found the gun in a cupboard. Couldn't find the shells . . . '

His legs suddenly gave way and Gavin Leach grunted as he took his weight.

'Put him back on Joel's bed, Gavin. I'll get some warm water and clean him up properly — and we'll see what he has to say for himself.'

Angie held the door while Gavin struggled through with the big, inert stranger.

What kind of man was this? she wondered. A man who would knowingly face armed strangers with an empty shotgun.

4

'Get Tough!'

Link Cady didn't like this 'Lucky' son of a bitch. He decided almost as soon as he set eyes on the battered stranger as he sat around on the porch smoking, head bandaged, raking those scary eyes around the yard. He had walked around for a while, limping, and Link figured it wouldn't be long before he was in the saddle, poking his nose into every corner of the A-Bar-W.

Link had his reasons for not wanting that. He could manage the greenhorn kid, no problem, but this new one looked mighty tough. Well, Cady was a tough man in his own right, too, had been kicked about since he could walk, when he first went to the orphanage. It was a case of take it and cower and make life more miserable than it already was, or find some way of fighting back.

By the time he was eight years old, Link knew how he could get back at all the 'guardians' who had beat on him and abused him, men and women. They gave him a job in the kitchen filling the coffee and tea for a luncheon spread the orphanage was providing for visiting do-gooders. Only two days before he had discovered where the iron-jawed matron kept the Epsom Salts that she dosed the kids with when they fussed . . . so he added a liberal — *very* liberal — quantity of the salts to the urns. In the general chaos that ensued, Link ran away, jumped a train west, and had made his own way ever since.

Link walked across to where Gavin Leach was saddling a horse at the corrals.

'Him on the porch — he stayin' on? Looks like he thinks he's the new boss.'

Gavin looked sharply at Cady. 'Don't be stupid. Sis is just letting him rest up until he's feeling better. He's taken a hell of a beating in that desert, crossed it north to south.'

Link snorted. 'He *says*!'

'Why would he lie? And Sis says it's the only way he could've gotten to the section of the basin I found him in.'

'Yeah? Well, what the hell was he doin' in Carnaby Desert in the first place? You think to ask him that?'

'They tell me that you don't pry into a man's business out here, Link. He'll tell us in his own good time or he won't. He hasn't regained his memory yet.'

Again Link snorted. 'You believe that? Listen, I've had my run-ins with tough sheriffs over the years. I've had the cuffs snapped on me just as tight as they'd go — and they left bruises and raw skin on my wrists, just like them on this *hombre*'s wrists. You ask me, he's on the dodge.'

Gavin thinned his lips and turned back to tightening the cinchstrap.

That part had been worrying him, too . . .

* * *

Claiborne's face was still bruised but some of the swelling had gone down and his neck wasn't quite so stiff. But enough discomfort remained to keep his hatred for 'Lucky' burning at red heat.

He sniffed and spat before mounting the steps to the big ranch house, went inside and down the passage to where Rafferty awaited him in what he called his den.

The walls were decorated with the heads of reindeer, mountain lion and one bear, fierce in expression with the enlarged teeth the taxidermist had given it. Fancy weapons were set in racks: Purdey hand-made shotguns with filigree gold and silver wire decorations; Harrison & Richardson hunting rifles with engraved bolts and actions; ornate revolvers in glass-fronted cases. Interspersed between the weapons were paintings of Ireland, one of an ancient castle with partially crumbled walls in a large ornate gilt frame. Claiborne figured that if ever he quit here, he would take along some of those fancy guns . . .

'Ah, Clay,' Rafferty greeted his ramrod, looking up from a pile of mail that had been brought to him from town. 'What have you found out about that hardcase at the Bancroft place?'

'Nothin' yet, chief. I've seen Windy Nichols. He's sendin' wires all over the place, but says he ain't had any word of prisoners on the run in this neck of the woods.'

The rancher made an exasperated sound. 'Dammit! The man came in across the desert! That's not 'this neck of the woods'! Tell Nichols to start looking further afield. I saw those marks on his wrists, they were still raw. That ranny's escaped custody from somewhere not long ago — and I want to know *where* and when.'

Claiborne nodded. 'OK, but I don't see the worry, chief. He's tough, but I figure he just bought into that deal because Angie'd been takin' care of him — I don't think she sent for him, if that's what's botherin' you.'

It was quiet in the room for what seemed like a long time to Claiborne.

'I — don't know,' Rafferty admitted slowly. 'But I can't take the chance of someone coming in here to start snooping around.' He tapped the letter he had been reading when the ramrod had entered. 'From the group in Chicago — they're tightening the deadline. They want returns on their investment, *pronto*. We know there have been complaints about the way we — acquired some of the land around here — They may not be provable but one of the law agencies could be suspicious enough to send in someone to check things out.'

Claiborne arched his eyebrows. 'That drifter? With them 'cuff marks on him . . . ?'

'A good enough cover, don't you think? Make us believe he's on the run from the law.'

The ramrod thought Rafferty was paranoid, although that wasn't a word in his vocabulary, but he figured that the big Irish son of a bitch was being hassled by his 'friends' back East and jumping at every shadow that didn't seem to fit in place around here.

He said nothing.

'I want to know what he's doing on the Bancroft place, Clay. If he saddles-up and rides out within the next few days, have someone follow him, though I must admit I'll feel quite a relief if that's what he does. It'll mean he's just been recuperating there as it appears and is moving on. But if he starts snooping around — well, I'll certainly want to know that, too!'

'Whatever you say, chief.' Claiborne paused at the door. 'If Angie won't sell because she don't want the family graves flooded — well, d'you have to pussyfoot around with her? Why not move in rough, get tough, run her off, and that greenhorn kid brother with her.'

Rafferty smiled thinly. 'I'm tempted, Clay, oh, believe me, *I am sorely tempted* to do just that, but it will be prudent to satisfy ourselves about this stranger first.'

As Claiborne nodded and went out, he murmured, 'Prudent, my ass. I'd as soon put a bullet in him right now and settle it for sure.'

* * *

Lucky was at the wash bench near the kitchen door when he saw Gavin walking towards the corrals, carrying a rifle. Angie was hanging out washing nearby and, as he patted his sore face dry — it was still sun-raw and tender — he said, 'First time I've seen the kid with a gun. Is he any good with it?'

Angie took a wooden clothes peg from between her teeth and pushed it over the folds of a dress on the strung rope of the line. She looked at the man for a moment before shaking her head.

'I think he's not a bad shot but he

doesn't like guns much.'

'Then why's he toting one?' The stranger gestured to where Gavin was now sliding the rifle into a scabbard and attaching it by rawhide thongs to the saddle.

'He saw some of Rafferty's riders on our land yesterday. They rode away when he tried to approach them and ask what they were doing.'

Lucky nodded, eyes narrowing as he watched the kid. He started forward around the side of the house, saying quietly, 'He's tying it on all wrong . . . ' He raised his voice. 'Hey, kid! Wait up.'

Gavin turned as he saw Lucky coming towards him, still limping slightly. 'You're walking better.'

'Getting there. Gavin, you've tied that scabbard wrong. The rifle's upside down in it and it's tilted too low. Your breech'll be full of grit and dust in no time — and water if it rains.'

As he spoke he shouldered Gavin aside, untied the rawhide thongs, arranged the scabbard at a slight downward angle, butt towards the rear.

Gavin frowned, hesitated, then said quietly, 'I thought the butt should be facing forward?'

'That's OK — in dry country. But you come from a place that gets a lot of rain like me, you have it this way, butt angled up and to the rear. You might have to lean a mite to free the gun, but you can drape your slicker folds over it and keep it dry, too. Worth that extra effort to twist and lean. A gun that works is what you want, not one jammed with grit or rusting from too much water.'

Gavin nodded his thanks. Gathering the reins, one boot in stirrup, he asked casually, 'You speak from experience, I take it?'

Lucky hesitated, rubbed at his head bandage. 'Well — it seems to be just something I know. Where you headed, kid?'

Gavin swung into the saddle. 'Just riding. Familiarizing myself with the place — I don't want to make the mistake of crossing Rafferty's line again.' He smiled. 'You might not be around to rescue me.'

The stranger shrugged that off. 'Hardly recollect doing anything. Just reacted, I guess. How about I come with you?'

'Well, d'you feel up to it?'

'You saddle me a horse and I'll see if I can borrow a hat and some more of Walt's clothes — he seems to've been about my size . . . ' As he started back to the house, Gavin dismounted, looped his reins over the corral rail and ran his eyes over the remuda, wondering what kind of horse to pick for Lucky Whoever-he-was.

He chose a claybank and had it saddled and waiting when Lucky came back, wearing a checked shirt and whipcord trousers, both of which had belonged to Walt Bancroft, but his boots were his own.

Gavin knew, too, that it was Walt's old Colt, complete with bullet belt and holster, that the man carried in his left hand. He paused and buckled it on and Gavin frowned. Lucky did it with such ease and even a certain amount of grace, so that when the holster settled and he tied down the base to his leg, the gun rig looked right at home. And the way Lucky set the weapon in the holster told Gavin that here was a man used to guns and quite at home with them.

'Let's go,' he said and mounted the claybank. 'We find a lonely draw, we'll take a little time out and I'll show you how to shoot — OK?'

Gavin said nothing as he mounted his own horse. But his heart was beating faster. He'd never felt easy about guns somehow . . .

And Angie stared over the sheet she was hanging on the clothes line, noticing that gun on the stranger's hip, looking a little apprehensive.

From behind the barn, Link Cady watched, too, pursing his lips thoughtfully, as the two men rode out.

* * *

Gavin Leach knew of a couple of isolated draws that he had found on his rides around A-Bar-W but he didn't go near them during the morning, showing Lucky where he had figured out the boundaries to be.

'Pretty big place,' the man allowed. 'Lush valley — be a pity to see it disappear under water.'

'Well, yes. But I guess you can see where government would be interested in such a scheme to bring the desert back to life.'

'What? Flood this fertile valley, to bring life to a desert not much bigger?' Lucky shook his head. 'Don't make much sense to me — Think of how much it'd cost.'

Gavin nodded. 'Yes, I have. At college we touched on a little engineering, along with several other subjects, just giving us a taste to see who might be interested in what, you know? I reckon it'd take hundreds of thousands to pull off . . . But, of course, the dam wouldn't be used just for the desert, there's all that country to the west and south that could benefit if pipelines were built.'

'You're talking about things on a mighty big scale, kid. You ask me, it's Rafferty's ego that's bigger'n anything else.'

Leach snapped his head around. 'What? You mean — you think he's doing it for *his own satisfaction*?'

Lucky shrugged. 'His family have left their mark, way back, if you can believe him. He seems to be on the outer with his family. Could be he sees this as a chance to show 'em all that he can leave his mark on this country, too — and no doubt make a good profit as well.'

Gavin blew out his cheeks. 'Seems a bit far-fetched if you ask me,' he allowed but Lucky didn't seem to hear.

'That looks like the entrance to a draw yonder,' he said. 'Let's go see . . . '

It was a draw and Lucky insisted that they set things up so he could give Gavin some lessons in firearms' handling.

'Look, I don't like guns . . . '

'Then why bring that rifle?'

'Well, I am a bit uneasy riding alone out here.'

'If you don't know how to use a gun, kid, leave it at home — or take time to learn. What'll it be?'

Gavin hesitated, licked his lips and finally nodded. 'I guess I want to be able to protect Angie, and if it means learning how to shoot then so be it. I suppose you know what you're doing, Lucky.'

Gavin said this a little strangely and Lucky merely grunted and began pacing out a range.

He set up stones and chips of wood, a broken whiskey bottle Gavin found by a rock, and even some of the shards of shattered glass.

'Kind of small, aren't they?'

'They'll catch the light and reflect it — make a good target, practice for shooting against the sun, too, but it's not something I'd recommend. OK. First piece of wood's on that hummock, twenty feet away. Shoot at it with the rifle.'

He had to show the kid how to hold the Winchester properly, get the metal curve of the butt snugly into his shoulder so as to save bruising, to grip firmly.

'Hold that fore-grip with your left hand cupped, fingers wrapped around the wood, then pull back firmly — not too hard or your fingers'll go numb and you lose the feel of the gun — OK. Sight so that the tip of the foreblade settles dead-centre in the V of the rear sight, but level with the top of the arms . . . *level* with the top of the V! You shoot like that, and you'll only dig a hole at the base of the hummock. Not too high, damnit! You're not trying to bring down that hawk. OK. That's reasonable — now squeeze the trigger — don't jerk — Jesus, I said *don't jerk*!'

The rifle crashed and the sound batted at their ears and the horses started and snorted — and nothing happened to the piece of wood. No dirt even sprayed from the hummock.

But way down the line, the bullet ricocheted from a lichen-scabbed boulder and chewed a handful of dirt from the high edge of the draw.

'What happened?' Gavin asked, bewildered. 'I sighted just as you said . . .'

'But you *jerked* the trigger like you were trying to pull it out of the action! *Squeeze*! You ever give a girl a little squeeze round the waist, sort of testing the lie of the land for something a bit more intimate later? No? Well, kid, you got a *lot* to learn — and, it seems, not just about guns!'

Gavin flushed. 'All right, all right! Let's stick to the subject . . . I shot wrong. Well, show me how to do it right! Now we've started I might as well do the best I can.'

Lucky smiled thinly. 'Good attitude, kid.'

Time ran away.

It was afternoon and the draw stank of powder-smoke, was filled with tendrils of grey fog. The small hummocks closest to the men were ragged lumps of dirt, diminished in size from all the bullets chewing away at them. The whiskey bottle was in pieces. Smaller sections of glass were no more than splinters. Slabs of bark were riddled and twigs were splintered enough to be used as tooth picks.

Gavin complained his trigger finger had a blister on it and his hands were cramped and his shoulder was bruised.

'That's when you lost your concentration,' Lucky told him without sympathy. 'You gotta *think* when you're shooting. Right now you'll have to do it consciously. With a little practice, all I've taught you will come naturally.'

'When? By the time my hair turns grey?'

Lucky grinned, punched Gavin lightly on the sore shoulder and the kid winced and swore, rubbing hard.

'You're not a bad shot. Need lots of practice, but doing OK.'

Leach blinked, surprised. 'Then why've you been cussing me so much? Telling me what a lousy shot I am?'

'Make sure you stayed awake. You looked kinda bleary-eyed there for a while.'

'Maybe you were boring me!'

Lucky conceded that with a grin and a shrug. 'Well, kid, like I said, you did OK — for the first lesson. We'll do a little each day till you can hit what you aim at five times outa six — you want to try a six-gun, by the way?'

Gavin shook his head vigorously. 'Not today, thank you!' Then something seemed to occur to him. 'You haven't showed me what you can do with a gun.'

Lucky was sober now. 'Throwing down a challenge, eh? Well, let's see . . . ' He reached out and took the rifle from Gavin, glanced up, then threw the Winchester to his shoulder and fired.

Gavin squinted, shading his eyes, saw an eruption of feathers and the mangled body of a hunting hawk in its final swoop on its target hurtling to the ground.

'My God! That bird must've been moving at forty miles an hour!'

'All in how you lead a moving target, kid.'

He threw up the rifle again and lever and trigger worked in smooth blurs as shot after shot rent the heat of afternoon. The short, splintered neck of the bottle disintegrated, sticks no larger than half the length of a man's little finger leapt wildly into the air, individual stones no bigger than a thumbnail shattered and buzzed.

Gavin was impressed and his eyes were slightly wide as he turned to Lucky who was already reloading the rifle's magazine.

'Never be caught with an empty gun, kid. If you can, leave one shot always and reload quick as possible.'

'All right. How about the Colt? Are you any good?'

'Average.'

Lucky pointed to a small bush with his left hand, and then the Colt was banging and slamming in his right fist and the bush was stripped of its thin branches and leaves one by one. He stopped shooting at five and dropped the loading gate for Gavin to see that he had left one cartridge in the cylinder, ready to come up under the hammer.

'Precaution.'

'You seem to know all this stuff like an expert — I don't suppose I should ask but were you ever a lawman?'

Lucky laughed. 'Me? Not me, kid.'

Gavin Gavin sobered. 'Then — you learnt all this on the *other* side of the law?'

'Now why would you ask a man such a thing?' Lucky wanted to know, thumbing home new shells into the Colt. 'Don't you know that could get your head shot off?'

'I — er — I knew it was risky but I wanted to know — still do. You're an intriguing man, Lucky.'

'I've been called lots of things, but never that, far as I can remember.' He glanced up at the sky and the heeled-over sun. 'Guess we better be heading back . . . '

As they mounted and turned towards the mouth of the draw, Gavin put his mount alongside the clay-bank and, when Lucky looked at him, said, 'You haven't lost your memory at all, have you?'

Lucky's face didn't change but he didn't answer.

'You've made a couple of mistakes — said you came from a place that had a lot of rain — are a bit too adamant that you were never a lawman; something of 'methinks he protesteth too much', if the Bard will forgive me — and at supper last night when Sis asked if you wanted chilli sauce on your steak you said, 'I never use it — Did once in Mexico at a *hidalgo's* fiesta, made me sick on the spot. Embarrassing — 'course, I'd had more than my share of tequila, too. I've passed on chilli ever since.' Sis didn't appear to notice, but it seemed to me you were recalling details you wouldn't know if you really had lost your memory . . . '

They had ridden as far as the river before Lucky answered, looking levelly at Gavin Leach.

'Seems like I slipped up, doesn't it, kid? You're a lot damn sharper than I figured.'

5

Man of Mystery

Link Cady was riding the river when he saw something in midstream that caught his attention. He couldn't quite make it out, put his mount into the murky water.

Turned out to be a battered old burlap sack with a dead kitten in it. He tossed it away, started to turn his mount, when a voice cracked from the far bank — on the Rafferty side.

'You're trespassin', Cady! No! Hold it right there or I'll shoot. I'm within my rights! You're past the mid-line of the river!'

It was McColl, with Lindsey by his side. Both held rifles on Link and he swallowed, raised his hands and at their instructions, kneed his mount across.

'Listen, fellers, I just seen what I

thought was an old hat caught on the edge of the sandbank and . . . '

McColl hit him across the side of the head with his rifle barrel. He swayed in the saddle and Lindsey grabbed the reins and urged Link's mount up onto the bank.

While he was dazed they rode him back through the brush and into a campsite where Claiborne was sitting on a log, smoking, and nursing a tin mug of coffee. The ramrod glanced up and showed interest when he recognized the dazed Link Cady. McColl halted the horses and pushed Cady out of the saddle. He grunted when he hit the ground, rolled over to hands and knees, started to his feet.

But Lindsey kicked him between the shoulders and he staggered forward, fell again to hands and knees only a few feet from Claiborne.

'Trespassin', Clay. Was crossin' the river when we caught him.'

'Now why would you want to do that, Link?'

'I wasn't! An old sack that looked like a hat was caught up, an — ' He gasped and clawed at his eyes as Claiborne tossed the remains of his hot coffee at his face.

Claiborne stood, hitched at his trouser belt and brushed a hand across his nostrils, sniffing. 'You better quit lyin', Link, 'cause I'm gonna ask you some questions 'bout the new ranny on A Bar W.'

'Hell, I dunno nothin' about him! Nobody does. Says he's lost his memory.'

'You believe that, Link?'

'I dunno — he was pretty much beat when Gav brought him in . . . '

'What's he done since?'

Link felt this was progress, co-operating with Claiborne, but he kept his eye on the big, brutal man's fists. 'Nothin' much — too tuckered, I guess.'

'We seen him ridin' with Gav yest'y,' said McColl. He flicked his gaze to Claiborne. 'Heard some shootin' way off, too, Clay.'

The ramrod's eyes narrowed. 'Did

you now. How about that, Link? Know anythin' about it?'

Cady licked his lips, nodded. 'Matter of fact, I do. I kinda followed Gav and this Lucky as he calls hisself. They just rode for a spell, then went into a draw and — you ready for this? — Lucky give the kid a whole bunch of shootin' lessons: how to handle a rifle and a six-gun. They was there for hours.'

The three Rafferty men exchanged glances and Claiborne asked, 'He do any shootin' hisself? This Lucky, I mean.'

Link snorted, smiling crookedly. 'I should smile he did! Man, he's a dead shot with a rifle — and as for a six-gun. Well, I never even seen him draw and he stripped a small bush of its leaves and branches, Colt blastin' like a Gatlin' gun!'

Again the Rafferty men exchanged glances. McColl and Lindsey looked a mite worried, but Claiborne kept his face blank.

'Would you tag him as a gunfighter?'

Link stiffened: he hadn't expected that question and he looked thoughtful before answering. 'Ye-ah — yeah! I would! That's exactly what I'd call him, the way he used them weapons — a goddamn gunfighter!'

Claiborne poured more coffee from the blackened, bubbling pot and Link stiffened, but the man took a couple of sips, looking at Cady steadily.

'So Angie's hired herself a fast gun . . . '

Link looked startled. 'Well — I dunno as she's *hired* him.'

'He's there, ain't he? Workin' for her, teachin' the kid how to shoot.'

'He's still recoverin' from crossin' the Carnaby.'

'But Gavin brought him in, eh? How you know the kid wasn't *s'posed* to meet him out there? Feller lost his hoss, mebbe, had to make the rest of the way afoot and was lucky enough to be picked up by the kid.' He snorted again, spat. 'That's where the 'Lucky' comes in, eh? He coulda died out there.'

'Almost did, accordin' to Angie.'

Claiborne drank a gulp of coffee. 'Ye-ah — Angie — well, if she's hirin' gunfighters, she sure ain't ready to sell and the chief wants her place pronto.' He stood suddenly, tossed his coffee into the fire, much to Link's relief. 'Link, old son, I'm the one s'posed to make Angie see reason and if I don't Mr Rafferty'll gut and flay me alive — I got no hankerin' for that, so tell you what I'm gonna do.'

On the last word, he swung a boot viciously into Link's face. The man lifted completely off his hands and knees and rolled almost into the fire. Claiborne stepped up, nudged him into the edge of the flames and coals with a boot, holding him there. Link screamed, shirt smouldering.

McColl and Lindsey looked uncomfortable as they smelled burning flesh. Then Claiborne eased up the pressure and Link, sobbing, pushed himself back.

'Mac, Lin — hold this son of a bitch upright.'

By the time they had obeyed, Claiborne had pulled on a pair of sweat-hardened leather work-gloves and he faced the sagging Cady, no longer the tough young ranny he liked to think he was.

'You don't work for Angie no more, Link,' Claiborne told the frightened man. 'You don't work for no one around here. When I'm finished with you here, you just ride on outa the valley and don't come back — you savvy?'

Link just stared out of pain-filled eyes, nodded slowly.

Then Claiborne grinned crookedly and said, 'If you can ride, that is . . . ' And the first blow took Link in the midriff and contorted his features as he gagged and retched.

Claiborne moved his boots wide, settled his shoulders and began swinging blow after blow into the cowboy's body, working up to his face, stepping around him to slam punches into his kidneys and spine. McColl and Lindsey cursed the sagging cowboy, snarling at him to 'Stand up!' but Link's rubbery legs wouldn't hold him.

After a while, breathing hard, sniffing and hawking, Claiborne wiped a sleeve across his nostrils and gasped, 'Let him drop.'

McColl and Lindsey released Link and he fell on his face, shuddering, blood on the ground under him, his clothes torn and red-soaked, his breathing sounding wet and slobbering.

Then Claiborne started in with his boots.

* * *

At supper the previous night, in the kitchen of Angie's house, with old Horseshoe dragging his wooden leg as he served what he called his 'sonofabitch stew', one of his prized, ex-traildrive recipes, the man called 'Lucky' sipped some water from the glass beside him and saw Angie and Gavin staring at him expectantly.

'OK, my name's Lucky Montana. Well, 'Lucky' was tagged onto me by some tinhorn a while back and it's kind of stuck. Montana's a family name. Spanish, somewheres way back.'

'And why did you say you'd lost your memory, Mr Montana?' Angie asked, somewhat frostily.

'Habit — I like to know who I'm with and the surroundings before I admit to anything. Even my name.'

'I guess that's fair enough, Sis.'

Angie didn't look at her brother, kept her gaze on Lucky's still bruised face. 'It sounds to me the way a man who has something to hide might act.'

Lucky drank some more water, toyed with the glass, gaze lowered, not answering.

'I know I'm not supposed to pry, Mr Montana, but you're staying in my house and I believe I have a right to know something at least of your background — your true background.'

He nodded, sighed. 'I guess — OK. Could be I'm on the dodge.'

'*Could* be?'

He stared at her now, soberly, eyes flat and unreadable. He turned the almost empty glass between his fingers. Gavin waited, leaning forward a little in his tension. Angie met and held Lucky's gaze and tried to hide the discomfort she felt.

She sensed that here was a mighty dangerous man.

'Come from up north — a long ways north. I've been in some trouble. Found it hard to settle after the war and got in with a bad bunch . . . '

'Of course!' she said sardonically. 'It wasn't your fault, you were just led astray!'

His cold eyes never wavered. 'No, I was the leader of the bad bunch,' he said flatly, and she showed her surprise as Gavin whistled softly. 'Never mind that — it was a long time ago and I've tamed down some since. Got married.'

'Ah! Of course! The good woman! You seem to have been reading the same books I have, Mr Montana. Full of clichés!'

His face was bleak now and she knew she had ragged him just a little too much.

'She *was* a good woman. But she died. And I went out and killed the man who caused her death. Trouble was, he had a lot of important friends and they hired a gunfighter named Dawson so I had to go on the run. He nearly caught me at Rapid City, Dakota, and then some damn lawman picked me up for stealing the horse I got away on in a dump called Murphy's Creek . . . '

'You do have rather bad luck, don't you?' She didn't sound so sarcastic now, regarded him more thoughtfully.

He nodded. 'That's why I say the nickname never did fit. Anyway, this lawman decided to take me back to Casper, Wyoming, where the Cattlemen's Association would pay him a bounty for the return of one of their horses — and use me as an example to anyone else with ideas of stealing one of their broncs — makin' sure they'd forget all about 'em, pronto.'

He put a hand round his neck, grimaced hideously.

'They — they were going to hang you?' Gavin asked, frowning, and when Lucky nodded, said, 'Without a trial?'

'Never got that far. Some wild bunch hit the train we were on and he was convinced they were trying to rescue me. We left the train and made a run through the timber, but came out on a cliff top over a river — seventy feet straight down.' He paused and they could see his thoughts turn inwards as he relived that heart-stopping moment. 'Damn fool panicked, grabbed my arm and jumped, dragging me with him.'

'*Seventy feet*!' exclaimed Gavin Leach.

'Felt like seven hundred before we hit the river,' admitted Montana slowly, remembering . . .

Wind rushed past hard enough to whip the hat from his head, almost turning his eyeballs inside out.

He would never forget that shocking feeling of his stomach travelling upwards from its normal position into the back of his throat. They began to twist in mid-air and through the blur of wind-induced tears he saw the countryside turn sideways, then upside down, then spin around. He opened his mouth to yell and the wind smashed past his teeth, ballooned his cheeks, roared in his throat and his lungs felt as if they would burst outwards through his ribs.

The sheriff was yelling — and then they hit.

No one could ever tell Lucky Montana that water was soft to land on.

They were lucky inasmuch as they hit a deep part of the river but it felt to Montana as if he had landed on compacted dirt. What breath he had left was smashed from him, the world disappeared in a rocket-trail of stars and bursting lights and his head was filled with a bubbling roar that threatened to explode his brain.

Something hard hit him alongside the head and more red starbursts formed a curtain behind his eyes. It might have been a rock, floating debris, even one of the sheriff's boots, for he could feel the toppling body of his captor tangling with his own flailing limbs.

It got mighty wild after that. Wrenching sensations so that he thought his body was coming apart. He wished his hands were free of the goddamn handcuffs and was grateful at least that they were in front of him and not behind his back. He tried his best to use his arms and boots to fend off obstructions. The other man's body didn't seem to want to leave him: it rolled and twisted into his path several times.

Now and again the current thrust him up enough to gasp a lungful of air — he didn't know how the lawman fared in this respect. Underwater the light was murky green, sometimes much darker. He bounced off the river bottom at least a dozen times, feeling the rough gravel shred his clothes — and his skin. 'Up' and 'down' were directions he no longer knew. It was all a swirl and tumbling and twisting and bouncing until finally he began retching sand and water and found he had washed-up on a sandbank. Water was only inches deep over the bar and he had the feeling he had been out to it for a time and was just coming round. His vision was strange, blurred, distorting things, but he recognized the sheriff's body lying a few feet away, legs trailing in the water.

Head throbbing, bleeding from a temple wound, Montana, still gagging, crawled across awkwardly with his manacled hands, the iron cuffs having torn and bruised his wrists badly enough for them to bleed. He rolled the sheriff onto his back — and vomited when he saw the raw, shredded pulp that was all that was left of the man's face. The lawman must have bounced off a lot more rocks than he had . . .

Afterwards, he searched the body's torn and sodden clothing and found the key to the handcuffs snagged in a corner of a jacket pocket. His fingers were mighty stiff and sore and bleeding but he managed to manipulate the key into the lock of the left cuff and then the right one was easy.

He started to fling the cuffs away, paused, made himself look at the sheriff's face and mutilated head once more. His own mother wouldn't know him . . . Working quickly, he put the cuffs on the sheriff and threw the key away.

With luck — maybe living up to his nickname for once — when the body was found they would think it was the prisoner who had drowned and been mutilated by the river. Sooner or later they would find out the body showed signs of age that didn't fit Montana's description but by then he ought to be many miles away.

With a little luck . . .

'And you claim your nickname isn't appropriate!' Angie Bancroft said in the kitchen. They were eating their stew now and had been while Montana told his story. 'I'd say you had phenomonal luck, Mr Montana! *Good* luck.'

Gavin agreed.

'Never mind the 'Mr Montana' — might as well call me 'Lucky', I guess.'

'But how did you get way down here?' Gavin asked. 'Casper, Wyoming is a long way north.'

'I followed the river and came to a small town on the banks, stole a skiff and some grub, let the current take me. I was still pretty well tuckered out and I washed up somewhere south, awoke in the river one night, the skiff having overturned. Got ashore somehow, collapsed, and when I came to, heard cows and riders, saw a small ranch. Skirted around to where I could see the buildings, just a shack and a rope corral. Stole a horse but was seen and they chased me into the desert where they shot the horse from under me — and left me, with no food or water or even a gun. Next I know I woke up in a bough shelter and saw Claiborne and his pards working on Gavin . . . '

They were silent, toying with what was left of their food now. Angie looked at Montana and he caught her eye. He smiled. 'OK — I really was lucky.'

'Lucky Montana. Perhaps I was lucky, too — that you turned up here when I need help so badly. Will you stay on? Help me fight off Rafferty?'

'I've seen him shoot, Sis,' Gavin added excitedly. 'We could sure use a man like him . . . what d'you say, Lucky?'

He sighed, looked from one to the other.

'Well, maybe my luck's changed for the better. Guess I might's well stick around and see.'

6

Gloves are Off!

It was Montana who found Link Cady.

Lucky was riding the west boundary, familiarizing himself with the lay of Rafferty's land as much as that of A-Bar-W. The Irishman's spread ran mighty close in places, butting right up against an invisible 'line' so that it was anyone's guess where one ranch ended and the other began. Lucky Montana made a mental note to have Angie fence in this part. It would be too easy to accuse riders of trespassing and such accusations usually ended in a fight of some kind.

He spotted a couple of riders hitting the timber on a low knoll across on Rafferty's and shortly after caught a flash of sun on a lens. He smiled crookedly: they were watching him.

That was fine by him — it didn't bother Montana and he even waved once but the lens followed him.

Turning where the line seemed to deviate around a hogback — though it might have run right over it, splitting it down the middle — he would need to check a survey map to be sure — he glimpsed movement on top of a lopside butte. He guessed by the look of it that it was the one Gavin had pointed out yesterday from another angle and told him was called Broken Tooth. Without seeming to do so, he watched the top as he rode but didn't see any more movement. It might have been a cloud shadow, or a gust of wind tipping the pale underside of brush foliage to the sunlight. He veered away and headed for country that started to rise. If he got high enough, he could see better over onto Rafferty's side — maybe flush the man with the glasses, too.

The ledge was weather-worn up here, with long stretches of flat rock that angled down to a clearly defined edge.

Curious to see what lay beyond that ledge, he rode across, the horse not keen to go too close. So he dismounted, put a rock on the reins — he didn't want to find himself afoot this far from the ranch house if the animal decided to run off. He wasn't sure why he took his rifle with him, old habits, he supposed later, but he carried the Winchester Angie had given him in his right hand as he approached the edge, frowning when he saw scrape marks in the shale leading to a broken section. He could almost hear the iron horseshoes making those marks as the animal was pulled reluctantly closer to the edge.

He eased up a step at a time, and looked over. He caught his breath — there was a drop of at least a hundred feet onto a steep slope that ended in a jumble of big rocks.

And lying among these was the carcass of a horse. Some ten yards away and a little upslope was the body of a man. Montana glanced up as a shadow passed over him and he knew then what had caught his eye up on the butte earlier: vultures gathering. Must've seen him coming and perched along the edge of the butte, patiently waiting for him to ride on . . .

The horse was a piebald, one that Link Cady had favoured, and when he thought about it he had seen the cowboy riding out on it this morning right after breakfast. In fact, he had tracked Link for a time when he had come across a trail earlier and the sign led him through brush-choked draws to a small canyon where there were about forty cows penned in by cut lodgepoles. There had been a small camp and he had found a neckerchief he had seen Link wearing, crumpled it and put it in a saddle-bag.

He'd intended to ask Link some questions about those mavericks when he saw him . . . He had left the cattle where they were and continued on his ride. He could see the river and the trail but there was no further sign of Link.

So he had kept on, ending up here, looking on a crumpled body far below. There would be no questions about any mavericks now.

He jumped as there was a puff of rock dust a foot from his right boot swiftly followed by the whipcrack of a rifle. Montana went down to one knee, twisting so that he was facing back towards Broken Tooth butte, rifle coming to his shoulder. He was exposed here but he needed to get that damn bushwhacker's head down before he made a run for cover.

His eagle eyes picked out the drifting gunsmoke up there, allowed for the direction of the wind and moved his rifle barrel slightly to his right. Another bullet ricocheted off the edge of the broken rock but he forced himself not to flinch, got off two fast hammering shots. Rock chips sprayed right underneath the new spurt of gunsmoke and he saw the blur as the hidden rifle lifted when the man threw himself backwards.

Montana was on his feet and running, crouched double, crossing the open stretch and zigzagging towards his horse which was standing with ears pricked, sniffing the hot mountain air. Lucky slapped at the reins as he ran past, clutching the strips of leather, dragging the startled mount's head around and in towards sheltering rocks. He vaulted into the saddle, paused briefly, then rowelled hard and with authority. The horse whinnied and its hind legs buckled for an instant before the shoes managed to get a grip on the shale, sparks flying.

He lunged the animal back the way he had come, racing it to where he had seen the movement on the high ground. Vultures wheeled high on the thermals, giving him a rough clue as to the ambusher's whereabouts. He set the horse at the steep slope, the animal stumbling and almost falling. As it did so, three bullets cut air around his body, one close enough to tug at the flapping corner of Walt Bancroft's soft leather vest that Angie had given him.

But he weaved the horse through the rocks and when he came into an open section, took the rein ends between his teeth, stood in the stirrups and brought the rifle up to his shoulder again. He raked the area up there where he knew the man to be, saw the flash of a grey shirt, a dark-coloured hat, before they disappeared behind a rock.

Montana settled back into the saddle, still holding the reins in his teeth as the animal grunted and heaved up the slope. He slipped cartridges from his belt loops and thumbed home four into the Winchester's loading gate.

Above the clatter and stertorous breathing of his mount, he heard the rattle of hoofs on rocks clearly — from above. He bared his teeth in a tight grin, sheathed the rifle now, took the reins in his hands and used them in concert with his knees and shifting weight, taking the struggling mount through the rocks, climbing all the time, using as much shelter as he could manage.

There was so long between gunfire from above that he was thinking maybe he had got in a lucky shot and hit the son of a bitch bad enough so he couldn't shoot. And hard on the thought came three hammering, booming shots, one of which almost took his head off as it sent his hat spinning.

Close! Much closer than he figured!

The killer was smarter than he had figured, too. He had quit the saddle, allowing his horse to run on riderless, waited until Montana came into view.

Lucky was leaving the horse in a headlong dive behind a rock that was almost a perfect sphere as he figured things out. He saw the patch of dirt and wrenched his body so that he landed on it, jarring and grunting. The man above shot down at him and bullets kicked dirt and whined off rocks all round him.

He had to stand up to get in a shot like that! Lucky thought and immediately slid around the curved base of his shelter, hesitated briefly, then stepped out into the open.

And there was the killer, standing on top of a rock, working his rifle lever as he aimed down into the small crevice where Montana had landed. He must have seen Lucky out of the corner of his eye and spun swiftly, rifle coming round.

Montana, crouching, fired with the butt against his hip, two fast shots that spurted dust from the killer's shirt and knocked the man flailing from his perch. The body hit hard, leg jammed between two rocks, the smoking rifle clattering. Montana levered in a fresh shell, went in warily, soon stood over the unmoving man. He saw by the smashed mouth and general violent rearrangement of the man's face that it was McColl, the man he had hit with the sapling, full force, out at Midget Mountain that day . . .

McColl was dead.

'You're trespassing, feller,' Montana told him quietly. 'A long way into A-Bar-W land here — and the only reason I can think of that brought you here was to push Link Cady and his horse off the rim.'

There was blood on McColl's hands and shirt front, dried blood, smeared, like a man would get carrying something or someone already dead or nearly so, having been badly beaten first.

The fresh bullet wounds Lucky had given him hadn't bled much because they had both been right smack through the middle of the man's heart, stopping it instantly.

* * *

Angie Bancroft, watching through the parlour window, gasped and put a hand to her mouth as she watched the rider coming into the yard, a travois dragging behind his weary mount, a bundle of bloody rags resting between the splayed poles.

Instinctively, she knew whoever it was on that *travois* was dead . . .

She called Gavin and together they went outside and met Montana as he dismounted wearily.

'It's Link. Someone — I think McColl — beat him and then pushed him over a cliff near Broken Tooth, with his piebald, trying to make it look like an accident.'

Palefaced, Angie whispered, 'Just like Walt's . . . '

They had questions, of course, but Angie could see how his ride had taken its toll, got him seated on the small porch and brought him a glass of fresh lemonade. He drank, nodded his thanks, then told them about the gunfight with McColl.

'You nearly caught him at it, eh?' Gavin asked but Lucky didn't seem too sure.

'Saw two men riding into some brush and one of them put field-glasses on me soon afterward. The sun kept flashing off the lens — and I figured he was mighty careless, but I think he wanted to hold my attention while the other one — McColl — slipped back across the river and tried to bushwhack me. Reckon they were on their way back after throwing Link off that cliff.'

Gavin nodded to the *travois* where old Horseshoe had now come to look at what it held. 'What makes you think Link was beaten first? I mean, there's not too much left to see.'

'Gavin!' Angie said sharply but Lucky said, 'He's got bruises on his side — in the shape of a riding boot. Ribs are all stove-in, of course, but there's a big bruise on his belly — I've seen enough men stomped half to death to recognize a boot-heel's mark . . .'

'That's enough!' Angie was white-faced, worried. 'D'you think McColl, and whoever was riding with him — '

'Would've been Lindsey,' Gavin put in tightly. 'They always stick together.

'Whoever it was,' Angie continued, 'd'you think they beat Link, Lucky?'

'Be my guess, but he needn't have been beat-up on your land. Could've dragged him across earlier and done it on Rafferty's place, then tried to make it look like an accident when they went too far.'

'I believe it was probably Claiborne,' she said quietly, hands clasped tightly. 'He's beaten men badly before this. Other ranchers who didn't want to sell had cowhands beaten and driven off or were sometimes attacked themselves by Claiborne . . . but why Link?'

'You just said it, Sis — you don't want to sell, so they beat him and probably told him to clear the valley, but it was too late so . . . ' He shrugged, nodded towards the *travois*.

'Or they might've been trying to find out something about me.'

They looked sharply at Montana.

'I'm the mystery man. They must be wondering if you'd sent for me, Angie.'

'Sent for you? Why?'

'Hired a hardcase for fighting pay.' Montana saw her face straighten as she thought about this.

She put a hand to her mouth. 'My God! If Rafferty thinks that, he'll believe I'm ready to fight, I mean, really *fight* him!' Looking shaken, she sat down slowly on the stoop. 'Who knows what he'll do? As long as I just refused his offers to buy, I didn't believe he would do too much to hassle me . . . '

'You don't know that, Sis! Look what happened to Billy Shumaker? They burned him out, his eldest son was shot and might never walk again — and Halliday always claimed that it was Rafferty's men who drove his herd off Bison Butte. Killed two hundred prime beeves and left him stony broke.'

'So Rafferty knows how to play rough . . . '

She sighed, staring into space. 'Nothing was ever proved — but then that's not surprising with a sheriff like Windy Nichols investigating.' She looked at Montana. 'It seems to me, Lucky, that now the gloves are off.'

He nodded. 'Glad you see that. No use me riding out, not now they've killed Link. They won't stop; can't afford to now they've tipped their hand.

Angie, we're gonna have to get ready for a range war.'

She tightened at his words, looked from Montana to Gavin to Old Horseshoe as he limped up towards the porch.

This was her crew — all she had to stand between her and Rafferty.

She shivered, felt instinctively that it wasn't enough and that if Sean Rafferty went all-out — well, she would lose A-Bar-W.

7

'Who is He?'

Sheriff Windy Nichols was dozing in his chair, head thrown back, tonsils rattling as he snored, boots up on the desk.

Rafferty and Claiborne entered and banged on the edge of the desk but the lawman snored on. The rancher nodded and Claiborne swept Nichols' boots off the desk. They slammed down to the floor with a thud, jarring the lawman awake, a curse on his lips as he fought to stay in his chair, grabbing an arm as it swivelled, glaring at his visitors.

His face straightened abruptly and he leapt awkwardly to his feet when he recognized Sean Rafferty.

'Ah — howdy, Sean. Just catchin' up on a bit of shut-eye. Busy night last night.'

'No wonder you find it hard to sleep

at night when you sleep all day, Sheriff,' the rancher said sardonically. He flicked a kerchief at the straightback chair opposite the desk and sat down slowly, folded his hands over the silver top of his ebony cane.

Claiborne leaned a beefy shoulder against the wall near the gun cabinet, rugged face unsmiling.

Nichols ran a hand around his jaw and the day-old stubble rasped. 'I looked into McColl's shootin', like you asked, Sean, but I couldn't find anything worthwhile.' He lowered his voice conspiratorily. 'Less'n you count his tracks were well into A-Bar-W land. I'd say that's where he was shot but — what the hell was he doin' trespassin' so far onto Angie's place?'

'Forget McColl — he had plenty of enemies, and I *know* that this new man of Angie's was one of them. Lindsey's pretty sure he killed Mac but there's no way to prove it.'

'Well, whoever it was nailed him dead centre through the ticker.'

'Link said this Lucky was a dead-shot,' Claiborne allowed, but neither man took any notice of him.

'What've you found out so far?' Rafferty asked Nichols and the sheriff looked mighty uncomfortable.

'Hardly anythin', Sean — look, you gotta unnerstan' that I ain't got much to go on. Feller's found staggerin' in the desert, says he's got no memory of bein' there — I mean, how can I say different?'

Rafferty sighed, leaned forward a little. 'We know now that he came down from the north, a long way north according to Link. You send some telegrams to lawmen up that way, far as Montana if you have to. Ask about anyone wanted using the nickname of 'Lucky' and anything they've got on him — is that so hard?'

Nichols shrugged and took a cheroot from a vest pocket and lit up. 'Ain't hard, Sean, but it's costly — '

Rafferty flicked his gaze to Claiborne who moved swiftly and kicked the chair

Nichols sat in. It spun wildly, Nichols grabbing at the arm, shouting 'Hey!' and then Claiborne stopped it abruptly and the sheriff slid off the seat, scrabbled wildly to keep from sprawling on the floor.

'God-damn! What the hell you doin', Clay?'

'Mr Rafferty pays you plenty! So just *send the goddamn telegraphs*!' Claiborne grabbed his shirt front and thumped him down into his chair. The burning cheroot fell into the sheriff's lap and he scrabbled wildly for it, picked it up, burning his fingers. Claiborne snatched it from him and rammed the burning end against the lawman's ear.

Windy Nichols screamed and writhed, doubled up as he clapped a hand to his stinging ear, obviously scared now.

Nichols looked up at Rafferty, tears of pain in his eyes. 'Judas, Sean, I done what you asked! I sent heaps of telegraphs . . . '

'To all the wrong places,' Rafferty

told him calmly. 'Now you send 'em north this time — and you find out who this son of a bitch *is*! I want an answer in two days. If I don't get one, Clay here will come visit you . . .'

'Aw, no need for that, Sean.'

Rafferty stood. 'I hope not. Now get on to it, Windy. Two days maximum.'

They left then and Nichols dropped back into his chair, still muttering curses as he wet his fingers with spittle and rubbed it on his burning earlobe. He felt a stir of cold hatred but swiftly put it down. He knew he would never do anything about the anger and resentment he felt for Rafferty and that snake, Claiborne.

Instead, he took out a ledger from his desk and began searching for the names of lawmen in the far north, his hand shaking noticeably.

* * *

Rafferty and Claiborne were walking towards the livery where they had left their mounts when the ramrod suddenly stopped, reaching out a hand to grab his boss's arm, stopping the rancher in mid-stride and earning him a glowering look.

'Chief! There he is! Goddamnit — there he *is*!'

Rafferty recognized Lucky Montana from his visit to Angie's.

He was just coming out of the general store with young Gavin Leach, each man carrying a gunnysack of supplies towards mounts tethered at the hitch rail.

'Time we found out just how good this feller is, ain't it, chief?' Claiborne asked tightly. His eyes narrowed as he watched Angie's men tie their sacks on the horses. 'I mean, he blind-sided me once, took us by surprise with a damn shotgun which I still figure likely wasn't even loaded — wonder how good he is in a square-off.'

'No gunplay, Clay — not just yet.' Rafferty said quickly. 'Remember Mac — it had to've been Lucky who killed him. The kid couldn't do it, Link was out of it, and that only leaves Horseshoe or the girl. It had to've been Lucky.'

'Just another reason to brace him, chief! What d'you say?'

Rafferty hesitated: violent confrontation wasn't his style at this stage of the game, or unless he was forced into it. But Claiborne had a legitimate beef with this man. It would look OK, and test them both — and those damn investors *were* crowding him; he needed to show them he was doing *something* . . .

'I hope you're up to it, Clay!' he said finally.

Claiborne snorted and spat in the dust, hitching at his trouser belt. 'Send someone for the sawbones, Chief — Lucky's 'luck' is about to run out.'

He was moving away with long strides before he even finished speaking and when only a few yards from Montana and Gavin, the young greenhorn spotted Claiborne, swiftly spoke a warning to his companion.

'Trouble!'

Lucky looked up casually, tightened his rope on the grubsack and turned to face the storming Claiborne, looking at his ease.

'I want to talk to you!' gritted Claiborne, still striding in fast.

'No you don't,' Montana replied. 'What you want to do is beat my head in — or try to. See how you go.'

And Gavin Leach gasped as Montana stepped forward, weaved to one side and drove a fist into Claiborne's midriff.

The Rafferty ramrod grunted and doubled up, sliding back a pace or two. Montana followed, lifted a knee into his face and when he straightened slammed two left jabs into his face, hooked with a right and knocked Claiborne off the boardwalk to flounder in the street. He stepped down as Claiborne shook his head and instinctively fought to his feet.

Montana stepped forward to slam him again but his ankle turned in a rain-eroded gutter and he stumbled. His blow passed over Claiborne's right shoulder and the man lunged forward, getting the point of his left shoulder into Montana's mid-section. Lucky grunted and grabbed at the man's thick body as the ramrod's weight carried him back and down.

They rolled and kicked and elbowed and punched and snarled as they fought to get their feet under them. The horses at the hitch rack whinnied and shied and stomped and Claiborne yelled as a hoof gouged his riding boot. Lucky got a knee into the man's chest, heaved him away, rolled to hands and knees and jumped upright.

The Rafferty ramrod was only a second behind him and they met again with boots dug in, hips swivelling as they traded blow after blow, skin tearing, blood splashing. Lucky threw up a left forearm, parrying a blow, but it was a feint and Clay got him with his other fist alongside the jaw. Montana's head snapped sideways and he staggered. Claiborne bulled in, fists cocked, then hammering, his sheer weight driving Montana backwards. Then Lucky stopped, stepped nimbly to the left, twisting side-on at the same time. Claiborne stumbled with the force of the blow he had swung and Lucky clipped him on the ear, moved around and hooked him twice in the ribs, each blow bringing a loud grunt of pain from the other, Clay's feet leaving the ground. Then Montana drove a straight right with his shoulder behind it into Claiborne's face, but it was a little off and didn't finish the fight as Lucky had expected.

The ramrod floundered, dodged a boot, and thrust up like a piston rising in a steam cylinder, met Lucky's charge with legs braced. Montana staggered back as he met the solid wall of muscle and flesh. Claiborne sniffed, wiped the back of a hand across his bleeding nose — and that habit, only a second or two

— cost him a punch under the left eye that sent him reeling, his neck feeling as if it had snapped.

His arms flayed at the air and he spun in a kind of macabre dance, and when he got his balance, Lucky Montana was waiting with cocked fists. They hammered Clay from jaw to brisket, Montana's elbows working, fists blurring as they bruised ribs and solar plexus. Claibourne clutched at his assailant, trying to stay on his feet. His legs were caving in and Lucky stepped back. Claiborne reached desperately, fell forward — right onto a rising knee.

He went down hard and was slow to attempt getting up this time, the world swimming dizzily around him. Lucky, breathing hard, face smeared with blood, stepped forward, and drove a boot into Clay's side.

The man rolled over, drawing up his knees. Montana towered above him, nudged him roughly with a boot toe, and when the sick ramrod made no attempt to rise, reached down and twisted his fingers in the long greasy hair.

Claiborne yelled as he was lifted, feeling as if his scalp was tearing away. He thrashed and flailed but when his head was just above Montana's waist level, Lucky said, 'Link sent this!'

And drove a clubbed fist down into that ugly, bloody face. Folk who had gathered to watch heard the nose go and the teeth *clunk* together hard enough to break, or at least chip. A dreadful shudder passed clear through Claiborne's entire body and his eyes rolled up, showing the whites. Lucky hit him again, between the eyes, and let him go.

Rafferty's ramrod fell face first into the dust, no more fight left in him.

Lucky Montana stood there, swaying on rubbery legs, breathing hard, chest heaving as he fumbled for a kerchief and dabbed at his bloody face. Then he felt Gavin Leach leading him to the horse trough and the gaping spectators opened out to let them through.

It was quite a spectacle to see a man like Claiborne spread out in the dust, beaten down and bloody.

After sluicing water on his face, Montana looked up and saw Rafferty standing on the walk. He tossed the Irishman a mocking salute.

'You'll need better men than that,' he panted, but Rafferty showed no reaction, merely turned and spoke to Sheriff Nichols who had come running up, carrying a sawn-off shotgun down at his side. The rancher paid no attention to his battered foreman as someone dragged Clay over to the walk clear of the traffic. The man groaned as he started to come to slowly — and mighty painfully. But Rafferty pointed to Lucky Montana and snapped at the lawman.

'Arrest that man! He started the fight — I sent Clay across to tell him I'd like a word and next thing he's beating on him!'

Plenty in the crowd murmured — a lot of people had seen how the fight started and they were on Montana's side. Many of them had felt Claiborne's bullying fists over the years. Nichols licked his lips, but at a savage glare from Rafferty he stepped down and started towards Montana.

'I want a word with you about the shootin' of McColl anyways, mister!' the sheriff said, bringing the shotgun up into both hands, a thumb poised over a hammer.

'Save your breath, Sheriff,' Lucky said, still breathing a little hard. 'McColl laid for me at Broken Tooth, bushwhacked me.' He held out the punctured corner of the leather vest and showed the bullet hole. 'If someone'll hand me my hat, I'll show you a hole in the brim — fired from above. I can take you to the place, show you fresh bullet marks on rocks, all from above where McColl lay. I can show you his boot prints on the edge of the cliff above where I found Link Cady and his horse amongst the rocks below.'

Nichols blinked. 'You sayin' Mac

pushed Link off?'

Lucky shook his head. 'No — I'm saying he *threw* him off, his body, leastways. Because Claiborne had already beat him to death. They were trying to make it look like an accident, just as they did with Walt Bancroft, but he spotted me riding in and decided to square a couple things he figured he owed me.'

'This man's crazy,' Rafferty said easily. 'You'd do everyone a favour by locking him up and checking his background, Sheriff.'

Montana set his hard gaze on the rancher. 'Take a look at Claiborne's boots. Splashed with brown marks — it's Link Cady's dried blood. I found bootmarks on Link's ribs. Check Clay's trousers, too. They're splashed with more blood, not from the fight, but a long time before when he beat up on Link.'

Nichols was bewildered but Rafferty's bleak gaze told him what to do. He moved the ball of his thumb swiftly to the spur of the gun hammer, aiming to cock the weapon.

There was the crash of a gunshot that scattered the crowd and made Rafferty leap for his life as the shot-gun spun from Nichols' grip and the sheriff yelped, grabbed at his numbed fingers and stared at the bullet burn across the back of his hand. He snapped his gaze up fearfully and saw the smoking six-gun braced against Lucky Montana's hip.

Gavin Leach, white-faced, stood about a yard away, staring. The crowd gaped and Claiborne, half-conscious, let his aching, swollen jaw drop a couple of inches.

'Sheriff,' Montana said slowly, 'you've got no reason to arrest me. I don't aim to let you arrest me. You try again and maybe my next bullet'll do more than just tear a gun outa your hands.'

'I-I can charge you with attempted murder, resistin' lawful arrest, woundin' a lawman . . . ' blustered Nichols but paused when Lucky merely shook his head slowly.

'You can do those things, Sheriff, but only if you want to die. And you don't look to me like the kinda lawman who's willing to lay his life on the line.'

Nichols swallowed and Rafferty snorted in disgust and strode away angrily towards the livery. The sheriff, wrapping a kerchief around his bleeding hand, started after him.

'Wait up, Mr Rafferty! I-I cain't do nothin'! You seen him! Half-brother to a bolt of lightnin'!'

'Get those telegraphs away!' Rafferty snapped, entering the livery.

By that time, Gavin and Montana were riding slowly out of town towards the A Bar W trail.

'You're in plenty of trouble now,' Gavin opined,

'Been in worse.'

'But — you wounded a lawman!'

'He's not a lawman: he's Rafferty's man.'

Gavin stared a while. 'I've never met anyone like you, Lucky.'

'We're a dying breed. Oops! Mebbe I

could've worded that better.' Lucky winced, putting a hand swiftly up against his aching jaw. 'That Claiborne packs a wallop.'

'Yes, he's a tough customer, all right. But did you need to hit him that last time?' Gavin asked tautly, and Montana looked at him through a puffed eye on that side.

'Why not?'

'Well, he was already beat. Seemed unnecessary to me.'

'Now he'll remember it — new experience for him.'

After a dozen more paces, the kid said, 'Why'd you say that about Link? 'This one's for Link!' I mean, he wasn't much of a man and you didn't seem to take to him.'

'He worked for Angie, didn't he? Took his beating while on her payroll.'

'Ye-es, but he was obviously going to steal from her — I mean, those mavericks you found hidden away.'

Montana hitched slightly in the saddle, unnerved the kid the way he looked at him out of that battered, still bleeding face.

'Kid, you've got a lot to learn. A man don't have to be a saint seven ways to Sunday just because he rides for the same brand — what matters is, good or bad, if he rides alongside you, he's your pard for the time being and if anything happens to him, the same thing could happen to you. So you fight — on his behalf as much as yours. You fight for the brand and whoever rides for it, no matter whether you like 'em or not.'

Gavin flushed, then said, 'I never expected to hear that kind of philosophy from a — an admitted outlaw!'

Montana smiled faintly and it was obvious it hurt to do it.

'Like I said, kid, you've still got a lot to learn.'

8

Gunslinger

Angie Bancroft wasn't pleased with the news.

'That was rather extreme, wasn't it, drawing your gun on a lawman, whether he's straight or crooked?'

Montana arched his eyebrows. 'He was cocking the hammer on a shotgun.'

'And Lucky beat him!' Gavin put in, unable to keep the excitement from his voice. 'I couldn't believe it. Half the town was there and they couldn't believe it either! He drew and fired while Nichols was still cocking the hammer — and the sheriff wasn't doing it in slow motion.'

Angie frowned. 'You have a reputation as — as a gunslinger?' she asked Montana.

He shrugged. 'Up north a few

might've heard of me — small frog in a big pond. There're others faster.'

'I'd sure like to see 'em!' Gavin said, with a sceptical chuckle.

Montana was sober. 'There's a man named Dawson . . . '

'The man your enemies hired . . . ?' Angie said slowly.

He nodded. 'Hell in a hand-basket with a six-gun.'

'Is he still looking for you?'

'Guess so. They say once he takes a job he don't quit till it's finished — even when the hire money runs out, he's been known to keep on till he gets his man.'

Her frown deepened. 'Then he could trail you here?'

Lucky hesitated. 'Doubt it. That dead sheriff I put the handcuffs on ought to hold things for a while. If you want me to move on, Angie, say so. Don't be afraid to speak up.'

She tossed her head, met his gaze steadily. 'I won't. I just hope you haven't brought a lot of trouble down on yourself, and indirectly A Bar W, by shooting at Windy Nichols.'

'If I have, I'll handle it — and keep you out of it.'

'You told me a man rides and fights for the brand he works for,' Gavin said slowly. 'Shouldn't that work the other way round, too?'

Lucky smiled slowly: his injuries felt a little better since Angie had doctored them with iodine and arnica. 'I'd like to think so, kid, but sometimes it's easier and wiser for a rancher to disown some troublemaker she's hired.'

Angie looked indignant. 'That's not the case here! I hired you to help me keep this ranch. Any trouble you find yourself in is my trouble, too, and you can rely on the fact that I'll back you to the hilt.'

Montana nodded briefly, hitched at his gunbelt. 'Well we all seem to know what we ought to do, so what's next, Angie?'

'I was thinking maybe you had a suggestion? I mean, I don't want to carry this fight to Rafferty and give him reason to use Nichols and his version of the law against us, or an excuse to call in a crew on fighting wages.'

She and Gavin both looked expectantly at Lucky Montana.

'I think we should let things lie for now. I'll take a ride through the valley, have a talk with the few spreads you told me still remain.'

'Only because they're on the fringe, or up too high for Rafferty to bother with, but there are still a couple of the ranchers who sold out to him under pressure living on their places until he's ready to flood the valley. He agreed to that.'

'OK, I'll go see 'em. Give me a week, maybe. That'll keep Nichols off your back if I'm not here, anyway.'

Gavin looked alarmed. 'What if Rafferty makes a move?'

'He won't — he's not sure of me yet. He thinks I could be a drifter, looking to hire out my gun, an outlaw on the run, maybe even undercover law.

Because he's up to something that's not as legal as he tries to make it appear.'

Angie looked puzzled. 'What gives you that idea? It seems legal enough, buying our ranches, his scheme backed by businessmen back East — and the government, he claims.'

'Not sure the government's in it right now. It'll help, I guess, if he comes up with an acceptable plan. The men who control the public pursestrings usually want ironclad guarantees before they invest a dollar. As for 'businessmen', they're in it for profit and won't look too closely at his methods. I think he'll sit tight till he's sure I'm not any real threat to him, just someone on your payroll, Angie.'

'I hope you're right.' She looked worried now.

He smiled crookedly. 'I think Rafferty knows enough about me already to be leery. Heard him tell Nichols to send off some telegraphs as he went into the livery. Reckon they'll be to check up on me. It'll take a week at least for him to get all replies and I'll be back here by then.'

As he stood to leave, setting his bullet-clipped hat squarely on his head, she moved in and placed a hand on his forearm, looking up into his battered face.

'Take care, Lucky. Try and live up to your nickname.'

'Do my best. Gav, you want to get me a sack of grub and some spare ammo?'

At the corral, while Montana was finishing saddling his claybank, Gavin brought out the food and ammunition. He tied them on behind the cantle and asked, 'Those replies to Nichols' wires, Lucky — just the way you said about it taking a week, made me think that maybe Nichols or Rafferty could expect something about you they might not want to hear . . . '

Montana stepped up into the saddle, grunting a little with small stabs of pain from his bruises and stiff joints.

'Whatever they hear they won't like,

kid — guarantee that.'

He nodded, wheeled the horse and rode off across the sun-hammered pastures towards the hills.

Young Gavin pursed his lips thoughtfully, then, as Angie came out onto the porch with a bowl of peas to shell, he called, 'Sis, I'm going riding — think I'll have a bit more practice with my guns.' As her head snapped up at his words, he added, 'No use kidding ourselves, sis, it's going to get down to shooting any time now . . . I have to be ready.'

She knew he was right. Her heart beat faster, and she felt afraid, but she couldn't find the words to stop him.

* * *

The first rancher met Lucky with a rifle, standing in the doorway of the small shack not far from the banks of the Viper River. He looked work-worn and tired, his clothes patched, hair straggly, and he was unshaven. There was movement behind him in the shack and Lucky heard a child's voice, whining for something, a woman remonstrating.

'That's far enough, mister.' The man lifted the rifle and squinted as Montana halted the claybank and leaned his crossed hands on the saddlehorn in the universal sign that he had no hostile intentions. The man ran his eyes over the silent Montana. 'You look like a gunslinger to me.'

Lucky straightened in the saddle, the movement making the rancher tense. 'Relax, *amigo*, I'm not a Rafferty man.'

'You say — what d'you want?'

'Just come to see how you're getting on. Rafferty give you a deadline?'

The man squinted again, moved his rifle to a better position for shooting. 'Deadline? Well, he said we could stay on till he's ready to flood. Dunno when that is.'

'You get your money?'

'Not yet.' The man was tightening up and Lucky watched him warily: a nervous man with a cocked gun pointing at you wasn't anything to take casually. 'We stayed because we got nowheres else to go till he pays up.'

'When did he say he'd do that?'

'You ask a lot of questions, stranger.'

'Bad habit of mine. Name's Lucky Montana.'

It meant nothing to the rancher who said his name was McGovern. 'Why you want to know these things?'

'Working for Angie Bancroft. Had a few run-ins with Rafferty and Claiborne. Like to know all I can about a man who's after my hide.'

McGovern studied him more closely. 'A drunk went through here late at night, whoopin' and a'hollerin'. I come out to tell him to shut up and he said he just had to let everyone in the valley know he'd seen Claiborne hammered into the dust on Main Street — that wouldn'ta been you done it, would it?'

'Aw shucks,' Montana said, putting on an exaggerated bashful look, smiling at the same time.

The rancher snorted. 'My God! Listen, we ain't got much, but you're welcome to anythin' we have. That Claiborne son of a bitch beat my two cowhands silly and made threats agin Nan and the kids — it's why I agreed to sell. You gotta tell me what you done to that hardcase bastard.'

'Not much to tell, but I'll trade it for whatever you can give me by way of information.'

'Done deal, pard — you step on down and come in.'

He lowered the gun and stood to one side of the door. Montana swung down easily and doffed his hat as he entered the draughty shack.

* * *

The next place along had three tough-looking *hombres* working on it, removing heavy, Eastern-made furniture from the log house and stacking it on a couple of Conestoga covered wagons. Their mounts wore the Rafferty brand.

The one who came to meet Montana as he rode in slowly didn't have a gun in his hand, but he wore his six-gun tied down and kept a hand on the butt as he spat a stream of tobacco juice, looking up at the rider. His two companions went on bringing out furniture.

'You're trespassin', mister, Mr Rafferty owns this place now.' He was broad and muscular but not more than medium height and his eyes were restless, never staying on Lucky's face more than a few seconds.

'Where're the folk who built this place?'

'Who knows? Who cares? They've gone, and Mr Rafferty said to take the furniture they left as part of the deal. Now I've told you more'n you need to know. Turn round and ride on out.'

'Looks like good quality furniture,' Montana remarked as he watched the other two struggle to load a heavy mahogany sideboy with carved front and doors. 'Like the stuff they'd brought out with 'em when they migrated.'

'So? They were immigrants, couldn't make a go of it. Mr Rafferty gave 'em a good price.'

'Good for him, but what about the immigrants?'

The man stepped back, his hand tightening on the gun butt. 'I told you to vamoose!'

'Heard you. This was the Higgins place, wasn't it? The husband had some kind of a fall he never really spoke much about — busted both his legs. And his two men quit on him after being beaten up in a staged bar-room brawl. No wonder he couldn't make a go of it.'

'Been talkin' to that gossipin' McGovern, ain't you?' The broad man whistled shrilly once, not turning, and the other two stopped their work and came striding across. They were cut from the same mould as the man who faced Montana. 'Told this sonuver to move along twice — don't seem to want to do it. Guess we'll have to help him . . . '

He jerked his head towards Montana and the two men lunged at the horse. Lucky rowelled the claybank abruptly and it whickered as it leapt forward. The startled men jumped aside and Montana leaned from the saddle, kicked one in the neck and knocked him sprawling, yanked the horse's head around violently as the other man grabbed for the bridle.

The claybank's head smashed into the man and he stumbled back, both hands going up to his face. Blood ran between the fingers as his legs gave way and he sat down, dazed.

The broad man lifted his six-gun in a fast movement, but it was Montana's Colt that roared and he yelled, floundered as he dropped his gun and clutched at his bleeding arm. Lucky jumped the horse into him, knocking him flat, allowed the animal to step on him, the man screaming now.

Montana wheeled the horse, smoking gun still in his hand. He looked down coldly at the three floundering men.

'You'd be wise to cart that furniture into town. The Higginses are staying with her sister in a cabin on the north side, much too damn small . . . like McGovern, they're waiting for Rafferty to square-up what he owes 'em. You give 'em their furniture and they'll be able to afford to rent a decent place until he pays 'em. McGovern says Mrs Higgins is expecting. Got all that? Because I'll check it's done.'

It was the man who had greeted him who spoke, biting back the pain from his bullet-burned arm. 'Rafferty'll kill us.'

'He doesn't, I will,' Montana said, without expression and rode on out, leaving them staring after him.

The one who had been kicked in the neck could hardly speak but he rasped, 'Hell with this — I'm ridin' out.'

'Me, too,' said the man whose face

had been mangled by the horse's swinging head.

The broad man staggered to his feet, face tight with pain. 'You ain't goin' nowhere — not till we deliver this load to the Higginses — then I'll come with you. I ain't gonna be the one to stay behind and tell Rafferty what happened.' He looked after Lucky Montana riding out along the river by now. 'That son of a bitch is a gunslinger if ever I seen one and Rafferty ain't payin' us no fightin' wages . . . '

* * *

Angie Bancroft had more than 200 head of cattle grazing free in her river pasture.

The majority of them had been mavericks that her husband and the cowhands they had hired had rounded-up in the hills, brought down to the river grass and branded them with the A Bar W. They had wintered well there and now with spring moving along nicely after a little rain, the grass was lush and the cows were packing on the beef.

By the time summer was here they would be ready for driving to the railhead and shipping to the meat houses. She was looking forward to getting a good price because her herd had come down from the hills earlier than others in the valley and she hoped her trail drive would be first out of the valley. Besides, there were no other herds worthy of the name ready for the drive to railhead, not now Rafferty was buying out everyone. As for Rafferty's own herds, well, he would move them at any time, bullying his way up-valley, letting his cows feed on the grass of the small ranches, promising to pay once his beef was sold, but never doing it.

Angie hoped Lucky Montana would still be here when trail-drive time came around. She had a feeling that this year she was going to need all the help she could get.

And a man like Montana, with his

guns, was just what the doctor ordered . . .

But Angie needn't have worried about the coming trail drive. For two nights after Lucky had started his ride through the Viper River Valley, a small band of dark riders crossed the river from the direction of Rafferty's and paused at the barbed wire fence that kept the cattle from wandering into the river.

'Remember, don't cut the wire,' a muffled voice said quietly. 'Work on the posts, snap 'em off at ground level, or pull 'em out. When the wire slacks off, lay it on the ground or as close as it'll go . . . '

There were four men and they were all masked with bandannas covering the lower halves of their faces. The cows were scattered through the pasture, not needing nighthawks, being a small herd in a fenced section of lush grass. They were content and wouldn't wander far. The fence was there just to make sure.

The riders tore it down along the river side of the pasture, set their horses across and then rode in on the sleeping cows. They had smoke pots with them, a mixture of gunpowder and greasy rags with short fuses, in old preserve jars.

At a word from the leader, matches flared and fuses spluttered and the pots were hurled amongst the bunches of cattle. The powder flashed without exploding, but it hissed and crackled and made the pots jump as if they were living things, flaring brightly, terrifyingly. Some hit the cows and the beasts bawled as hide singed and burning powder spattered them, smoke stinging eyes and rasping at nostrils.

The men rode around the frantic cows, pushing them into several small bunches, then driving them together into one large bunch.

By now they were hard to control and the flares were dying, but a pall of thick smoke hung like a curtain between them and the house so they turned towards the only way out — over and through the sagging fence and into the river.

There were men waiting on the far bank, riding out into the water, turning back the first of the swimming, eye-rolling, bawling cows that tried to make it to Rafferty land.

The other men were crowding them from behind and the two lots met and mixed it up, shoulder to shoulder, horns gouging, panicked steers leaping on top of others, cloven hoofs tearing flesh and bringing more pain and more panic.

The river churned as the cows battled each other and the riders, churned and foamed until the muddy waters took on a reddish hue, the colour visible even on this moonless night.

The men crossed upstream from the drowning chaos, met with the others, and rode back to the Rafferty bunk-house, only two staying behind to wipe out their tracks and collect the remains of the smoke pots from the trampled pasture.

They were gone by the time lights

showed in the distant house, the blood-chilling bawling of the steers finally loud enough to rouse the inhabitants.

A little while later, gunshots crackled through the night along the river as crippled steers were put out of their misery and Angie and Gavin began to count their losses.

Even Old Horseshoe limped down to help, bringing a battered pot of his infamous coffee and a couple of tin cups.

But even that powerful brew failed to settle Angie's nerves.

She had been counting on that herd to see her through, the money helping her to fend off Rafferty.

Without it she knew she would go under.

9

Bushwhacked

Angie and Gavin stood on the river-bank, smoking rifles down at their sides, old Horseshoe standing in the background with his battered black coffee pot.

'It was Rafferty,' Gavin said tightly.

Angie glanced at him sharply: she knew it had to be connected to Sean Rafferty in some way but she didn't care for the kid's sudden cold tone or the unaccustomed hard look in his eyes. As he spoke and surveyed the slaughter, he was pushing fresh cartridges through the loading gate of the hot rifle. He rested it against a rock, took out his Colt and checked the loads in the cylinder.

'We can't go off half-cocked on this, Gavin,' she said quickly. 'If we make any kind of move against Rafferty he'll use Windy Nichols to cause us no end of trouble, maybe throw us in jail — and in no time at all he'd have his hands on A Bar W.'

'Like hell he will!' There it was again, that bleakness in his face and voice, like she had seen and heard in Lucky Montana when he had braced Rafferty and his men that time with the unloaded shotgun. 'There's broken glass all over the pasture, blackened patches — Horseshoe said they're from smoke pots.'

Angie looked levelly at the old cook. 'Smoke pots . . . ?'

'Some call 'em flash pots,' Horseshoe told her. 'Pack a preserve jar with some gunpowder and ram greasy rags on top. Set it off with a fuse of just a strip of burnin' rag and toss 'em in among a herd. They flash, smoke like crazy, but there's no bang. Scare the cows outa their hides. We used it in the army to stampede Injun ponies before we hit their camp.'

Angie had seen the snapped-off fence posts and had at first believed it was a stampede set off by some natural force that had terrified the herd. But she had wondered about those streaked black flowers on the ground in several places . . .

'Gavin!' she snapped suddenly, aware that her brother was running towards his horse, ground-hitched ten yards back. 'What're you doing?'

'Going to brace Rafferty, Sis. This is my fault. I should've been riding nighthawk and it wouldn't've happened.'

'You little fool! If you had been, you'd be dead now!' She started to run after him but Gavin was already jumping into the saddle, ramming his rifle home in the scabbard, rein ends between his teeth as he did so, using his knees to turn his horse. 'Gavin! Please! Don't . . . '

'I'm going to have it out with Rafferty once and for all! I'll be back, Sis!

He splashed the mount into the river and urged it across, the noise of the river drowning his sister's screamed words.

He disappeared into the brush on the other side rowelling his horse brutally, heading fast into Rafferty land.

She rounded on Horseshoe. 'Why didn't you stop him!' she shouted unfairly, but the old man sniffed and shrugged.

'Kid's got the right notions, Angie. You can thank Lucky Montana for that.'

'To hell with Lucky Montana! I could kill him for planting such notions in Gavin's head!' Tears flooded suddenly. Her voice broke. 'He — he'll be killed! He's still only a boy, Horseshoe! He thinks because he can shoot pretty good — that — that he can — '

'I can still ride,' cut in Horseshoe abruptly. 'You just gimme a boost up into your saddle, Angie, and gimme that rifle. I'll catch up with Gav.'

'I-I can't let you do that, Horseshoe — you — '

'Angie, I'm the best one, the only one to go after him.' He snatched the rifle from her suddenly and stepped up onto a rock beside her tethered horse, balancing on his good leg. 'You gonna gimme me a boost or do I do it myself? Gav's gettin' closer to Rafferty all the time.'

Crying with anger and frustration and outright fear, Angie helped settle the oldster into the saddle. She jumped back as he kicked the horse away with his good foot and turned it towards the river.

'Horseshoe! Be careful!' she called after him, as he rode into the river. 'Bring him back safely — and you, too.'

⋆ ⋆ ⋆

Gavin rode much faster than Horseshoe — he didn't even know the oldster was behind him. He pulled ahead, weaving his mount through dry washes and draws, unfamiliar with Rafferty's land. He rode into several dead ends, wheeled around, swearing, disoriented, and, after the fourth time, felt his belly knot as he saw a rider coming out of timber on a rise above him, from the way he had just come.

Heart hammering, he reached for his rifle, but paused when he saw it was Horseshoe. He blinked. 'What the — what're you doing here?'

'Come to back you up,' called Horseshoe, and started the mount down the slope. 'Promised Angie I'd bring you back safe.'

Anger burned Gavin's ears. 'Dammit, I can do this! I know what to do and I don't need your help!'

'Well, you got it whether you — '

Gavin's horse jumped and almost threw him as a rifle whipcracked from a line of boulders on a ledge above where the A Bar W men were. As he fought the animal to a standstill, he watched in horror as Horseshoe was knocked out of the saddle, hit the slope awkwardly and started to slide and roll down, arms flopping limply.

Only now did the kid pull his rifle from the scabbard, his gaze searching out the bushwhacker's position. In disbelief he watched as the man stood up, sighting down his rifle, disdaining cover so as to get in a good shot.

He was either mighty brave, or mighty stupid, Gavin thought, even as he threw himself violently out of the saddle. The bushwhacker fired and for the first time in his life, Gavin Leach found out what it was like to have a bullet driving into his flesh.

He twisted in mid-air, smashed to the ground, rifle flying from his grasp, hat gone, blood matting his pale-brown hair.

* * *

When Lindsey rode in and told Sean Rafferty he had shot both Gavin Leach and old Horseshoe, obviously mighty pleased with himself, the rancher went very still, looked back out of eyes like dark beads.

'You shot 'em *dead*?'

'I got Horseshoe in the chest, blew him clean outa the saddle, an' I got the kid in the head! His hair was all bloody and he never moved a finger after tumblin' off his hoss, chief.' Lindsey was still excited.

'*Did you go down and check?*'

Lindsey swallowed, licked his lips, didn't have to reply. Rafferty swore, clenching his fists. He glanced at Claiborne who was leaning against the wall by the door, arms folded. 'Go back with this idiot and make sure those two are dead!'

'If they're not?' Clay asked, and flinched at the whipcrack tone his boss used.

'I said *make sure they're dead!*'

Claiborne flushed. 'I savvy, chief.'

Rafferty looked worried now, toying with a pen on his desk. 'Either way, that damn drifter's going to come here looking for Lindsey — if not me! So you get back here fast, whatever you find.'

Claiborne paused as he set his hat on his head. 'Chief, he'll be after Lin, all right — so why don't we send him up into the hills for a few days?'

'What?' Lindsey asked, startled.

But the rancher nodded slowly. 'Good idea, Clay. You heard, Lin. Get some camping gear, go back to where you shot Angie's men, make sure they're dead, then head for the hills. We'll send for you when it's safe to come back.'

'Wait up! Montana'll come after me! I need some back-up if you're gonna use me as bait.' Lindsey was noticeably sweating now.

Claiborne smiled crookedly. 'You'll get your backup, you damn fool — you just won't see me is all. Nor will Mr *Un*lucky Montana!'

* * *

The Viper River Valley was sure lush country, Montana allowed, as he made his way down the snake-like course of the river. So far he had called in at six spreads whose owners had been forced to sell to Rafferty by various means — most barely legal, some highly illegal, with terror raids or beatings and shootings.

It soon became obvious that Rafferty hadn't actually laid out much money. All the contracts were for final settlement to be made when the last ranch in the valley has been acquired by Sean Rafferty's 'Viper River Valley Development Association'.

The Irish rancher had paid at most only ten per cent of the agreed purchase price, the balance to be paid when Angie Bancroft sold Rafferty the A Bar W. It was yet another way for Rafferty to increase pressure on Angie: the other ranchers would want the rest of their money as soon as possible so would urge her to sell quickly.

Angie had said nothing to Montana about such pressure but the opportunity for it to happen was definitely there.

Most of the ranches were empty but

a couple, like Asa McGovern, stayed on, waiting for the final payment, wishing they hadn't given in to Rafferty's force and signed the sale contract in the first place.

The last ranch, at the far northern end of the valley, where it began to spread out onto the plains beyond, was still inhabited by the original settlers, a middle-aged couple named Tate and Emma Pritchard. They watched Lucky approaching the house and even from twenty yards away he could see the tension in them.

He waved but it didn't relax them. The man looked solid, his clothes old and patched but clean. There was a good deal of grey in his hair although McGovern had said he was only in his mid-fifties. The woman barely came to her husband's shoulder, her colourless hair drawn back tightly, showing her pink scalp in front but doing nothing to smooth the careworn wrinkles. There were bags under her blue eyes and she looked sad.

Montana stopped the sorrel a few yards out from the stoop which was made of packed earth rammed into a log frame, the logs notched for stability and strength like the cabin itself. Must be hard to give up a place like this, Lucky thought. *Obviously it had been built for permanence. Now . . .*

'Howdy folks. Name's Montana. Been making the rounds of the valley and spreads bought by Rafferty.'

Tate Pritchard looked at him with his square jaw thrusting a little, silent, unsmiling. Montana gave him a minute but when he didn't reply or ask him to step down, he added, 'Maybe 'bought' is the wrong word. Hate to tell you, but the way I see it, none of you are going to get any more money out of Sean Rafferty. I believe he's gonna run you out of the valley with no more than what you happen to be wearing at the time.'

Pritchard replied this time, his face colouring. 'Well, you're just the kind of visitor we been lookin' for, bringin' us good news like that!' He spat.

'Sorry, Mr Pritchard. I just wanted to get you talking. But I believe it's true. And I think you do, too.'

Emma took her husband's arm. 'We suspect it's true, but we have to hope we're wrong, Mr Montana.'

'I'd be happy for you to call me 'Lucky', ma'am. I didn't come here to . . . ' His words trailed off when he saw the frowns on their faces and the way Emma tightened her grip on Tate's arm. 'What's wrong?'

Tate took a deep breath. 'We heard there was someone workin' his way through the valley, checkin' out the ranches. Everyone figures you work for Rafferty.'

'Not so. You have my word I'm Angie's man.'

Tate hesitated, nodded to his wife as she said, 'Asa McGovern rode down last night. Said to watch out for a man calling himself 'Lucky'.'

'Well, that's me — Lucky Montana. Not necessarily a true nickname but

I'm here to help in any way I can.'

Pritchard squinted sceptically. 'How?'

'Well, we might get round to that a little later.' Montana took a folded paper from his pocket and studied it. 'You're the last spread up this way, but there's one out on the edge of the plains, the Westmeier spread — Rafferty make them an offer, too?' As he asked, Emma went into the house and Tate said, 'Westmeier still works his place. He's just outside the valley, but he's had his troubles of late — stampedes, fences cut so his remuda wandered onto a patch of loco weed — kinda thing we all had before Rafferty turned up on the doorstep with his offer to buy.' His mouth twisted bitterly. 'On his conditions. I figure Westmeier's on his list.'

Then Emma emerged from the house holding a grubby envelope which she held up to Montana. He took it, obviously puzzled. 'Asa McGovern asked us to give this to you when you showed up. He was very nervous, wouldn't even stay for coffee, said he had to get back to Nan right away.'

Intrigued, Montana opened the envelope, swiftly read the few lines of childish words written on a piece of torn paper:

Yu best cum bak — angjie lost herd. Kid and Hossshu shot

McG

Lucky went very still, staring, reading the brief message again, taking long enough for Pritchard to ask with concern:

'Everythin' all right? Mac wouldn't tell us nothin'.'

'Worried about his wife and the baby, I guess — Rafferty's crowding Angie. Seems Gavin and Horseshoe have been shot. I'd best be going.'

As he lifted the reins, Emma said, 'Wait — your grubsack looks mighty thin. We can spare a little food.'

'Thanks, ma'am, but I'll ride straight

through — be back at A Bar W by morning. Good luck.'

* * *

When Lucky Montana rode the foam-streaked horse into the Bancroft ranch yard early the next morning, Angie appeared, holding the same shotgun he had used to drive off Rafferty and Claiborne. It seemed like a long time ago now and he realized quite a deal had happened since he had shown up here.

'It's me, Angie,' he called, riding in out of the sun that was just lifting above the range like a ball of blinding white gold. She lowered the gun a little. 'I got word that Gavin and Horseshoe have been shot.'

He dismounted, loosened the cinch strap even as he spoke and she lowered the gun even more. She pushed back a stray strand of hair from her face and he saw the weariness and the deep-etched worry lines clearly.

'Horseshoe's dead,' she told him heavily.

'I don't know how Gavin managed to bring him back in his condition . . . '

Montana mounted the porch steps. 'The kid OK?'

'He has a head wound — I think he's starting to come round now. He passed out after bringing in Horseshoe.'

He was beside her now, took her arm to steady her, urging her back through the doorway. 'Let's see what he's got to say for himself.'

Gavin was conscious, lying in his bed in his room, but it was clear he wasn't too aware of his surroundings right now. Montana talked the woman into making a cup of coffee while he sat with Gavin, giving him time to get his bearings. He thought it best to keep Angie busy.

He sat beside the bed, touched Gavin's shoulder, and the kid's eyes fluttered half-open, a small movement in his pale gaunt face beneath the bandages swathing his head.

Speaking quietly, Lucky told him his name and that he had been head-shot and was in his own bedroom at his sister's ranch, repeating the information several times until Gavin's eyes opened all the way and stared at Montana blankly for a moment. Then he gave a wan smile.

'Howdy — Lucky. I-I went after Rafferty like a — damn fool. Got Horseshoe killed . . . '

'No. He did the right thing riding after you, kid. You see who did the bushwhacking?'

The kid thought for a few moments, then nodded slowly. 'I saw him. So confident I wouldn't . . . give him any trouble after he shot . . . Horseshoe that he-he stood up, in the . . . open, took his time drawing his bead . . . ' He shook his head roughly, grimacing. 'Like I didn't count. I was way too slow getting my rifle out, Lucky . . . '

'Who was it, Gavin?'

'L-Lindsey.'

Montana nodded gently, patting Gavin's shoulder. 'Just take it easy, kid. I'll handle things now.'

Gavin tried to struggle up, but it was too much. Gasping, he said, 'But it's *my* job! She's my . . . sister!'

'You proved you're game. You just got a little to learn about being trail-smart is all. Leave this with me.'

The wounded man wanted to argue, tried to hold Montana's sleeve as he stood, but his grip was way too weak. His words were slurred and trailed off before Lucky reached the bedroom door. 'Rest easy, Gav. You did good.'

In the kitchen, Angie was pouring coffe and she looked at him quizzically. 'How is he?'

'He'll be OK — just a scalp crease. Knocked him off-centre for a while. McGovern's note said something about you losing a herd?'

She nodded, brought the coffee to the table and sat down opposite him. He drank his coffee despite its scalding heat and she knew he needed something to boost his flagging energy after riding all night from the far end of the valley.

Angie told him about the stampeding of the herd into the river, the broken fence and the signs of the flash pots.

'Used them so they didn't need to shoot off their guns to stampede the herd. Gavin says it was Lindsey who bushwhacked him and Horseshoe.'

As she poured him another cup of coffee, she looked up at him. 'You're going after him, aren't you?'

He didn't answer and, genuinely puzzled, she asked, 'Why? You don't have to — ' She stopped abruptly and nodded gently, still watching his face. 'Of course you do! You're that kind of a man, aren't you? But it's risky, Lucky! Rafferty's obviously going all-out now to drive me off this land. He won't hesitate to order your death!'

'He likely did that long ago. But I'll nail Lindsey. That'll shake him up, make him leery about his next move.'

She frowned. 'I know you're a very hard man, Lucky, and you're used to danger, but why are you helping us? I mean, I'm more grateful than I can say for what you've done but you're a total stranger! You rode in here and — '

'I was *toted* in here, Angie — by your brother. And you doctored me.'

'Is that your answer? *The* answer? You feel you owe us something?'

'Good a reason as any.' He stood abruptly. 'I'd be obliged for a box of cartridges if you can spare some, and then I'll be on my way.'

Seeing him off on a fresh mount, a high-shouldered sorrel gelding, she said, 'Please take care, Lucky. Try to live up to your nickname, will you?'

'I'll try to *live*, Angie. That's what counts.'

She waved him off and called, 'Rafferty might've sent Lindsey away by now, knowing you'll come.'

'I'm counting on it.'

10

Meanest Gun Alive

Sean Rafferty was smoking, alone in his office, trying to figure his next move, when he heard men calling greetings to someone arriving in the yard.

His heart started pounding before he realized that if it was Lucky Montana no one would be shouting 'Howdy!' Annoyed with himself, he thrust back his chair, went to the window and drew the curtain aside. He frowned. Sheriff Windy Nichols was dismounting in the yard. There was a rider with him, a lanky string of a man whom Rafferty had never seen before.

The first thing he noticed was the man's height — six feet four, maybe a little more — his rawhide leanness, then he saw the guns.

This stranger wore two of them, in a

Mexican Border *buscadero* rig, which was one wide belt with two holsters. And this one had *two* rows of cartridges. Here was a man who didn't aim to run low on ammunition. But his hips were so negligible that Rafferty wondered how they supported the weight of two heavy Colts and so many bullets.

But the man moved easily, settled the guns comfortably — Rafferty noted the holster bases were tied down to the man's thighs, though not too low — and then adjusted his hat a little, shading his eyes. His clothes were trail dusted but seemed of good quality. He followed the sheriff towards the house with long, lithe strides, looking around in a movement that seemed casual but one which the Irish rancher had seen on other men — Lucky Montana for instance.

This newcomer was a gunfighter.

He felt the tension grow as he watched the sheriff and the tall man come up onto the porch, went back thoughtfully to his desk and sat down.

When the two new arrivals came in, Rafferty was smoking easily as he toted up tally figures in the ranch ledger, glanced up casually, one finger holding down a number in his list as if it might jump off the page.

'Sheriff,' he greeted evenly, his eyes on the tall man who stood at ease, hands down at his sides, head not moving. But Rafferty knew he hadn't missed a thing.

'Howdy, Sean. Din' see Clay around. He out on the range?'

Rafferty nodded, looking directly at the tall man now. 'He's about his chores, just as you are with yours. What can I do for you? And your friend . . .'

Nichols took the hint. 'Aw, yeah.' He turned towards the tall man. 'Brad, like you to meet Mr Sean Rafferty, biggest man in the valley and goin' to get way bigger when he floods it and makes the desert bloom.'

Rafferty, showing his annoyance now, glared at the sheriff. Neither he nor the tall man made any move to shake hands.

'And this is . . . ?' the rancher ground between his teeth, looking steadily at the tall man now.

'Oh — Brad Dawson. He's lookin' for a man named Lucky Montana. I thought of that feller workin' for Angie Bancroft . . . I got a reply to one of my wires to a sheriff up in Wyoming, too, Sean, says there's a fugitive wanted for killin' a range detective up that way. Goes by the name of Lucky Montana. So when Brad turned up lookin' for a feller of that name, I thought of you.'

Rafferty was leery now. Was this lanky gunslinger a deputy lawman of some kind and this fool of a sheriff didn't realize it?

'Why me? He doesn't work for me,' he said carefully.

Nichols tugged at one earlobe. 'No, but I knew you had an — interest — in him. You see, Brad's a bounty hunter. An' he's chasin' down the re-ward on Lucky Montana.'

Rafferty felt a lot easier hearing that. 'I see — what I *don't* see is why you brought him here.'

'Aw, come on, Sean,' Nichols said with a wary smile. 'Brad ain't got no illusions. He heard on the way down about Montana joinin' up with Angie, which makes him your enemy.'

'Reckoned I'd get more accurate information from an enemy than one of Montana's friends,' Brad said, speaking for the first time, and in a deep, easy-on-the-ear voice, one full of confidence, and a touch of weary arrogance, too. 'I'll take him outa your hair for you, Sean.' If he noticed the stiffening of Rafferty's shoulders at the familiarity he didn't show it. 'I been chasin' this son of a bitch for more'n a year and this is the closest I've gotten to him — except for a time in Rapid City. I almost had him, but made the mistake of callin' on local law for back-up . . . made a mess of it and give him a chance to get away.'

He sounded bitter and there was a

twist to his mouth, a narrowing of the cold grey eyes. Rafferty knew this man hated Lucky Montana with a passion. He figured it would be more than just the reward that was driving him.

Bounty hunters were usually cold, dispassionate men who saw their quarry not as human beings but merely as a face on a wanted dodger with a certain number of figures following a dollar sign.

But this man had a personal stake in bringing down Montana, and that suited Rafferty fine. Just in case Claiborne didn't manage to get him.

'Seems we best have a little talk — over a couple of drinks, I think.' Rafferty got to his feet and went to a cabinet where cut crystal decanters stood. As he took down glasses and poured liquor into them, he said, casually, 'I wonder if I've heard of you, Brad? What was your surname again?'

'Dawson. And if you ain't heard of me before this, you're sure gonna. And so's a lot of other people. They know me up north as the 'Meanest Gun Alive'.'

* * *

Lucky Montana was suspicious.

He rode back to the area Gavin Leach had described as being the place where he and Horseshoe had been ambushed, and saw fresh sign around the dark-brown bloodstains.

Someone had been checking this place recently, he allowed silently, sitting back on his haunches, close to a boulder in case he needed cover quickly. He saw where Gavin had said he had seen Lindsey standing up, drawing a bead on him.

There was no one up there now, but if this was a set-up, they likely wouldn't want to kill him on Rafferty land, too — it could get sticky explaining how two of Angie's men had been shot at on Rafferty property. But he was sure they would push the unwritten law of 'trespass' that a man could shoot anyone not having legitimate business on his land.

Seemed to him, someone had come back to make sure Gavin and Horseshoe were dead. They had split here — one man riding for the hills, the other heading back to the Rafferty headquarters.

Or so the tracks showed. Plainly — *very* plainly — as if to make sure whoever came here couldn't miss them.

He figured it was Claiborne who had gone back to the ranch: he knew the tracks of the man's horse, a long-stepping grey with small feet. There was even a few silvery-grey hairs caught on the coarse surface of the boulder beside him where the horse had rubbed against it.

He glanced again up to the ridge from where Lindsey had shot Gavin Leach. The tracks that led there were larger and he knew these, too: they belonged to Lindsey's piebald.

So they had set him on the run, or he had decided to run himself when it seemed the 'dead' men weren't dead at all — not both of them, anyway.

Lucky figured Rafferty would know he would be the one to come looking, even if the kid was still alive.

He stood slowly, keeping the rifle at the ready as he looked around slowly.

'OK, gents — I'll play your game. But it'll be by my rules.'

The trail led him into the hills, going away from the river, into wild country that Rafferty claimed as part of his spread. A mighty good place for an ambush.

So he rode with rifle out, the butt resting on his thigh, hawk eyes raking the country ahead and to either side. He circled twice, cutting back across the trail, but Lindsey hadn't tried anything fancy. He was just running scared, putting as much distance between himself and Montana in the shortest possible time.

Lindsey would be scared, and rightly so: he knew he was a dead man if Montana got within gunshot range.

The heat of the day had increased considerably now and Montana was feeling it. Lack of sleep drugged him and he was not as alert as he might have been. He was aware of this and kept shaking his head occasionally, rolling a cigarette awkwardly as he kept riding. He took off his hat and poured some canteen water over his head. But he was a long way from the river up here so he used the water frugally: he didn't know when he might be able to refill the bottle.

In mid-afternoon, his horse was blowing, the sorrel's legs more used to flatter country than the steep, broken ground of these mountains. Foam slid over the dark-red glistening hide and the air snorted noisily through the flared nostrils.

Lucky knew he had to rest the animal — and himself.

He found a small brush-lined gulch not far from the top of the crest, already filled with cooling shadows. This was the place: he was impatient to get closer to Lindsey but the man had managed to hold his lead. He knew this country well and Montana figured he would need all his senses honed to a fine edge if he was to come out of this alive.

Fatigue overtook him. He punched in the crown of his hat with the bullet-holed brim, gave the horse half the water in his canteen, swigged a mouthful himself. He badly wanted a cigarette but figured the smell of tobacco would hang in the still air up here and maybe give away his position, so he settled down, hat brim over his eyes, rifle beside him under his right hand, a cartridge in the breech, thumb resting on the hammer spur.

But he fell into a deep sleep despite his resolve to only catnap, allow his weary body to recover some energy . . .

He started awake, hammer spur going back under his thumb, the rifle swinging up smoothly across his body so that it literally fell into his cupped left hand under the wooden forestock. But he stayed his finger on the trigger.

There was no one menacing him.

His alarm was real, though, because it was daylight and early sunshine slashed across his face as his hat fell to one side. Montana's heart was thudding against his ribs and he wasted a little breath cussing — but was glad to see the gusting steam of his words issuing from his bitter-twisted mouth. *At least it was still early, the mountains still under their usual morning chill.*

He got moving as fast as he could, chewing on jerky, knowing the horse had grazed on the succulent young brush that choked the gulch. The rifle was in his right hand as he rode out of the gulch, figuring to find some water so he could refill his canteen. There was little more than a mouthful left now . . .

Then the rifle shot came from above and to his left, the bullet thrumming past his face. Then he was going out of the saddle, to the left, towards the gunman, because the brush was thicker there. The sorrel whinnied and plunged downslope, but only to a group of rocks which would have afforded Montana much better cover although there was too much open ground to cross first. But he rolled under the brush, poked his rifle through a gap in the branches and triggered. The bullet ricocheted somewhere below the crest and he heard a man laugh.

'Thought you was s'posed to be a good shot, Montana! My old granny could do better'n that!'

Lucky couldn't believe it: Lindsey had been stupid enough to *come back* looking for him! He had sacrificed his lead and come looking to see if Montana was indeed following him this morning.

'You must have a death-wish, Lindsey!' Montana called, rolling to his right, and sliding back a few feet.

Lindsey had been waiting for the movement, of course, and raked the brush where Lucky had been originally. Montana heard the man swear, triggered again without aiming. Lindsey laughed again.

'Christ, I dunno why they say you're a good shot! You couldn't hit a hoss if it was standin' in front of you!'

Lindsey raked the brush again and waited. But there was no answering shot this time. The ambusher levered in another shell — and thought he heard a half-stifled moan from below. He grinned tightly, moved his position, threw the rifle to his shoulder, but held his fire.

If he climbed up to a boulder above his position he would get a better view of the brush where Montana lay — hopefully bleeding with Lindsey's bullet deep inside him . . .

He took one last look below, saw no further movement down there, and leapt up, clambering wildly up the face of the big rock above him. It was awkward with the rifle in one hand and his body made a fine target against the light grey basalt. He reached the top, started to rise, turning, and his blood froze.

Lucky Montana was standing on the

slope not ten yards away, rifle held across his body, shaking his head slowly.

'You'd be the dumbest son of a bitch I've ever met, Lindsey,' Montana said, as the Rafferty man made an effort to stand straight and get his rifle up.

Montana's Winchester blurred to his shoulder and there were two bullets in Lindsey before he unkinked his spine. His body arched and twisted as it was flung from the boulder, slid downslope, bringing a small bow wave of gravel and twigs with it. It crashed into the brush where Montana had been hiding originally and when he walked across, rifle barrel pointed at the man, hammer cocked, he knew he didn't have to put another shot into him.

He was dead and, likely, already standing in line at the gates of Hell . . .

Lucky rode the sorrel up to the crest, found Lindsey's piebald tethered to a bush under a scraggly tree and lifted the heavy canteen from the saddle. It was nearly full and he took a long drink, gave some to the sorrel. He unsaddled the piebald and turned it loose, taking the grubsack.

He had no intention of toting Lindsey's body back: the animals could have it. But he relented enough to stack some loose rocks over it, before mounting again and turning the sorrel across the face of the mountain, figuring he wouldn't ride back the way he had come in case Claiborne or some other Rafferty man was waiting to ambush him.

It was a good enough move — but not *quite* good enough.

Claiborne rose out of the rocks behind Lucky Montana, slightly above the cowboy's trail.

'Hey! See how lucky you are this time, Montana!' Clay couldn't resist calling, as he fired hard on the last word as Montana wrenched in the saddle, swinging his rifle up.

Too late.

Claiborne's slug slammed into him, rocking him violently in the saddle, the rifle going off but the bullet carving a path through the tree tops. He slammed across the sorrel's neck, startling it so that it whinnied and lunged away at a run, the reek of gunpowder rasping its nostrils as Lucky held on, rifle under the horse's head.

Claiborne fired several shots, bullets spurting dust, exploding bark from trees all round Montana.

He was too weak and dazed to guide the horse, feeling the crushing pain in his chest, the blood soaking his shirt and smearing across the saddle.

He knew he was hit badly — it had to be bad if it was in the chest — and wondered if his luck had finally run out as the horse plunged on across the mountain face, and the world jarred and faded in and out of focus.

One thought he had before he reached the uncaring stage, was — *How far was Claiborne behind him . . . ?*

11

Dead Man's Ears

Claiborne was savagely angry at himself.

Goddamnittohell! He'd had the man dead centre in his sights but that son of a bitch had lived up to his nickname, twisted a little in the saddle and instead of the bullet going squarely into his chest, it was Clay's impression that it had ripped across the front. Probably tore up the muscle and caused plenty of pain and bleeding, but that wasn't what he wanted: he wanted Montana *dead*!

Now the man had disappeared into the high timber and his damn horse had decided to play — using that frustrating, blood-pressure-lifting game of walking just beyond reach, standing still until he approached and put out a hand for the bridle, then backing-up, turning and trotting off, tail high and contemptuous, a whinny as if to say 'you can't catch me!' In no time at all he was sweating and cussing so bad that his throat was dry and raspy.

Finally — *finally* — the damn jughead had stopped and allowed him to grab the bridle. Claiborne was rough with it, getting a good grip before he sheathed his rifle in the saddle scabbard and, when he climbed on board, he twisted the ears brutally, ramming home the spurs and raking viciously with the rowels. The horse, no doubt sorry it had decided to be playful, snorted and put on a burst of speed as Claiborne continued to rowel and jab without mercy.

Timber slowed the animal and then Claiborne had to check for tracks and blood and that slowed him even further. His mouth tightened as he examined splashes of fresh blood. Looked like the man was still mostly conscious, for he was weaving that big sorrel between the trees and brush, not plunging straight ahead and leaving a trail a blind man could follow.

But he knew if the bullet had gouged Montana's chest it would have taken out a good deal of flesh and there were plenty of blood splashes to confirm that. The man was mighty tough or riding by pure instinct. Many another man would be down by now, sprawled amongst the leaves and twigs and other forest floor detritus, moaning and bleeding, fumbling to reach his gun and having not a hope in hell of doing it before Clay would kill him.

But not this *hombre*! Tough as white cedar with a core of mountain granite. No matter! He was hit and had to be weakening by the minute — and Claiborne was on his trail and wouldn't turn back until he had the man dead. He'd take his head back to Rafferty to prove that Lucky Montana's luck had finally and irrevocably run out.

The thought cheered him up some, but he still wanted to see that hardcase in his sights before dark this day.

* * *

Montana was still in the saddle but he didn't know for how much longer.

He had wrapped the reins around the saddlehorn and then awkwardly tied the remaining ends around his left wrist, using his teeth. The leather cut into his flesh and blood trickled over the back of his hand. He had managed to yank off his neckerchief and stuff it over the deep bullet gouge across the thick muscles of his chest, but he knew he was still bleeding plenty. The gouge was a trough, no doubt filled with bits of grit and grease from the lead missile, not to mention shreds of dirty cotton from his shirt. If loss of blood didn't kill him, it was a good bet that infection would do the job.

But these thoughts only came to him intermittently as he swayed in the saddle, the horse slowed way down by this time. They were still climbing and when they reached the crest he worked the panting animal over through timber and vegetation that was way too thin to offer much cover. He slipped almost all the way out of the saddle. Only the rein tying his wrist to the saddlehorn saved him, the pain knifing through him and waking up his brain with its messages of agony.

Straining, he fought until he was half upright, just as he topped-out on the knife edge of the mountain ridge.

A hornet buzzed wildly from a sapling over to his left and downslope a few yards. He knew what it was: shooting upslope was always difficult and the killer had fired too low. His vision was blurred but he saw movement way back down the mountain, figuring it was Claiborne, but he didn't actually see enough detail to definitely identify the man. It would be logical though: spook Lindsey into making a run for it, holding back and allowing Montana to get behind Lindsey, even to kill the man — that way his mouth was shut permanently. Then Claiborne would come in behind Montana and finish the job.

Yeah! His chest was proof enough of what Claiborne intended . . .

He made no attempt to shoot back now. He was too tuckered out for one thing and it was too awkward to get at his rifle in the scabbard under his left leg for another. He could easily draw his six-gun, but he would only waste lead at this distance.

Then a wave of pain and dizziness swept over him and he flopped sideways again as the rifle below hammered several shots. He heard the ricochets but none of them sounded close. Hardly knowing what he was doing, operating on pure instinct, he nudged the horse down the slope on the far side.

It seemed like a wild ride to him and yet the horse wasn't moving very fast. It, too, was weary and weakened by the long, steep climb and the constant dragging and shifting of the wounded rider's weight. It propped its forelegs on the steep incline and slid and skidded through a thin screen of brush, beginning to snort as it tried to keep control.

'Good boy! Good boy!' he slurred encouragingly. 'Ke-keep goin' . . . Keep on . . . '

The words became unintelligible but the horse kept descending, legs quivering with the strain. Lucky's overheated brain told him that Claiborne would be coming, whipping his mount, driving it relentlessly now that he was this close. The man would be impatient to ride in for the kill.

He tried to lift his head, twist his upper body, so he could look back but the pain suddenly became a broadsword blade searching for his heart. He cried out loud and felt the horse going down under him, falling, sliding, toppling, dragging his left arm almost out of its socket. Somehow a firework exploded inside his skull and then he was nowhere that he knew because it was pitch black and there was nothing to see — or hear — or feel.

Just — nothing.

* * *

Claiborne was sweating and breathing hard by the time his horse managed to reach the crest and stumble over onto the narrow strip of flat ground before the steep slope started.

He wiped sweat out of his eyes, sitting slumped in the saddle, shoulders hunched, chin on his chest. *Goddamn but that Lucky must be tough! Up and over, then down the other side with a bullet in him and spraying blood all over the countryside. Why, Claiborne himself felt tuckered out . . .*

He abruptly stopped his thoughts as he wiped his eyes again and saw below an unbelievable sight: Lucky Montana was down! Leastways, his horse was and the man was pinned across the still sliding sorrel, one arm somehow caught up on the saddlehorn.

The sorrel ploughed through bush

after bush although it was slowing noticeably now, beginning to turn a little and, even as he watched, it caught up on a thicker bush and quivered to a stop. The horse struggled to get on its feet but Montana's unmoving body seemed to prevent it in some way.

Claiborne slid the rifle out of the scabbard, swung a leg over the saddle and dropped to the ground. The grey was panting and snorting and stamping about but he ignored it, stretched out behind a flat slab of shale and settled in, elbow braced, the rifle coming to his shoulder.

He concentrated on his sights, bared his teeth as he saw that Montana was still trapped and fouling the horse's efforts. Mind, the animal itself must be hurt some as well as near exhausted from the climb and the run through the timber before that.

Claiborne drew a careful bead on Montana's sprawled body. It was jerking and flopping with the movements of the horse but he could pin down the spot where the bullet would go in this time: slap-bang in the middle of that wide spread of blood across Montana's shirt front.

'So long, you son of a bitch!'

Claiborne gritted the words exultantly and his finger began to squeeze the trigger.

Then he froze as cold steel pressed into the back of his head — hatless now as he had removed it so he could sight better — and a voice he didn't know, but which sounded even colder than the touch of the gun barrel, said softly, 'Uh-uh, Claiborne — he's mine! Now you just show some good sense, lower the gun hammer, ease off the trigger, and lay the rifle down on the rock. Then turn over slowly without tryin' to get up . . . OK?' Claiborne, stiff with shock, didn't move and the gun eased up its pressure on his head — but only for a moment.

It came back in a short, sharp swing and he felt as if the back of his head had been smashed in. '*OK, I said*?'

'*Jesus*! Yeah, yeah — *OK*!'

He did as ordered, wanted to turn and look at this stranger who had come up on him from behind, his movements masked by the grey's stomping and heavy breathing, and his own fierce concentration on the rifle sights. Steel fingers gripped his shoulder, yanked him off the flat rock, and spun him onto his back.

Blinking, Claiborne stared up at the tall, lanky man holding the gun on him — and got his first good look at Brad Dawson, Meanest Gun Alive . . .

Behind him, looking weary and worried, but hard-eyed, stood Sheriff Windy Nichols.

'Who the hell's this, Windy?' Claiborne grated.

'Sean's new trouble-shooter, Clay. Named Dawson,' the lawman answered. 'He — '

'I got an interest in Lucky Montana,' Dawson cut in, in that mellow voice. 'Now you, you get on that asthmatic jughead, ride the hell back to the ranch and check with Sean — if you gimme one little bitty piece of trouble, I got his permission to shoot the eyes outa your head — which I can, and will, do at twenty paces. You want me to try . . . ?'

'Christ, *no*' Claiborne backed away, still sprawled, watching the gun warily. 'You're — *Brad* Dawson? The bounty hunter from up north, the one they call Meanest Gun Alive?'

'In the flesh, mister. I don't see you climbin' into that saddle . . . '

Claiborne got carefully to his feet, started to pick up his rifle, but Dawson kicked it out of reach. 'Shuck the gun-belt, too,' the bounty hunter ordered and Claiborne swallowed his protest and obeyed, looking at Nichols.

'What's goin' on, Windy?'

'Plain, enough, ain't it?' the sheriff growled. 'Dawson's Sean's top gun now — I just come along to save him from killin' you if you fussed about.'

Claiborne didn't like that but he glanced at Dawson, ran a tongue across his lips and nodded curtly. 'OK — I'll get the straight of this from the chief.'

'Aah — just get the hell outa here!' Dawson snapped, and Clay knew enough not to rile the man any further. 'Go back and relax — I'll bring you Montana's ears by supper-time.'

In two minutes Clay was back over the crest with the sheriff riding by his side, watched with narrowed eyes by Brad Dawson. The grey picked its way down the easier slope on that side, and the further he drew away, the more angry Claiborne became. He paused halfway down, looked up to where Dawson stood watching him.

But all Claiborne did was to snarl a curse and turn his horse, recklessly spurring down the mountain. Nichols followed at a good pace, anxious to get away from the cold-eyed gunslinger.

Dawson watched until he could see both men riding out onto the flats and heading back up valley, before holstering his six-gun and turning to look down the slope on his side.

It appeared that Montana had come

round and was trying to free his left hand from the saddlehorn. Dawson smiled and started down on foot, in sliding sideways movements, never taking his eyes off Lucky Montana who didn't seem aware of him yet.

Lucky strained to free his hand from the reins that had trapped him. The horse was still struggling to get up and if he did so, and started to run in panic — well, Montana would be in for a mighty rough ride, so he had to free himself quickly.

Then suddenly a gloved hand holding a jack knife reached from behind and slashed the reins. Montana rolled off the horse and it heaved, snorting, to its feet, cantered off a little way and stopped, watching, its ears pricked.

Montana lay there, feeling the returning blood sending stabs of lightning-like pain through his arm. He rubbed the wrist hard and looked up at his rescuer, expecting Claiborne to be there, gloating.

He stiffened when he saw Dawson

and winced at pain in his chest as he tried to sit up. '*You*!'

'Yeah, Lucky — finally caught up with you after all this time.' Dawson had holstered his six-gun now and stood with boots spread a little, hands on hips, though close to his twin gun butts. 'And ain't you a *mess*! Look like you're about ready to die — are you?'

Dawson's voice was mocking and Montana stared up at him with pain-filled eyes.

'Not . . . quite . . . yet . . . '

Dawson grinned and stepped forward.

'Well, let's see, huh? I promised Rafferty I'd bring him your ears by supper-time — and the sun's already slidin' into the west . . . '

* * *

It was full dark when Dawson rode back to the Rafferty spread. A quarter moon was hanging in the east, dusty red and glowing like the devil's left eye.

He wasn't surprised when Claiborne's voice called from the bunkhouse porch where the man lounged in a chair made from an empty cask padded with burlap.

'You're late, gunslinger. Couldn't be that Montana give you the slip after all, could it?'

Dawson turned from fumbling with the flap of a saddle-bag towards where he knew Claiborne to be seated, likely with other silent cowboys waiting to hear what he had to say.

He held up something dangling on a leather thong.

'These what you're worried about, Clay? Told you I'd bring back Montana's ears and here they are. Wanna close look? Or have you got a weak belly and you're afraid of losin' your supper?'

12

Settle the Score

Sean Rafferty always ate alone in his dining-room, at a polished mahogany oval table. He took his time with his meals, believing that proper digestion was necessary for a man to function properly, both physicaly and mentally.

He was dabbing at his lips after drinking the final sip of his coffee and brandy when Dawson came in unannounced and held up his trophy, dropping it onto the table amongst the empty dishes.

'That's all that's left of Mr Lucky Montana.'

Rafferty shot to his feet, his heavy padded chair toppling as the legs caught in the carpet pile. '*Get those filthy things off my table!*' he roared. '*Get them off, I said!*'

Dawson arched his eyebrows, picked up the bloody ears by the thong. 'Take it easy — they won't hurt you.'

'The hell do you mean crashing in here during my meal? Get out! We'll talk later.'

Dawson's eyes narrowed as he hooked the thong holding the wrinkled ears over the hilt of his hunting knife, keeping his deadly gaze on the rancher — who was looking decidedly less belligerent now as the gunfighter said, very quietly, 'I'm used to more courtesy than that, Sean. You want to rephrase anythin' . . . ?'

Rafferty forced himself to stay calm, flapped a hand as he righted his chair and dropped into it. 'Forgive me, Brad. Those — things — gave me a start. They're all bloody. Does that mean he was still alive when you . . . ?'

'Well, he hadn't quite started along the road to Hell. You owe me some money, I'm thinkin' . . . '

Rafferty watched the man's hands, still too close to the gun butts for the rancher's liking. 'Of course. I can send to town for it tomorrow — '

'Or we could ride in together and get it. You pay me and then I head back north with the ears and use them to collect the bounty they got on Montana as well.'

'Ye-es — but I've just had another idea, Brad. Sit down.'

Dawson made himself comfortable. 'What's this big idea you've got?'

'You don't give a damn for a man's — standing, do you?' Rafferty couldn't hide his annoyance.

'You mean 'my betters'? Hell, far as I'm concerned I ain't yet met a man I consider is better'n me, Sean. Present company included.'

Rafferty's face flushed and he snapped, 'Don't be impertinent!'

Dawson sighed and started to get up. 'Look, you gonna tell me your idea or you gonna give me a lesson in manners? I'm damn hungry and I'm tired.'

Rafferty quickly held up a placating hand, forced a crooked smile. 'I won't waste any more of your time, Brad, I promise.' Dawson sat again, waiting impatiently. 'I was thinking — seeing as you've killed Montana and Horseshoe's dead and Angie's kid brother is laid up wounded — '

'How you know that?'

'I've had a man watching her place. Anyway, considering those things and that I am being pressured hard by my backers to finish the acquisition of land in the valley' — he paused, spread his hands — 'well, now would seem a good time to force the issue, *make* Angie Bancroft sign the sale contract.'

Dawson appeared just as casual and relaxed as earlier but there was a growing spark of interest in his bleak eyes. 'These fellers you got waitin' in the wings — your backers — they gonna give you money soon as you sign up this Bancroft woman? I mean *give* you money, not just promise it?'

Rafferty hesitated, more watchful now, but he nodded slowly. 'Yes. I need working capital so I can show my good faith to the Lands Commissioner and then — '

'Then he'll put up *his* cash, or make it available to you . . . right?'

'That's right.' Rafferty spoke a little slower now, carefully studying this gunfighter. 'You seem to know something about this kind of thing, Brad?'

Dawson shrugged. 'Wasn't always a gunfighter and bounty hunter — worked for a big lumber company in Oregon once. I was a foreman and the company got into trouble, needed investors and got a little gov'ment money to help 'em out buildin' a string of new army forts. But the company directors split the gov'ment money and lit out for parts unknown. Was my first bounty-huntin' chore, bringin' 'em in . . . '

He let the rest drift off but it appeared to satisfy Rafferty although he seemed much more wary now.

'That your idea?' Dawson asked softly. 'Let some of that gov'ment money stick to your fingers?'

Rafferty stood slowly. 'Shall we get Claiborne and go see Angie right now?'

Dawson stood. 'How about we leave it till mornin'? I need to get on the outside of some supper first.' He paused behind his chair, looking down at Rafferty. 'Might be an idea if you took that slimy sheriff along. His signature as a witness could help show it's all above board and bind the contract a little tighter.'

'Yes, that's fine. Windy is staying here overnight. He and Clay didn't get in till just before dark — fortuitous, eh?'

Dawson went out and Rafferty sat back, lips pursed, drumming thick fingers on the edge of the table.

That gunslinger wasn't as dumb as he looked . . .

* * *

The man Rafferty had had watching the Bancroft place was called Bo Clanton and he was yawning, just waking up when he heard the riders coming down the slope of the hogback rise where he had been all night. *He hadn't expected anyone this early*. Then he recognized Rafferty in the lead, followed by that new gunslinger Dawson, Claiborne and Windy Nichols bringing up the rear

Bo felt guilty because he had slept past sun-up, so before Rafferty could throw a question at him he said, 'Everythin's hunky-dory, Mr Rafferty. No visitors durin' the night.'

He hadn't even been awake long enough to study the ranch yard beyond the rise, but Rafferty didn't seem aware of this. 'Then there's still only Angie and the kid there?' he asked.

Bo nodded enthusiastically. 'That's the way it is, Mr Rafferty.'

'All right, Bo, you can go on back to the ranch and have a decent breakfast.'

Bo Clanton's hunger was more or less legendary on every ranch he had ever worked and he departed quickly, eager to front-up to the breakfast table and a heaping pile of greasy food.

By then, Claiborne, belly down at the crest, was focusing his field-glasses on the house below.

'Smoke comin' outa the kitchen chimney,' he reported, sweeping the lenses around slowly. 'No extra hosses I can make out. Montana's sorrel ain't there, leastways — '

'Were you expecting it?' Rafferty asked curtly and Clay shrugged, looking hard at Dawson.

'Just checkin' — them ears could belong to anybody.'

Dawson stepped forward and kicked Claiborne hard in the ribs. The man gasped, grabbed at his side, rolling over, face contorted. He fumbled for his six-gun but Dawson's boot pinned the hand to his body. The gunfighter shook his head.

'Don't be a bigger fool than you already are, Clay,' he said easily. 'You're lucky I don't kill you . . . '

'Please leave it until after we have Angie's name on the bill of sale,' Rafferty said tiredly, glaring at both men. 'If you are both ready, gentlemen . . . ?'

Sheriff Windy Nichols ran a tongue over his lips, plainly wanting no part of this, but not game enough to say so.

Riding in a tight group, they crested the hogback and rode down into the yard.

By the time they were dismounting at the corrals, Angie Bancroft stood on the porch, holding the long-barrelled Greener as if she knew what she was doing — which she did.

'*Far enough!*' she called, her voice steady, lifting the gun and pointing it in their direction.

Immediately, Claiborne grinned and started moving away from the others, towards the right-hand corner of the house. Angie looked bothered, trying to make a quick decision: where did she aim the gun now? At Claiborne — or the others? Then Nichols, at a word from Rafferty, began to edge towards the left-hand corner of the house.

'Stop!' Angie cried, lifting the gun as

she thumbed back the hammers with audible clicks.

Nichols froze but Claiborne laughed and kept moving.

'You pull the triggers, Angie, and you shoot off both barrels, you'll maybe get Windy *or* me, but only one of us — and you'll still have three to face. Why don't you show good sense and put down the Greener and listen to what Mr Rafferty has to say?'

As he was speaking he kept moving and on his last words he took three long steps and disappeared around the house corner. When Angie snapped her head back the other way, she was just in time to see Windy Nichols' lower leg as he jumped out of sight around the left-hand corner.

When she swung back, she cried out in alarm: Brad Dawson was standing almost on top of her, reaching for the shotgun, forcing her hand away from the hammers, as he twisted the weapon from her grip.

'There now, lady, ain't that better?

No decisions to make, no gun to kick you in the belly or the chest. Just you, and Mr Rafferty's proposition . . . '

As he wrenched the gun from her grip with one hand, he grabbed one of her arms with the other, led her to the top of the steps and moved away, unloading the Greener. He tossed the gun in one direction and the two shells in another.

Angie, white-faced, breathing hard, faced Rafferty now, Claiborne and Nichols coming back from around the sides of the house. 'What d'you want?' she demanded. 'You've killed Horse-shoe and my brother's worsening by the minute . . . Montana never returned so I assume you killed him, too?'

'Forget Montana — his luck's run right out.' Dawson grinned and indicated the ears on their thong, dangling from his bone knife handle.

She grimaced and looked at him coldly. 'Lucky said you were a cold-blooded murderer!'

Dawson bowed slightly. 'He musta

been feelin' good — usually he calls me a lot worse'n that.' He grabbed her arm and, as she struggled, he spoke to Rafferty. 'You ready, Sean?'

'Yes — let's do this in comfort,' Rafferty smiled, in a good mood now. He started up the steps, and chuckled as Dawson dragged Angie through the door into the parlour.

'You keep watch outside, Clay,' the Irishman said over his shoulder and, as Windy Nichols followed the others inside, Claiborne scowled and dropped into one of the split-cane chairs on the porch, reaching for his tobacco sack.

He felt left out of things — something that was happening more and more since the arrival of that son of a bitch Dawson . . .

Then he jumped at the crash of a gunshot inside, leapt up and went through the door with his six-gun in his hand, but there was no trouble. It seemed that Gavin Leach had been propped up with cushions on the sofa, bandages around his head, and he had dragged a pistol out from somewhere and taken a shot at either Rafferty or Dawson.

Too bad he missed! Then Dawson slapped him across the face, tore the Colt from his grip with his other hand. The bounty-hunter glanced at Claiborne.

'Nice fast move, Clay, but everythin's under control. Go finish your doze on the porch.'

Claiborne scowled and went outside, his jaw jutting like Bison Butte above the whitewater rapids at the bend of the river . . .

Angie pulled free of Nichols' grip on her arm and knelt swiftly beside Gavin. One side of his face was reddened, white finger-shapes showing through the patch of colour. 'Are you all right, Gav?'

'Sure, Sis.' The young wounded man glared at Dawson who had a mocking look on his face, totally unconcerned. 'Take more than a slap from that killer to put me off my grub!'

Dawson grunted, 'I'd say she's all yours now, Sean.'

'Sit down at the table, please, Angie,' Rafferty requested and, when she tilted her jaw at him defiantly, he merely nodded slightly to Dawson who dragged her to the small table, pulled out a straight-back chair and sat her down on it roughly.

'Take it easy, damn you!' Gavin said, thrusting up onto his elbow but going pale with the effort.

Rafferty spread a sheaf of papers in front of Angie and Windy Nichols brought over an ink bottle and nib pen from the small writing bureau in the corner, setting them near her right hand. The rancher flicked through the three or four pages of closely written words.

'I'm sure you would be bored with all the legalese, Angie, so I'll explain it to you simply: this is a contract for sale of your land and its goods and chattels to myself — '

'Then you might as well throw it into the kitchen stove,' she told him defiantly. 'I have no intention of signing any such document.'

Dawson winked at Gavin and next instant he was standing behind the wounded man, holding his hair brutally, dislodging the bandage, revealing part of the head wound, almost pulling the hair strands out of the kid's scalp. His hunting knife blade rested casually against Gavin's left ear.

Angie paled and her eyes went involuntarily to the ears dangling on the leather thong on Dawson's belt. 'No!' she cried.

Rafferty smiled like a hungry snake suddenly finding food and offered her the pen, handle first, the nib already loaded with ink. 'Just beside your printed name on the last page, if you will, Angie, my dear. I will date it later, so you won't be inconvenienced . . . Hmm?'

Angie made no move to take the pen, looked at Gavin now. He was still writhing, but not so violently, as his hair was held taut and his scalp felt as if it was tearing away from his skull. Sweat sheened his gaunt face. 'Sis . . . don't . . . do . . . it!'

'It's all the same to me, kid. Been wantin' to try and slice off an ear with just one stroke but they always struggle and make me saw away. You any idea how tough that cartilage is?'

'*Stop it!*' Angie croaked, looking sick. 'What kind of a monster are you?'

Dawson shrugged. 'Aw, I dunno — just your average bloody-handed fiend, I guess. Nothin' fancy . . . '

'Sis! Don't sign it!'

'You notice how his voice begins to sound like a woman's?' Dawson said, smiling. 'How about we try for soprano?'

Angie desperately swung towards Rafferty. 'Stop him, can't you?'

'*You're* the one who can stop him, my dear,' the Irishman said with a smiling smirk, as he thrust the pen towards her. 'Perhaps just a small nick to start with, Brad?'

'Sis!' Gavin tried to wrench his head aside and she snatched the pen quickly and scrawled her signature where Rafferty indicated, slumping in her chair.

'Aw, hell!' Dawson said, obviously disappointed. He thrust Gavin's face roughly into the pile of cushions and the kid rubbed hard at his stinging scalp, a thin trickle of blood crawling down his face. 'Shouldn't've done it, Sis!'

'I had to! You know I had to!' She glared at Rafferty, shaking. 'Well, you have everything now — I suppose you're going to throw me off my land right away?'

'Oh, I'm not a hard man, despite what you may think, Angie. I have no objection to you nursing your young brother back to health before moving out. I'll extend you the same courtesy as I did the others in the valley: you can wait until my money comes through from the government.'

'I signed a bill of sale for A-Bar-W and I want the full purchase price within twenty-four hours!'

'Ah, but see, you didn't take time to read the fine print, my dear. Ten per cent down payment, it says. You agreed to wait for the other ninety per cent until after I am paid the government subsidy. Oh, Sheriff Nichols, would you be good enough to witness my signature?'

'Sure thing, Sean.'

The two men bent over the paper, signing their names, while Angie stood trembling, hands clasped in front of her, face bloodless.

'It's too late to worry now, Sis,' Gavin said quietly. 'There's nothing anyone can do now you've signed.'

'Aw, I dunno — I reckon this can be sorted out easily enough.'

They all looked up quickly — for it had been Brad Dawson who had spoken.

Something in his tone chilled Rafferty although Dawson's guns were still holstered and his knife had been returned to its sheath.

'What the devil's this?' the Irishman

hissed and Nichols, frowning, out of his depth with this sudden switch, started to edge towards the door.

'Wait up there, Sheriff. Like a word with you. And with Mr Rafferty. Ma'am, if you'd move a'ways to your left . . . '

A trifle dazed, Angie moved as ordered. Dawson's eyes were on the sheriff and Rafferty — both men were tensed, wary, trying to figure things out. Dawson winked at both men and Gavin held his breath, glancing at his sister who seemed in shock.

'You wanna join us now, *amigo*?'

They stiffened as Dawson raised his voice and then Lucky Montana, looking trail stained and weary, moving stiffly, appeared in the hall doorway, coming through from the back of the house, a bandage showing at the neck of his torn, bloodstained shirt. He had a cocked six-gun in his right hand. Angie gasped.

'I don't believe in ghosts,' she said slowly, 'so . . . '

Lucky seemed grateful to be able to lean a shoulder against the door jamb. He smiled crookedly at Rafferty. 'Still got both ears, Sean — see?'

Rafferty's face enpurpled and his eyes narrowed, veins stood out in his throat and on his forehead as he swivelled his hate-filled gaze at Dawson. 'You double-crossing son of a bitch!'

Brad Dawson laughed. 'Hey, figured an Irishman from the peat bogs could come up with somethin' a bit more colourful than that, Sean.'

Rafferty was shaking now. 'No bogs, damn you! I was only eight years old when I came here. I've been away far too long, but I've never forgotten those emerald green fields on the old estate.'

'Might've been better if you had, Sean,' Dawson told him quietly. 'Bit of a wild dream you had about reclaimin' the family estate after all these years, wasn't it?'

Rafferty's head jerked, jaw thrusting. 'What d'you know about it?'

'A lot more than you want me to,

Sean.' Rafferty obviously didn't understand, looking from the silent Montana back to Dawson and the latter said, 'Had a lot of complaints from folk in the valley about the way you were buyin' 'em out. Small deposit and keepin' 'em waitin' with no real guarantee you were gonna pay up.'

'I resent that! I fully intended — '

'No you didn't,' Dawson cut in coldly, and Rafferty subsided at his tone, sensing he was close to big trouble here. 'There were too many complaints so we took a much closer look at you then, Sean. Learned about how your stepmother had cheated you out of a share in the family estate and then, through drink and scheming lovers, lost whatever money was left and allowed it all to fall into ruin.'

'Yes, the bitch!' Rafferty gritted, unable to hold back his hatred for the old woman far across the seas. 'That's why I worked so hard to get the money to buy it back, but — I had only enough for the deposit . . . '

'But it left you mighty short of cash, after you sent the money over to Ireland, agreein' to find the rest by a certain date.'

Rafferty seemed calmer now, cold, in fact, accepting that his deception had been discovered. But his eyes were murderous.

'Which is why you could only afford to pay the ranchers a small deposit. You needed their land because the gov'ment won't put in any money to your scheme until you have it. And when they do, Sean, you'll be on the next ship out of New York with all those thousands, headed for County Antrim . . . right?'

'That was my plan, yes,' Rafferty said heavily. 'And I'd like to know how you know so much about it!'

'Well, it's finished now, Rafferty,' said Montana, drawing all eyes. 'The whole deal's in ruins, just like your mouldy old castle.'

Before Montana could say any more, Windy Nichols, ever ready to cover his own back, asked, 'Who are you fellers, anyway? You sure ain't talkin' like any gunslinger or outlaw I know.'

Everyone in the room was hanging on the reply and Dawson glanced at Montana, then said, 'Speakin' for myself, I'm a Special Investigator for the Federal Lands Commissioner. I kind of deputized Lucky here, caught up with him just before Murphy Creek, and figured I could use a man like him, good with a gun, quick-thinkin' — so I put it to him: help me nail this Irish son of a bitch who's trying to steal gov'ment money and I'd see that they took away all them wanted dodgers out on him. That, or I took him in and he could stare ten, twelve years in jail right in the face. 'Course that damn fool of a range detective who tried to claim a bounty on him almost wrecked things, but Lucky knows which side his bread's buttered. He kept his part of the bargain when the kid there rescued him from the desert — so I reckoned it was up to me to keep my part — and here we are . . . just needed to actually witness one of your slimy deals, Sean — and this was the big one, wasn't it? Get Angie's place and you could put in your claim to the Lands Commissioner.'

The look on Rafferty's face should have killed both men where they stood but there was fear mixed with the hatred, too. He said, angrily, 'I have a letter from the commissioner himself advising me he is willing to sink many hundreds of thousands of dollars into my scheme. He recognizes it as a project worthy of government support, one that will be of benefit to everyone, a public-spirited plan to take this state forward into the next century. And, by a happy coincidence this happens to be the commissioner's home state.'

'You sound like a politician, Sean. Havin' been born here is why he wanted to make *damn* sure everything's well and truly above board. Very damn sure!' Dawson said flatly, and it clearly shook Rafferty.

'Not such a 'happy coincidence' after

all, eh, Rafferty?' Montana said. 'That was one thing to upset your plans — and then there was me.'

'But you — you're an outlaw!' said Angie suddenly. 'By your own admission!' She glanced at Dawson. 'And you said this bounty-hunter was pursuing you and wouldn't give up!'

'All true, Angie. When Dawson finally ran me down and put his deal to me, I had no choice. I'd been on the run for too long. I was glad to make any deal to get the bounty off my head.'

'I don't understand,' Angie said. 'You were really near death in the desert when Gavin found you — that wasn't faked.'

'Damn right it wasn't. It was only pure chance that the river we jumped into joined the Viper and carried me this way — I figured it was a sign, maybe a change of luck. The original idea was for me to work for Rafferty: thought he wouldn't be suspicious of anyone with so many wanted dodgers out on him.'

Rafferty stirred, very tense now, his eyes the colour of mud. But he remained silent.

'But after Gav took me to Angie's I reckoned it'd be better if I worked for her, seeing as she was one of Rafferty's enemies; that way he wouldn't figure I was investigating him. But you were still suspicious, weren't you, Sean?'

'With that much money at stake? I wasn't going to take anything at face value. I admit you had me fooled, Montana: I thought you really were just a killer on the run.' His face abruptly crumpled and his voice trembled, choking with his emotion. '*Damn* you! You and this — this cadaverous gunslinger have ruined my plans! All I wanted was to regain my family's honour, show those smug brothers of mine that I could make our estate in Ireland flourish again; I was the one who could give the Rafferty name back the respect it deserves! I — I . . . '

'Well, chief, sounds to me like this is as good a time as any to get rid of these interferin' bastards.'

The words were hurled into the room by Claiborne in the porch doorway, eyes hard and murderous, legs planted firmly, six-gun in hand. He swung the weapon onto Dawson first and let the hammer slip from under his thumb, baring his teeth in satisfaction. But the look turned to one of shock — and pain — as Dawson's twin guns came up flaming before Claiborne's hammer fell.

Three bullets smashed into him, the impact driving him back to the rail where his hips struck, somersaulting him over to fall flat on his face in the yard.

By then, Lucky Montana's Colt was blazing and Windy Nichols cried out as a bullet shattered his elbow. The sheriff fell to his knees, dropping his gun, screaming in pain. Rafferty dived for the door, gun out, shooting wildly.

One shot struck Nichols and knocked him flat. Dawson lunged after the rancher but stopped as if he had run into a tree suddenly growing in the doorway. He spun and went down, clutching at his side. Stumbling a little, Montana stepped forward and shot over Dawson's head. He brought down Rafferty in a cloud of dust, the big Irishman twisting to fire back — and keep firing until his gun was empty. Or until Montana's next bullet slammed the life out of him — it never was clear which.

Splinters flew from the doorway all around Montana but none touched him before Rafferty fell back and died, coughing red blood down his shirt front.

When he turned back into the room, Lucky saw Angie working over Dawson who was slumped against a wall, his open shirt revealing a bloody hole in his side.

Montana looked as he reloaded his gun. 'Your land's safe now, Angie.'

Her eyes were moist as she raised them to Lucky's gaunt face. 'Thanks to you two.'

'Say,' asked Gavin, managing to rise to a half-sitting position as he addressed

Dawson. 'Whose ears were they, anyway?'

'Lindsey's. He din' have no more use for 'em.'

Angie shuddered slightly. 'What're you two going to do now? Your job's finished, isn't it?'

Dawson and Montana exchanged glances.

'Well, Rafferty's took care of,' Dawson said slowly, pushing Angie aside suddenly so that she gave a small cry as she fell against the wall. He struggled up, grimacing, bloody, one gun down at his side in his right hand. He was looking at Montana. 'Lucky, you could've just rid out after Angie doctored you when the kid brought you in from the desert. But you never . . . why?'

Montana was tense now. 'We had a deal.'

Dawson smiled and shook his head slowly. 'Knew it! I'd trailed you for a year and all that time I told myself *Hell, this feller's tough as they come but he's got one weakness*. Know what it is, Lucky? *Honour!* You're a goddamned man of honour!'

'Some might see it as a weakness — I don't.'

'No — well, I do. And I've never been honourable. Thanks for your help, *amigo*, but you still got some big bounties on you.'

'You — you promised to get them removed!' Angie said, shocked. 'You gave Lucky your word!'

'Like I said, never was much on this 'code' thing.' His gun started to lift. 'Sorry, *amigo*, we could make a good partnership but you'd foul-up tryin' for fair play. Me? I'll take the cash in hand.'

Both guns crashed together and Angie screamed, throwing herself aside. Dawson slammed back against the wall, his eyes wide open in shock — or pain. He half-turned, his gun firing again into the floor. Then he collapsed, silently.

Lucky looked down at him, lowered his gun hammer.

'Well, he might've been the *meanest* gun alive,' observed Gavin slowly, 'but he sure wasn't the *fastest*!'

Montana helped the shaking Angie to her feet. She looked up into his face. 'You'll have to ride out now.'

He nodded. 'Kinda used to it.'

'Will you come back sometime? When you feel it's safe . . . ?

He smiled slowly. 'Why not? A man never knows his luck.'

THE END

Other titles in the
Linford Western Library:

THE HIGH COUNTRY YANKEE

Elliot Conway

Joel Garretson quit his job as Chief of Scouts to travel to Texas and claim his piece of land. He needed to forget the killings he had seen — and done — fighting the Sioux and the Crow in Montana . . . But he soon has to confront Texas *pistoleros* and then, aided by a bunch of ex-Missouri brush boys, he faces the task of rescuing two women held by *comancheros* in their stronghold . . . In the territory of the Llana Estacado, New Mexico, the violent blood-letting will commence . . .

Dear Reader,

If you've been enjoying Bachelo[illegible] wonderful stories written by Kate Hoffmann, JoAnn Ross and Candace Schuler have made you eager to understand the legend of the grand pink mansion on Wilshire Boulevard, you're about to be rewarded. *Timeless Love*, the last book in the series, finally reveals the identity of the mysterious woman whose ghost haunts the mirror in Apartment 1-G—the ghost who can make a person's greatest fear or greatest hope come true.

Not that Morgan Delacourt believes in any of that hokum. He's never seen the mystery lady in the mirror. Given his hard-scrabble background and his years of struggle, he knows that a person realizes his hopes through hard work, talent and commitment. Legends have nothing to do with it.

But on the greatest day of his life, a day his career as a cartoonist transforms him into a millionaire, tragedy strikes, forcing him to rethink *everything* he's ever believed in. The ghost in the mirror has a double, a real woman, and fate has thrown her into Morgan's path—into harm's way.

Has Morgan killed her? Can he save her? Can a sexy, footloose, fun-loving bachelor come to terms with love and destiny? After everything has gone so wrong, can the ghost ever make things right?

Read on! And please write!

Judith

Judith Arnold
c/o Harlequin Temptation
225 Duncan Mill Road
Don Mills, Ontario, M3B 3K9
Canada

Come live and love in L.A. with the tenants of Bachelor Arms

Bachelor Arms is a trendy apartment building with some very colorful tenants. Meet three confirmed bachelors who are determined to stay single, until three very special women turn their lives upside down; college friends who reunite to plan a wedding; a cynical and sexy lawyer; a director who's renowned for his hedonistic life-style, and many more…including one very mysterious and legendary tenant. And while everyone tries to ignore the legend, every once in a while something strange happens….

Each of these fascinating people has a tale of success or failure, love or heartbreak. But their stories don't stay a secret for long in the hallways of Bachelor Arms.

Bachelor Arms is a captivating place, home to an eclectic group of neighbors. All of them have one thing in common, though—the feeling of community that is very much a part of living at Bachelor Arms.

BACHELOR ARMS

BACHELOR HUSBAND Kate Hoffmann	February 1995
THE STRONG SILENT TYPE Kate Hoffmann	March 1995
A HAPPILY UNMARRIED MAN Kate Hoffmann	April 1995
NEVER A BRIDE JoAnn Ross	May 1995
FOR RICHER OR POORER JoAnn Ross	June 1995
THREE GROOMS AND A WEDDING JoAnn Ross	July 1995
LOVERS AND STRANGERS Candace Schuler	August 1995
SEDUCED AND BETRAYED Candace Schuler	September 1995
PASSION AND SCANDAL Candace Schuler	October 1995
THE LADY IN THE MIRROR Judith Arnold	November 1995
TIMELESS LOVE Judith Arnold	December 1995

THE TENANTS OF BACHELOR ARMS

Ken Amberson: The odd superintendent who knows more than he admits about the legend of Bachelor Arms.

Eddie Cassidy: Local bartender at Flynn's next door. He's looking for his big break as a screenwriter.

Morgan Delacourt: He liked his isolation…until his fate was irrevocably twined with the legend of Bachelor Arms.

Jill Foyle: This sexy, recently divorced interior designer moved to L.A. to begin a new life.

Natasha Kuryan: This elderly Russian-born femme fatale was a makeup artist to the stars of yesterday.

Clint McCreary: A cynical ex-cop who's looking for his runaway sister. Then he's back to New York where he belongs. But Bachelor Arms has its own effect on people.

Brenda Muir: Young, enthusiastic would-be actress who supports herself as a waitress.

Bobbie-Sue O'Hara: Brenda's best friend. She works as an actress and waitress but knows that real power lies on the other side of the camera.

Bob Robinson: This barfly seems to live at Flynn's and has an opinion about everyone and everything.

Theodore "Teddy" Smith: The resident Lothario—any new female in the building puts a sparkle in his eye.

TIMELESS LOVE

Judith Arnold

Harlequin Books

TORONTO • NEW YORK • LONDON
AMSTERDAM • PARIS • SYDNEY • HAMBURG
STOCKHOLM • ATHENS • TOKYO • MILAN
MADRID • WARSAW • BUDAPEST • AUCKLAND

To Fred and Greg,

Who are so proud of their mom for writing a book with a ghost in it.

ISBN 0-373-25665-5

TIMELESS LOVE

This edition published by arrangement with Harlequin Books S.A.

Printed in U.S.A.

1

LESS THAN AN HOUR AGO, Morgan Delacourt became a millionaire. So far, he liked it. He liked it just fine.

He supposed there was a downside to being incredibly wealthy, and in time, once the exhilaration wore off, he'd learn about it firsthand. He would probably be pestered for loans by all his freeloading relatives in West Virginia. Uncle Sam would surely help himself to a hefty chunk in taxes. Morgan would no doubt hear from every charity known to man, and then some.

But even if he gave grand sums of cash to the government, all the do-gooder societies that stumbled upon his address and all the damned Delacourts who crawled out from under their moss-covered rocks, Morgan would still have more than enough money for himself. The first million was going to turn into two million pretty fast, and two million was going to turn into four. The way his lawyer had explained these syndication deals . . . Well, Morgan didn't have all the details down. He understood the big picture, though.

The big picture was, he was rich.

The early evening drive from his lawyer's office home to his apartment in the old pink mansion on Wilshire Boulevard offered him a chance to accustom himself to his wealth, give some thought to it, fantasize a little. It wasn't as if he'd been impoverished before the contracts had been signed. Over the past few years, as Mongo the Magnificent had transformed from an underground comic book hero with a cult following to a character in occasional animated specials on a late-night comedy show on TV, and from that to the star of his own weekly series, Morgan had seen his earnings increase in a pretty steady curve. Until an hour ago, he could safely describe himself as comfortably upper middle class, quite an accomplishment for a college dropout whose parents could be charitably described as just this side of hillbillies.

But upper middle class wasn't the same as rich. Upper middle class meant driving a five-year-old Ford Escort. Rich meant trading in the Escort for something with leather seats, a quadraphonic CD system and a serious engine.

Steering around the corner onto Wilshire, Morgan marveled at his good fortune. Rich, he decided, meant not renting an apartment but owning a house, a big one. Down near the beach in Venice, or north of the city in one of the canyons. With a real swimming pool, not a hole sealed in cement like the onetime pool his windows overlooked in the courtyard of Bachelor Arms. Now that he was a millionaire, it made no sense to rent. Concepts like *equity* and *property* were going to start playing a major role in his life. The thought made him smile.

He rolled down the window of his car to let the balmy twilight breeze waft in. It tangled into his hair like a lover's fingers.

Hey. Millionaires collected lovers by the dozens, didn't they?

The hell with that, he thought with a laugh. One lover would do. A smart, sweet woman, preferably blond, stacked and sexually insatiable, who didn't love him for his wealth even though his wealth might be the most efficient way to hook her.

He was still grinning as he reached the block where the Bachelor Arms building stood, pink and hulking. He was too jazzed to go directly home. An appearance at Flynn's was called for.

Not just an appearance—a celebration. Morgan would treat everyone in the place to a drink. Eddie would go for it, even if he might be a little jealous. The poor guy had been tending bar at Flynn's forever, and trying to sell his screenplay for longer than that. But he was always up for a party, and Morgan had something to party about tonight.

Champagne, he decided. Lots of it, every bottle in the bar's cellar. Corks popping, bubbles frothing over the lips of bottles and the rims of glasses. Money was no object. All that mattered, as far as Morgan was concerned, was spreading the joy, sharing his triumph, making the entire universe as happy as he was. Christmas had arrived three weeks early for Morgan, and he was in a giving mood.

Something streaked across his consciousness, darting into his peripheral vision. A woman, practically flying through the front door of Bachelor Arms. She was petite, chalky pale, with flags of black hair streaming back from a face etched in horror as she raced toward the street. She might have been screaming, but with the traffic noise spilling in through his open windows he couldn't hear her.

Two people chased her down the walk, yelling at her to stop. He recognized them. The man—Clint, Morgan believed his name was—had moved into apartment 1-G about a month ago, and the woman was around a lot; Morgan figured her to be Clint's girlfriend. They were shouting something at the crazed woman, calling to her, pleading. The front door slammed so hard behind them that the wreath Ken Amberson had hung last weekend fell off.

The woman didn't stop. She continued her mad dash toward the street, charging at Morgan's car without acknowledging it or him or anything at all. She was staring at something, but it wasn't the curb or the busy road beyond. What she saw had nothing to do with Morgan.

He jammed his foot on the brake; his car skidded. He pounded the horn with his fist. She didn't react. She didn't break stride. She was obviously running away from something, heedless of what she was running toward.

There was a thud. A ghastly crackle as the safety glass of his windshield fractured into a crystalline web.

And then Morgan was the one screaming.

HOPE FELT HERSELF plummeting into a deep, dark crevice. The fall didn't hurt. The walls of the crevice were cushioned, dulling sensation. She experienced no pain, no discomfort and—for the first time since she'd stared into the mirror—no fear.

All she had were her thoughts.

Sound echoed around her, a blur of voices mingling with the distant din of automobiles cruising past. One voice cried, "Don't move her!" It was joined by other voices: "Get a blanket!" and "Somebody call the police!" and "Stand back, give her air!"

And another voice, both far away and much too close, a man's voice, low and husky and stretched by a faint drawl: "Oh God, oh God, I'm so sorry..."

"It wasn't your fault, man. I saw the whole thing—"

"She ran right into you—"

"There was no way you could have avoided her—"

And then his voice again, choked and rough-edged, ignoring all the other voices and speaking only to her: "Hang on. Don't you dare give up. You just hang on, now. I'm not going to let you go...."

Shadows enveloped her, seeping into her consciousness like ink into a blotter. Listening to the babble of so many frenzied voices exhausted her. She wanted to rest, to shut herself off from the hysteria on the other side of the shadows. She wanted peace.

Her mind withdrew, searching for a quiet place amid the chaos. She slid back, nestling deeper into the darkness, seeking the tranquillity of her life before she'd looked into the mirror....

They'd entered the store just like any other customers that morning. A man and a woman, obviously in love. She could tell by the way they held hands, the way they bowed their heads toward each other and exchanged intimate whispers. The man was tall, with thick black hair and a wariness in his eyes. The woman was his opposite, fair in coloring, her smile radiating sunshine brightness and trust.

While Hope rang up two *Gone With the Wind* posters for a customer, the couple wandered up one aisle and down the other, apparently interested in the movie memorabilia and knickknacks Reel Stuff carried. When she had first taken a job behind the counter at the Sunset Boulevard shop, she had been amazed that consumers would be willing to shell out so much money for useless junk: Davy Crockett caps, copies of Frankenstein's monster's neck bolts and Bill Bojangles Robinson's tap shoes, "Stella Dallas" hankies and *The Great Escape* action figures. But tourists, nostalgia fans and browsers filled the shop daily, buying, accumulating, handing Hope their credit cards and keeping her too busy to do what she'd moved to Los Angeles to do.

Not that she was complaining. She was grateful for the job. It paid enough for her to be able to afford a tiny but safe efficiency apartment near the University of Southern

California. More than that, it immersed her in Tinseltown lore. She'd never been a film buff, nor one of those rabid gossips who devoured the tabloids in search of nasty news about showbiz celebrities. Yet if her grandmother had been telling the truth, the mansion that rightly belonged to Hope was somehow related to Hollywood's glamorous past. She needed to educate herself about that past if she was ever going to figure out whether Gramma had been telling the truth.

The dark man and the blond woman waited patiently until all the other customers had left the store. Then they approached the counter. "Can I help you?" Hope asked.

The man looked at his companion uncertainly. "Go ahead," she urged him.

He turned back to Hope and cleared his throat. "This is going to sound crazy," he muttered.

Hope suppressed a laugh. Just yesterday someone had come in looking for a replica of King Kong's palm, from the scene where the giant ape cradled Fay Wray in his hand. Last week an intense young man had inquired about the availability of leeches of the sort that attacked Humphrey Bogart in *The African Queen.* Several rowdy fellows had asked whether the store could order a life-size pod like those the zombies emerged from in *Invasion of the Body Snatchers;* they wanted to have a stripper leap out of the pod at their friend's bachelor party.

"I'm used to crazy requests," Hope assured the man on the other side of the counter. "Fire away."

"Well..." He looked earnest and uneasy. His grip on the blond woman's hand tightened visibly. "Look, I'm a normal guy, okay? I used to be a cop back in New York. I'm a lawyer, now. I just joined the county D.A.'s staff."

Hope nodded politely, curious about just how crazy his question was going to be, given his eagerness to prove himself sane.

"Anyway, the point is, I'm not a nut case. I'm just an average guy."

He most certainly wasn't average. He was remarkably good-looking, and with his gruff East Coast accent and demeanor, he was unlike most of the super mellow southern Californians she'd met since moving to Los Angeles.

"My name is Clint McCreary," the man went on. "And...the thing is, I think I've seen you somewhere else."

Hope frowned slightly. She was sure she'd never met him before.

"The thing is . . ." He grew progressively more nervous. "The place I think I've seen you is a mirror in my living room."

Hope let out a hoot. Wasn't that just like L.A.? The more normal they seemed, the more demented they truly were. "You've seen me in a mirror," she repeated, humoring him.

"In my living room. I got the apartment cheap because it was supposedly haunted—or maybe because it had such an ugly mirror on the living room wall. The landlord refused to remove it. Everyone said a ghost lived in the mirror, and if you saw her..." He drifted off, evidently reading Hope's utter disbelief in her face.

The blond woman leaped in to assist him. "He really is sane," she said, then dug into the pocket of her denim skirt and pulled out a small leather envelope, from which she removed a business card. "I'm his fiancée, Jessie Gale. I run a shelter for runaway kids, Rainbow House."

Rainbow House. Hope had heard of the place. She'd seen flyers posted in the neighborhood where she lived. As a matter of fact, she was pretty sure she'd seen the house itself. "That's over near the USC campus, isn't it?" she asked, then confirmed her hunch when she read the address printed on Jessie Gale's business card.

"It's a private social services agency," Jessie Gale said. "And I can vouch for Clint. We're both mentally healthy."

"By California standards," Hope said with a grin.

"I haven't seen the ghost, but Clint has," Jessie continued. "He claims she looks exactly like you."

"Poor thing. Is she planning to have her nose fixed?" Still smiling, Hope gestured toward her own long, narrow nose.

"She's beautiful," Clint McCreary said laconically, his gaze zeroing in on her.

The implied compliment silenced Hope. How could she laugh at a man—no matter how much of a lunatic he seemed—when he was calling her beautiful?

"I've been trying to track you down for weeks," said Clint, jolting her. He'd been tracking her down? *Stalking* her? The very idea sent a shiver along her spine.

Things like this didn't happen in Kansas. In Los Angeles, though, a vast, crowded, threatening city... Big, rugged-looking men waltzed into stores and announced to the sales clerk that they'd been following her for weeks.

She wished she wasn't all alone in the shop. Her boss wasn't due to arrive until three o'clock. The telephone was at the other end of the counter, next to the cash register. She started to edge discreetly toward it.

Jessie Gale must have read Hope's panic in her face, because she quickly reached out and patted Hope's hand. Hope flinched and recoiled, backing up to the wall behind her and eyeing the telephone frantically.

"Please," Jessie murmured, "you're perfectly safe. We don't mean to cause you any trouble. It's just that you look exactly like the ghost in Clint's mirror." She rolled her eyes and smiled, obviously aware of how ridiculous that sounded.

"If you haven't seen the ghost, how do you know I look like her?" Hope asked dubiously, wondering why she was prolonging the discussion.

"I trust Clint. And you can, too. He would never hurt you."

"I only want to know who you are," he explained, sounding a bit too reasonable.

Hope glowered at him. "You already do know who I am. You tracked me down."

"What I really want to know is how you got into my mirror. And why."

"I'm not in your mirror," Hope argued, then laughed at the absurdity of the conversation. Of course she wasn't in his mirror! She didn't know him from Adam.

Remembering that he was a complete stranger who'd been tracking her for weeks, she stopped laughing. His sweetheart seemed harmless, but he was a man who had just claimed that he'd seen Hope in his mirror and had been stalking her. Hope wasn't foolish enough to let down her guard. She sidled a few inches closer to the telephone.

"Tell her about the legend," Jessie coached him.

He looked as uncomfortable as Hope felt. "I don't believe any of this," he insisted. "But Bachelor Arms—that's the building where we're living. It's a big old pink mansion on Wilshire Boulevard that was divided into apartments years ago."

An old mansion. Los Angeles was undoubtedly filled with old mansions, many of which had undoubtedly been divided into apartments. Hope had been living in the city long enough to know that Wilshire Boulevard was a major thoroughfare that spanned Los Angeles from east to west. None of this was relevant to her.

Yet his words resonated inside her: *an old mansion.* She could tell herself a dozen times that she didn't care, that whatever this man was telling her had nothing to do with the old mansion Hope's grandmother had prattled about, the mansion Gramma had never seen, the mansion that might well never have existed anywhere but in her mind....

Hope had come to Los Angeles to find one particular old mansion—assuming Gramma hadn't been talking rot, as Hope's mother had always insisted she was. But if the mansion that had so preoccupied Gramma did in fact exist, it certainly wouldn't have been called Bachelor Arms, or been pink, or had a ghost in residence.

"There's a legend that if you see the ghost in the mirror, either your greatest hope or your greatest fear will come true," Clint continued. "Well, I saw the ghost—or whatever the hell it was—this lady who could have been your twin. Anyway, I saw her in the mirror."

"And which did you get?" Hope asked in spite of herself. "Your greatest hope or your greatest fear?"

"My greatest fear." He gave Jessie a long, adoring gaze. "The thing was, it turned out my greatest fear was actually my greatest hope." He seemed almost embarrassed at the transparency of his love for the woman at his side, and quickly shrugged it off. "I don't believe any of this, but what the hell. The damned legend did a number on me."

Hope fidgeted with a stack of price labels. None of what Clint McCreary was saying made sense. She didn't care about his hopes or his fears or his ghosts. She didn't want to hear about his old mansion, the legend, any of it.

But she herself was haunted, not by a ghost but by Gramma's words: *They said her greatest hope was that I would grow up happy and loved, and her greatest fear was that I would come to a sorrowful end. She died in the mansion, without ever knowing. That old mansion is mine now, Hope. And someday it will be yours—if you can ever find it. It was my mother's and it's now mine, and when I die it will be yours....*

THE WAIL OF A SIREN sliced through her reverie, jarring her, dragging her out of the shadows and into the world of pain. Her entire body ached, but the keenest pain arose from the side of her head, from her right cheek back through her temple and into her skull.

She heard urgent voices now, brisk voices shouting numbers and readings, blood pressure and pulse. Something sharp pierced her arm. Someone thumped her chest. If she'd had any strength at all she would have screamed at them all to go away and let her drift back to where it was peaceful, back to the life she'd been living before she'd stupidly agreed to visit Clint McCreary and Jessie Gale at their apartment in an old mansion with a mirror in it, an old mansion possessed by tragedy and loss and a woman who could have been Hope's twin, but wasn't.

Through the drone of voices and the sob of the siren, Hope heard the other voice, that now familiar drawl, husky and unexpectedly consoling: "You're going to be all right, I promise. Don't you worry about anything. They're going to take care of you. I'll make sure of it. All you've got to do is hang on. I'll do everything else."

"It hurts," she tried to say, but her mouth didn't want to move. She felt tears burning tracks along her cheeks, but her hands didn't want to move either, and no one else bothered to wipe the moisture away.

"They're going to take you away now," the low drawl told her. No one else addressed her. They spoke only to each other, shouting more readings, more numbers, strange jargon. But he hadn't forgotten that Hope was there, a person inside the body everyone else was working on. He kept talking to her, his voice a constant, an incantation. "They're going to take you to the hospital, darlin'. Don't you worry about a thing. I'll do the worrying. God knows I have enough to answer for. You just put it all out of your mind."

Put what out of her mind? she wanted to ask. The mirror? The ghost? Gramma's legacy?

"Could someone wipe her cheeks?" he asked, his voice veering from her. "She's crying, for God's sake! Could someone just—"

Abruptly she was lifted, her body held stiff and then set onto a gurney. She tried to open her eyes so she could see what was going on, but she lacked the strength. And if she opened her eyes, Lord only knew what she would see.

There was only one thing she wanted to see: the man with the soothing voice. The man who had promised to make sure of everything, who wasn't going to let her go. The man who seemed to think he had something to answer for.

But she was being borne away, torn from him. And she let herself slide back into the crevice again, deep into the cool, painless shadows.

BARRY WAS IN A RAGE. "What the hell is wrong with you, Morgan? Why did you talk to the cops without my being there? Don't you have the sense you were born with?"

Barry could have said anything he wanted. Morgan wasn't listening. His gaze remained on the three doctors huddling at the opposite end of the hall. He was only faintly aware of his lawyer's ranting, the hum of the vending machines displaying snacks and drinks along one wall, the odd yellow light staining the air of the hospital's ICU wing.

The third man in the small lounge turned from the window and approached Barry. "He wasn't at fault, okay?" Clint McCreary defended Morgan. "Yeah, he talked to the cops. So did I. So did ten other eyewitnesses. We all saw the same thing, Mr. Loomis. She ran straight into Morgan's car. He tried to stop, he tried to steer out of the way, he tried everything humanly possible to avoid hitting her."

"Thanks for that testimony." Barry snorted, then lit one of his scented black cigarettes. Morgan smelled it and found himself wishing he could bum one for himself. He hadn't had a cigarette since high school, but if ever there was a time a man needed to smoke, it was now.

He dug his hands into the pockets of his jeans and watched the doctors conferring at the far end of the corridor, dressed in their green scrubs and looking like refugees from a pajama party. Maybe they weren't talking about his victim at all. Maybe they were discussing their weekend golf games or their children's antics. It took all Morgan's willpower not to storm down the hall, collar one of them and demand to know whether she was going to be all right.

Behind him, he could hear the *tap-tap* of Barry pacing the lounge in his leather-soled loafers. "I'm his lawyer, okay? I don't know who you are, but—"

"I'm a neighbor of Morgan's," Clint said. "Also a lawyer. Also an ex-cop. I saw what went down. Your client is clean and clear."

"Until the girl wakes up and sues him for every penny he has." Barry tap-tapped back across the lounge to Morgan and tugged his sleeve, demanding his attention.

Morgan turned and glared at his bristling, impeccably groomed lawyer. Was this the same man who, just hours ago, had navigated him through a very complex negotiation that transformed him into a millionaire? It seemed like another lifetime.

"Barry," he muttered, "lay off."

"You told them you would pay for everything." Barry waved down the hall toward the ICU nurses' station. "What the hell were you thinking, making an offer like that?"

"She has insurance. All I said was, I'd pay her deductibles."

"And you insisted that she have a private room, and flowers every day. Come on, Morgan. She's a vegetable—what does she need flowers for?"

Morgan almost punched Barry. He restrained himself because he knew it wouldn't do any good, and because most of his fury was sparked not by Barry's blunt statement but by the very real possibility that he was speaking the truth.

What if she never woke up? What if that pale, slender woman with the long black hair and the garish bruise bluing the right half of her face never regained consciousness? It didn't matter that the accident wasn't Morgan's fault. It didn't matter that the police had cleared him of any responsibility for it. In his heart, he knew he'd done this terrible thing to her.

"And meanwhile, your windshield is shot to hell. If it's true she ran into you, maybe you ought to be suing her for damages."

"Barry." Morgan's hands clenched inside his pockets. Barry Loomis was an excellent lawyer. He'd taken damned good care of Morgan's career during the six years Morgan had been living in L.A. But his concept of morality was about as substantial as a dewdrop on a hot summer day. "Go away, okay?"

"Positioning yourself to be her benefactor is like confessing guilt, Morgan. By covering her bills, you're establishing liability—"

"Go away," he repeated firmly. "Go home. Have a drink. Leave me alone."

Barry shook his head and glanced at Clint. "I love this guy," he said quietly. Morgan knew he meant it. A good attorney was supposed to do exactly what Barry was doing: protecting his client, from others or from himself. The only thing wrong with Barry's attempt was that Morgan didn't want protecting.

He wanted to right a tragic wrong. And he wasn't sure it could ever be made right.

He swiveled away from Barry and nodded when he felt his lawyer's hand squeeze his shoulder. The *tap-tap* sound of Barry's loafers receded as he left the lounge.

Morgan glanced toward the trio of doctors once more. They were still huddling. One of them threw back his head and laughed.

"He's right, you know," Clint told Morgan. "You're under no legal obligation here."

"Some obligations can't be measured legal or not legal," Morgan argued. "She's hurt. *I did it.*" The words settled in his soul, heavy, oppressive, causing his gut to clutch and his eyes to burn. *I did it.* "You don't have to stick around," he added. "I appreciate your giving me a lift to the hospital, but I can find my own way home later."

"I *do* need to stick around," Clint argued, moseying over to the soda machine and stuffing a couple of dollar bills into it. Two cans of cola tumbled down the chute. Clint brought one to Morgan. "This whole thing is at least as much my fault as yours."

Clint forced a smile of thanks and snapped the tab open. "How do you figure that?" he asked, shooting a quick glance down the hall to monitor the doctors.

"She was visiting Jessie and me when she flipped out."

"She's a friend of yours? Oh, God..." A fresh wave of guilt crashed over him, churning, tugging him under. "Oh, God, I—"

"She isn't a friend, not exactly." Clint took a swig of soda, then sighed. "I'm living in apartment 1-G, you know."

"Yeah, everyone was buzzing about it when you moved in. That apartment scared the hell out of the last tenant. All that garbage about the ghost in the mirror—he just took off and never looked back."

"I wish I could call it garbage." Clint sighed and took another swig of soda. "I don't believe in ghosts any more than the next guy. The thing of it is, though...I saw something in the mirror."

"You did?" Morgan had been hearing wild tales about the mirror in apartment 1-G since he'd moved into Bachelor Arms a couple of years ago. Some tenants claimed to have seen her; some claimed the whole story was nothing more than a mess of cow manure. But it was always good for a laugh.

Morgan hadn't had much to do with Clint McCreary in the few weeks Clint had been living in 1-G. They'd shared a few minutes in the laundry room a while back, and they occasionally ran into each other at the front door. Morgan had no basis for judging his new neighbor. But he seemed like a reasonable sort, no bull about him. And he'd been a rock during the accident, talking to the police, arranging for a wrecker to tow Morgan's car to the body shop, driving Morgan to the hospital, getting Barry off Morgan's back just now.

"What did you see in the mirror?" he asked Clint, unsure of whether Clint's answer was going to destroy Morgan's positive impression of him.

Clint had the good grace to look uncomfortable. "What I saw was a woman who looked exactly like Hope."

"Hope?"

"That's the name of the woman you hit. Hope Henley."

"She was in your mirror?" Either Clint was talking crazy, or Morgan had lost his ability to process spoken English.

"Someone who looked exactly like her," Clint explained. "I kept seeing Hope near where Jessie—my fiancée—works, and she looked so much like the lady I saw in the mirror it was spooky. So I tracked her down and invited her to the apartment to see the mirror. She came by after she got off work today."

"You're kidding. You invited her to look at a ghost in your mirror, and she actually came?"

"She seemed pretty nervous about the whole thing—not that I blame her. I think she came only because Jessie would be there. Jessie's a social worker. She knows how to get through to people and make them feel safe. Although the truth is, Hope seemed kind of curious, too—not just about the mirror but about Bachelor Arms and that *Believe the Legend* plaque. Let's face it, the whole thing is pretty bizarre."

"Amen to that."

"But..." Clint chose his words carefully. "Whatever her reasons, she came. And she looked into the mirror, and she—she just freaked out. I don't know what she saw. All *I* saw was her reflection. But she..." He shook his head, apparently at a loss. "She went berserk. She flew out of the apartment before we could stop her. She just started running and didn't stop."

"From something she saw in the mirror?" It was Morgan's turn to shake his head, in disbelief. "Even with her face all bruised up and puffy, I don't see how a woman like her could scare herself with her own reflection. She's a nice-looking woman."

"So's the ghost."

Morgan mulled over Clint's statement. It implied that Clint had seen the ghost—which, in turn, implied that Clint was bonkers, which allowed Morgan to discount everything he'd just said.

Clint shook his head again. "I saw what I saw. God alone knows what Hope saw. Whatever it was, it terrified her."

"Terrified her so much she ran straight into rush hour traffic?" Morgan drank some soda to keep from saying what he was thinking—that the whole lot of them could use a few weeks at the funny farm, Clint for alleging he'd seen the ghost, Hope for her suicidal sprint into Morgan's car . . . and Morgan for caring so much, for feeling so profoundly guilty, for volunteering anything, everything, his money and his heart and his soul if it could bring the poor woman back to life.

"Excuse me?" The voice behind him was mild, gentle. He spun around to find one of the doctors standing at the entry to the lounge, still in her green scrubs, with a pale blue face mask draped around her throat like a necklace. "Mr. Delacourt?"

"Yes." If he was deranged—if they *all* were—he didn't care. All he cared about was Hope Henley.

"The brain scans look good," the doctor reported. "There's minimal swelling and no hemorrhaging."

"What does that mean?"

"There's less likelihood for lasting brain damage if she pulls through."

"*If?*" He pounced on the word. "*If* she pulls through?"

"I'm sorry, Mr. Delacourt. But none of us is willing to place odds at this point. With the kind of head injury she sustained, we just can't tell if she'll improve or take a turn for the worse. That's why we have her in intensive care. We're going to keep her on support—"

"I want to see her."

"I don't think that's possible," the doctor said sympathetically. "Only next of kin—"

"I'm paying for that room," he snapped, squaring his shoulders and staring down at the woman. "Until this hospital locates her next of kin, I'm it. And I'm going to see her."

"She isn't going to see you," the doctor warned. "She's unconscious, Mr. Delacourt, and—"

"You don't know what she's going to see," he said, his Appalachian drawl stretching out the words and giving them the flavor of a warning. There was nothing more to say, nothing more to argue about. He was going to see the woman he'd almost killed, and no damned doctor was going to stand in his way.

2

THE ROOM WAS a cramped cubicle barely big enough for her hospital bed and all the equipment she was hooked up to. She shaped a slender island in the center of the mattress, her body raising a hilly ridge beneath the blanket, her head squared on the pillow. Her skin was as pale as the bed linens—or, more accurately, her arms and throat and about three-quarters of her face were pale. The fourth quarter—an area sloping from her right cheekbone down to the hinge of her jaw and into her scalp—was a livid purplish blue. A bandage slashed from the outer edge of her eyebrow to her ear.

Darker than the bruise was her hair, a long, silky black mane framing her face. If the doctors had had to perform brain surgery, they would have shaved it all off.

Cripes. Morgan didn't want to think about brain surgery. He didn't want to think about her injuries, or her unnatural stillness, or her fragility. He didn't want to think about the practical jokes fate played on people, and he definitely didn't want to think about the mystery of the mirror in apartment 1-G.

"Hey, there," he drawled, taking a seat on the window ledge. The room held no chairs. Obviously visitors weren't supposed to make themselves at home.

He didn't care. Through the glass front wall of the room he could see the nurses monitoring the ICU patients, alternately peering into the rooms or reading data from the bank of monitors arrayed at their work counter. Yet despite the hustle-bustle of the nurses' station, Hope Henley's room seemed peaceful. It smelled not of antiseptic but of flowers. At his behest, the hospital had placed a huge bouquet on the wheeled bed table at her side.

The doctor who had spoken to Morgan in the waiting lounge was right: Hope couldn't see the flowers, and she couldn't see him. But he refused to act as if she were as bad off as she actually was.

"How's it going?" he asked, trying not to feel self-conscious. He didn't expect any sort of response from her, but he kept his tone conversational, just in case. "Looks like you got yourself a nasty bruise," he observed. "I hope it doesn't hurt too bad. Damn. I *know* it hurts."

His voice splintered, and he took a couple of deep breaths to smooth it out. "I will never be able to live this down, Hope," he whispered, wishing she didn't look like something carved out of cold white marble. Was it possible that her existence had been reduced to nothing more than the electrical impulses making her heart monitor beep in a steady, dreary rhythm? Could it be that Morgan had destroyed every other shred of life inside her?

"I don't expect forgiveness," he murmured. "I don't deserve it. They all told me it wasn't my fault, but..."

He closed his eyes and took another breath. He was not going to break down, he was not going to blubber and wail and tell her the accident was worse for him than it was for her. It wasn't. She was suffering, she was floating on some private plane of existence that excluded him and the hospital and quite possibly the planet earth. He wasn't going to behave as if he were suffering more than she was.

What he was going to do was pull her back to earth, if he could.

"My name is Morgan Delacourt, and I know your name is Hope Henley," he said. He felt stupid, chatting as if he were trying to pick her up at a bar. "This is a hell of a way to get acquainted, isn't it?"

She didn't answer. She didn't move, didn't twitch, didn't do anything. If his words were registering on her in any way, he couldn't tell.

The monitor above her bed continued its monotonous pulsing. The ventilation system hissed softly. The only other sound was Morgan's voice, and when he stopped talking the room grew eerily quiet.

"Hope, I don't know if you can hear me, but . . . I want you to come back. If you come back, if you open your eyes and come back to life, I swear to God I'll do anything I can to make it worth your while.

"I know you don't know me. You probably want to be surrounded by your loved ones, and I sure as hell don't qualify as one of them. I reckon they're trying to track down your family right now. The police found some ID stuff in your wallet. But there was no name of a person to call in case of emergency, so they said they'd talk to your landlord and your neighbors and see if they can find out who your people are."

He wondered whether she had a family like his, a huge, unwieldy tribe of blood-kin and in-laws. Somehow, he doubted it. She seemed so isolated in the bed, and the fact that there was no person listed to call in case of an emergency—no husband, no parents, no siblings—left him with the impression that she'd been spared the blessings and banes of a large family.

He himself had the sort of family that congregated in July at an annual family picnic, where everyone intended to have a good time but things invariably degenerated as old recriminations and feuds were given a full airing—and damn, but those picnics *were* a good time, recriminations, feuds and all. Christmas was another fine occasion for dredging up old resentments, nursing old grudges, reminding his sister Louise about the time she gave his perfectly broken-in baseball glove to Wynn Ewell because she had a whopping crush on him, and not only did Wynn refuse to give it back but he also called Louise a pig. Morgan had gotten his nose broken in the ensuing fistfight—although he had managed to reclaim his glove and Louise's dignity, and leave Wynn with a Technicolor shiner. Wynn later married Morgan's cousin Charlotte, and sure enough, every year at Christmas Wynn and Morgan chided each other about that fight, while Louise made porcine noises behind Wynn's back.

In a few weeks, the three of them would go through the same routine. Without all the infantile squabbling, it wouldn't feel like a real Christmas. "I hate to think they'd have to call your mama to tell her you've been hurt so close to Christmas," he said to Hope.

No response.

He shifted on the ledge, trying to arrange his lanky body more comfortably. "Then again, maybe you'll be all better by Christmas. Wouldn't that be great? Or Chanukah, or whatever you celebrate. Some of my friends celebrate Kwanza at this time of year. That's an African harvest festival. I'd never even heard of it before I came to L.A. This city is amazing that way—so many people, so many cultures. Where I come from—Bailey Notch, West Virginia, population four hundred, and half of 'em are relations of mine—well, you don't learn about things like Kwanza."

His awkwardness gradually faded. He didn't bother pausing for her to answer, didn't search her for any indication that she could hear a blasted word he said. He just kept talking, his feet propped on an aluminum bar of her bed's frame and his attention on her delicate, wounded face.

"My dad works for the county highway department. That sounds mighty grandiose, considering there's no highways anywhere near Bailey Notch. What he does is patch potholes. My mom takes care of the garden. It's actually a small farm, enough to keep the family fed through much of the winter. I'm the youngest of five kids and the only unmarried one. The others all got hitched right out of school, but here I am, closing in on thirty and still a bachelor. They think that's some kind of odd." Whenever he teased Louise about her long-ago crush on Wynn Ewell, she always retorted that at least she and Wynn had grown up and settled down, and by the time she'd reached Morgan's current age she'd already had two babies, and what had he accomplished that was anywhere near that significant?

He could never come up with a proper response. When Louise put it that way, his siring of Mongo the Magnificent seemed like a pretty feeble accomplishment, even if it was making him very rich.

"My folks think Hollywood is a strange place to live. I can't get any of them to visit me, ever. I'll be making a trip east for the holiday. First class this year." He shook his head in amazement at his own good fortune. "I'm not real big on holidays. Maybe it has to do with being far from my family—not that I have any desire to move back there. It's just . . . I don't know. I do like it out here in L.A. Everybody else bitches about the place, but I've seen worse. At least the weather here is terrific."

Jeez. Was he actually babbling about the weather? He must be boring her to tears.

She wasn't crying, though. And he could think of nothing that would make him happier than if she opened her eyes and yelled at him to shut up.

"I don't know how long the doctors are going to let me stay here with you. But it seems to me you shouldn't be left alone with nothing but high-tech machines for company. You can't read, you can't watch the tube, you can't fix yourself some cheese and crackers. The least you deserve is company.

"I wish I could give you more than that. I offered to donate blood, but they said you didn't need a transfusion. And the flowers . . . I don't know much about flowers, but I could describe them to you: there's some pale pink ones and some bright yellow and orange ones that look kind of like little pompoms, and a couple of long, skinny ones like blue-and-yellow flags, and a bunch of ferns, all bushy and green. And a couple of red roses. I wish you could see them, Hope."

He exhaled. The flowers were going to die before she ever saw them. He planned to order more, even though he knew they would die, too. He wondered when she would see flowers again—in a hospital room, in a garden, in her own home.

"If it would make any difference," he said quietly, "I'd buy you acres of flowers. Mountains of them. I'd buy every last flower in California and have them shipped here, just for you. If it would make any difference, I'd stop talking—or talk more. I wish you could tell me. I just wish you could give me a sign."

She didn't move. Didn't speak. Didn't flutter her velvet-lashed eyelids. Didn't do a goddamn thing.

"Give me a sign, Hope."

She let out a small, wistful sigh. It carried a hint of her voice, a hint of her soul.

Elation filled him. He refused to accept that her sigh might have had nothing to do with him. He was looking for a sign, and this was her sign. His words must be reaching her, somehow.

"All right," he said, settling back on the ledge and allowing himself a smile. "Now we're talking. Now we're getting something accomplished. I know you're in there, sweetheart. And I'm not going anywhere till you come on out and show yourself. I'm not going anywhere."

She sighed again. Maybe it was boredom, maybe pain.

Or maybe, just maybe, it was her way of telling him she wanted him to stay.

SHE FELT AS IF she were listening to a radio station with a weak signal. His voice drifted in and out, sometimes clear but more often a remote mumble accompanied by crackling static. Yet she treasured his warm, husky drawl. It seemed to anchor her, to keep her from slipping away.

She wondered who he was, and what he was trying to tell her. The specifics didn't seem important, though. All that mattered was that as long as his voice was still reaching her, she knew she wasn't dead.

Except for his voice, she didn't hear much. But then, what, other than the echo of her own thoughts, could she have expected to hear in the depths of a great, dark chasm?

She struggled to figure out exactly what had happened to her. Memories skittered toward her and then evanesced before she could actually make sense of them, like glints of light in a mirror.

A mirror. She'd seen something in the mirror.

I want you to come back, the man was saying. Come back where? To the mirror?

She knew the voice didn't belong to the man who'd invited her to see it. Clint was his name, the man who lived with the mirror. She glommed onto that one lucid memory, refusing to let it go: Clint and his fiancée—Jessie—and their cozy apartment in the grand pink mansion with the turquoise trim. Hope had gone inside. She had thought Clint and Jessie were a bit screwy, but she'd gone inside their living room because the mansion struck her fancy. Maybe, just maybe—

Darkness crashed over her in a wave, tearing the memories from her grasp and washing them away. It would be so easy just to sink deeper and deeper, so deep she could never emerge. But the man was speaking to her, his voice like a lifeline tied around her waist, refusing her the freedom of simply plunging to her death.

If you come back, I swear to God....

Wouldn't it be nice to have a man adore her so much he made vows to God on her behalf? She'd done her share of dating, but she had always been extremely cautious around men. Probably because her father had walked out on the family when she was three. Her mother's second husband hadn't been much of an improvement, and her third—the one she was married to now—was no great shakes, either. And Hope's grandmother had always said it all began with a man, a cad, a sinner who'd left Gramma's mother in trouble.

Gramma, talk to me, she murmured soundlessly. *Tell me what it's like to die. Tell me if I should be afraid. Tell me everything I need to know, and I'll tell you what I saw in the mirror.*

"No way," the man was saying, his voice raised slightly, less the husky, romantic drawl she'd grown accustomed to than a sharp reproach. "You can't make me leave. Visiting hours are till nine—I don't care that the Intensive Care Unit has its own rules. You can take those rules and shove them."

Hope heard a blur of words, a woman's voice. Then the man spoke again. "All right, so she needs to rest. She's resting. Does it look like I'm dancing the polka with her?"

Hope surprised herself by laughing. Not really—she couldn't move. She was drugged and fatigued and weak. But she laughed inside, in her soul. And that laughter proved to her that she truly did want to survive.

She wished she could thank the man, whoever he was. Not only had he sworn to God about her, but now he was fighting for her. He believed in her.

He continued to ramble, his voice once again directed to her, a hoarse male lullaby. She couldn't make out the words and she didn't care. All that mattered was that he was with her, keeping her alive. He wasn't leaving her, he wasn't giving up on her. He didn't walk away from the edge she'd tumbled over, but instead remained there, reaching for her, refusing to let her fall the rest of the way.

It was almost enough to make her love him.

"SHE'S GOT TO HATE ME," Morgan groaned.

He and Clint were seated facing each other at one of the tables in the rear of Flynn's. Clint was drinking beer, Morgan Wild Turkey. He didn't have to drive home, seeing as the bar was next door to Bachelor Arms, and he had every intention of getting good and ripped.

Morgan's new neighbor had insisted on accompanying him to the bar. For some reason, Clint felt as responsible for the accident as Morgan did. It risked turning into a competition, the two of them vying for guilt rights. A few more drinks, and Morgan just might ask Clint to step outside so they could settle the issue with their fists.

He didn't want to fight with Clint, but he *did* want to punch something. Instead, he took another swig of bourbon.

"What if she's permanently crippled or something? What if she winds up blind, or deaf?"

"She ran into you," Clint reminded him. "She looked in the mirror and ran into you."

"I've been hearing crackpot stories about that damned mirror since the day I moved into Bachelor Arms," Morgan grumbled. "I'm not going to say I believe the ghost exists—or doesn't exist. I've heard all the stories about the bachelors who lived in the mansion back in the thirties, and all their wild orgies, and the starlet who drowned in the pool."

Clint drummed his fingers against the table, looking deceptively calm. "Did you ever hear who the starlet was? What she looked like?"

"Ask Bob." Morgan gestured toward the bar, where Bob Robinson sat. A regular fixture at Flynn's, Bob had never met a subject he didn't consider himself an expert in. "He'll tell you about the starlet."

"He already did. For hours," Clint said, then grinned. "I was wondering . . ." His smile faded into a look of embarrassment. "You know, I hate admitting I saw the ghost, but I was wondering, just hypothetically. . . Let's say the ghost in the mirror is the spirit of the drowned starlet, who happens to look exactly like Hope. Maybe Hope is a relative of the starlet. It's possible, isn't it?"

"Yeah, sure." Morgan took another belt of bourbon and wondered why it wasn't having the desired effect on him. His nerves were razor sharp, his thoughts relentlessly clear. "It's also possible that a meteor is going to land on our heads in ten minutes. Maybe more possible than a drowned starlet choosing to spend her afterlife in a mirror in your apartment."

Bobbie-Sue, Morgan's neighbor at Bachelor Arms and his favorite waitress at Flynn's, sauntered over, a fresh bowl of peanuts on her tray. "Hi, guys," she drawled in her lush Dixie accent. "I heard about the accident, Morgan. I'm real sorry."

"Don't be sorry for me," he retorted bitterly. "I'm not the one with an oxygen tube up my nose."

He didn't miss the *poor Morgan* look Clint and Bobbie-Sue exchanged. The smile Bobbie-Sue sent him was as artificial as NutraSweet. "Weren't you and your lawyer going to meet today with that production company?"

"Yeah." He wished he could sound just a little more cheerful about it.

"And?"

"The deal flew."

"No kidding? Morgan, that's phenomenal! Mongo the Magnificent is going to be on weekly TV?"

"That's right." He emptied his glass and sighed wearily.

"And you're going to be rich."

"Funny thing, Bobbie-Sue—rich doesn't seem worth a helluva lot when you've hit a lady with your car."

Bobbie-Sue exchanged another look with Clint. "All right, then, sugar—I stand corrected. You're going to feel sorry for yourself."

"I'm going to save that lady's life."

"Is that a fact? And what are you going to do with it once you've saved it?" Before he could answer—before he could *think* of an answer—Bobbie-Sue set his empty glass on her tray. "You want this thing refilled?"

"Yeah. Maybe it'll help."

"It never does, Morgan," she murmured, leaning over and brushing a kiss on his cheek before she lifted her tray and departed.

"Mongo the Magnificent," Clint said thoughtfully. "Isn't he a comic book superhero?"

"He started out in the comic books, but he's about to have his own weekly TV show. We're going into production in early January. But he's not just a straight superhero. He's supposed to be a spoof of superheroes."

"You're—what? His producer?"

"His creator. His daddy. His alter ego."

"Wow, I'm impressed." Clint gave Morgan a respectful nod. "Mongo's got a magic wand or something."

"Yeah. Him and that wand of his. It's supposed to be a phallic in-joke." Morgan shook his head. Just hours ago, Mongo had been the source of such pride and excitement. Now, talking about his new venture did nothing for him. "The premise is, he's a nerdy kid who wants to be a magician. But every time he uses the wand he transforms into someone else with a super power. He never knows what the super power is going to be, though. It's an adventure concept for kids, but there's all sorts of subversive jokes tossed in for the grown-ups."

Clint took a sip of beer. "Is he heroic enough to save the world?"

"Sometimes. Unlike me," Morgan added morosely. "Who am I kidding? I can't save Hope's life. Wand or no wand, I can't perform magic."

"Stuff happens," Clint observed. "You've just got to do what you have to do to get through it."

"Yeah. Like drink heavily."

"You could toss back bourbon after bourbon, from here till tomorrow, and you're not going to get drunk."

"How do you know that?"

"You've already had three, and it hasn't done the trick, has it?"

Morgan conceded with a sigh. "So, what am I going to do?"

"You're going to keep on the hospital's case, and make sure they do everything they can for Hope. I've got to tell you, Morgan, I've got a vested interest in this, too. I need her to recover so I can ask her what the hell she saw in my mirror." He chuckled sadly. "Jessie's been driving me crazy. She believes in ghosts and yet she's never seen the thing. I *don't* believe in them, but I saw it. And Hope saw something, too."

"And it made her dive headlong into my windshield."

"Like I said, she's got to pull through so we can find out what she saw. Do your magic, Mongo. Maybe you've got a super power—you just haven't figured out what it is."

Morgan didn't have any power at all. The only thing Clint was right about was that downing bourbon wasn't getting him drunk. It was nearly midnight; Clint said he had work in the morning and was ready to turn in.

Morgan worked when he wanted to—which was more often than most people. He had an office downtown, and as part of the contract he'd signed that afternoon, the production company was going to set him up in a much larger studio in a building with full animation facilities. But he did much of his best work at the drafting table in the tiny second bedroom in his apartment. The drawings he created there were usually pretty rudimentary, but they inspired him. They generated the stories, jump-started them. A few frames sketched out at the drafting table were all it took for him to formulate the entire plot for a thirty-page book or a twenty-two minute show.

If that was the only magic he had access to, it wasn't anywhere near enough.

When Clint insisted on paying the bar tab, Morgan didn't argue. If he hadn't come to blows with Clint over whose fault the accident had been, he wasn't going to come to blows with him over who was going to pick up the bill.

They exited into a balmy night, warm for early December. Although the interior of Flynn's hadn't yet been trimmed with seasonal decorations, small white lights had been strung around the door. Lights and tinsel were as close as L.A. ever got to a white Christmas.

Morgan and Clint strolled the short distance to Bachelor Arms in contemplative silence. The amber light above the front porch illuminated the plaque beside the door: *Believe the Legend.* Morgan had heard his neighbors discuss the legend often enough, all that bull-hickey about how once you saw the ghost your greatest hope or your greatest fear would come true.

Morgan had never encountered the ghost, but fear was closing in on him. Fear that Hope wouldn't live. Fear that he would have her death on his conscience, that he would wear guilt and sorrow in his soul for all his days. Fear that if she didn't recover, he would never recover, either.

His greatest hope was . . . Hope herself. She was a total stranger to him, someone destiny had literally thrown in his path. She wasn't a friend, she wasn't a colleague, and she sure as hell wasn't a potential sexual conquest. She wasn't even his type. He'd always been partial to blondes with macromammaries.

As if he weren't already wallowing in enough guilt to drown a navy, he was inundated by a fresh ocean of it. How could he be thinking of Hope in sexual terms? Even worse, how could he be finding fault with her physical attributes? He was more despicable than he'd realized.

Once they'd entered Bachelor Arms, Clint walked directly to his apartment. "Get some sleep, Morgan," he advised. "Things'll look better in the morning."

"Sure," Morgan grunted. "As my mother always said, 'It is always darkest before it turns completely black.'"

Clint smiled. "You want to look in my mirror? Maybe you'll see something in it."

"If I look in your mirror I'm going to see a jerk in need of a haircut," Morgan said, starting up the stairs. "Thanks for the drinks, Clint."

At the top of the stairway, he strode down the hall to his apartment at the rear of the house. The message light on his answering machine was ominously dark—usually it flashed like a distress signal, the tape crammed with invitations, messages from his publisher, admonitions from Barry.

Tonight, no one had called.

Tonight, there was nothing to say.

He locked the door and headed to his drafting table in the back bedroom, detouring into the kitchen for a bottle of bourbon. He didn't bother to turn on the lamp above the sloping surface of the desk, or to line up a sheet of paper and gather his pencils. Sitting in the old leather swivel chair, he rested his elbows on the desk and gazed out the window at the paved-over pool in the courtyard.

So a woman had drowned there sixty years ago. So the house had a colorful history. So people liked to talk about legends, to spook newcomers and spin yarns about a mirror.

What did any of it matter? An innocent young woman was fighting for her life, and regardless of what anybody said, it was all Morgan's fault.

3

SHE FELT LOST WITHOUT HIM. He'd said goodbye—she remembered that, but she had no sense of time, so she wasn't sure how long ago he'd left her. All she knew was that without his voice to guide her, she was suspended in a void, a realm of darkness.

Soon the vacuum created by his absence filled with other voices, not from outside her but from within her free-floating mind. She heard her mother scolding, "Wake up and smell the coffee, Hope." And "I'll say this about your Gramma—the older she gets, the nuttier she gets. She just dwells on that same old story about the mansion until I want to scream." And "Take a good look at her, Hope. Does she look like an heiress to you?"

Gramma hadn't looked like an heiress. She'd looked like what she was: a farm wife and then a farm widow, a strong, stubborn Midwesterner with eyes as dark as Hope's and hair that went from black to white, one stroke at a time, as if Father Time had used a paintbrush on her. Gramma had dressed in sturdy clothes and had developed thick muscles in her arms from physical labor. After Hope's mother's second marriage, Hope had spent more and more time on the farm, an hour south of her mother's house in Topeka. She didn't get along with her stepfather, and her mother always said Hope and Gramma were two of a kind, two dreamers.

So what if Gramma didn't look like an heiress? So what if her stories didn't always make sense? They were great stories, and Hope was an eager audience for them.

"I was five when the lawyer tracked me down," Gramma would say. "He found me at my family's house—my adopted family, but of course they were the only family I ever knew. The lawyer told me he'd been searching for me for years, because in her will my mother had left me her house in Los Angeles. He told me it was a big, fancy mansion. The problem was, her parents had somehow fudged the deed and sold the house to a bank to cover their debts in the stock market crash. That crash destroyed so much, Hope. The Depression made everybody poor, not just farm folk like us but high rollers in Hollywood."

Hope could listen to Gramma's wonderful stories for hours. She listened to them now, in the thick sleep that claimed her. Gramma's voice replaced the voice of the man, soothing Hope, relaxing her, fending off her fear.

"My birth mother's parents had put the deed to their house in her name to protect it from debtors, but then my mother died. Died insane, maybe killed herself because she'd never known whether her baby—that was me—was okay. A rotter had gotten her in trouble, you see, and in those days women didn't have the choices they have now. An unmarried woman carrying a fatherless child—the shame was enormous. And my mother wasn't just *anyone*. She was a rich, beautiful debutante, a child of great wealth and prestige who'd brought this terrible shame down on her family. The lawyer told me my mother was taken to a secret place up the coast in Monterey, where she gave birth to me, and then they took me away from her. Just tore me out of her arms and put me on a train to Kansas, where my dear folks, bless their hearts, raised me like I was their own. And that debauched young woman was sent back to her parents' mansion in Hollywood, where she went mad longing for me."

"But you were only five when the lawyer found you, Gramma. How can you remember everything he told you?"

"Some things a person never forgets. Like mother love. I know that my birth mother loved me so much she died of a broken heart from losing her only child."

"How do you know she owned the mansion?"

"That was why the lawyer came in search of me—because the house had been hers and she'd written in her will that she left her estate to her sole surviving daughter, which was me. It took the lawyer years to find me, though, and by then the bank had taken over the house. The mansion was broken into a few apartments, and a group of movie stars, party boys, had taken up residence in it. Three bachelors, all of them film stars. The lawyer said it might take years of fighting for me to get title to the house, and my parents, sweet souls that they were, said it wasn't worth the fight. They said I was their daughter now, and I belonged in Kansas, and Hollywood was a snake pit. So we never fought for the mansion. But it was mine, Hope. It was mine."

Hope had never been quite convinced. Much as she loved her grandmother, she couldn't deny that the woman tended to be flaky at times. She'd refused to move off the farm when Hope's grandfather had died. She'd continued to can her own vegetables and drive her own tractor and labor right alongside the hired hands to bring in her crops each year. And she'd continued to insist that she was the legal owner of a mansion in Hollywood, which at some point had been occupied by some movie stars. Hope could respect her grandmother's fortitude and independence, but the story of the mansion in Hollywood was a little hard to swallow.

Gramma's belief in her alleged inheritance grew even stronger once she'd been diagnosed with lymphoma. The old woman would talk about nothing except her legacy in California, the lawyer who had searched for her, the young, unwed mother who had gone mad from losing her, the parents who had stolen the mansion, the inheritance that was due Gramma.

Hope had spent the last few months of her grandmother's life nursing her and making her comfortable. She would have said anything to ease her grandmother's mind. That was how deathbed promises came about.

I tried to find your mother's home, Gramma, just like I promised, she called into the black void. *I came to Hollywood to find the house your mother bequeathed to you, and you bequeathed to me. I'm not sure it exists, but I promised you I'd look for it and I did find a big, old mansion that was broken into apartments. There was a mirror, Gramma . . .*

"Good morning, darlin'."

He was back! Her friend, her savior had come back. The dark loosened its grip on her, and she felt herself floating up, away from her grandmother, away from the memories. The right side of her face felt tender, achy with sensation. Her fingers flexed and fluttered against the blanket. After her long, lightless trance, she was coming back to life.

"Hot damn—a fellow could think you were happy to see him. Is all that activity for me, or have you been squirming all night long?"

She tried to force her eyes open, tried to shape her mouth around a word. All she could manage was a low, weary moan.

"Does it hurt, sweetheart? You want me to get them to bring you a painkiller?"

She moaned again. It seemed the only sound she was capable of.

"Hey!" His voice was directed elsewhere. "Hey, get in here! She's waking up!"

No, not yet, she wanted to protest. She was tired, her head throbbed, she wasn't ready to face the world. All she wanted was to listen to the man's low, sexy voice.

She felt a cold hand on her arm, a pinch on her right eyelid as someone lifted it. A blinding pinpoint of light bored into her skull. She let out a tiny cry of protest and her eyelid was released. A babble of conversation ensued, and Hope searched through the mumble for the man's voice. She didn't hear it, and her heart wanted to break.

The mumbling faded, leaving silence in its wake. Then, when she was about to give up and sink back into the dark, she heard him, his tone underlined with muted laughter. "Well, I reckon that was the most exciting thing that ever happened in their lives. I see the hospital delivered you some fresh flowers. Lots of yellow ones this time. I don't know what these things are—the pom-pom ones, and something that looks like dyed daisies. They're awfully pretty, Hope. I wish you could see them."

She became aware of a fragrance—not flowers but coffee. Suddenly she was desperate for a cup of coffee.

"So, what should I talk about? Let's see... It's nine-thirty. I almost got hauled bodily out of the hospital this morning when I asked for a visitor's pass, because visiting hours don't officially start till two in the afternoon. I discovered you don't need a visitor's pass to get upstairs if you pretend to be a doctor. I just sauntered down the hall like I owned the place, and took the staff elevator. I had two cardiologists sharing the ride up with me, chatting up a storm on the subject of angioplasty. I nodded a lot. They must've thought I was some kind of expert."

He stopped talking. Was he drinking his coffee? If she could figure out how to open her eyes, how to speak, she would ask him for a sip. At that moment, she believed her survival depended solely on a good, strong hit of caffeine.

"It's raining outside. Drizzling. Damn, I can't believe I'm yakking about the weather again." Pause. "Clint telephoned me from his office this morning. Remember Clint? He's the guy you were visiting when you... Well, anyway, he says the police talked to your boss and told him you'd be missing some time at work." Pause. "I didn't sleep well last night."

She tried to recall whether she'd slept at all. Who could tell? The line between sleep and delirium had evaporated in her mind.

"Every time I drifted off," he said, "I saw you. I saw the way you looked the instant you were hit, and then the way you looked lying on the street..." He cleared his throat. "I don't know, maybe I should avoid heavy topics, but Hope, this is all we've got, this situation. This is what we're all about here, isn't it?"

No, she wanted to say. *We're about much, much more.*

The only problem was, she didn't know what it was.

And the only other problem was, she still hadn't figured out how to talk.

"Every time I closed my eyes, I pictured you lying in that hospital bed, with tubes going into you, and you were so still and frail, and... man, I just..." His voice dissolved into a sigh.

She flexed her hands again, and moaned again—anything to let him know she heard him. She felt a hand against hers, not the same hand as before but a healing hand, warm and hard and large, folding around her fingers, enveloping her. *His* hand. If he couldn't talk to her one way, he would talk to her another, through touch, through his quiet, powerful clasp.

She wanted to assure him she would be okay. She wanted to tell him about her grandmother and her legacy, and even about the mirror, if she could ever bring herself to come to terms with the spiritual lightning that had all but electrocuted her when she'd confronted the silver glass in apartment 1-G. She wanted to talk to this man the way he talked to her, slow and easy and affectionate.

Since that was impossible, she squeezed his hand.

HER FINGERS WERE SOFT and cool, the ripple of motion in them so faint anyone else might not have noticed. Morgan noticed, though. He noticed everything about her: the arch of her eyebrows, the fullness of her lower lip, the sleek curve of her chin, the slope of her throat. The way her nostrils flared when she inhaled, and her breasts rose and fell beneath the blanket.

It scared him, how aware he was. He and Hope were trapped together in a strange web, threads of guilt and fear, pain and faith tying them to each other and imprisoning them. It scared him like nothing had ever scared him before.

Yet she had gripped his hand and sighed, and moaned and given him every sign he could possibly ask for—short of sitting up and slapping him five—that she was aware of him, too.

He wished he hadn't noticed her lips. They were a sweet strawberry pink. Hope really was pretty. Despite her matted hair, despite the bruise discoloring her right cheek, Hope Henley was a remarkably beautiful woman.

He felt even more guilty for noticing that.

If he hadn't struck her with his car, he would never have given her a second look. Well, maybe a second—but definitely not a third. She wasn't his type.

And yet . . .

Her hand was like a whisper of silk within his, so soft and small and slender it made him wonder whether the rest of her was that soft. The doctors had told him that other than some internal bruising, her body had escaped the accident relatively unscathed.

Why was he thinking about her body? Why, when she was lying in bed, totally helpless thanks to him, was he contemplating the modest curve of her bosom and the satin smoothness of her skin? Why, when he'd always been partial to blondes, was he admiring the stark contrast between her black, black hair and her creamy complexion?

She gave his hand another almost imperceptible squeeze. She was trying to tell him something. "Hey," he said, and her hand moved again, a quiet stroke of her fingertips.

Maybe she wanted him to talk. He'd already discussed the weather. Time to think of some other innocuous subject.

"Clint told me you work at a store that sells movie memorabilia. He said the store was full of all sorts of ticky-tacky stuff—Scarlett O'Hara and Rhett Butler dolls, and Fred Astaire-style top hats, and those glass balls filled with fake snow, with a sled labeled Rosebud inside them. I bet it's fun working there—if you like old movies. I used to go to the movies when I was a kid. We'd all pile in the back of the truck and drive to the theater in town, and they'd be showing a Billy Jack movie. It seems like they were *always* showing a Billy Jack movie, or else a spaghetti western."

He laughed, remembering how he and his cousin Floyd would hoot and snort at those self-righteous vigilante movies. But any movie was better than nothing to do on a Saturday afternoon in Bailey Notch.

"If you're into old movie lore, you really ought to check out Bachelor Arms. That's the building where you were visiting Clint and Jessie. I live there, too. A long time ago, the mansion was split up into three huge apartments, and three high-living bachelor movie stars lived there. That's how it got to be called Bachelor Arms—on account of those bachelors. There's a woman living at Bachelor Arms now, Natasha Kuryan, a really neat lady who's been around forever. When she was young, she went to some of the parties the bachelors used to host, back in the thirties. They were major bashes. All kinds of film people used to come. People sure knew how to live it up in those days."

Her hand, he realized, had been growing more and more tense within the curve of his. Her pretty pink lips moved, as if she were struggling to say something.

"What, Hope? Come on, you can tell me. I know you can hear me—now tell me what it is. You can tell me anything, honey. Just spit it out."

"True." She lacked the voice to speak, but the word emerged on a hoarse gasp.

"What's true, Hope?"

"It's true," she croaked.

He ought to inform the nurses that Hope was talking—yet he believed her words were meant for him alone. "What, Hope? What's true? Open your eyes, now. Come on, darlin'. Look at me. Tell me what's true."

Her dense black lashes twitched. She gripped his hand so tightly she practically cut off the circulation in his thumb. And then, with what seemed to be excruciating effort, she opened her eyes to him.

Oh, God, they were so dark. Large and lovely and impenetrably dark. She appeared stunned as she stared at him. Did she recognize him? Had she glimpsed him through the windshield in the instant his car slammed into her? Did she believe she had come face-to-face with the devil himself?

"Hey, there," he murmured. "It's me."

Her eyes widened as she gazed up at him. She worked her mouth, ran the tip of her tongue over her lips, and breathed a single word, so quietly he saw more than heard it. "Morgan."

SHE WASN'T SURE how she'd known his name. He must have told her. He'd told her a great deal, most of it muddled but all of it recorded in some form in her chaotic mind. His name was Morgan.

And he was beautiful. She supposed that after her long, troubled hours of sightlessness, the first person she saw would be beautiful to her, no matter who it was. But Morgan...

He was something to behold.

He had hair the color of brandy, brown with licks of red fire burning through it. It fell in unruly waves to his shoulders, framing an open, even face. His eyes were the same brandy shade beneath the twin slashes of his eyebrows. His lips were thin, quirked in a tentative smile.

She drank in the sight of him, the man who had kept her from plunging to her death, the man whose voice had connected her to the world of the living. If she could sort through the miles and miles of memory tape in her head, she might be able to piece together more about his identity. She was positive he'd told her about himself. Surely he must have explained why he'd stayed by her side while she'd been floundering in the dark.

For now, she knew the important things: He was Morgan. He had saved her life. He resided in the pink house with the mirror, where movie stars used to live, the big, old mansion where a spirit in a mirror had appeared before Hope and frightened her to her soul. A mirror where she had seen herself and someone else—where she'd seen herself *in* someone else.

The woman in the mirror had said, "My greatest hope has come true. You've come back."

Hope didn't believe in ghosts. But to see one—one who looked like her, who spoke to her and beckoned to her, who'd tried to draw Hope into her arms, right into the mirror... Merely remembering made Hope's heart pound with abject dread.

The monitor beside her bed started to beep dangerously fast. "Nurse!" Morgan shouted through the open door, apparently alarmed by the racing heart monitor. "Something's going on! Hurry!"

The nurse was already in the door. "Stand back," she ordered Morgan. "Get away from the bed. You shouldn't even be in here."

Hope tightened her grip on him. She didn't care what the nurse said. She wasn't going to let go of him.

"Please, sir, stand back!"

"I'm not in your way," Morgan snapped. "You've got access to all of her except her right hand, and as long as she wants me holding it, I'm going to hold it."

The small room grew crowded as a doctor and then another nurse rushed through the door. Hope was blinded by another pinprick of light, and voices filled the room like fog, blurring her ability to think. Panicked, she clung to Morgan's hand and focused on him.

In contrast to the commotion, he looked serene, his amber eyes on her and only her, his smile growing more confident and his hand snug around hers. While the doctors and nurses murmured importantly, he simply stood at her side, leaning his elbows against the bed frame railing and grinning at her. He had broad shoulders and lean, sinewy forearms, visible where he'd rolled the sleeves of his shirt up to his elbows. Her gaze journeyed down his torso to the belt riding his narrow hips. He was wearing blue jeans, not fashionably styled ones but real ones, work pants, the kind of jeans she and Gramma used to wear when they weeded the vegetable garden.

God, he was beautiful.

"Thank you," she murmured, although she couldn't even hear her own voice.

His smile deepened, rising to illuminate his eyes. The doctors and nurses could have been functioning in a parallel dimension for all Hope cared. Morgan had heard her. He knew her gratitude was for him.

A motor vibrated beneath her, raising the top half of her bed and lifting her into a sitting position. A doctor settled on the edge of her bed and tucked his hand under her chin to steer her attention to him. She would have protested, but Morgan gave her hand a quiet, reassuring squeeze. He wasn't going anywhere. She could look at the doctor without losing Morgan.

"Do you know who you are?" the doctor asked.

Stupid question. Of course she knew who she was. She nodded, because it was easier than speaking.

The doctor smiled encouragingly. "Can you tell me your name?"

"Hope Henley," she said in a scratchy whisper.

"How old are you?"

Considering she seemed to have died and come back to life in the last several hours, she felt incredibly old. "Twenty-five," she said.

"Do you know where you are?"

In a hospital room. In a bed. In California. "With Morgan," she answered, stating what mattered.

The doctor shot a glance at Morgan, who gave her hand another private squeeze. "How do you feel?" the doctor asked her.

"My head hurts."

"No surprise there." The doctor proceeded to put her through a series of tests: following his finger with her eyes, reciting the alphabet, distinguishing left from right. The exertion tired her, and after a while she closed her eyes and shook her head.

"She's had enough," Morgan said, once again her savior.

"I think we can transfer her out of ICU," the doctor decided. "We can move her down to the third floor. I'd like to get her up on her feet, try her on clear liquids—"

"I want her in a private room," Morgan said.

"Her insurance stipulates a semiprivate room," a nurse piped up.

"I already spoke with the administrators. You can bill me for the extra cost. I want her in a private room. With a television, a window, and anything else her heart desires. Is that clear?"

"Mr. Delacourt—"

"Anything she asks for. Send the bill to me. I don't want to hear about what's covered and what's not covered. I want her to have what she needs."

"I'll call the business office," a nurse said. "If I get confirmation on that, we'll find a private room for her."

Her eyes still shut, Hope sank into the pillow. Let them chatter, let them bicker. It was all too much for her. She felt dizzy, overwhelmed by everything except the comforting hand closed around hers.

She would get what she needed. Morgan would see to it. Morgan would make sure of everything.

"MORGAN."

He sent her a rakish grin. "Yes, darlin'?"

"Why are you here?"

His smile waned and he sighed. "Try to remember, Hope. See if you can remember."

She gazed across the room at him. Her third day out of intensive care, she'd finally stopped experiencing double vision. She could see the spacious private room, the palms outside the window and the botanical harvest of blossoms festooning the sill, the small bureau and the night table. She could see the lace bed jacket Jessie Gale and Clint McCreary had brought her—a bed jacket! She'd never owned such a garment in her life—and hanging on the wall near her bathroom, a poster from the film *Awakenings*, which had been about patients emerging from deep comas.

But mostly she could see Morgan Delacourt. He sat in the tweed-covered easy chair near the window, a glory of tawny hair and solemn eyes and the most virile physique ever bestowed upon a man.

He'd been with her as much as possible, considering that the doctors were forever dragging her out of her room for tests and sessions with the physical therapists. Other than the double vision problem, she'd been beset by dizzy spells whenever she'd stood up. But her memory was clear, her verbal skills had returned, and even the doctors were using the term *miraculous* in discussing her recovery.

When she wasn't being probed and prodded, examined and exercised, she was with Morgan. He would arrive every morning at nine with a jumbo cup of gourmet coffee for her from one of the coffee boutiques near the hospital. He would also bring a copy of the *Los Angeles Times,* which he would read to her because her double vision prevented her from reading it herself. Once he'd shared everything from the editorials to the advice columns and the comic strips with her, he would set the paper aside and they would talk.

"Don't you have to be at work?" she asked him the first day, and he'd told her about his career as the creator of Mongo the Magnificent. He'd described the story lines he was toying with for upcoming comic books and the half hour series a production company was preparing for television broadcast.

"Aren't you bored, sitting there and watching me heal? It must be like watching paint dry," she'd remarked, and he'd smiled and said he could think of nothing less boring than watching a woman overcome a terrible injury.

"Why are you here, Morgan?" she'd asked, so many times she'd lost count. "I'm glad you're here, but . . . *why?* Why me? Why did you choose me to worry about?"

Whenever she asked that, he would lose his smile. "Don't you know? If you can't remember, Hope, then you've got a lot more healing to do."

What she remembered was hearing his voice, low and husky and stretched around a delicious mountain drawl, practically from the moment she'd banged her head and lost consciousness. He must have witnessed the accident—the details of which she wasn't quite clear on. She'd been running, running from the mirror, and then suddenly everything had gone dark, everything had slammed shut inside her and the world had vanished.

Except for his voice. It had been there all along, telling her to hang on, begging her to come back. She recalled his voice finding her in the darkness, luring her, seducing her back to life. She recalled believing that whoever he was, she loved him.

Now that she was getting to know him, she was embarrassed by that overblown sentiment—and yet she couldn't quite convince herself that she *didn't* love him. Perhaps if he was older, or colder, perhaps if he wasn't such a gorgeous hunk, if he didn't have that beguiling drawl . . .

Of course she didn't *really* love him. Her days in the hospital were an aberration. Just as her vision and balance had been thrown out of alignment, so had her heart. A conk on the head could wreak havoc on a woman's affections.

But Morgan had such a warm, genuine smile. And his eyes were a color she'd never seen before, maple brown and honey gold, with glints of sunshine mixed in. And his touch . . . oh, yes, she remembered his touch. It had been about as unromantic as a touch could be, but her body had come to life—literally—when his hand had taken hers.

"Hope." He rose from the chair, crossed to her bed, and lowered himself gently onto the mattress beside her. When he sandwiched her hand between his, she felt herself come to life even more. She tried to persuade herself it had nothing to do with the penetrating radiance of his eyes, the sensuous tilt of his lips, his strong posture and his large, masculine grip. "I really want you to remember who I am to you. I want you to remember what happened, or we'll never get past this."

"You talked to me," she said, snuggling her fingers inside his hands. "I do remember, Morgan—you talked and talked until somebody pulled me away from you."

"Medical technicians pulled you away from me, Hope. They put you on a gurney and lifted you into an ambulance."

"Yes, I remember that." Impatience nipped at her. Why did Morgan keep making her rehash the accident again and again? What was she missing? Why couldn't he just tell her?

"Do you remember how you got hurt?"

She felt the leather surface of his palm against her fingertips. His hands dwarfed hers. Not surprising; once, when she'd stood up and suffered a staggering wave of vertigo, he'd leaped from his chair to steady her, and he'd towered above her. She wasn't exactly statuesque, but she wasn't so very short, either. Morgan must easily stand more than six feet tall, and his hands were proportionate to the rest of him.

"Do you remember, Hope?"

"I was running. There was an accident..."

"Do you remember the accident?"

She frowned, even though frowning made her facial bruises throb. She closed her eyes. She remembered her irrational fear of being sucked into the mirror, of being absorbed by the woman on the other side, the woman who seemed to recognize Hope and welcome her, and want her for some reason, some unspoken purpose. Hope remembered bolting, propelled by sheer fright. She remembered fleeing from the room, from the pink mansion. She remembered tearing down the front walk to... the *street*.

"A car," she said, her voice catching on a sob. "A bright red car."

"Yes."

"I was hit by a car."

"Yes." She opened her eyes and found Morgan's face just inches from hers. "I was the driver of that car, Hope."

"You?"

"It was my car that hit you. I did this to you."

"No." She refused to look away from him, refused to accept what he was saying. "It was an accident."

"It was my car. I was driving. I hit you. It's my fault you almost died."

"No." Her vision was indeed clear—clear enough to see the grief in his eyes, the anger and anguish and outright sorrow. "It wasn't your fault, Morgan. You can't think that."

"I was at the wheel—"

"No, listen to me. You saved my life. That's why you're here—because you saved my life."

"I could have killed you."

"But I'm alive." It dawned on her that for once, he needed comfort more than she did. He was the one suffering, in pain, racked by remorse. "You saved my life, Morgan," she whispered, sliding her hand free of his and wrapping her arms around his shoulders, embracing him, wishing she could hug all his sadness out of him.

He drew her to himself. "If you hadn't gotten better—"

"But I did get better."

"—I would never be able to forgive myself."

"I'm better," she swore, resting her cheek against the firm expanse of his shoulder. Hugging him revived her just as holding his hand had. It made her vision sharper, her mind steadier. "I'm better because of you."

"I still can't forgive myself," he admitted, his voice gruff with emotion.

"You'll have to forgive yourself," she whispered. "If I can heal, you can heal."

He closed his arms more snugly around her and buried his face in her hair. She felt safer in his arms than she'd ever felt before. Even if he'd been driving the car that struck her. Even if he'd been a part of the terrible accident that had nearly cost her her life.

She felt safe with Morgan, safe and secure and curiously content, as if she belonged in his arms, as if he could protect her from all the pain and fear that had battered her over the past few days.

As if he could protect her from all the pain and fear that the future might send her way.

4

"IT'S NOT LIKE I wouldn't do the same thing in your shoes," Ted remarked, "but do you really want her hanging around full-time?"

Morgan drained his beer bottle and glanced up at his illuminated living room window. He was seated outside in the courtyard, sharing a drink with his neighbor, Theodore Smith, who by some strange quirk of fate was dateless that night. Ted was the resident Lothario of Bachelor Arms, and if there was a reason he wouldn't want an unattached young woman camping out in his apartment, it was probably because he'd rather have a whole harem of unattached women camping out there.

"I mean, Morgan, ol' boy, letting her move in with you... It's a very big step."

"Oh, come on. She's not moving in. She's just staying for a few days."

"A few days can expand into a few more days, and a few more, until the next thing you know, she's taken over your lease. Have you considered all the ramifications?"

"There's an old saying," Morgan drawled, his gaze lingering on the light-filled window one story above him, "that if you save someone's life, you're responsible for that person forever."

"Forever is a long time, buddy."

"I know. And I didn't save her life. I practically killed her. But she doesn't see it that way. She thinks it's thanks to me she's alive."

"It was a bad accident. Maybe her brain got scrambled."

Morgan shook his head and laughed, although in truth he found nothing funny about the situation. "You're right, Ted," he muttered. "If anyone's brain is scrambled, it's mine, for bringing her back here."

"Why did you do it, then?"

He mulled over his answer. Part of him believed he'd brought her back to his apartment because her dark, wistful eyes had somehow sent him into an irrational trance. Part of him believed that, despite his usual taste in women, the thought of a dainty beauty like Hope Henley spending a few nights under his roof appealed to his baser male instincts. Part of him even liked having her so dependent on him, if only for a while.

He couldn't admit to that, though, so he told Ted the logical reasons, the ones he'd told himself that morning when he and Hope had come up with this solution. "The hospital wasn't going to release her unless she could have around-the-clock home care. She still gets dizzy spells sometimes, and her vision blurs. But she said she couldn't bear another night in the hospital. I can't say I blame her. Hospitals are depressing."

"Full of mysterious germs, too. Sometimes staying in a hospital can make you sicker than you already are."

Morgan concurred with a nod. "Anyway, I offered to hire a nurse to stay with her, but she wouldn't hear of it. Her apartment's an efficiency; there's no room for a nurse to stay with her. She suggested just a day nurse, but *I* wouldn't hear of *that*. If something happened to her at night, and she had nobody there to help her . . ." He didn't bother to finish the thought.

"So you said, 'What the hell—move in with me.'"

Not in so many words, but yes, that was pretty much how it happened. Morgan was astonished that he'd made the suggestion, astonished that she'd accepted—and then maybe not so astonished, after all. No one other than Clint, Jessie and Morgan had bothered to visit Hope in the hospital; she obviously didn't have many friends in town. When he'd asked her about her family, she'd mumbled something about a mother and stepfather in Chicago. Her tone of voice had informed him that she wasn't close with them.

Which left him. Him and his spacious two-bedroom apartment, with a friendly group of neighbors to help him keep an eye on her.

"I told her she'd be welcome, and she took me up on it. She's got it in her head that when she was in the coma, the sound of my voice kept her from going under for good. She seemed pretty pleased about staying at my apartment for her recuperation."

"Obviously she hasn't heard about your way with women," Ted teased, giving his eyebrows a Groucholike twitch.

"I'm not going to have a way with her. I hit her with my car, for God's sake. Do you really think she's going to want to dance the dance of time with me?"

"Why not? According to Brenda and Bobbie-Sue, you've got the cutest buns in Bachelor Arms."

Morgan snorted a laugh. "Did they tell you that?"

"They're sly gals. They check out all the guys."

"And always find us wanting."

Morgan didn't really want to talk about Brenda and Bobbie-Sue, the two alluring waitresses and wanna-be actresses who lived in Bachelor Arms. For that matter, he didn't want to talk about Hope, the alluring sales clerk who'd run into the path of his car five days ago. He didn't want to talk about anything at all, but Ted was watching him expectantly, obligating him to explain himself further. "I figured, if I brought Hope here, there would be plenty of people around to stay with her. Natasha Kuryan said she'd be happy to keep Hope company if I had to go out. But since I've got a drafting table in my apartment, I can be around pretty much all the time."

"Have you and Hope worked out the sleeping arrangements?"

"She's got my bedroom. I've got the foldout couch in my office."

"If she isn't going to share the bed with you, why not give her the foldout couch?"

"That was what she said, too. She made a little speech about how she didn't want to put me out—like my ramming into her with my car didn't put *her* out any. The lady's recovering from a near-death experience. I'm not going to ask her to sleep on a couch."

"Who says chivalry isn't dead?"

Morgan gazed up at his window again. As the surreal pink of the dusk sky faded into mauve, the rectangle of light appeared brighter. Natasha was with Hope now, helping her to settle in. Earlier that afternoon, Clint's fiancée Jessie had driven Hope to her apartment to pick up some clothing and toiletries, while Morgan had cleaned his apartment, changed the sheets on his bed and made a quick run to the grocery store, wondering, as he roamed up and down the aisles, what she liked to eat.

He would find out soon enough. Tomorrow morning he would be facing her over his first cup of coffee, a prospect that sent a twinge of nerves through his body. He wasn't used to spending the morning with a woman—at least, not unless he'd first had the privilege of spending the night with her.

He absolutely had to put a hold on all thoughts about spending the night with Hope. He had to pretend that having her toothbrush and face cream lined up on his bathroom counter didn't seem strange, and clearing out a drawer in his bureau for her hadn't made him feel an intimacy toward her he wasn't prepared to acknowledge.

From the instant she'd bounced off his windshield to this moment, when he'd realized he was in the way in his own apartment, his entire existence had seemed out of control. Within just a few short days, he'd gone from being a happy-go-lucky comic book artist to a millionaire to an uneasy man who'd just invited a near stranger to store her lingerie in a drawer where he used to store his socks and boxers. It was just too . . . out of control.

Natasha Kuryan would get him through it. She was the grande dame of Bachelor Arms, and for whatever reason, she'd always been fond of Morgan. When he'd first moved into Bachelor Arms a few years back, Natasha had helped him to negotiate the ins and outs of the neighborhood. She'd run interference for him with Ken Amberson, the landlord, and during a few excruciatingly lean periods, when royalty checks had gotten delayed and story ideas had gotten nixed, she'd discreetly extended invitations for dinner so Morgan wouldn't have to live on peanut butter on toast sandwiches three times a day. Once he'd started earning real money, he'd made sure Natasha's wine supply never dropped below a certain level, and he remembered her birthday with flowers, even though he had no idea how old she was.

Natasha tended to be eccentric—although, as far as Morgan was concerned, anyone who'd lived as long and colorful a life as she had earned the right to be eccentric. Just because she dressed like a Gypsy and piled her waist-long silver hair in a haphazard knot on her head didn't mean she wouldn't serve as a damned good companion for a recovering accident victim.

In fact, the minute she'd entered his apartment, she and Hope had hit it off, making him feel extraneous. Grabbing a beer, he'd left them jabbering like old friends and exiled himself to the courtyard.

"The thing about women . . ." Ted said, then grinned. "They're wonderful, you know? I adore them. But live with one? Even for a few days? Sheesh. Turn your back, and she's going to start rearranging your silverware drawer."

"My silverware drawer could use some rearranging," Morgan muttered.

"She's going to hang nylons on the towel racks in the bathroom."

"I doubt it. She isn't going to be dressing up." Betraying him, his imagination conjured a picture of filmy stockings draped in his bathroom. Filmy *black* stockings, retaining the curved shape of Hope's legs. Several times in the past few days, he'd been treated to the sight of her bare legs, exposed beneath the knee-length hem of her hospital gown. They were great legs. Superb legs. The sort of legs guys couldn't help noticing—and imagining in sheer black stockings.

Another window above him lit up—his kitchen. He didn't want Natasha cooking for his guest, and he didn't want his guest having to cook, either. She ought to be taking it easy. The sooner she regained her strength and equilibrium, the sooner he could resume living the life of a carefree millionaire bachelor.

"I'd better go see what those two are up to," he said, rising and lifting his empty bottle from the arm of the chair.

"Listen, Morgan—if this lady is as pretty as Clint says, would you mind if I dropped by later?"

"To make a pass at her?" Morgan rolled his eyes. "Yeah, Ted, I would mind."

"I understand," Ted said, feigning innocence. "She's all yours."

Morgan almost retorted that soon she would be all her own, on her own, and this whole peculiar episode would be over. But a protest would only give Ted more ammunition to taunt him with, so he merely smiled and bade his neighbor good-night.

He entered the building and climbed the stairs to the second floor. As soon as he edged open the door, he heard Hope and Natasha chattering as blithely as when he'd left them a half hour ago. Their voices floated from the kitchen on an aromatic waft of air.

He walked as far as the doorway, where he found Hope seated at the table and Natasha standing at the stove, stirring a pot of soup with a cooking ladle. She had tossed her turquoise-and-violet scarf over the back of a chair, and stubborn strands of hair had escaped from the convoluted twist on her head and drizzled like silver streamers past her shoulders.

She must have heard Morgan's footsteps, because she immediately turned and wagged the ladle accusingly at him. "I can't believe you have so many cans of that manufactured soup. Shame on you, Morgan Delacourt."

Morgan knew better than to take Natasha's scolding to heart, especially when she was smiling so broadly. "I don't know how to make soup from scratch."

"Well, lucky for you, I've managed to salvage this with a few herbs and spices and some fresh vegetables. It might almost taste palatable. Keep stirring it until it starts to simmer, and then feed that girl. She needs some fat on her bones." Natasha tapped the ladle emphatically against the side of the pot, then placed it on the counter and grinned at Hope. "You and I shall continue our talk later."

"I'm looking forward to it," Hope said, her smile directed at Natasha but her eyes on Morgan. As Natasha gathered her scarf, Hope pushed herself to her feet. Morgan quickly moved to her side, in case she was going to stumble.

Her smile tensed; she seemed annoyed by his hovering. Not that he could blame her. He hated people hovering over him, too. But he'd be damned if he'd let her keel over in his kitchen.

She teetered slightly, her cheeks pale, her gaze darting from him with chagrin. He wanted to remind her that healing took time, that she had to be patient, that given what she'd been through, it was a miracle that she was standing at all. He nixed the lecture, though, and simply cupped his hand under her elbow to steady her.

She was fine-boned, yet he sensed strength in her arm, a small but effective muscle swelling toward her shoulder. Her skin was as soft as a baby's.

He wished he hadn't noticed.

She shot him a quick look. He wasn't sure if she resented his touch, but she seemed to resent her own weakness more. Frustration flared in her eyes.

Morgan was frustrated, too—only it had less to do with her wobbly balance than with the fact that this petite dark-haired woman could turn him on without doing a darned thing. He was frustrated that, more than the aroma of the soup he smelled *her,* the faint, tangy fragrance of her shampoo, the freshly laundered scent of her short-sleeved cotton sweater. He was frustrated by her fragility and her strength, and the sweet curve of her lower lip as she bit it and concentrated on remaining upright.

The hell with her rearranging his silverware drawer. What Morgan really had to protect against was her rearranging his hormones.

She wasn't his type, he reminded himself. Given his newfound affluence, he could have his pick of nubile, buxom blondes, women he'd met under more auspicious circumstances. Just because taking Hope's arm made him feel all sorts of old-fashioned protective male urges didn't mean he and Hope had anything going, other than an utterly screwed-up acquaintanceship forged in guilt.

Natasha was yammering about the soup—"Don't add any salt. Those canned soups are eighty percent salt, so don't you add another grain. Honestly, Morgan, if you're going to buy canned soup, buy the low-sodium kind"—and Morgan focused on her to keep from focusing on Hope. He walked both women to the door, where Natasha flung her scarf around her shoulder with a dramatic flourish.

"Thanks for the health class, Natasha," he said, smiling to melt the sarcasm from his words. "And seriously, thanks for helping out with everything."

"My pleasure," Natasha said, then turned her astute gaze to Hope. "And thank *you*, dear, for being such a good listener."

"As long as you're willing to talk, I'm willing to listen," Hope said.

"Then we have many more conversations to look forward to. I am usually willing to talk forever. Ask Morgan, he'll tell you. Good night, children." With that, Natasha strolled away.

Hope and Morgan lingered on the threshold until Natasha had disappeared, and then he remembered the soup simmering on the stove and started back to the kitchen. Hope hesitated for a moment, frowning as she stared down the hallway. "Is my eyesight really that bad, or is there a bass fiddle leaning against the wall?"

Morgan turned to glance in the direction she was pointing and chuckled. Sure enough, what appeared to be the carrying case of a towering bass viol stood upright by one of the doors. "That's apartment 2-C," he said. "I guess someone's living in there."

"You guess?"

"That apartment changes hands so often, no one ever knows who's there. Either the new tenant is a musician or he's an assassin with a very large gun."

Hope peered up at him, as if uncertain how to take him. Instead of questioning him, she eased her arm from his grasp and walked in slow, measured steps back to the kitchen. "I'll check the soup."

"Hey. You're a guest here," he said, chasing her into the kitchen. She was already at the stove, turning off the burner and giving the pot a final stir. "You shouldn't be cooking."

"I'm not cooking."

"Sit down," he ordered her, prying the ladle from her hand.

Standing so close to him, she had to crane her head upward to look him in the eye. "I'm not your patient, Morgan. And I don't like feeling helpless."

"You aren't helpless," he agreed, noting with some irony that when he stared into her dark, fathomless eyes, *he* was the one who felt helpless. He wanted to protect her, he wanted to pamper her—yet in that one brief moment, as she stood inches from him and gazed up at him, he was aware of her steely strength, her flinty ego, her determination not to be protected and pampered.

He almost wished she would suffer another dizzy spell. How was he going to atone for his sins if she refused to let him take care of her?

"You really don't want to be here, do you?" he murmured. Her hair was so thick and dark, it seemed to absorb the light from the overhead fixture, to suck it in. He felt himself being sucked in, too, absorbed by her steady gaze, by the stubborn set of her mouth.

"I really *do* want to be here," she refuted him, then abruptly turned away.

Did that mean she liked him? Or was simply lonely? Or wanted to avoid her own home, for some reason?

He watched her take a seat. Her movements were careful, almost stiff, and he saw the way she gripped the table as she lowered herself into the chair.

She wasn't as strong as she wanted him to think. Not physically, at least. Mentally, emotionally...he had a feeling she was a hell of a lot stronger than he was. And that bothered him.

He carried two steaming bowls of soup to the table, then dug a box of crackers from the back of a cabinet. "What would you like to drink?" he asked. "I've got beer, soda, some hard stuff—"

"Water would be fine," she said.

He filled two glasses at the sink and joined her at the table. It had always seemed big to him when he ate alone, its circular surface large enough to hold not only his meal but an open newspaper or a box of take-out pizza. But sitting opposite Hope, he felt as if the table had shrunk. She was too close.

As long as she was living in his apartment, she was going to be too close. Yet he had no desire to ask her to leave. More than simple remorse made him want her in his kitchen, eating his doctored soup.

"You're from Chicago originally?" he asked, bothered by how shamefully little he knew about her.

She shook her head. "Kansas."

"I thought you said your mother—"

"She's living in Chicago now. But I grew up in Topeka, and I went to the state university, and I spent the last couple of years on my grandmother's farm a ways south of the city."

"No kidding? You're a hick, just like me." He smiled, a little of his tension ebbing. "My folks weren't professional farmers, but where I come from, growing your own vegetables costs less than buying them, so everyone cultivates an acre or two."

Her spoon halfway to her mouth, she paused, a flicker of light glimmering in her eyes. "Bailey Notch, West Virginia," she said, both startled and pleased.

Morgan was startled, too. "How'd you know that?"

"You told me."

"You mean... when you were out of it? Back in intensive care, when you were all but dead to the world? The only reason I was talking was to try to drown out the sound of your heart monitor. I didn't know you could hear me."

"I didn't know I could hear you, either." She swallowed her soup, shook her head and grinned. "But I knew your voice, right from the start. And I knew your name. When I opened my eyes, I saw you—and I knew it was *you*."

He wasn't convinced. "I got coldcocked once in high school, during a football scrimmage. I collided with Wynn Ewell—man, that guy caused me more trouble when I was a kid—and since he outweighed me by about fifty pounds, I wound up seeing stars. But I was out for less than a minute, and I don't remember a damned thing."

"I don't remember much, Morgan. I hardly even remember the accident. But I seem to remember things you said."

"Yeah?" Intrigued, he leaned back in his chair and appraised her. Dressed in that pale pink sweater and slim-fitting jeans, with her hair long and loose and her smile dimpling her cheeks, she looked younger than her years. "What else did I tell you?"

"You told me your town is full of your relatives, and you're going to fly home to see them for Christmas." She seemed to be gazing at the air around him, concentrating, trying to dredge up her memories of his long-winded monologues. "You argued with the doctors." She thought some more. "You described flowers to me. You brought me flowers, and you described them to me." Her eyes seemed to glisten with moisture.

"Hey," he said quietly, afraid that she was going to start weeping. He groped along the counter behind him for the box of tissues he kept there, and passed them to her as the first tears trickled down her cheeks.

"I'm sorry," she whispered, wiping her eyes and blowing her nose. "I don't know why I... I mean, I'm not usually a sentimental sop, but those flowers, Morgan..."

"You never even saw them."

"Yes, I did. You described them for me, and I saw them in my mind." She sniffled a bit more, smiling bravely through her tears. "It was so kind of you."

"It was penance, nothing more. A way to pay off my guilt."

"No." One final sniffle, and she squared her shoulders. "Those flowers helped me get better, Morgan. They had nothing to do with your guilt. You gave them to me to help me recover."

He opened his mouth to argue, then shut it. Maybe she was right. No amount of flowers—not even a huge, expensive bouquet every day for a million years—could pay off his guilt. But if they'd helped to heal her, they were worth immeasurably more than what they'd cost him.

Clearly embarrassed by her maudlin display, she dug into her soup. After a few spoonfuls, she seemed to have regained her composure. "Natasha is a wonder, isn't she."

"She's a neat lady," Morgan agreed.

"She's a font of information about this house."

"Bachelor Arms? Yeah, she goes way back here. She's been living here since right after World War II. But she'd already been in Hollywood for years by then. She used to work in the film industry."

"Was she an actress? She's so beautiful."

Morgan smiled. It was hard to think of a wizened woman who, by his estimation, had to be in her eighties at least, as beautiful. Yet Natasha had a hard to describe radiance, a star bright glow about her. He was inexplicably pleased that Hope saw Natasha the way he did.

"I don't think she ever appeared in a film. She was a makeup artist. She was in charge of making everyone else beautiful. Ask her about the time she had to wax Errol Flynn's mustache during the filming of *The Adventures of Robin Hood*. It's quite a story."

Hope shared his grin. "She was telling me about the three bachelor movie stars who used to live in this house—they hosted some wild parties on the premises. She was a guest at some of them."

"Oh, yeah. Natasha's got lots of stories. Get her started, and she really will go on forever."

"I wasn't kidding when I said I was a willing audience. I want to hear everything she can tell me about this house and its history. I'm very interested in it."

Morgan heard something in her voice, something tough and leathery and difficult to interpret. The house had its legends and its lore, but Morgan had never gotten all that caught up in them. He'd never seen the alleged ghost in the mirror in 1-G—to be sure, he'd been more than a little horrified when his apparently sane neighbor Clint claimed he *had* seen the ghost.

Hollywood was chock-full of flamboyant folks. No doubt half the city believed in the supernatural—ghosts, numerology, astrology and all that New Age mysticism stuff. But as far as Morgan was concerned, fantasy belonged in comic books, not in real life.

"Why this house?" he asked. "What do you find so interesting about it?"

Hope set down her spoon and studied him thoughtfully. "I think," she said, then sighed, apparently anxious about what she was going to tell him. "This is going to sound very odd, Morgan, but . . . I think I own Bachelor Arms."

5

SHE SHOULDN'T HAVE told him. The way he gaped at her, he was probably thinking she had lapsed back into a state of delirium.

Perhaps she had.

But ever since she'd seen the spirit in the mirror in apartment 1-G, she'd *known*. She hadn't wanted to believe that something as absurd as a phantom in a mirror could be true. In fact, at times she hadn't even wanted to believe her grandmother's stories about being tracked down by a lawyer and informed of her inheritance.

The whole thing was so very strange, and at heart Hope was not a strange person. She took pride in her solid midwestern roots. She enjoyed the earthy simplicity of farming, and when she'd gone to college she had chosen the eminently practical major of business administration. If her grandmother hadn't taken ill, Hope would have kept her job at a market research firm, or gone on for a master's degree—or both.

She had never in her life bought a lottery ticket. The most she'd ever paid for a garment was one hundred twenty dollars for a Liz Claiborne dress. She had never even *dreamed* of being an heiress, nor had she put much faith in luck. Flights of fancy were not her style.

And yet . . . she was positive the house she was sitting in right that very minute, the great pink mansion with its funky turquoise trim, its Spanish-style roof and its colorful legacy, was the same house her grandmother had told her about, the house where many years ago a young woman had lost her child and died of grief. And today the ghost of that young woman floated in a mirror, waiting for her daughter to come home.

It was preposterous, of course. It was totally illogical.

Yet Hope believed it.

There was no way of explaining this to Morgan without sounding like a raving maniac. But she couldn't imagine keeping secrets from him, not after he'd saved her life. He had been an essential presence during her long, dark night of unconsciousness. He was a vital part of everything that had happened to her since she'd seen the ghost.

It was only fair to tell him she'd had more than one reason for accepting his invitation to stay with him. When he had asked her to live at Bachelor Arms for a few days, the place where it had all started, the place that had so frightened her she'd nearly killed herself running away from it—she'd had to say yes. Not just because she was too weak and wobbly to be on her own, not only because Morgan seemed so desperate to compensate her for what truly wasn't his fault, but to spend some time under the roof of this house that had haunted her grandmother and now haunted her.

Gazing across the table at Morgan, noticing the puzzlement creasing his brow into a frown, she was forced to acknowledge another reason she'd agreed to stay with him. That reason had nothing to do with her health or the deathbed promise her grandmother had extracted from her. Observing his face, seeing through his bemusement to the clear, vivid amber of his eyes, his sensual mouth, his firm chin and his broad, strong shoulders . . .

She'd agreed to stay with him because she was attracted to him.

She had better forget about his sex appeal. He had no personal interest in her. That his voice had penetrated her coma to soothe and lull her, that she was more preoccupied with him than with the damnable ghost in the mirror downstairs—none of it was relevant. She was here to heal and to ease his troubled conscience, nothing more.

"Run that by me again," he drawled, a hint of laughter shining in his eyes even as he continued to scowl at her.

"You think I'm crazy."

"Your words, not mine."

She sighed, realizing there was no way she could possibly explain herself to Morgan without sounding even crazier. "Forget I said anything."

"How the hell could you *own* this house? You just told me you're from Kansas, and you work in a souvenir shop. Bachelor Arms isn't the sort of place that a saleswoman would own. It must be worth a million dollars, give or take."

"Oh, I don't know about that," she demurred, admitting privately that he was probably right. It was a huge building on a prime piece of real estate. The land alone must be worth a fortune.

"If you own this house—" he seemed to choke on a laugh "—why are you working as a sales clerk?"

"I don't have title to the house yet, Morgan. There was a will..." Reading his skepticism in his face, she faltered.

"A will," he prompted her.

"My grandmother's mother's will. I have to find it first. It will prove the house was my grandmother's. And she left it to me."

"Oh. Of course." He didn't bother to stifle his laughter. "Let me see if I've got this straight—there's a missing will that says you own Bachelor Arms."

"It says my grandmother owns it. But she passed away last summer, and she left the house to me."

"Does that make you my landlord?"

"No, I—"

"Or does it just mean you're richer than sin? Because if you are, maybe *I* ought to charge *you* rent."

"I wish you would," she retorted, tired of being mocked. "I'm taking advantage of you, staying here as your guest. You've already spent your own money to pay for my private room at the hospital, and all those flowers—"

"Yeah, the flowers. Man, I spent an arm and a leg on those. I ought to send you a bill." He shook his head, laughing even harder. "Come to think of it, I ought to send you more flowers. I could do quite nicely for myself, wooing a rich heiress like you. Just let me know—before I incur any more expenses—am I competing with any Maserati-driving European playboys?"

"Don't make fun of me." She wanted to pout, but his laughter was infectious. A giggle escaped her. "I know it sounds ridiculous. But some day when you aren't busy laughing at me, I'll explain it to you."

"I can't wait, darlin'." His laughter waned, although he was still smiling as he glanced at her empty bowl. "You want any more soup? Cripes, you're probably used to eating caviar on toast points, and instead I'm making you eat like a prole. Tomorrow I'll pick up some well-aged steaks."

"The soup was fine. And I don't want any more, thank you." His teasing was beginning to grate on her, as was his comment about trying to woo her. The only time he would ever mention wooing her, it would be as the punch line of a joke. That shouldn't have hurt, but it did.

She rose from her chair, determined to help him clear the dishes. Before dizziness had a chance to seize her, he darted around the table, planted his hands on her shoulders and pushed her, gently but firmly, back into her seat. "I'll do the dishes," he said quietly.

Yet instead of gathering their bowls and spoons, he remained behind her for a long moment, his hands molded to her shoulders. They were large, his fingers blunt-tipped, not what she would expect of an artist—even if he was only a comic book artist. His nails were clean and square, his knuckles thick. His were hands that could easily arch around a football or wield a hammer and nails, hands that could span her waist, or tangle into her hair, or caress her cheek and ignite dark thoughts in her soul.

They were hands that could lift an unconscious woman out of the abyss and carry her back to life.

They were hands that belonged to a man who thought she was a few cards shy of a full deck.

She couldn't really blame him for thinking she was insane, but she wasn't sure she could share living quarters with him if he was going to patronize her—either physically, by not letting her help him with the simplest of kitchen chores, or emotionally, by acting as if she were in desperate need of a straitjacket and a padded cell.

"I'm sorry I mentioned the house," she mumbled, staring glumly at the dishes he refused to let her bring to the sink.

"I'm sorry I laughed at you," he conceded. "You can't help it if things are still a little squirrely in your mind. It's amazing you're doing as well as you are."

"This has nothing to do with the accident. I came to Hollywood to find my grandmother's house." She bit her lip, then let out a long breath, as if she could blow the subject out of the room. "Never mind."

He finished clearing the table in silence. She refused to turn in her chair to watch him wash the dishes, but the sounds of washing conjured a mental picture of his strong, hard hands glistening in the sudsy water, wiping and rinsing the bowls with unexpected grace. At last she heard the water shut off, and he moved back into view, drying his hands on a towel. "I'm sorry," he said again, peering earnestly down at her. "I have no idea who owns this house. Ken Amberson runs things, and we all call him the landlord. But he's actually more of a super. As I recall, some corporate entity is named as the owner on the lease."

She perked up. "Do you have a copy of your lease, Morgan? Could I see it?" If she could learn the name of the corporation, she would have a place to start her investigation, evidence more concrete than a ghost in the mirror and her grandmother's sometimes incoherent rambling.

"God knows where it is. I'll try to dig it up tomorrow. Tonight, though, I think you ought to get some rest. You're less than twenty-four hours out of the hospital. I really think you should take it easy."

"I *am* taking it easy. You won't even let me pick up a spoon."

"And now I'm going to set you up with some TV, or whatever you'd like to unwind with."

"I don't watch much TV," she said, her anger dissolving. He wasn't teasing her now, and he couldn't help it if his eyes, his smile, his touch provoked inappropriate responses in her. He was trying to be nice, and the least she could do was be nice in return. "I usually read in the evenings, but I forgot to bring any books with me."

"I've got books," he assured her, taking her hand and helping her out of her chair.

She tried to pretend he was the physical therapist at the hospital. She'd never felt anything the least bit personal when the therapist had eased her to her feet and assisted her in her exercises. But then, the therapist hadn't filled her unconscious mind with his healing voice. And he hadn't had such startlingly beautiful eyes, such defiantly long hair, such a lean, lanky build.

"Do you know what I'd really like to read?" she asked, swallowing to clear the catch in her throat. "A Mongo the Magnificent comic book. I've never read one before."

"Never read a Mongo comic? Shame on you!" He led her through the doorway and into the living room. "They're Nobel Prize quality literature. I can't believe you've lived as long as you have and never read a Mongo story."

He was laughing at himself as much as at her, and she played along. "I'm ashamed to admit it, Morgan. Instead of reading Mongo, I was wasting time with hacks like Shakespeare and Mark Twain."

"We'll just have to rectify this terrible lack in your life." He guided her to an easy chair, nudged over an ottoman with his foot, and turned on the lamp at her elbow. As soon as she had sunk deep into the overstuffed cushions, he left the room. When he returned, he was carrying a half dozen comic books. "Here you go. Classics, every one of them. A huge improvement over Shakespeare and Twain."

"Thanks," she said, smiling up at him as he laid the stack of comic books in her lap.

"Can I get you anything else? A cup of coffee? A shot of whisky?"

"No. I'll be fine. You can watch TV if you'd like—it won't bother me." She gestured toward the shelves of entertainment equipment against the opposite wall: stereo components, stacks of CDs and videotapes, and a television set.

He considered her suggestion, then shook his head. "I'm going to put in some time at my drafting table. I've got a couple of story ideas I want to tinker with. I'll be just the other side of that door—" he indicated a door in the arched hallway leading out of the living room "—so if you need anything, just holler."

"I'll be fine," she repeated.

"I mean it, Hope. Anything at all. Even if you want to talk about your grandmother's will. I'll be there—and I promise I won't laugh at you."

That was a promise Hope wouldn't test; she doubted he would be able to keep it. She sent him a quick, cool smile and then focused on the stack of comic books in her lap. What she needed right then was for him to leave, so she wouldn't have to stare into his riveting eyes and think about how easily he'd laughed at her before, how he'd assumed she was suffering from some post-traumatic dementia. She wanted him far enough away that she would no longer remember how his hands felt on her.

She doubted there was any place far enough away for that. But he took her unspoken cue and left the room, leaving her with her unwanted memory of his touch—and his Mongo comic books.

She opened the first one and began to read.

MIDNIGHT FOUND HIM still hunched over his drafting table. The hinged lamp cast a bright white circle on the blank sheet he'd clipped to the table's surface. The last sheet of paper he'd had there now lay wadded up on the floor, along with nine other wads, all of them bearing sketches that went nowhere. Behind him his computer hummed; the screen-saver pattern—a cascade of dancing magic wands—reminded him of how much time had passed since he'd touched the keyboard. He used the computer to write scripts and plots, but his ideas for Mongo stories nearly always germinated visually, through drawing.

Right now, unfortunately, the only thing germinating was restlessness. Five days had elapsed since he'd signed the damned contract, five days lost to worry about Hope and his own culpability. He ought to have five days' worth of ideas pouring out of him.

But all he could think about was the woman in his bed.

At around ten o'clock, after the third or fourth aborted drawing had found its crumpled way to the floor, he'd risen from his chair and walked into the living room to check on her. The easy chair had been empty, and when he'd hurried down the hall to the master bedroom, he'd found her fast asleep in his bed. Unlike at the hospital, her face looked smooth and free of discomfort. This was real sleep, contented sleep, not the sleep of someone racked with pain and jangled gray matter. Hope almost looked as if she belonged in his bed.

He was rattled by the understanding that she'd walked to the bedroom without his assistance, that she'd gotten herself washed and into bed without his knowledge. It wasn't just that he wanted to shadow her every step; she would go even more nuts than she already was if he made a pest of himself like that. But the thought of her prowling around his house, making herself so very much at home in it . . .

He wasn't sure he was ready for it.

She'd been the picture of serenity in his bed, her hair spread around her face in splashes of black, her eyelids shaping two fringed crescents and her lips pursed in the shape of a kiss. A lesser man might have been tempted to tear off his clothes and join her under the covers.

Given how tempted Morgan had been, he could only conclude that he was a lesser man.

Leaving her to her sweet dreams, he'd left his bedroom, then detoured into the bathroom. He hadn't really expected to see black stockings dangling from the towel rack, but their absence had disappointed him. She *had* left something in the bathroom, though—and not just her neatly arranged toiletries. She'd left a scent, something fresh and minty, a fragrance that made him want to U-turn and head straight back to his bedroom, to his bed, to her.

Lesser he might be, but he exercised enormous self-control and returned to the spare bedroom, to his useless, dreary drawings and his hissing computer.

He started a new sketch. With light, jabbing strokes of his pencil, he drew his hero—a caricature of himself, a long, lanky fellow with stringy hair and a jutting chin—waving his wand. A house emerged from the tip of Morgan's pencil, resembling Bachelor Arms in an uncanny way. A lovely young woman was trapped in the house. She had long, black hair. She stood before her reflection in a mirror. . . .

Man, she was making him nutty, too. If he'd known her insanity was contagious, he wouldn't have let her move in.

"Are you working?" Her voice was like liquid silver gliding through the silence.

Startled, he spun around in his chair. She hovered in the doorway, a pale apparition in an oversize white sleep shirt that fell to her knees. Her arms, her legs, her face were so fair, she seemed almost ethereal—except for the sleep-rumpled black hair cascading down around her shoulders.

If Morgan believed in ghosts, he would have thought he was looking at one now. But he didn't believe in ghosts, and he realized that he was looking at a slightly drowsy, slightly dizzy, extremely pretty woman.

He sprang out of his chair as she leaned against the door frame. "I'm all right," she murmured, but that was another thing he didn't believe. Within an instant, he had his arm around her and was leading her to the couch. He hadn't opened it into a bed yet—which was probably just as well. If he had, he would have been hard-pressed not to fling her down across it—and himself down across her.

"I thought you were sleeping," he said, hastening back to his chair the moment she was safely on the couch. God, but her waist was tiny. Which wasn't to say she was skinny. There were definite swells above and below that ridiculously narrow waist. Nicely rounded hips and breasts. And nicely rounded knees, and calves, and—

"I *was* sleeping," she said, apparently oblivious of the effect she was having on him. She tucked her legs under her and leaned back into the cushions. "But then I woke up, and I didn't recognize where I was. I was all disoriented. When I got out of bed, I saw the light coming from this room. I hope I haven't interrupted anything."

"You haven't." He waved at the balled-up papers littering his floor. "It hasn't been the most productive night of my life."

"I loved your comic books," she said, then grinned sheepishly. "That sounds silly coming from an adult, doesn't it."

"Like hell it does," he said with pretended indignation. "Lots of adults read Mongo."

"You can add one more adult to your fans. The stories were really funny. They had action and adventure, just like other comic books, but they also were hilarious."

Her compliments touched him more deeply than he would have liked. "Thank you."

"The character of Mongo, himself—he's so sweet. And cute."

"Cute? He's a geek who just happens to be armed with a magic wand."

"He's not a geek," she argued, as if she understood his hero more than he did. "He's adorable. So shy and self-effacing, and he's got all that great hair—"

"Stringy hair," Morgan muttered, reflexively brushing an errant lock of his own hair out of his eyes.

"And the wand motif... It cracked me up. It's so—so—"

"So what?"

"Well, you know." Her cheeks flamed pink and she averted her eyes.

"Manly," he supplied.

"Well, yes." Her blush grew even more intense. She almost looked feverish.

"I don't suppose the kids who read the books see it that way. The jokes tend to work on two levels, one for children and one for adults."

"I noticed." She recovered from her embarrassment and smiled at him. "Mongo is based on you, isn't he?"

"Yeah, sure. I'm a geek with a magic wand."

"You're not a geek," she protested, then evidently thought better of commenting on his wand. "Did you ever want to be a magician?"

"I was a magician like Mongo, unfortunately. I never knew how my tricks were going to work out. When I was, oh, about twelve or so, I saw a magic show on TV. I thought it was cool. So I went out and started buying magic paraphernalia and books that explained how the tricks were done—but I always botched things. I'd make a quarter disappear in a handkerchief, but then, when the quarter was supposed to reappear, it wouldn't. And then five minutes later it would drop out of my sleeve. Or I'd put a scarf in a hat, and I was supposed to pull out silk flowers, but instead the scarf would come out—only it would have changed color. I don't know what I was doing wrong, but the audiences loved it. It became my act—the bumbling magician who never knew what was going to happen next. Even Wynn Ewell used to pay fifty cents for the joy of watching me screw up."

"Wynn Ewell," she echoed quizzically

"At one time, my nemesis. Currently, my cousin by marriage."

Hope gazed around the office. It was Morgan's favorite room in the apartment, except for those occasions when he had a woman in his bedroom. Everything he needed was here: not just the drafting table, his pens and his computer, but a portable CD player, a rug so old and faded he could no longer remember what color it used to be, and a few important books—among them *Alice in Wonderland, The Hobbit,* and an album of photos of Elvis impersonators. On the walls hung framed posters of some of his favorite cartoon characters: Walt Disney's Goofy, the X-Men, Calvin and Hobbes, Bart Simpson, and Zonker from "Doonesbury."

"What's the computer for?" she asked.

"Plotting, mostly. Writing story lines and scripts."

"Scripts?"

"Mongo's about to become a regular on TV."

"Really?" Her eyes grew round and she nodded. "You told me about that in the hospital."

"I might have mentioned it. We're just starting production. They're going to broadcast a couple of previews at the end of the summer, and then go into the regular weekly schedule in mid-September."

"That's so exciting." She eyed an encyclopedia of magic tricks lying open on the counter next to the computer. "What's your marketing strategy?"

"My what?"

"Well, if you're going to have a show about a comic book character, you've got the perfect setup for merchandising. What are you planning?"

Morgan scoffed. "I don't plan. I leave that to the paper pushers." Hope looked disapproving, and he goaded her. "What? You think I'm an idiot?"

She shook her head modestly. "It's none of my business."

"Say it anyway."

"Well, only that . . ." She ruminated for a minute, then pressed onward. "Mongo's your invention, Morgan. He's your property. You ought to retain the licensing rights to him."

Morgan leaned forward, intrigued by what she was saying and more than a little astounded that she could be discussing business strategies so lucidly at half-past midnight. "Licensing rights?"

"You know, like—if the show goes on television, you're going to create a market for, oh, I don't know. Mongo dolls. Mongo board games. Mongo magic trick sets."

"You think so?"

"Or greeting cards. Or T-shirts. Look at Disney." She waved toward the Goofy poster on his wall. "They have stores all over the country, devoted to selling Disney-related merchandise."

"Mongo isn't exactly in the same league as Mickey Mouse," Morgan reminded her, although her analysis fascinated him. "You don't actually think someone would want to open a chain of Mongo stores, do you?"

"No. But there'll be tie-ins, especially if the show's a hit. Which I'm sure it will be."

He couldn't help smiling. "How can you be sure?"

"I read those comic books you gave me. They're very clever."

"Clever doesn't always sell."

"But Mongo will. If he's on TV, people who never read comic books are going to discover him. It could become very big."

He leaned back in his chair and regarded her thoughtfully. For a woman who'd gotten a major thump on the head, and who became delusional when it came to Bachelor Arms and her grandmother, Hope seemed mighty shrewd about business. Shrewder than Morgan. Shrewder, maybe, than his lawyer. "I'll have to go over my contracts and make sure I'm protected."

"You'd better. There could be a ton of money in those licensing rights, Morgan."

"How do you know all this?"

"I majored in business at college. Marketing."

"Would you—" He hesitated, wondering whether he ought to trust her with something as important as his career. He recalled her off-the-wall claim that Bachelor Arms belonged to her, and her insistence that Morgan had saved her life, and every other zany thing she'd ever said to him. Yet despite her bouts of irrationality, he couldn't deny that in this one instance she was making a hell of a lot of sense. "Would you thumb through my contract and make sure my lawyer didn't blow it? Not right now, of course—it's the middle of the night. But tomorrow, after you've had some coffee—"

"It's the least I could do for you. Of course I'll look through it." She smiled shyly. "You'll also let me look through your lease, won't you?"

"Anything you want. I'll trade you Bachelor Arms for a genuine Mongo wristwatch."

"His magic wand can be the minute hand."

"I thought I explained what his magic wand stands for."

Her cheeks flushed with color again. If he had truly offended her, she would have fled from his office. But, embarrassed though she was, she remained on his couch, curled up like a soft, sweet kitten, begging to be stroked.

His own magic wand stirred to life.

How could he not be turned on by her? She was a beautiful woman and a business whiz, and she was lounging in his office in a baggy nightshirt. He wondered what she had on under it. He wondered what she would do if he joined her on the couch.

He swiveled in his chair, turning away from her just long enough to reach behind him and switch off his drafting lamp. The light in the room dropped to a muted golden glow. When he swiveled back to her, he noticed that her smile was gone, her eyes profoundly dark.

"It's getting late," he observed, figuring he could turn this thing into a time-to-hit-the-sack moment if she gave him any indication that she was unreceptive.

"It got late a long time ago," she murmured.

The air in the room hummed like his computer, churning with electricity, circuitry, more information than he could assimilate at the moment. The couch suddenly seemed miles away from his drafting table. Hope shifted against the cushions, tilted her head, frowned slightly as he rose from his chair.

He wished he would come to his senses. He wished he could remember that he preferred blondes, that he preferred his women sane and simple, that the circumstances that had brought Hope Henley into his life were not conducive to romance.

But it was as if he were behind the wheel of his car once more. Hope was there, straight ahead, directly in front of him. And he couldn't seem to stop.

6

NOTHING COULD HAVE prepared her for his kiss.

It wasn't that she was surprised by it. She had known, even before he'd risen from his chair, that he was going to cross the room to her, sit down beside her on the couch and claim her mouth with his. She'd felt the yearning that swept through the room like a sudden gust, roiling the air, altering the atmosphere between her and Morgan, wrapping around them and drawing them together.

Oh, yes, she'd seen it coming, the way you could sometimes see a storm rising up from the flat Kansas horizon, miles and miles away but approaching, bearing down on you. You stand transfixed, aware that you can't outrun the storm or do much to protect yourself from it, but must simply brace yourself and wait for it to reach you.

Yet anticipating it was one thing, and experiencing it was another. When Morgan pulled her into his arms and lowered his mouth to hers, she felt buffeted, deluged, completely at the storm's mercy.

It was only a kiss.

It was so much more than a kiss.

It was the passion of a tall, limber man with a quirky sense of humor and a stubborn trace of a hillbilly accent, a large-handed, large-hearted man, using whatever strange, magical powers he possessed to bend her to his will.

When she'd been in the hospital, she might have died, but he wouldn't let her. When she was ready to leave the hospital, she would have returned to her own home, but he wouldn't let her. And now, when she ought to have pointed out that this was a bad idea, that someone—namely herself—was going to wind up hurt if they got involved, he wouldn't let her.

It wasn't as if he were preventing her from speaking—although the moment his lips brushed against hers she discovered that her mouth had much more important things to do than talk. She knew that if she so much as sighed the wrong way, or turned her face an inch to the side, or gave any indication that she didn't want his kiss, he would back off.

What he wouldn't do was allow her to deny the truth. And the truth was, she wanted his lips on hers, his arms around her, his lean, hard chest crushing her breasts as she leaned against him. She wanted everything Morgan Delacourt had to give her. And if she wound up hurt . . . She supposed recovering from whatever his kiss did to her would be no worse than recovering from what his car had done to her a few days ago.

His mouth seemed designed for no other purpose but to arouse her. He brushed his lips against hers, then pressed, then nipped. Sliding his hand around to the nape of her neck and up into her hair, he cupped her head and held it steady as he slanted his mouth over hers, caressed and cajoled and coaxed her lips apart.

His tongue moved inside her mouth as if it belonged there, as if he'd kissed her a million times before—and yet everything about this felt new to Hope. She'd been kissed in her past, but never by a magician. Never by someone who had saved her life.

A shudder of sensation gripped her between her shoulder blades, slithered down her spine and settled in her hips. It left her feeling warm and liquid, as if she could pour herself onto Morgan, take his shape, cling like sweet syrup to the planes and angles of his body.

She circled her arms around his shoulders, and he lifted her into his lap. His hands glided down her back, tracing her spine through the thin cotton of her nightshirt. When he reached her waist, he splayed his fingers downward along the curve of her bottom and stroked her hipbones with his thumbs.

Another shudder seized her, causing her stomach to clench and her hands to fist in his hair. She opened her mouth fully, and he groaned. One of his hands journeyed forward and up until he reached the curve of her breast.

"Morgan," she whispered, although she couldn't hear her voice. It was like when she'd been in the hospital, certain she was talking to him although no sound came out. Her lips moved as they had then, but only to kiss him again and again, to tease his lower lip with her teeth and skim her tongue over his.

He didn't speak, either, and yet she could hear his words, his plea. His hands told her, his mouth, his broken sighs, his fingers seeking the swollen tip of her breast and his erection straining against her as he shifted his legs under her. She might as well have heard him shout out loud that he wanted her. The message came across clearly.

She heard another voice, then, neither his nor hers, a pale whisper emerging from deep within the chasm of her memory: *He doesn't love you.*

She wanted to argue that it didn't matter, this wasn't about love. It was about a burning, churning hunger that encompassed them both, that could be satisfied only one way. It was about being alive, in every sense. It was about embracing sensation, celebrating survival, sharing one more intimacy with a man whose destiny was already intimately entwined with hers.

He doesn't love you, the voice reverberated inside her. *I loved a man who didn't love me, and I lost my child because of it, and I went mad with grief. Never give yourself to a man who doesn't love you, or you will go mad with grief, too.*

The ghost. She saw the glitter of a mirror in the dark of her closed eyes, a streak of light, the negative image of her own shadow emerging from another time, another place, a moment when a woman loved a man who didn't love her, and lost her mind and her life because of it.

"No," Hope moaned.

She was addressing the ghost, but Morgan naturally assumed she was talking to him. He drew in a shaky breath and eased his lips from hers. Slowly, tenderly, he stroked his hands up and down her back. She realized she was trembling, and she cuddled deeper into his embrace, partly for the comfort he offered and partly because she was too mortified to look at him.

"Bad idea, huh." He sounded friendly enough; the only sign that he was at all frustrated was the almost imperceptible tightness in his tone, and the very perceptible bulge beneath his fly as he shifted his legs again.

"No." She sighed, burrowing her face into his strong, solid chest. "No, it's just . . ."

"Just a bad idea." His hands came to rest on her shoulders, and he carefully pushed her far enough from himself that he could see her face. "After all you've been through, I must be one hell of a bastard to try anything with you."

"You're not one hell of a bastard," she managed to say, wishing she didn't have to gaze into his beautiful eyes. "This was my fault."

"Here we go again, arguing over who gets to take the blame." He shook his head and gave her a lopsided smile. "The last thing you need right now is what I've got."

She wanted to argue, but she didn't know what to say—except that she *did* need what he had. Not sex but protection. Strength. A firm tether to the present.

"Don't sweat it, Hope. It won't happen again," he promised.

But she wanted it to happen again. She wanted him to kiss her the way he'd kissed her just now, to kiss her so fiercely she tingled from her scalp to her toenails. She wanted him to hold her in his powerful arms and run his hands over her body, and . . .

And she didn't want a damned ghost getting in the way and reminding her of what a stupid thing it would be to make love with Morgan.

"I should get you to bed," he said, then laughed and shook his head. "Lousy choice of words."

"Morgan—" She faltered and lowered her gaze. "You must think I'm horrible, leading you on and then stopping you so abruptly."

"Were you leading me on?" His laughter grew more natural, and a quick glance downward informed her that his body had subsided. "I thought I was doing the leading, honey, acting like a domineering macho man."

She knew he was kidding, but she wasn't in the mood to share his amusement. "One thing you aren't is a macho man."

"Ouch. You sure know how to hurt a guy."

His teasing only made her feel worse. "I *don't* know how to hurt a guy, Morgan. I've never hurt a guy before—not knowingly, anyway."

"Like hell." He was still chuckling. "I bet you've broken a million hearts."

"There aren't a million hearts in Topeka, Kansas." And even if there were, Hope wouldn't have broken any of them. She'd never been a femme fatale. Men tended to overlook her when there were taller, more striking women around. Hope had always been quiet, reserved, the kind of girl guys didn't pay much attention to—and that had suited her well enough.

"Anyway, this kind of hurt isn't fatal. I'll get over it." He nudged her the rest of the way off his lap and stretched his legs. His gaze intersected with hers, and his smile vanished. "You'll probably never trust me again."

"Oh, Morgan..." Tears threatened. Of course she trusted him—trusted him even more than before, given how quickly he'd withdrawn when she'd said no. It was herself she couldn't trust, her own treacherous longing for him, and the part of her—an ever increasing part—that seemed locked in some hallucinatory world of ghosts and voices and her grandmother's strange legacy. She blinked rapidly, not wanting to cry in front of him. "It's *me*," she mumbled, staring at her knees. "I'm sure you think I'm a nut case, saying I own this house and then coming on to you, and then shutting you down like... like..."

"Like a woman recovering from a bad accident," he completed for her.

He *did* consider her a nut case—even if he was willing to invent a plausible excuse for her nuttiness.

"I think I'll get myself to bed," she said, unfolding her legs and pushing herself to stand.

Almost at once the dizziness swamped her. She felt her knees start to buckle, her body to sway—and in an instant she was high off the ground, cradled in Morgan's arms.

"Put me down," she demanded. To be carried to bed—and then abandoned there, alone—was more than she could bear.

Ignoring her, he moved in long, brisk strides out of the room and down the hall to his bedroom.

"This is humiliating," she complained, hooking her hands around his neck to keep from tumbling out of his arms.

"Oh, come on. You weigh hardly anything."

"It's not my weight that's humiliating, it's—" *My weakness*, she wanted to say.

"Just call me Mongo the Magnificent. Me and my macho magic wand can lift a full-grown woman without popping a bead of sweat." He shoved the bedroom door wider with his toe and hit the light switch with his elbow. "Not that you grew all that full. How tall are you, anyway?"

"Tall enough," she muttered.

He lowered her onto the center of the mattress, as if deliberately to avoid leaving room for himself beside her. "There," he said, smoothing the sheet out under her. "Comfortable?"

Not as comfortable as she'd been in his arms. She didn't want him to make love to her. She didn't need a ghost to remind her that she wasn't ready for that. But simply to be held by him, enveloped in his warmth . . . That would be the perfect way to fall asleep.

"I'm sorry," she said for the umpteenth time.

He straightened up and shoved a thick shock of honey-colored hair from his face. "We can't keep apologizing to each other all the time, Hope."

"Then maybe we'll have to stop doing things that require apologies."

"Either that, or we ought to go ahead and do what we want, and forget the guilt."

Hope almost said she'd be willing to forget her guilt if he would forget his. Lying in his bed and gazing up at him, she was keenly aware of his eyes roaming over her scantily clad body, igniting small sparks of heat wherever they paused—at her ankles, at her breasts, under her chin, in the slope where the cotton fabric of her nightshirt settled between her legs.

She didn't feel the least bit guilty about wanting his hands to touch her as his gaze did, wanting to feel his blunt-tipped fingers on her ankles and her breasts, her throat and her thighs. Unlike the accident, which she was still convinced was more her fault than his, the emotion in Morgan Delacourt's bedroom in the heart of the night had nothing to do with guilt.

It had to do with lust. And with the dire warning of a ghost from generations past: *He doesn't love you. You will go mad with grief.*

It was the ghost who was making Hope mad. It was her confounded belief that the ghost existed, and the shocking realization that a haunted pink mansion in Southern California could somehow be the home her grandmother had willed to her, and the understanding that all that had stood between her and death was the tenacity a comic book creator who just happened to be the sexiest man Hope had ever known. *That* was what was making her mad.

But the ghost called out to her again. *Never give yourself to a man who doesn't love you.* Her mother hadn't offered her that wise advice. Neither had her grandmother. Only a ghost—her mother's mother's mother, a chimera from the past, the lady in the mirror—told Hope what she knew in her heart to be true.

With a sigh, she pulled the blanket over her body, hiding herself from Morgan's view. "Good night," she murmured, wondering if he could hear the disappointment in her voice.

He backed up to the door and switched off the light. "Good night," he said, and she could hear the disappointment in his.

"BREAKFAST IN BED," Natasha Kuryan announced.

Hope groaned and blinked her eyes. For one groggy minute, she saw two overlapping Natashas—two thick silver manes of hair, two fuchsia paisley scarves draped over four shoulders, two swirling green skirts, two benign smiles. Two mugs of coffee emitting twin coils of steam.

It reminded her of staring into the mirror in apartment 1-G and seeing double: herself and the ghost, overlapping, drawing more and more tightly into focus until they risked becoming one.

The memory shook her, and she closed her eyes and willed it away. She was sick and tired of the damned ghost—and annoyed that Natasha and not Morgan was waking her up. If Natasha was here, Morgan was probably gone.

The elderly woman confirmed her suspicion by reporting, "Morgan phoned me a while ago and said he had to go to his studio for a while. It's after ten. He told me to let you sleep, but enough is enough. If you sleep any longer, you won't be able to sleep tonight."

Like last night, Hope thought miserably. Long after Morgan had left her alone in his bed, she'd lain awake, wishing...wishing he was with her, wishing his arms were around her, wishing he could silence the ghost.

Natasha balanced the tray carefully on the bed, then propped Hope's pillows against the brass headboard so she could sit. "It's fun fussing over someone for a change," she said. "When one gets to be my age, one is usually on the receiving end of the fussing. I rather prefer things this way. Morgan told me you take your coffee black."

Hope nodded, unnerved to think of Natasha and Morgan discussing her behind her back, even if all they'd talked about was her taste in coffee. She surveyed the tray's offerings: besides the coffee, a toasted English muffin and a glass of orange juice. She wasn't terribly hungry; the light breakfast would suffice.

Natasha crossed to the window and drew the drapes open, letting in an offensively bright spill of sunshine. Then she sat in an old, faded easy chair near the window and watched, eagle-eyed, while Hope bit into one of the muffin halves. "Morgan is worried about you," she remarked, as casually as if she were commenting on the sunny weather.

Hope eyed her curiously. Was he worried because he thought she was a temptress? Or because he thought she was seriously deranged? "What did he say?" she asked warily.

"Nothing specific. But I can tell. When he speaks your name, his eyes take on a strange glow."

"He shouldn't worry about me," Hope insisted, then took another bite of her muffin to keep from muttering that she wouldn't dare kiss him again, or even show herself outside the bedroom without being fully clothed.

"He cares a great deal about you," Natasha went on.

"It's just misplaced guilt." Hope reached for her coffee and took a sip. "And maybe a little panic."

Natasha only smiled.

The silence weighed heavily on Hope. She could hear herself swallow the coffee, hear her hair rustle against the linen pillowcase. "Have you ever seen the ghost?" she blurted out.

Natasha's smile didn't change. She shook her head.

"But other people have seen her?"

"Oh, yes."

"You believe she exists, then, don't you?"

Natasha settled back in her chair and knitted her worn, bony fingers together. "I do."

"Do you believe the legend?"

"That if you see her, your greatest hope or your greatest fear will come true?" When Natasha grinned, years peeled away from her face. Her eyes glinted with youthful amusement and delight. "I do, indeed."

"But you yourself haven't seen her."

"I have seen someone who might be her." Natasha smoothed the fringed edge of her scarf against her slim chest. She obviously relished talking about the myth that clung to Bachelor Arms. Her smile grew deeper, her gaze distant, as if she were peering through a long tunnel into the past. After a minute, her attention returned to Hope. "Has anyone told you about the movie starlet who drowned in the pool outside?"

"What pool?" Hope had looked out the windows yesterday and seen only a courtyard landscaped with a few trees and shrubs.

"It's paved over now. In the old days, though, it was an in-ground pool surrounded by a patio and lit by torch lamps. It was quite grand."

"It certainly sounds grand," Hope agreed. It also sounded awfully Hollywoodlike.

"The three bachelors who lived here back then—oh, we're talking some sixty years ago—they used to host the wildest parties around that pool."

Hope's breakfast went forgotten. She was even able to forget Morgan's disturbing sex appeal, the golden eyes and sensual mouth that had haunted her restless night as surely as the ghost had. She had an appetite only for Natasha's nostalgic reminiscences. "Wild parties?"

"Dreadfully decadent. The hooch flowed like water. Music played. People danced and danced until they collapsed in a heap."

"You didn't live here then, did you?"

"No, but I went to a few of those parties. The bachelors who lived here were a notorious group. Everyone wanted to be invited to one of their galas—particularly young starlets longing to see and be seen. Many directors attended the parties, and producers—people who could transform a starlet into a star, if they had a mind to."

"What happened to the starlet who drowned?"

"Well, she wanted to be a star, like all the rest. One of the men at the party—I don't know whether he was a director or an actor, but I'm sure he was someone who wielded great power in the industry. He brought the starlet indoors. Perhaps you've heard of the casting couch?"

Hope nodded.

"That was why he brought her into the house. The story was, they emerged after a short time, the starlet distraught and the man grumpy. Apparently he'd tried to seduce her, but she was too vain. She kept staring into the mirror in that downstairs suite, staring and staring at herself, and then she bolted from the house. She got lost in the crowd, and the next time anyone saw her, she was at the bottom of the pool, dead."

A chill skittered through Hope's nervous system. It was a juicy, colorful story, but also sad. She felt a pang of sorrow for the starlet, even though she had no connection to her. "Was it an accident, or did someone kill her?"

"That I can't say. But there are some who believe she's the ghost haunting Bachelor Arms."

"No," Hope firmly refuted Natasha. "No, she isn't the ghost. I'll bet what happened was, she saw the ghost when she was staring into the mirror. It wasn't vanity that made her stand in front of the mirror. She *saw* the ghost—and her greatest fear came true."

Natasha seemed intrigued that Hope, a complete outsider with the most tenuous connection to the building, should have such a strong opinion on the ghost's identity. "Everyone has always assumed it's the starlet's ghost in the mirror. If it isn't, whose ghost could it be?"

Hope didn't answer right away. She already had Morgan assuming she was bonkers; she didn't want Natasha thinking she was, too. But if anyone might believe her, the silver-haired woman with the wise, ancient eyes would. "The ghost looks exactly like me."

Natasha laughed in delight. "But of course! You've really come to Hollywood to become a star, haven't you. Morgan said you were working at that charming movie memorabilia shop—"

"No," Hope cut her off. "I'm not an actress, and I'll never be a star. I have no interest in show business."

"Then why come to Los Angeles? For the weather?"

Hope shook her head. "I saw the ghost, Natasha. Clint McCreary—the man living in 1-G—saw the ghost, and then he saw me, and he found out who I was and demanded that I see the ghost for myself. That ghost could be my twin." She sighed and gazed past her companion, staring into the bright morning sun until it nearly blinded her. "I came to Los Angeles to find that ghost. I might not have realized that when I came. But now that I've seen her... now that I'm over the shock of it, I know that was why I came. To find her."

"You wanted to find the ghost of a dead starlet?"

"It's not a starlet," Hope explained, forgiving Natasha's bewilderment. "The starlet looked into the mirror and saw the ghost, and her greatest fear came true. She must have been afraid of dying young, or of water. Maybe she didn't know how to swim. Or maybe she was suicidal, and her greatest hope came true—although that would be horrible. But the legend says that's what happens when you see the ghost."

"But if the ghost isn't the starlet, who could she possibly be?"

Hope squared her shoulders, bracing herself for the possibility that Natasha would laugh at her, or race to the telephone to summon the nice gentlemen in the white coats and arrange for them to take Hope away. "My great-grandmother," she said.

Natasha didn't laugh. She didn't run to the phone. She regarded Hope thoughtfully, her eyes aglitter, her mouth curved in a smile of amazement. "Your great-grandmother," she said. "How utterly lovely."

"HOW'S THE PATIENT?" Francine asked.

Morgan sent his assistant a doleful look, but refrained from telling her the truth: the patient was exasperating. The patient was making him crazy. The patient had lit a match under his hormones and heated them to boiling. The patient had insinuated herself into his dreams. The patient had arranged her lithe, slender body on his lap in such a way that his lap would never be the same again.

"She's improving," he muttered.

"I wish I could say the same for this month's story line. Your plot sucks lemons." Francine gestured toward the pages of script piled on his drafting table next to his current sketch.

"I'm having a little trouble concentrating, okay?"

"You're having a little trouble finding your razor, too, I see." Francine hoisted herself onto the counter across the room from him and swung her stilt-like legs back and forth. Morgan had always been fascinated by her legs, which were so long and skinny he wondered how they held her up. They made a mockery of her miniskirts—indeed, any skirt she wore was destined to be a miniskirt on her tall, reed thin frame. Still, her boyfriend thought she was a veritable goddess, a fact Francine reminded Morgan of every chance she got.

She was, in fact, a pretty irritating person, all around. But she was also indispensable to Morgan. She took care of everything else so he could take care of Mongo. And she never pulled her punches with him.

Much as he resented her brutal honesty at the moment, he had to admit she was right. The plot he'd been toying with for his next comic book stank.

He scooped up the script and dropped it into the wastebasket under the drafting table. "I'm open to ideas," he said.

"Where you went offtrack was having Mongo pull a red Ford Escort out of his hat. He's expecting to pull out a dove. What does a car have to do with a dove?"

"Nothing. That's the point."

"But the car is malevolent. You've got it doing a Steven King number, running down people as if it had a mind of its own."

More than sucked lemons, the plot sucked his too raw, too recent history. He lifted the drawing he'd been doing—of a red car running amok—and let it join the script in the recesses of the trash can.

"That was really productive." Francine snorted, curling her lip and shoving a thatch of dyed purple hair out of her eyes. "What else have you got up your sleeve?"

"A magic mirror," Morgan suggested.

"Here you are, on the cusp of major stardom—and me on the cusp of a major raise, hint, hint—and you can't come up with an original idea."

"What's unoriginal about a magic mirror?"

"It's been done. Check out *Snow White*. 'Mirror, mirror, on the wall . . .'" The phone on the other end of the counter rang. Francine stretched her elongated body out on the counter and lifted the receiver. "Mongo the Magnificent's office, can I help you?" she recited, then crooked a beckoning finger at Morgan. "It's your lawyer."

Too weary to walk across the room, he coasted across it on his wheeled chair, extending his legs to brake himself against the supply cabinet. He took the receiver from Francine and sent her a look which was supposed to convey that he wanted privacy.

She ignored him, instead glomming onto the computer and typing what was no doubt a much better script than anything he'd come up with since he'd rammed into Hope with his car a week ago. Sighing, he swiveled so his back was to Francine. "Yeah, Barry?"

"How's the patient?" Barry asked, sounding as snide as Francine.

"She's fine." *I'm the one who's a wreck.*

"The lady hasn't filed a suit against you yet. No papers have been served, as far as I know."

"She's not going to sue me." *She's got more devious ways of bringing me down,* he added silently. *She'll brainwash me into believing I'm hot for underendowed black-*

haired women who harbor inexplicable delusions about mirrors, and then she'll torture me until I die of unfulfilled lust.

"Have you received any bills from the hospital?"

"Oh, come on, Barry—you know how bureaucracies operate. They won't be billing me for months."

"Something to look forward to. I was thinking, maybe you should have the hospital send the bills to me. I'd like to review the charges before—"

"Licensing," Morgan cut him off. He didn't want to talk about hospitals and bills. He'd much rather talk about the one thing Hope Henley had said last night that *did* make sense.

"Morgan, they aren't going to rescind your license. They didn't even give you a traffic ticket. I'm sure—"

"I'm not talking about my driver's license. I'm talking about licensing Mongo merchandise."

Barry fell silent. He was obviously surprised; Morgan rarely showed much interest in contractual issues. Barry handled everything, told Morgan where to sign and what everything was worth to him, and Morgan was content not to be hassled by the ins and outs of his publishing and broadcasting deals.

But he should be hassled by them. Hope was right to encourage him to pay attention. "Is there something in that new million-dollar contract about licensing?" he asked his lawyer.

"Of course. I got you the best terms I could, Morgan. You own the licenses, but any money earned on Mongo products gets split fifty-fifty between you and the producers, for the life of the contract. I would have preferred a better split, but this was the best I could do. They claim the TV show is going to create the entire market, and on that basis they deserve a cut of the profits. I can't really argue that logic."

"Okay." Morgan had no idea what such a split could be worth to him. He only wanted to make sure there was something in the contract about it.

"You've never worried about those details in the past, Morgan. You know I take care of your interests—even when you fight me every inch of the way. What's going on?"

"Nothing. I just thought I ought to know."

"Well, now you know." Again Barry lapsed into silence for a moment. "Is everything okay?" he finally asked, sounding less like an attorney than a concerned friend.

"Everything's fine." Even if Morgan couldn't have sex with Hope, even if she wound up giving him a lethal dose of frustration, he was grateful to her for making him think like a businessman for once in his life. "Barry, I've got work to do," he said. "You can call the hospital and give them your address if you want. They can send the bills to you; it'll make my life simpler. I'll talk to you later."

Before Barry could question him further, he hung up. Still in his wheeled chair, he skidded along the counter to his computer and nudged Francine out of the way. "Go sort the mail," he ordered her. "I've got a dynamite story idea."

Francine eyed him skeptically. "Not dynamite. You had Mongo's wand turn into a bomb last year."

Giving her a friendly shove toward her office next door to his workroom, he commandeered the keyboard and began to shape his concept: instead of a dove, what would come out of Mongo's magic top hat was an army of plastic Mongo dolls.

Smiling, Morgan began to create.

7

KEN AMBERSON was standing on the front steps as Morgan strolled up the walk from his car.

He'd had an incredibly prolific day, creating an entire plot and rough-sketching a good eight pages, based on the idea of Mongo dolls escaping from the magic hat, being purchased by unwitting parents for their children, and then turning on their new owners. Tomorrow, Morgan would have Mongo use his good magic to recapture all the evil dolls and neutralize their bad magic.

In fact, he'd been so pleased with his productivity, he'd left the studio early and visited a few car dealerships on his way home. He'd sat in a Jaguar; he'd fondled the gear stick of a Porsche 911; he'd inhaled the leather aroma of a BMW's upholstery. The local body shop had replaced his old Ford's windshield the day after the accident, but as far as Morgan was concerned, the best thing about the repair was that it upped the Ford's trade-in value. Definitely, a pricey new car was in his future.

Things were straightening out. Life was getting back to normal. He was feeling like a successful millionaire once more, a Mongo mogul, the founder of an empire in its infancy. When Morgan got home, not only would he be able to resist Hope Henley's allure, but he would spend the night dreaming about gorgeous buxom blondes: Heather Locklear. Claudia Schiffer. Both of them at the same time.

Ken Amberson's glowering mug couldn't dampen Morgan's spirits as he neared the house. The building manager, a short, balding fellow given to appearing at odd moments and engaging in long-winded dialogues with himself, appeared to have been waiting for Morgan, because he sprang to life the instant Morgan was within hearing distance. "That friend of yours is trouble," Ken grumbled.

Morgan faltered a step, then continued onto the porch. Obviously Ken had a bug up his butt, but that wasn't news. "Hello to you, too," Morgan said evenly, wondering what Hope had done to incur the old guy's wrath. "Warm evening, isn't it?"

"Your girlfriend's out of here, Delacourt, I'm warning you. If she doesn't settle down, she's out."

Morgan caught himself before admitting that Hope wasn't his girlfriend. For one thing, the particulars of his relationship with Hope were none of Ken's business. For another, no matter how much he wanted to dream about Heather and Claudia, he hadn't forgotten what it was like to kiss Hope. He hadn't forgotten the velvet texture of her lips, the whisper of her sighs, the way her compact body had writhed against him when his hands had moved over her back, her waist, her breasts.

If she wasn't his girlfriend, he wasn't sure what she was. And he didn't feel like analyzing the question with Ken Amberson. "What's wrong?" he asked innocently. "Is she causing trouble?"

"Is she? Her and Natasha, and Jill Foyle—the lot of 'em. It's a rebellion, is what it is."

"A rebellion?" Morgan ought to have been concerned, but he burst into laughter instead. The thought of sweet, old Natasha, and Jill Foyle, a spirited forty-something divorcée who served as the building's unofficial den mother, and Hope Henley, a charming if slightly deranged accident victim, joining forces in some sort of insurrection was nothing short of hilarious. "Geez. Should I put on a bulletproof vest before I go inside?"

"She's taking the house over, your sweetie is. I know she got knocked on the head, but that doesn't give her the right to take the place over."

Morgan's amusement faded slightly. He hadn't bothered to dig up his lease that morning. He'd been too anxious to clear out of the apartment before Hope woke up, so he wouldn't have to look into her magnificent onyx eyes once more, and relive the kiss she'd given him last night, and wrestle with his longing to live another kiss with her, and another until it was too late. Instead, he'd run for cover, leaving Natasha to deal with his raven-haired, screwball temptress. He'd figured that if Hope was still hung up on her weird notion about owning Bachelor Arms by the time he got home from work, they could go over his lease in the evening.

Had she taken matters into her own hands in his absence? Had she banded together with Natasha, just the sort of romantic who would be partial to lost causes, and Jill, who'd do anything if it was wild and crazy but not harmful to one's health, and had the three of them somehow managed to establish Hope's ownership of the building? Had Hope torn up everybody's lease? Had she listed the mansion for sale? Had she fired Amberson?

Worse, was she going to evict Morgan?

"She's really too weak to take anything over," he said, recalling the way she teetered whenever she stood up too quickly. And the way she'd nearly swooned into his arms, and the way he'd literally swept her off her feet and cradled her against him and she'd circled her hands around his shoulders so her fingertips brushed erotically against the nape of his neck....

For a weak lady, she'd done some pretty powerful things to him. He'd be wise to remember the strength that lurked inside her fragile body.

"The whole place is in upheaval," Amberson complained. "Tell her to cut it out, or she's history. I don't care whether she's the love of your life, Delacourt. Either she pipes down or she's gone."

"She's not the love of my life," Morgan argued, as much to convince himself as to set the building manager straight. He eased past him and pushed open the front door.

He was greeted by a boisterous swell of laughter. Male laughter, female laughter, exuberant voices, cheerful shouting, happiness filling a transformed front hall. A huge fir stood in the shelter of the stairway, which was draped with sprigs of holly. Poinsettias and cinnamon-scented red candles adorned the mail table and the ledges. Silver foil stars hung on threads from the ceiling. The entry was redolent of pine and spice, a glorious seasonal perfume he wasn't used to smelling in southern California.

His neighbors were clearly enjoying an epidemic of holiday fever. Natasha sat on the stairs, stringing gumdrops for the tree. Several steps above her, Ted Smith was reaching over the railing to affix a porcelain angel to the top branch of the tree. Clint McCreary and his fiancée, Jessie, were overseeing the hanging of glass-ball ornaments and candy canes on the lower branches. Bobbie-Sue and Brenda were busy tying red velvet bows along the stairway railing. Jill wove among the group, carrying a tray filled with cheese and crackers, wedges of apple and glasses of wine.

If this was a rebellion, Morgan wanted to know where he could join up. "Hey! This is great!" he hollered above the din, then rethought his assessment. It was *almost* great. Something was missing.

Hope.

Natasha must have read his mind. "She's resting upstairs. She was looking a bit peaked, so I made her lie down."

The joyous celebration lost its grip on him. If he hadn't misunderstood Ken Amberson, Hope was the force behind this transformation of Bachelor Arms. But the general could no longer lead her troops. She was back at the army hospital, too weary to go on.

With a quick nod, he raced up the stairs, taking two at a time. He expected to find his apartment door unlocked, and it was. Shouldering the door open, he hurried through the living room and down the hall to his bedroom.

She lay atop the neatly made bed, dressed in jeans and a white button-front shirt of some soft, loose fabric. Her eyes were closed, her cheeks pale, her lips pursed. Morgan must have made plenty of noise entering, though, because as soon as he crossed the threshold her eyes fluttered open.

The lamp was off, and the rosy dusk light seeping through the window didn't do much to brighten the room. But he could see every detail of her: her delectable pink lips, the delicate line of her throat, the oval hollow where her collarbones met. The olive-shaped bone of her wrist. The pale bruise shadowing her hairline on the right side of her face. The curve of her feet inside white cotton socks. The arch of her cheeks as she smiled.

"Hi," she mumbled, her voice thick with sleep.

He'd charged into the room prepared to rescue her—from who the hell knew what—but he'd felt a strange panic at the thought of her being too exhausted to enjoy the festivities she'd launched. That she greeted him so calmly unnerved him. It was almost as if she belonged here, as if this home were hers. *Theirs.* And her seductively drowsy voice . . .

"How are you feeling?" he asked briskly, shaking off both his worry over the news that she'd lacked the energy to help with the decorations and his unwelcome arousal at the sight of her, rumpled and luscious, sprawled out across his bed. "Natasha said you were peaked."

"Peaked." Hope chuckled. "That's such a Natasha word."

She started to sit up, but Morgan nudged her back against the pillows, then sat on the bed next to her. He realized at once that the whole scene was much too intimate. He almost blurted out that he wanted her to remain lying down until she was fully awake and less prone to dizziness, but there was no discreet way for him to say he wanted her on her back without making the suggestion sound lewd.

Her eyes widened slightly, and he knew she was just as aware of his nearness as he was of her. Her hip was less than an inch from his, her body luxuriating against the blanket, her lips parted as a sultry yawn escaped her. Her breasts shifted beneath the shapeless fabric of her shirt as she sighed. Even though she and Morgan were both fully clothed, he felt his temperature rise, along with a certain part of his anatomy.

Claudia who? Heather who? He wanted Hope Henley. Only her. All of her.

He wished he could turn off his thoughts, but he couldn't. Nor could he tear his gaze from her. He couldn't stop admiring her plump lower lip and her profoundly dark eyes, her narrow waist and the slight flare of her hips. When her hand stirred at her side, a wicked sector of his brain did a quick calculation of how far her fingers were from his groin. Not terribly far at all. All she'd have to do was follow a route across a couple of inches of blanket to his left thigh, scale th denim surface and round the top, up another inch or so an she'd be at ground zero.

He smothered a moan as she lifted her hand to her face and brushed a strand of ha from her cheek. He and ground zero were safe for now, ut he couldn't say he was pleased about having averted dis ter.

"We've been decorating the hous " she said.

"I noticed." He wondered if he soun d as tightly strung to her as to himself.

"I remembered you talking about the er holidays people celebrate at this time of year. When vas in the hospital, I think...."

Her comment startled him. She'd been uncon s, yet so much of what he'd said to h gotten through and taken hold. He couldn't recall half the things he'd talked about, but she seemed to remember every word. Holidays? Yeah, he'd probably run at the mouth on that subject.

"The downstairs hall looked so plain—I mean, given the holiday season and all. I hadn't really thought about it myself. But the ghost..." She bit her lip and turned to gaze past him at the window. The pink light of the sunset made her cheeks look even more flushed than they were.

Morgan stifled a sigh. Her mention of the ghost reminded him that, no matter how horny her presence made him, she was a crackpot. "What about the ghost?" he asked warily.

"Well, she told me about how the house used to be decorated at Christmastime when she lived here. The tree by the stairs, and the ribbons along the railing, and the candles.... I just thought, the house would look so lovely, all decorated the way it used to be when she was alive."

"She told you this." Morgan forced patience into his tone. "Did you see her in the mirror again?"

"No. Clint and Jessie were out most of the day, and when they got home they let me come in to look at the mirror. I didn't see her there. But Morgan, I don't have to see her to hear her. She's been talking to me."

"Uh-huh."

"You think I'm crazy." She sounded disconsolate.

"No, I don't—but damn it, Hope, you had a concussion. The doctors were concerned that . . ."

"That what?" she goaded him when he hesitated.

"That there could be brain damage."

At that, she shoved herself up to sit. "I do *not* have brain damage."

"Okay, okay," he said, hastening to console her. God knew, if she *did* have brain damage, getting all riled up might trigger a convulsion or something. He would have to be more tactful. "Look, I'm sure the ghost talks to you. I'm not questioning that—"

"You most certainly are!"

"—but I think, maybe . . ." He let out a long breath and managed a smile. "Maybe we ought to get some dinner." Anything to change the subject, to steer her away from her fixation with the ghost. "As a matter of fact," he said as a sudden brainstorm hit him, "why don't we go out for dinner? That soup you had last night is pretty much the limit of my cooking. What do you say we hit a restaurant tonight?" *And I can get you out of this house, away from your stupid ghost.*

His invitation mollified her. "Okay," she said, smiling shyly. "That would be nice."

"I seem to recall promising you a juicy steak last night."

Hope's smile increased. "I don't eat steak."

He scanned her dainty figure and snorted. "I should have known. You're a vegetarian, and you talk to ghosts. Lady, you were made for L.A."

"I'm not a vegetarian, and I don't talk to ghosts," she corrected him, although she looked more amused than insulted. "The ghost talks to me. And I eat poultry and fish. Just not red meat."

"So we can go to a real restaurant?" At her nod, he relaxed a bit. "Why don't you freshen up a little, and then we'll hit the road."

He extended his hand to her, but she swung her legs over the side of the bed and stood without his help. Evidently, she forgave him enough to go out for dinner with him, but not enough to let him assist her to her feet. Either that, or she didn't trust him to behave himself if she touched him.

He wasn't sure he trusted himself. If she touched him, if she draped her slender fingers around his forearm for balance, or leaned into his shoulder for leverage, he might well drag her onto his lap, where she'd made such a glorious impression on him last night, and they might never get around to dinner. Hope might be crazy, she might have suffered brain damage from the accident, she might talk—or listen—to ghosts, but she obviously had all her wits about her when it came to protecting herself from Morgan.

Watching her walk steadily out of his bedroom and into the bathroom, he tried to assure himself that he was happy she was showing signs of health. But if she was going to be healthy, he really wished she'd quit her obsession with the ghost. There were plenty of things a healthy woman and a man could do together, and talking about ghosts was way down on Morgan's list.

HE THOUGHT SHE WAS deranged—but she already knew that. And she couldn't really argue the point. *She* thought she was deranged, too.

But she had heard the ghost. The lost lady, dead but alive in a mirror, had been whispering to her ever since the accident. The stronger Hope grew, the clearer the ghost's voice became.

Last night she had warned Hope not to get involved with Morgan. Today she had regaled Hope with stories about how her family had celebrated Christmas back in the good old days, when they'd been flush with money. She'd described to Hope the decorations they'd strung about the mansion, the extravagant parties they'd hosted, the lavish gifts they'd exchanged. Interspersed with the ghost's holiday tales were laments about the infant daughter she had given up and the man who had broken her heart. *The only pain greater than to lose one's love is to lose one's child,* the ghost had mourned. *Don't give your heart away as I did. Don't let a cad take the most precious gift you have. If you do, you'll never recover. I never did. I grieve for him still, and for my own foolishness.*

Natasha had reassured Hope that hearing voices was perfectly normal—although Natasha herself was hardly a poster child for normalcy. "Joan of Arc heard voices," Natasha had remarked, to which Hope had pointed out that Joan of Arc had also been burned at the stake.

And while hearing voices was one thing, believing the voices came from a ghost in a mirror was quite another. Hope had suffered a serious head injury just days ago; why shouldn't Morgan conclude that she had incurred brain damage?

She decided Morgan was right to suggest that they leave the house and the holiday revelry Hope had started with her insistence that Bachelor Arms needed to be dressed for the season. Perhaps the ghost could abandon the mirror in 1-G to follow Hope around Bachelor Arms, but surely the ghost wouldn't follow Hope all the way to the small Japanese restaurant Morgan took her to.

The dining room was dimly lit and exquisitely decorated, with fans and silk screens hanging on the walls and shojis breaking the room into private dining alcoves. A hostess in a resplendent silk kimono instructed Hope and Morgan to remove their shoes before ushering them to a low ebony dining table in a cozy nook behind a screen. She left them with menus and chopsticks.

"Have you ever eaten Japanese food before?" Morgan asked as Hope arranged herself on one of the cushions on the floor beside the table.

She shook her head.

"Don't worry. You'll like it. Just don't order the steak." He dropped onto the cushion next to her, crossing his long legs under the table, and shook her chopsticks from their paper sleeve. "You know how to use these?"

Grinning, she shook her head again. "I guess I'm a hick. Japanese food hasn't made a big dent on the restaurant scene in Topeka."

"Oh, sure, you're a hick, all right. Us hillbillies have always considered folks from Kansas the ultimate in hickness." He laughed, then added, "A few years ago, if anybody had given me chopsticks I probably would have used them for campfire kindling. Here, hold this stick like so..." He cupped one hand beneath hers and wrapped his other arm around her shoulders so he could reach her hand from the other side. Then he attempted to mold her fingers into the correct position.

She tried to concentrate on the chopsticks, but concentration was impossible when he had his arm wrapped around her so snugly. His hands were large and strong around hers, maneuvering her fingers and causing a totally unwelcome heat to thread its way up her arm and into her body. The tip of his thumb was as big as the entire top joint of hers, and her knuckles seemed to vanish in the curve of his palm. When she turned from the sight of their hands twined together around the chopsticks, she glimpsed the red highlights in his hair, shimmering beneath a paper lantern above his head, and the golden sparks of laughter in his eyes. She remembered the way his eyes had glowed, warm and sultry, when he'd kissed her, and the way his big, strong hands had stroked her body....

A shaky sigh escaped her, and the upper stick slipped and bounced against the table. "I'll never get the hang of this," she muttered.

"Sure you will. Just bend your fingers a bit more, like so...." He readjusted her hand, guided, cajoled. "Use your thumb like a fulcrum. Hold the bottom stick steady and move the top. You can do it."

She eased her hand out of his and placed the chopsticks firmly on the straw place mat. "If I drop food all over myself, I'm sending you the cleaning bill," she warned, letting him think she was tired of his instructions when she really only wanted him to stop touching her before she made a complete fool of herself.

"Pretend you're dealing with Mongo's magic wands," he said, tossing up both his chopsticks so they spun in the air, and then deftly catching them and beating a drumroll on the edge of the table with them.

"In other words, if I wave them around and say abracadabra, the food will magically end up in my mouth."

His smile had a condescending quality. "If you'd rather, I can get you some silverware."

"Not on your life." She had her pride. She smoothed her napkin in her lap and returned his smile, hers as stubborn as his was challenging.

He laughed, spun his chopsticks in the air once more, like a baton twirler, and then flipped them into the breast pocket of his shirt. She clapped politely, he bowed, and they both laughed. She could almost persuade herself that this was a real date, that the rapport she felt with him, the playful teasing, the showing off and the defiance, meant that they were a genuine couple, completely at ease with each other, prepared to continue on together into the future.

But they weren't a couple, genuine or otherwise. She was only his patient, his ticket to a clear conscience. Even though he *had* kissed her, and they'd spent the night under one roof, and he'd caressed her breasts, he'd stroked her tongue with his, he'd carried her to bed—

And left her there alone.

This wasn't a date. She'd be wise to remember that.

"Your car is all fixed," she noted belatedly.

"Did it bother you, riding in the deathmobile?" His expression suddenly grew solemn.

She studied her chopsticks, her ease in his company vanishing. When he smiled, when he had that devilish gleam in his eyes, she could gaze at him to her heart's content. But when he got serious, when guilt once again draped its cold, dreary mantle over him, she couldn't bear to see the way it altered him. "Your car doesn't bother me, Morgan. I still don't really remember the accident. Just flashes of it."

Morgan tucked his hand under her chin and steered her face back to him. "I didn't mean to upset you before, that stuff I said about brain damage. I'm sure, Hope, I'm absolutely positive—whatever you lost will come back to you in time. You'll have everything you started with."

"I'll have more than I started with," she refuted him, gently but firmly. "Not only will I have my memory of the accident, but I'll have the ghost."

What little light had lingered in his eyes disappeared. "I guess we ought to check out these menus," he muttered, letting his hand drop from her face.

"Why don't you like to talk about the ghost?" she said, pressing him. He scowled and lifted his menu, but she persevered. "I keep thinking you want me to talk about the accident, what I remember, what bothers me. But the most important part of it is the ghost, and you never want to talk about that."

"Because . . ." He exhaled. "Because that's the part that proves to me how far you are from a full recovery."

"To you, a full recovery means I believe the ghost is just a figment of my imagination."

"Well. . .yeah, it does. I know other people think they've seen the thing—but I don't give a damn about other people. You're the only one I care about. And you've taken the whole ghost thing much farther, talking to it—"

"I *don't* talk to it," she reminded him. "It talks to me."

"Whatever."

"Your friend Clint McCreary saw it. Do you think he's brain-damaged, too?"

"I've got my worries about him. But I didn't run him down with my car, so I don't feel quite the same level of personal responsibility when it comes to him."

"I'm hereby absolving you of responsibility. Okay?"

He opened his mouth and then shut it, saved from speaking by the arrival of a waitress with a pot of tea and two ceramic mugs. "Are you ready to order?" she asked as she poured the tea into the mugs.

Morgan glanced at Hope. She hadn't studied the menu, and even if she had she wouldn't have known what most of the food was. "Why don't you order for both of us?" she invited him.

"Okay." He requested a platter of shrimp and vegetable tempura and a pot of *yosinabe,* rice and a couple of Kirin beers. As soon as the waitress had departed from their cozy nook, Morgan offered Hope a bland smile. "I think you'll like those dishes. Lots of seafood. No red meat."

He might be finished with the subject of the ghost, but she wasn't. "Are you afraid of ghosts?"

He rolled his eyes, then relented with a half-baked smile. "Come on, Hope. How can I be afraid of something I don't believe in?" He reached for his cup of tea, then changed course and gathered her hand in his, instead. He gave it a gentle squeeze. "It isn't the ghost that bothers me. It's just. . . I want you healthy. When you talk about ghosts, it doesn't sound like you're all that healthy."

She discreetly slid her hand free and rested it in her lap. Whenever he touched her, she lost all track of the conversation. If anything made her crazy, it wasn't the ghost. It was Morgan. "I'm fine," she assured him. "I hardly had any dizzy spells today, and I only saw double once. I'm getting better, Morgan. I'm not brain-damaged."

"You're not a doctor. You can't be sure."

"Lots of crazy people believe the earth is round. That doesn't mean it's flat. And maybe some sane people believe in ghosts. Why not?"

He struggled with his answer. "I don't care what some sane people believe," he said, apparently having trouble putting his feelings into words. "I don't care about what anyone else believes. This is about you. The woman I hit with my car."

Not the woman he liked. Not the woman he desired. Not the woman he'd kissed last night, and held, and practically set on fire. Just the woman he'd hit with his car.

She tried not to be disappointed. "Why not look at it this way, Morgan—maybe the ghost is helping me."

"Helping you?" His tone was indulgent. "How is it helping you?"

"It's a she, not an it. And I think she feels more guilty about the accident than you do. She was the one who scared me in the first place. If it wasn't for her, I'd never have run into your car."

"Now, Hope—"

"It could even be argued," she continued, denying him a chance to patronize her, "that it's the ghost who's keeping me sane."

"Right." His eyes glowed, but not with laughter. His gaze was intense, laserlike, trying to penetrate her. "Explain to me how this ghost is keeping you sane."

Hope sipped her tea to avoid meeting that piercing gaze. "Well, she helped me to figure out what my grandmother was always babbling about, how she'd inherited the mansion and all. She put the pieces together for me."

"I take it, it hasn't occurred to you that your grandmother might have been even loonier than you," Morgan muttered.

"As a matter of fact, that did occur to me," she declared, refusing to let his needling vex her. "But the ghost confirmed a lot of what my grandmother used to tell me. And if it wasn't for the ghost..." She fell silent, feeling heat blossom in her cheeks.

"If it wasn't for the ghost, what?"

I would have made love with you last night, she almost admitted. The ghost had saved Hope from her own reckless, thoughtless passion.

If she told Morgan that, it would give him one more reason to resent the ghost.

Accepting the futility of trying to prove the ghost's existence to Morgan, she sighed and said what she really didn't want to say: "I can go back to my own place tonight, Morgan. I'm really okay. You don't have to put me up, or put up with me, or—"

"Hey." His tone was muted yet sharp, silencing her. She glanced at him, and his eyes locked onto hers, not moving when the waitress appeared around the side of the screen, carrying a tray laden with bowls of rice, bottles of beer, a straw platter of batter-fried shrimp and vegetables and a steaming kettle of stew. Hope would have acknowledged the waitress, but his gaze held her immobile. His mouth was set in a grim line.

Not until the waitress was gone did he speak again. "I haven't heard anyone say anything about your going home."

"It's my decision, Morgan." Her voice wavered, as if she weren't really sure it *was* her decision.

"I don't recall anyone saying you're one hundred percent back to normal. And frankly, toots, the more you talk about that damned ghost, the more inclined I am to believe you need more time to recuperate. I don't have any problem with you recuperating in my apartment. If *you* have a problem..." He halted, frowning. Evidently it had only just dawned on him that Hope might not wish to stay with him. "You could probably move in with Natasha."

"No." Much as she liked Natasha, Hope didn't want to live with her. She wanted to live with Morgan. She wanted that more than she should.

"Then you'll stay with me," he resolved, at last breaking from her and lifting his chopsticks.

She eyed him speculatively. "Even if I keep communicating with the ghost?"

"That's all the proof I need that you're not ready to go home," he said with a cocky smile. "Why don't you start with the shrimp? You don't need chopsticks for that—just use your fingers."

Ignoring the delicious-looking food arrayed before her, she persevered. "I've got to warn you, Morgan—I'm going to prove that that ghost is my great-grandmother."

"Be my guest," he said, his grin growing even cockier.

He was humoring her, and she resented it. "Not only am I going to prove she's my great-grandmother," she added fervently, "but I'm going to find out how she wound up alone and pregnant. A man broke her heart, Morgan, and I intend to find out what happened."

That brought him up short. His chopsticks frozen in midair, he gaped at her. "Wait a minute. You're going after *two* ghosts now?"

"I don't think he's a ghost. I'd rather think he's burning in hell. He destroyed her. I want to know why."

Morgan lowered his chopsticks, his eyes never leaving her, and sighed the sigh of someone whose patience was being sorely tested. "Why do you want to know why?"

"Because she gave her heart to him, and he broke it. She loved him, Morgan. I think she *still* loves him."

"She's dead," he argued, then shook his head, apparently writing Hope off as irredeemably psychotic.

"She's a ghost with a broken heart. No wonder she's haunting Bachelor Arms. Just like me; she's trying to heal. Maybe once she does, she'll go away."

"Hope." He stretched the word, massaged it, his husky drawl turning her name into something private and tender. "Hope. I really don't think you're crazy, but you're going to *make* yourself crazy over this stuff."

"Oh, no," she said with certainty. "I'm going to make myself all better. And the ghost, too. I'm going to make sure everyone mends. My head, her heart."

He gazed heavenward and groaned. Yet, to her great relief, when he lowered his gaze back to her, she saw the laughter return to his eyes. Laughter and bemusement and...grudging admiration. "If you can do that," he conceded, "you're a better magician than me and Mongo combined. Go for it, Hope. Make everyone all better."

8

IT SEEMED EASIER not to mention the ghost anymore, so by tacit agreement they didn't. For the rest of the meal, they discussed the Mongo dolls concept Morgan had come up with for the new comic book. He thanked Hope for having inspired the idea, and she modestly insisted she'd done nothing he had to thank her for.

He tried to accept that this woman, endearingly clumsy with her chopsticks yet incisive in her questions about his comic book plot, was missing a few important brain cells. Yet everything she said, from analyzing the dipping sauce for the teriyaki to probing whether the evil plastic Mongo dolls were a metaphor for artificial reproduction, intrigued him. She was one smart woman. Even if she wasn't so damned nice to look at, he would enjoy her company.

But she *was* damned nice to look at. Despite the soy sauce dripping down her chin. Despite the grain of rice glued to her cheek. She was so beautiful he wanted to kiss the rice from her skin and lick the sauce from her lips. Her quirky attachment to the ghost couldn't make him stop thinking of her skin, her lips, the black cascade of her hair and the fathomless darkness of her eyes.

He'd wanted to get her out of Bachelor Arms so she would stop talking about the ghost—and a fat lot of good that did him. Now, he wanted to delay going back to Bachelor Arms because once they got there, they'd be just steps from his bed, and he would be hard-pressed not to pick her up the way he had last night, and carry her those few steps. Only this time, he wouldn't just drop her onto the bed and walk away. He wouldn't be able to.

"The night is young," he remarked, once he'd paid the bill and escorted Hope from the restaurant. "How about, let's take a drive?" He was thinking they could cruise down to Venice. They could stroll along the boardwalk adjacent to the beach and gawk at the flamboyant crowds who hung out there. He wondered whether she would like the colorful neighborhood enough to visit him there, if that was where he finally decided to buy a house.

Not that she got to vote on where he would live once he spent some of his newly acquired wealth on a house. Not that he had any expectation of seeing her again, once she was fully recovered.

"Actually," she said, rolling down the sleeves of her blouse as cool evening air settled around them, "if you wouldn't mind, I'd really like to stop by my apartment and make sure everything's all right there. When I went there with Jessie yesterday, I was feeling so discombobulated, we were in and out in three minutes flat. I didn't even think to water my plants."

"Okay," Morgan agreed, curious to see where she lived.

She recited her address. "It's on the northern fringe of the USC campus. Once we get into the neighborhood I can give you directions."

He nodded, rolled down his window, and steered out of the restaurant's parking lot. The night might have been cool, but not so cool he couldn't have gotten into cruising across town in a convertible. On his next run through the luxury car dealerships, he would have to check out a few ragtop models.

For some reason, he couldn't conjure a picture of a voluptuous blonde sitting next to him in the convertible coupe of his dreams. He could picture only Hope.

Cripes. She was becoming as much an obsession with him as the ghost was with her. "Have you gotten any feel for the city yet?" he asked, weaving deftly through the clogged traffic. "I know you haven't been living here long."

"It doesn't feel like a city to me," she admitted. "It's more like a conglomeration of neighborhoods separated by freeways." She rolled her window down, too. "I like the weather, though."

"You like sixty-five degrees in December? I would've thought, with all that decorating you did back at the house, you'd be the sort to go into a funk if you didn't have a white Christmas."

Hope laughed. "One thing has nothing to do with another. I don't ski, I don't skate, and about the only thing I like about snow is going indoors and warming up. Decorating a house for the holidays is an entirely different matter. I happen to think tinsel is one of the greatest inventions in the history of the world. You can make a tree look like it's hung with icicles, without having to deal with actual ice."

"Who bought that tree, anyway? It's huge." Too huge for Hope and her sidekicks Natasha and Jill to manage.

"Jill Foyle called a friend of hers—a brawny male friend—and he offered to go with her to a tree stand and pick one out." She laughed again. "That little man who manages Bachelor Arms, Mr . . . Anderson, is it?"

"Amberson."

"Amberson. He just about blew a gasket when he saw Jill and her friend lugging an eight-foot pine tree into the house. He started ranting and raving about fire permits and pine sap sticking to the floor, and how if we dared to set up the tree he'd evict everyone."

"And you told him you're the secret owner of the building," Morgan teased, then kicked himself for having brought up Hope's alleged inheritance. That belief was one of the symptoms of her dementia.

Fortunately, she didn't pursue the subject. "I didn't have to tell him anything. Natasha leaped into the fray. She told him he was a hog's behind, and a Scrooge, to boot. The poor man ran from the house."

"Natasha can be terrifying when she puts her mind to it."

"Anyway, once we had the tree standing, other people began to join the merriment. One of those two pretty women, I think they're waitresses. One of them has a name that begins with a *B*, I think—"

"They both do. Bobbie-Sue and Brenda."

"Well, one of them raced to the store and returned with the silver foil stars and ribbons. Jill supplied the candles. A fellow named Teddy went down to the basement and returned with a box of old tree ornaments he found there."

"Maybe they were left by your great-granny." Damn! What was Morgan's problem? Why did he keep handing Hope openings to talk about all her crazy subjects?

Once again, she kept the conversation rational. "None of those ornaments were old enough to be antiques. I'll bet a previous tenant left them there."

"Maybe they're Amberson's. Maybe deep in his teeny-tiny heart a flicker of Christmas spirit still burns."

"Has he ever decorated the building before?"

"For Christmas?" Morgan thought back, then shook his head. "Just the wreath on the door. And it probably breaks his heart to do that."

"Turn left here," Hope said. "My place is just a few blocks up, that two-story beige building on the right."

The block was full of two-story beige buildings, most of them drab and just this side of seedy. It was clearly a neighborhood of students, ex-students, lifelong students, wanna-be students, and anyone who couldn't afford to live elsewhere. At the first empty parking space, Morgan pulled to the curb and turned off the engine.

Hope stared through the windshield at her building for a long moment, then sighed and lowered her gaze to her hands, which were clasped primly in her lap. "What's the problem?" Morgan asked.

She sighed again and raised her eyes to him. Her smile was brave but not particularly joyful. "It's strange, Morgan, but . . . it just doesn't feel like my home anymore."

He shrugged. "How long have you lived there? Only a few months, right?"

"Even so . . ." She shook her head, as if to erase her comment, and reached for the door handle.

Morgan extended his hand across her knees and clamped it over hers before she could open the door. "Even so, what?"

"Nothing," she said with another feeble smile.

"Even so, what?"

"Bachelor Arms feels more like home to me." The words came out in an embarrassed rush, and then she smiled nervously. "That's a ridiculous thing to say."

"Not so ridiculous if you believe Bachelor Arms belongs to you."

"But you don't believe it does. You think I'm brain-damaged."

"We're not talking about what I think. We're talking about what you feel."

She let her gaze meet his. Her eyes glistened, but she blinked away the moisture, clearly determined not to get emotional. "You're right. This place doesn't feel like my home because it *isn't* my home. It's just a furnished flat I took for a few months. I never intended to live the rest of my life here. Let's go." Her brisk tone signaled that she didn't wish to discuss it further.

They walked the half block to her building, and Morgan opened the outer door for her. Built into one wall of the foyer was a panel of mailboxes. Hope slid a small key into her box. It was empty.

"Someone must be taking in your mail for you," Morgan stated the obvious.

She shut the door with a quiet click. "I don't get much mail," she said. "Maybe nothing's come for me."

In a week? He kept his thoughts to himself, but really, that seemed an awfully long time for a woman all alone in a strange city to go without mail. He was thinking not of the junk that frequently crammed his box—advertisements, flyers, credit card offerings and the like—but of a note from Kansas or Chicago. Didn't she say her mother lived in Chicago?

She unlocked the inner door just as a man loomed into view, descending the stairs. He appeared to be in his mid-twenties, like Hope. He was tall and lanky, dressed in fashionably torn jeans, a T-shirt and a flannel shirt over that, and he carried a grungy backpack in one arm. His narrow face was capped by a shag of straight, flaxen hair.

"Peter!" she cried.

"Hope?" He scampered down the remaining stairs, hurled his backpack to the floor and enveloped her in a crushing hug. "Oh, wow! Hope! How are you, sweetheart?"

Morgan inched back a step and witnessed the passionate reunion. Passionate was definitely the word. The guy was obviously mighty special to Hope.

If he was her boyfriend, though, he wasn't a particularly attentive one. Where the hell had he been while Hope was in the hospital? Where had he been while she'd been lying in a coma, hovering near death?

Slowly, gingerly, Hope and the rangy blond man disengaged. "Now, tell me how you are," he demanded. "Tell me where you're staying. Tell me every detail."

"I don't know most of the details," she admitted, then smiled toward Morgan and waved him over. "I'm staying with Morgan Delacourt right now. He's . . . a friend of mine. Morgan, this is my neighbor, Peter Charney."

"How do you do?" Morgan shook the guy's hand.

The guy grinned eagerly at him, then turned back to study Hope. "You got out yesterday, I gather. I called the hospital a few times, but either you were at physical therapy or you were asleep and they didn't want to disturb you. And when I called yesterday, they said you'd been released."

"That's right."

"You look wonderful." Peter clamped his hands on her shoulders and angled her this way and that, scrutinizing her beneath the fluorescent hallway light. "Except for that bruise on the side of your cheek, there. Ooh, I don't like the looks of that." He clicked his tongue.

Hope brushed the bruised area with her hand. "It's much better, Peter. Really. It's faded a lot. I'm fine."

"Oh, God. You had me so worried." He released her, then sent Morgan another cheerful grin before focusing once more on Hope. "So, when are you coming back?"

"I can't live by myself yet," she explained. "The doctors discharged me only on the condition that I'd have someone with me twenty-four hours a day. Morgan has lots of neighbors who've been looking after me."

"I'd look after you, Hope," Peter insisted. The way he kept including Morgan in his smiles didn't mean squat, as far as Morgan was concerned. Whether or not this dude was Hope's boyfriend, he obviously had designs on her.

"You can't possibly look after me, not twenty-four hours a day. Peter is working on a Ph.D. in mathematics," she explained to Morgan. "He spends more time on campus than he does here. You're on your way to campus now, aren't you?" she guessed, eyeing his backpack.

"Gotta crunch them numbers," Peter said, then clasped Hope's shoulders once more and sighed happily. "Man, it is *so* good to see you. Listen, Alan's been watering your plants and taking in your mail."

"Great. I was wondering." To Morgan, she added, "Alan's our landlord."

"And he went through your refrigerator. You had some milk going bad in there, which he dumped. He gave me your oranges so they wouldn't rot. I hope you don't mind."

"Oh, sure I mind," she teased. "I'll send you a bill."

"Seriously, love—once you're all better, we'll go out and I'll buy you all the oranges you can handle. Speaking of which—" again he sent a friendly grin Morgan's way "—a few of us are planning to get an ice-cream fix around eleven o'clock. You want to join us?"

Hope smiled and shook her head. "Maybe another time."

"Turning down ice cream. That must have been quite a whack you took on the skull." He clicked his tongue again, then smiled and kissed her forehead. "I've got to run, Hope—but come home soon, won't you?"

"I'll try."

Peter scooped his backpack off the floor and loped toward the door. "Oh, by the way, Alan called your mother."

Hope said nothing. Her smile went icy.

"He found her number in your phone book. He said he thought someone ought to tell her you'd been in an accident. That's okay, isn't it?"

"It's fine," she said. Morgan knew he wasn't imagining the brittle edge to her voice. "Thanks for telling me, Peter."

"Yeah. Well." A final toothy grin, and he swung open the door. "You look great, Hope. I've missed you." With that, he sauntered through the foyer and out of the building.

Hope stood rigidly at the foot of the steps. Her smile waned; her face lost color. Morgan wanted to care about her apparent uneasiness, but he was just selfish enough to put his own concerns ahead of hers. "Is that your boyfriend?" he asked, trying to sound as if he didn't care, but not doing a very good job of it.

Hope shook off her mood and forced a smile. "Who, Peter? Hardly. He's gay."

"He is?" Morgan turned to stare at the door through which Peter had vanished. Suddenly he felt a heck of a lot better. Relieved, he gave Hope his full attention. "Are you all right?"

"I'm fine," she said, still in a cold, brittle voice. Starting up the stairs, she looked wobbly. She grabbed onto the railing so tightly her knuckles turned white.

She wasn't fine. Morgan sprinted up the stairs behind her and curved his hand around her upper arm. He didn't bother asking if she was dizzy; it was obvious she was, and he had the feeling she'd light into him if he made a big deal about it. She was obviously strung tight over something Peter had said.

Her mother.

She let Morgan walk her up the stairs, keeping her hand on the railing and laboring to plant her feet solidly, one step at a time, up to the second floor. If she resented his assistance, she did her best not to show it.

At the top of the stairs she unlocked her apartment door. It was pretty much what Morgan had expected: a small, tidy, cheerful room, furnished with old pieces but brightened by potted plants and a couple of colorful posters on the walls. The kitchen area took up one corner of the room—a small refrigerator, a two-burner stove and a sink. A large remnant rug covered most of the painted wood floor; a bureau stood near the bathroom door, a small TV perched on a bookshelf, a couple of chairs circled a steamer trunk that doubled as a coffee table, and a broad sofa shared a wall with two windows which overlooked the alley separating this building and the next.

"Well," she said quietly. "The plants are alive."

Not only were the plants alive, they looked perkier than Hope did. Morgan remained near the door while she clicked on a lamp and surveyed the apartment. She crossed to the kitchen and peeked inside the refrigerator. On the counter next to it she discovered a small pile of mail. She riffled through it and tossed it, unread, into the wastepaper basket near where Morgan was standing. The top envelope, he noticed, was a large white rectangle, hand addressed to Hope. Postmarked Chicago.

"That's from your mother," he said, lifting the card out of the trash can.

"Oh," she said, and her face went three shades paler.

"What?" he asked gently. If he'd been curious about where she lived, that was nothing compared to the curiosity he felt about the way a mere mention of her mother seemed to give her the willies.

"I guess I should read it," she said quickly, as if trying to compensate for having discarded it. She tore open the envelope, unfolded the card, skimmed the message and dropped the card back into the trash. It missed the can and landed on the floor.

Morgan picked it up. The front featured a trite drawing of flowers and ribbons and gold-embossed letters that said: Get Well Soon. Inside, the printed script read, "So sorry to hear you're ailing. Wishing you a speedy recovery." Below that, her mother had inked in, "Take care, Hope. Mom."

Sheesh. Total strangers—his neighbors at Bachelor Arms had displayed more compassion toward Hope. Most of them had never met her before, yet they'd taken her under their collective wing and let her decorate their house for the holidays. Clint and Jessie had visited her at the hospital and brought her a gift. Natasha had prepared soup for her. Jill had found a Christmas tree for her.

And her own mother had sent her a card. Gee whiz. What an effort she'd made for her own daughter, who'd almost died.

He gazed across the small room at Hope. She was leaning against the kitchen counter, staring out the window. Her face was as pale as the envelope her mother's card had come in, but her chin jutted out at a stubborn angle, and her mouth was set. Morgan wondered what would happen if she tried to speak, what words would come out, what anger, or bitterness, or pain.

He dropped the card into the trash, where it belonged, and ventured a step toward her. She turned abruptly, her eyes so dark with misery he halted, unsure of whether he should risk moving any closer.

"Have you talked to her?" he asked, gesturing toward the wastebasket.

"Of course I've talked to her." Hope's voice was papery, thin and dry.

"I mean, since the accident."

She inhaled deeply, let out her breath in a slow sigh and turned away. "No," she said, so softly he almost didn't hear her.

It was none of Morgan's business, and yet . . . It *was*, in some way. He'd nearly killed Hope. He'd taken responsibility for her. Her recovery was the most important thing going on in his life right now. If her mother was screwing up that recovery in any way, yeah, it was his business. "Are you going to talk to her?" he asked.

"I suppose I should." Hope sighed again, and reached behind her for the wall phone.

Morgan hadn't expected her to give in so quickly. Now that she was punching the phone's buttons, he wasn't sure what he was supposed to do. Her apartment wasn't big enough for him to exit discreetly into another room while she made her call. She hadn't asked him to leave, but he really didn't think he should hang around, eavesdropping.

He entered the bathroom and closed the door. He didn't have to use the facilities, so he checked out his reflection in the mirror above the sink, guzzled a glass of water and ran a comb through his hair. Through the door he heard little, just an occasional yes or no from Hope.

Tired of hiding in the small, stuffy bathroom, he edged the door open. "Well, I couldn't call you when I was in the hospital," she was saying, the phone pressed close to her ear and her body bowed, facing the wall. "And once I was out of the hospital, I didn't see the point in calling and worrying you. What would I have said? 'Hi, I've been in an accident, but I'm okay now.'" She listened for a minute. "I'm sorry I called so late. I know it's two hours later where you are. I'm sorry." Another pause. "Okay. Goodbye." She lowered the phone into its cradle and then went still, her shoulders still hunched, her back to Morgan.

He had never before felt such a strong urge to hug someone—and such deep misgivings about what might happen if he followed through on that hug. Hope didn't like it when he fussed over her. Yet she looked more fragile now, more crushed and battered, than when he'd slammed into her with his car.

He waited for a sign that it was safe to approach. After an endless minute, she straightened up. She seemed to waver slightly, but she gripped the edge of the counter to steady herself.

That was enough of a sign for him. Maybe she didn't want him treating her as if she were about to collapse—but she *was* about to collapse, and he wasn't going to stand by and watch her take a tumble. Two long strides carried him to her side, and then he had her in his arms. She sank against him without a trace of resistance. He held her tight, and she rested her head on his shoulder, her hands bunched against his chest, her eyes closed and her cheeks bone-dry.

"It's okay," he murmured. That was probably a lie, but he couldn't think of anything else to say. "It's okay."

"I woke her up," Hope said in that papery voice. "It was eleven-thirty their time, and they'd already gone to bed. She was annoyed."

"She's a bitch," he said, tossing aside discretion.

A poignant smile traced Hope's lips. "I guess she is."

"How did she wind up with such a nice daughter?"

Hope nestled closer to him. He closed his arms more snugly about her. "Thank you, but I'm not sure I'm all that nice."

"You are. You're incredibly nice," he insisted, realizing how true it was. *Nice* was such a boring word, so bland and clichéd that no one bothered with it anymore. No one thought about it—or, sad to say, *lived* it. But as soon as

Morgan had spoken, he'd understood Hope's appeal to him: not just her dark beauty, not just her mule-headedness and her self-sufficiency, but the fact that she didn't hassle him, didn't snap at him, didn't go out of her way to flaunt a fashionable cynicism. There was a kindness about her, a gentleness that tempered her underlying will of iron.

"My mother doesn't mean to be a bitch," she said, proving how nice she was by attempting to rationalize her mother's callousness. "She just . . ." A shaky sigh escaped her, and she reached up to cover her eyes. Morgan wished she would cry. He wanted her to let go, release her rage, vent the emotion that would destroy her from within if she didn't get rid of it. She didn't have to pretend to be strong in front of him; he knew how incredibly strong she truly was.

She did cry, not a big flood of tears or audible weeping, but a subdued dry sob. Morgan led her to the couch and sat, drawing her down beside him and curving his arm protectively around her. She rested against his shoulder, refusing to let her tears flow even as she cuddled close. He felt suppressed shudders racking her, but she wouldn't shed a single tear over her mother.

"It wasn't me, really," she said after a while. "She doesn't hate me, Morgan. It's just...my father left her when I was about three. He and my mother got married right out of high school, and they were too young, and suddenly I was there, this huge responsibility. I guess it was more than he could handle, so he packed up and left, and my mother was stuck with me. I was just never part of her dreams for herself, what she wanted, what she'd planned for. She was desperate to find another husband, and I was in the way."

Bitch, Morgan thought, but he limited his reaction to weaving his fingers through her hair, twirling through the silky strands and easing her closer against himself.

"She sent me to my grandparents' farm so she could meet men without having me underfoot," Hope told him. "When she got married a second time, she still shipped me off to Gramma's, because my stepfather wasn't crazy about me. She said it wasn't fair to him to have me around all the time. She said, 'No man wants to get stuck raising another man's child.'"

"It sounds like she found the perfect match—a guy as selfish as she was," Morgan noted wryly.

"Oh, I don't know, I . . ." A weary laugh escaped Hope. "You're right. I don't know why I'm trying to defend her. She was selfish. But . . . but maybe it wasn't such a bad thing. I didn't like my stepfather, he didn't like me, and we spent as little time together as possible. And I loved being at the farm. That's when my grandmother and I really became close."

"Even so—"

"And then my mother got another divorce when I was in high school. She was desperate to snag another husband. I don't know why. She had no professional skills, but she could have gotten a job. Or she could have helped out on the farm. My grandfather had died by then and Gramma could have used another pair of hands around the place. But my mother thought Gramma was crazy. She always did. Gramma was always talking about her mansion in Los Angeles, and the olden days in Hollywood, and the lawyer who tracked her down when she was a child—"

"What lawyer?"

Hope seemed to relax against him, her body molding to him as he combed his fingers consolingly through her hair again and again. "My grandmother was adopted at birth. She'd been born to an unmarried young woman in California. That woman's parents owned Bachelor Arms. Or at least I think so. The lawyer who found my grandmother told her about the house. He said her birth mother died, and technically the house belonged to my grandmother, only some bank was holding the title to it because of family debts. My grandmother swore there was a mansion, and I guess I was the only person who believed her. My mother just wrote her off as a crazy lady." Hope laughed again, a sad, wistful laugh. "Maybe spending so much time with Gramma made me crazy, too. Maybe I'm as crazy as you think I am, Morgan. Maybe there's no ghost. Maybe I'm just hearing voices and seeing things because I'm as crazy as my grandmother was. I don't know anymore."

"You're not crazy." An hour ago, a half hour, Morgan would never have said such a thing. But right now, with her curled up in his arms, with her soft, sweet voice filling the air and lulling him, he could almost believe her strange story about the ghost and her grandmother and the ownership of Bachelor Arms.

So what if her grandmother had been eccentric? At least she'd loved Hope, and raised her, and cared for her—unlike Hope's mother, who probably never saw a ghost or believed in anything she couldn't hold in her hand. Hope's grandmother had taken a child who should have been bitter and resentful, and turned her into a dreamer.

Morgan could understand dreamers. His kinfolk had thought he was crazy when he'd given up a scholarship and dropped out of college—and devoted himself to creating comic books, of all things. But that was his dream, and he'd devoted himself to it. If people thought he was crazy, well, maybe he was, a little.

He was crazy enough to believe in Hope. He was crazy enough to want to be a part of her crazy life.

His hand found the edge of her chin and tipped her face upward. Bowing, he dropped a light kiss on her lips. And another. And another, not as light.

She responded with a whisper of a sigh, the gradual lowering of her eyelids, the flexing of her hand against his chest . . . the generous parting of her lips.

His heart kicked against his ribs as her tongue lured him in. He recalled the first time he'd kissed her, the exciting combination of acceptance and resistance he'd sensed in her, the way she'd taken him in and then dueled with him, met him thrust for thrust, let him know he was there only because she wanted him there. It was the same this time, only better—because this time he wasn't just fueled by lust. He wanted *her*, Hope, a woman so strong her mother's neglect couldn't defeat her any more than a run-in with Morgan's car could.

He twisted on the sofa to face her, and she leaned back into the upholstery, taking him in her arms. Her fingers twisted into his hair, pulling him down; her lips moved with his, danced with his, let him lead and then balked, demanding her own turn at dominance.

He wanted to tell her it didn't matter that she was half under him, that he outweighed her by a good seventy pounds of lean, hard muscle. She was in charge; he was in her thrall. Wherever she led, he would follow.

She skimmed her hands down his back to his waist. He felt their warmth through his shirt, the frenzy of her fingers digging into the small of his back. Hot sensation gathered in his groin, making him ache, making him kiss her more deeply.

She moaned, opening wider, wriggling under him until her legs could tangle with his. "Hope," he whispered, gazing down into her pale, pretty face.

Her lips were damp, glistening. So were her eyes. She brought one hand to his face, cupping his cheek, studying him with what appeared to be astonishment.

"Are you okay?" he asked, unable to interpret her expression.

She smiled. "You make me feel so alive. When I thought I was dying, you brought me back to life. That's what you do to me, Morgan."

She made him feel pretty damned alive, too. In his head and below his belt. He was as alive as a man could be.

He bent to kiss her again. She slid her hand to his collar and inside. Her fingers trailed, cool yet fiery, against his neck. It occurred to him that her passion could be a result of desperation, anger at her mother, loneliness or any of a number of other negative things. But he had more faith in Hope than that. She was a woman who knew what she was doing—even when it made no sense. She was a woman who made choices.

Right now she was choosing him.

He grazed her cheeks, her forehead, the pale gray-blue bruise that had all but faded from the edge of her cheek. He pushed her thick black hair back from her face and shoulders and propped himself up so he could unbutton her blouse. He tugged the shirt from the waistband of her jeans and spread the fabric.

She was as petite as he'd known she would be, as slim and sleek as a bird, not an ounce of fat on her. Her breasts, enclosed in a lacy white bra, were small and firm and round, rising and falling with her every breath. Through the thin fabric he could see the dark circles of her nipples.

Just looking at her cranked up his arousal another few notches.

Sending a special prayer of thanks to whoever had invented front closures on bras, he popped open the clasp and brushed back the twin scraps of lace.

And decided, right then and there, that bigger wasn't always better. Nothing could be better than this. Nothing.

He slid lower on Hope so he could savor her compact, beautiful breasts with his hands, his lips, his tongue. He sucked one nipple into his mouth and felt her lurch beneath him. He squeezed and kneaded the other breast, and she writhed. The fever that had already caused one part of his body to swell to a nearly painful degree rose through him until his mind was feverish as well. It took all his willpower not to tear off her jeans and impale her, plunge inside her and love her until they were both screaming in ecstasy.

Her plans obviously paralleled his. She yanked at his shirt, gathering bunches of it in her hands, groping for the buttons. He reluctantly stopped kissing her long enough to remove the damned thing, and then her hands were all over his chest, stroking, skimming, lighting fires everywhere she touched him. He moved so she could reach his back, but she didn't bother with that. She went straight for his fly.

His head was spinning from her, his heart was shimmying. He forced his hands to remain steady, working the zipper of her jeans as she worked the zipper of his. When she slipped one smooth, cool hand inside his shorts he just about died.

And then he revived, stronger than ever. He was hot and hard and bursting with energy, with hunger, with a need to make her feel more alive than she'd ever felt before.

He shucked his jeans and shoved hers down her legs. Then he reached between her thighs. She gasped. So did he, when he felt her softness, her dampness, the trembling folds of flesh waiting for him. He explored her with his fingers, readying her even though she was more than ready, daring her, watching with a thrill of anticipation as she squirmed against him.

"Morgan, Morgan, I . . ." She moaned, her hips arching, her legs flexing restlessly.

He didn't know what she was going to say. But the sound of her speaking his name reminded him of what he had to say. "I didn't . . ." He moved deeper with his fingers, groaning along with her, feeling her arousal as keenly as his own. "I didn't think—I wasn't expecting this. . . ." His voice emerged in a breathless rasp. "Do you have anything here?"

She shook her head. He saw why she couldn't speak; she had her teeth clamped around her lower lip. Her eyes were closed, her head thrown back, and tiny beads of sweat dotted her upper lip. He wanted to kiss her there. He wanted to kiss her everywhere. He wanted to make her come and come until she was as alive as a woman could be, even if he couldn't be there with her.

He removed his hand, spread her legs, and pressed his mouth against her, his lips, his tongue. He heard her low, keening cry of pleasure as her hips rose against him and then sank in surrender. Her hands fisted against his shoulders and she cried again, an aria straight from her soul, nothing held back. She gave everything she could, and took everything he could give her, and he felt a vicarious fulfillment almost as powerful as the real thing.

A long minute later, he was up on top of her again, peering down at her as the tension ebbed from her face. Slowly, languidly, she opened her eyes. "Morgan?"

"Yes."

She looked flushed, happy yet stunned. "I'm sorry, I—"

"No," he drawled. "You're not sorry."

A timid smile teased her lips. "All right. I'm not sorry." The smile faded. "What about you?"

"I'm just peachy."

"I'm not . . . I don't do this—this kind of thing very often. I mean, with men."

He grinned. "Who do you do it with?"

Her face turned a vivid pink. "I mean, that I didn't have—that I don't keep protection on hand. It's just never—it's never been an issue before."

Her stammering amused him. Her awkwardness touched him. "Well, that's all right. We made do."

"Let me . . ." Her bashfulness seemed to increase. "I want . . ." And then she gave up talking and wedged her hands between their bodies until she could close them around him.

He was still rigid, raring to go. The sensation of her soft, silky palms on him sent a shock wave of sensation through him. "Hope—"

She cupped him against her abdomen and rocked her body beneath him. Her hands slid back and forth. The skin of her stomach was warm. She gazed up at him uncertainly and tightened her grip.

Heat lashed his spine, his hips. He didn't want to hurt her, but she was caressing him so erotically, moving her hands with a combination of delicacy and forcefulness that was beyond his ability to resist. He ground himself into her, pinned by her hands. He thrust against her belly, felt the pressure well up, grow unbearably hot, and explode in a spurt of liquid fire across her skin.

"Hope," he groaned, sinking against her in luscious exhaustion and smiling against the hollow of her throat. Her hands remained on him, touching him curiously, gingerly, as if she weren't quite sure what had happened or how she'd managed it.

He wasn't quite sure, either. He wasn't sure of anything anymore. Except that he believed Hope. Whatever she believed, he believed it, too. The woman had definitely made him as crazy as she was.

And at the moment, he didn't mind one bit.

9

WHAT IRONY, SHE THOUGHT. She had no protection in her own apartment. Not the kind Morgan meant, and not the kind—the nagging voice of her ghost—that could have protected her from her own foolish emotions.

Morgan emerged from the bathroom carrying a wet washcloth and a towel. Striding back across the room to her, he appeared utterly at ease with his nakedness. Hope herself wanted to find a blanket to hide under. She wasn't used to lolling about on her couch in the nude, in the company of a riveting, virile, equally nude man.

For that matter, she wasn't used to making love the way they had. In her past, pathetically scant experience, sex had resembled a kind of drill—in every sense of the word. It had all centered on one part of her anatomy, and one part of the man's. Hands and mouths hadn't entered into it in any real fashion.

Neither had minds and hearts.

The way Morgan had made love to her, the way she'd made love to him . . . It had been so intimate. So personal. And she wasn't used to that, either. She wasn't used to wanting a man so much, giving so much, feeling so much.

Gazing at Morgan's magnificently male body and remembering everything that had occurred between them, not just in the past ten minutes but ever since she'd had a too close encounter with his car, she was forced to acknowledge the truth: she had fallen totally, helplessly in love with him.

Where was that damned ghost when Hope needed her?

Morgan reached the sofa and nudged her hips until he had enough room to sit beside her. Then he spread the washcloth over her stomach. His tender ministrations, combined with the friction of the warm, damp cloth moving in cleansing circles across her skin, turned her on almost as much as his kisses had, his touch, his mouth on her...

Oh, God. She couldn't be so aroused again, so soon.

"What are you blushing about?" he asked.

She heard laughter in his tone and saw it in his gold-flecked eyes. "Why do you think I'm blushing? I'm embarrassed."

"By this?" He swabbed her belly one last time, then dried it with the towel, stroking her skin with light, deft swabs. "This is just biology, darlin'. Nothing embarrassing about it."

If she explained to him that her embarrassment was not about what he was doing to her now, but rather what he'd done to her before and what she felt merely by reminiscing about it, she would only embarrass herself even more. She scrambled for a more acceptable answer. "It's embarrassing that here I am, a single woman in my midtwenties, and I don't have any condoms in my home."

He laughed out loud. "I regret to inform you, Ms. Henley, that you've lost the Queen of Sophistication contest. But I already knew that. You're just a hick from Kansas," he teased.

"Believe me, Morgan—even in Kansas they've heard of condoms."

"Well, then, the subject shouldn't embarrass you." He tossed the towel onto the floor and stretched out next to her. She rolled onto her side and leaned against the back cushions, leaving him as much room as she could. He lay on his side, too, facing her, close enough to be able to plant a kiss on the tip of her nose without having to move. "Actually, this brought back some good old memories from high school."

"I never did anything like this in high school," she said indignantly, although his dimpled smile provoked a matching smile from her.

"I'm sure I was more of a scoundrel than you. Lots of girls swore they wouldn't go all the way back then, so a guy had to improvise. Flexibility was needed if you wanted to get your kicks on a Saturday night. There wasn't much to do in Bailey Notch, other than messing around."

"You could have gone to a Billy Jack movie," she said, then flinched. Where on earth had *that* come from?

Morgan seemed startled, too. His smile lost its playful edge as he studied her face, less than an inch from him. "You remember," he murmured. "You remember everything."

"What do I remember?" she asked, so baffled she forgot her embarrassment.

"The things I told you when you were in intensive care. You were out cold, Hope. Completely blacked out. I just kept talking and talking because I didn't know what else to do. And you remember everything I said. You heard me, didn't you? You heard every word."

"I don't remember," she said, then laughed uncertainly. Obviously she *did* remember. She just didn't remember remembering. Her memory was like the faint outline of a picture she might have glimpsed once, long ago; something was there, something she could almost perceive and comprehend. "You told me about Billy Jack movies, didn't you? You went to the movies in a truck."

"Hope, you scare me." But he didn't look scared. He looked turned on. And when he leaned toward her to kiss her mouth, she felt his desire in his lips, in his arms closing around her, in the swell of him probing between her thighs. The soul-deep heat that had barely subsided into a low simmer flared into a dangerous conflagration once again. She wanted him. She wanted him more than she had before—more of him, more of them together. And that scared her far more than her slowly reawakening memory could possibly scare him.

He pulled back, swearing under his breath and then chuckling at his own impatience. "We'd better not get started again—at least, not without a quick trip to a drugstore."

"You're right," she said, shocked to hear the regret in her voice. She didn't want to stop. She wanted him now, all of him, filling her, taking her. He was the man whose conversation about the movies of his youth had kept her from going under forever, whose persistence and steadfastness had made her love him when she'd been all but dead.

Now he was making her alive, and she wanted him so much she didn't care about the consequences.

But he was being responsible, refusing to let her repeat the mistake a woman had made three generations ago, when love had overcome caution and she'd wound up alone and pregnant and so haunted by her recklessness she'd been sentenced to haunt others to this very day. If Morgan hadn't backed off and opted to play it safe, would Hope have wound up a heartbroken ghost three generations from now, imprisoned inside a mirror? Would she have been locked into a timeless world, doomed because she'd loved unwisely and too well?

Just one more thing to thank him for, she thought with less charity than the occasion called for. Perhaps her ancestor in the mirror hadn't wanted to be saved, either. Perhaps she'd willingly brought her fate on herself.

For better or worse, Hope would never know that fate. Morgan was already off the couch, gathering his far-flung clothes.

She allowed herself one final admiring study of his beautiful body, the long, lightly haired legs, the sleek surface of his chest, the tracings of auburn hair across his pectorals and the denser hair at his groin. His shoulders were knotted with bone and muscle, his hands remarkably graceful for their size. His abdomen was flat, his bottom taut, his arousal still extremely evident.

Her embarrassment returned, making her cheeks burn. She quickly groped around the sofa upholstery for her bra, found it crammed between two cushions, and put it on.

She had expected to be a little less afflicted by lust by the time they were both dressed, but she wasn't. "Maybe we ought to go back to Bachelor Arms," she said, thinking that the only thing that would save her from loving Morgan would be a harsh scolding from the ghost.

He immediately agreed to her suggestion, for the wrong reason: "Yeah. My bed's a lot more comfortable than that couch—and unlike you, I keep certain necessities on hand."

She didn't mention that she was hoping to cool off by the time they got there. Lord knew, once they reached that comfortable bed of his, and his handy necessities, she might decide to throw her lot with love rather than caution.

She smoothed her shirt into the waistband of her jeans, stepped into her loafers, and crossed to the kitchen counter for her purse. When she turned, Morgan was close behind her. He looped his arm affectionately around her shoulders and dropped a kiss onto her brow.

It was ridiculous that he could turn her on by doing so little. Or maybe what was ridiculous was not what he did but how she reacted to it.

Mustering her willpower, she refused to kiss him back, but instead pulled her keys from her purse and started toward the door with him. It wasn't until she noticed the get well card lying in the wastebasket, the one her mother had sent her, that she suddenly felt weak.

Her faltering step caused Morgan to hold her more securely, sliding his hand under her arm and keeping her upright. "Maybe we should burn it," he suggested.

"No." She wasn't going to act as if it, too, were haunted. It was just a stiff paper rectangle with a corny picture and some all-purpose sentiments inscribed on it. It was just her mother's way of saying, "I'm your mother and I wish you the best." Her mother was the weak one, unable to stand on her own. Hope might be light-headed from the accident, she might occasionally suffer from double vision, but she would never depend on a man the way her mother depended on her assorted husbands.

She would depend on Morgan to get her down the stairs without stumbling, however. She would depend on him to hold the doors open for her, and usher her out into the crisp December night, and lead her to the car. She would depend on him to help her into her seat, and join her behind the wheel...and then kiss her again, sweetly, deeply, before he turned on the engine.

The warmth of his kiss lingered on her lips as he eased out of the parking space and cruised down the block. It lingered as he drove away from the apartment that no longer felt like her home and headed toward the mansion that felt so very much like she belonged there. It lingered as he followed a route north to Wilshire Boulevard and then west to Bachelor Arms, where Hope's history, and perhaps her future, awaited her.

The massive pink building was quiet when Morgan and Hope entered. The tree trimming party must have wound down hours ago. But the tree stood glittering in the shelter of the stairway, the ceiling light catching the shreds of tinsel and the shiny surfaces of the colored glass balls hanging from the fragrant boughs. *On Christmas eve, we would light all the candles,* the ghost whispered.

Hope swallowed, then squared her shoulders. She shouldn't be surprised; she had expected the ghost to be waiting for her here. She had *wanted* the ghost.

But she wanted Morgan more.

She glanced at him, wondering whether he too had heard the ghost. He had his back to her, checking the front door to make sure it was locked.

On Christmas eve, the man I loved came to me....

She wanted to clamp her hands over her ears, but she knew the ghost's voice would reach her anyway. Another glance at Morgan told her nothing. He was smiling at her, taking her hand, leading her up the stairs.

He pledged his love to me, and still I was betrayed. This man has pledged nothing to you, nothing at all.

He's given me life, Hope wanted to cry out. *He kept me from dying.* But she pressed her lips shut and accompanied Morgan upstairs to the second floor.

Outside apartment 2-C, the bass viol was gone. In its place was a pair of well-used running shoes. "I guess he's a physically fit musician," Morgan surmised, shooting a grin Hope's way. "Or a jogging gangster."

She wanted to share his laughter, but she was afraid that if she opened her mouth she'd wind up ranting about the ghost, and then Morgan would call her brain-damaged, and that would be the end of everything. Which would be for the best, she reminded herself, but still . . .

The tart pine fragrance of the Christmas tree followed them down the hall to Morgan's apartment and inside. He closed the door behind them, twisted the dead bolt, and took Hope in his arms.

I want this so much, she thought, melting in his embrace, in his hot, hungry kiss. *I want to be alive.*

But there was the ghost again, that niggling voice admonishing her about how a woman could be demolished by loving the wrong man, about how the only thing in life worse than losing one's heart was losing one's child. The ghost's sorrowful litany flooded Hope's skull until she let out a moan of protest.

"I know," Morgan murmured, running his hand through her hair again and again, pressing his hips to hers. "I know."

"You don't know," she wailed quietly. She leaned against him, struggling to catch her breath and calm her quivering nerves. She felt caught in a tug-of-war, the ghost and her own sense of self-preservation pulling one way, her yearning heart pulling the other.

"You're tired," he said.

He was giving her a tactful way out. Sighing, she leaned back and peered up at him. He looked wistful and perplexed and as frustrated as she felt.

"I'm tired," she admitted in a tiny voice, hating her cowardice but knowing that if she told him the truth—that she was once more in communication with the ghost—she would lose Morgan more surely than if the ghost's predictions came true.

"It's late. Why don't you go wash up? I'll join you later."

She nodded and took a step backward when he let his arms drop to his sides. Once again, Morgan was saving her life. And she felt guilty as hell about it.

HOURS LATER, he was still at his drafting table in the spare bedroom, sketching up a storm.

He hadn't stopped thinking about Hope, lying in his bed, waiting for him—or maybe *not* waiting for him. He wasn't sure if she wanted him there with her—but then, he wasn't sure of anything at the moment, except that the drawings he was coming up with were some of the best he'd ever done. Maybe he was sublimating all his libidinous energy, but he doubted that. When he'd been horny in the past, he'd never dealt with it through Mongo.

He was horny now. Merely thinking of Hope, mouthing her name, observing the black ink from the pen in his hand and thinking of Hope's black, black hair, caused his body to strain uncomfortably against the thick denim of his jeans. Yet here he was, scribbling away. And there she was, in bed without him.

He didn't consider himself all that much of a gentleman. When a woman indicated that she wanted him, and he was of a like mind, they went at it. He used precautions and he made sure the woman enjoyed the encounter as much as he did, but if both parties were ready, willing and able, it was a guaranteed go.

He and Hope had been on the same wavelength a couple of hours ago, at her apartment. He knew without a doubt that she desired him. As for himself, desire barely scratched the surface. He wanted her the way a drowning man wanted air.

Yet he was here, and she was there.

He finished outlining his ninth drawing of the night, then glanced at his watch. Nearly 2:00 a.m. It was too late to keep going, yet he wasn't sleepy. A college acquaintance of his had once described the experience of tripping on uppers. Morgan had never been tempted by drugs, but he imagined this was what it was like—a feeling of overwhelming cleverness, of amazing clarity. He felt as if, like Mongo, he was imbued with magical powers. He could conquer the world, and he could conquer the toy store chains with Mongo merchandise. He could pull miracles out of Mongo's top hat. He could wave his magic wand, and the world would fall at his feet.

He wanted to wave his magic wand, all right—but only for the benefit of one woman. Resolutely, he switched off the hinged lamp and heaved himself to his feet.

He should have felt stiff after sitting at the drafting table so long. But he felt loose and limber and pumped up. He felt like a man who had passed through the valley of buxom blondes and discovered heaven on the other side, in the form of a delicate dark-haired woman who should have been filled with bitterness but wasn't, who should have been wearing her troubled childhood like a coat of armor but didn't, who was too unsophisticated to keep contraceptives at her apartment and thus hadn't been able to indulge in the ultimate act with him—but who sent him to the moon and back, even though she hadn't really seemed to know what she was doing.

This must be love, he said—and then realized he hadn't said anything.

He wouldn't have said that, anyway. He didn't love Hope Henley. Their relationship had nothing to do with love. It was born in need and guilt, and it had progressed to healthy physical pleasure, and from there it would evolve into a smile-inducing memory. Love wasn't any part of it.

So why had he said that?

He *hadn't* said it. He'd just thought he had. He'd heard it said, but not by himself. He'd *thought* he'd heard it.

All right, so maybe he *was* a little sleepy. Maybe he had moved beyond sleepy to delirious.

Sighing, he rolled his head from side to side, stretched his back muscles, and sauntered out of the room. He took his time in the shower, waiting for exhaustion to hit. But the stinging hot spray only invigorated him. That, and the thought of Hope in his bed.

If he'd behaved like a gentleman earlier, he would have to behave like one again. He wouldn't wake her if she was sleeping. He would just slip into bed next to her and wrap his arms around her. Maybe she would dream of him. Maybe, if he was lucky, she'd wake up on her own.

Luck didn't look too promising, he thought a few minutes later when he tiptoed into his bedroom. She was fast asleep, but what really discouraged him was that she was wearing the baggy nightshirt she'd had on last night. If only she was in the altogether, he'd know he was welcome in his own bed. Now, he wasn't sure.

He clicked the bedside lamp to a low setting. She didn't stir. Her face looked tranquil, nestled into the fluffy down pillow. The bruise was almost completely gone.

Once it was, she'd be gone, too. How in the world could he have even considered the possibility that he loved her? She was just a beautiful woman. A beautiful, smart, determined woman. A beautiful, smart, determined woman who seemed able to haunt his every waking minute.

But it wasn't love.

He unwrapped the bath towel from around his waist and tossed it on a chair, then crawled under the blanket and turned off the lamp.

"Morgan?" she whispered.

So help him, if she asked him to leave, he wouldn't. Not after her display of wild ecstasy at her apartment. Not after he'd had a taste of what full-blown sex could be like with her.

"What?" he asked warily.

She was the one to close the distance between them. She rolled into his arms and settled against him, replacing the pillow with his shoulder.

His body shot to attention. "Did I wake you?" he asked in a deceptively relaxed voice.

"No. I've—I've been restless."

"Mmm." He trailed his fingers over her shoulder, damning the fabric that shielded her skin from him. "Me, too."

"I slept fitfully. There were dreams . . ."

About me? he wondered. *About us? About making the earth move?*

"Morgan. . . ." She sighed, then whispered, "Damn."

He continued to stroke her shoulder and arm, savoring her graceful curves, her slender strength. "Something tells me I'm not going to like this," he said, unable to stifle a chuckle.

"It's the ghost," she said.

"Ah." His hand fell still on her. He wasn't sure what to think—or what she expected him to think—but he had a feeling *damn* pretty well summed it up. "Care to elaborate?"

"What is there to elaborate? The ghost has been talking to me. That means I'm insane, doesn't it?"

He heard the bristling anger in her tone, and felt it in the rigidity of her shoulders even as her body nestled closer to him. "I never said you were insane," he consoled her, even though it was a lie. "All I said was that you got a pretty bad knock on the noodle—"

"You said I was brain-damaged," she sharply reminded him.

This was not the quickest route to a glorious interlude of lovemaking. There he was, lying stark buck naked in bed with a woman he yearned for the way bees yearned for pollen, the way flowers yearned for sunshine . . . the way dreamers yearned for hope. He had Hope—the woman and the emotion—in his grasp, so close her feminine heat permeated his skin and flooded his body. And he was not going to make love to her because earlier that evening he'd tossed off the observation that a bad knock on the noodle could lead to a temporary brain injury.

He was up against it. His only resort was to lie some more. "Hope, I didn't mean it."

"Of course you meant it. You think I'm brain-damaged."

"I think you're healing. And come on, honey—we were fine at your apartment, weren't we? The ghost has nothing to do with what's going on between you and me."

"The ghost wasn't at my apartment. She's here, at Bachelor Arms. She's been with me all night."

"Well, perhaps you could ask her to leave, now that I'm here," he said, hoping a little levity would help his case. "Unless you're into threesomes . . ."

Hope didn't laugh. "This has nothing to do with asking her to leave. It has to do with you thinking I'm insane because I'm aware of her."

"I don't think you're insane. I just think, maybe . . ." He struggled to come up with something pleasantly euphemistic. "You're in a delicate state."

"Given my delicate state, I'm not sure making love is such a good idea."

"I think it's a damned good idea," he argued.

"Do you?" She raised herself slightly and peered down at him, her silhouette visible in the dark. What he couldn't see with his eyes he could see with his mind: her angular chin, her long, narrow nose, the full, lush mouth he craved, the hypnotically dark eyes. "Surely you wouldn't want to take advantage of a brain-damaged woman."

He couldn't tell if she was being sarcastic or not. He suspected she wasn't. Sarcasm wasn't part of Hope Henley's repertory.

Which meant she was serious. "I wasn't aware that anyone was taking advantage of anyone," he snapped, wishing his indignation would register on his body. No matter how offended he was, he still wanted her. At least physically, he did.

"Oh, Morgan..." Her voice broke, and the plaintive sound of her suppressed sob suckered him but good. How could he be angry with her when she was obviously so torn apart by her silliness about the ghost? "Morgan, I'm sorry. I want to be with you, I do, but..."

"But?"

He felt moisture on his chest. Tears. Hope's tears. This woman who wouldn't cry for her heartless mother was crying for him, for what they both wanted but what her ghost hang-up was denying them. "I'm sorry, Morgan. I just can't."

He let her weep, let her tears streak across his skin. "Do you want me to sleep in the other room?" he asked.

"No," she said on a soft, ragged sigh, and she sniffled her tears to a close. "But you probably don't want to stay."

"I do," he said, surprising himself. He would have thought the best part of staying would be making love with her. But even though he couldn't do that, he could still hold her. He could still breathe in the faint scent of her skin cream, and he could let her hair spill like black silk around him, and he could feel the tight roundness of her breasts pressing against him through her shirt.

And if they got through the rest of the night, maybe she would have a change of heart in the morning.

"Sometimes I think you're right," she confessed, her voice hoarse after her bout of crying. "I am crazy."

"The only thing I'm right about is—" *We should make love,* he almost said, then thought better of it. Being pushy wouldn't accomplish anything. "You still have healing to do."

"I guess."

"Let's try to get some sleep, Hope. It's late."

"Okay." She settled back into his arms, slinging one hand across his waist and resting her head against his chest. After a minute she stopped shifting and rearranging herself, and her breathing grew more regular. He didn't know if she'd fallen asleep or was just faking it.

He himself was nowhere near falling asleep. His mind spun, presenting him with a dizzying array of notions. His work tonight had gone so well, uncommonly well. He'd been prolific, he'd been brilliant. Hope had inspired him.

He'd come in her hands, on her belly. Like a kid, like a lovesick adolescent. Like a protective man.

And now here he was again, protecting her. Not because he'd hurt her, not because he'd nearly killed her, but because her beauty and her obstinacy and her unshakable faith in the most outrageous things had gotten to him, and touched him, and changed him somehow.

This must be love, he heard himself say.

The room was silent. No one had spoken a word.

But he'd heard it coming from himself, a thought planted inside him, making itself felt in the oddest way.

He knew he was not going to sleep that night.

SHE SMELLED COFFEE. She recalled lying in the darkness in the hours after the accident, sinking deeper and deeper into the chasm, and then smelling coffee, craving coffee. That marvelous aroma had induced her to claw back out of the chasm, almost as much as Morgan's voice had.

She did remember everything, everything that had ever happened between her and Morgan, right from the start: the coffee, his words, his stalwart presence. His pleading. His support. His touch.

His touch yesterday, at her apartment.

Shuddering, she hauled herself out of bed. She was alone, although she knew he'd been with her last night. As besieged by insomnia as she'd been, once Morgan had gotten into bed with her she'd been able to sleep. Just having him close had made her feel safe, even though she knew he posed the greatest threat to her safety since she'd first seen the ghost in the mirror. With his arms around her, she'd known the ghost wouldn't bother her any more last night.

Standing, she felt a predictable wave of light-headedness. She waited until it passed, then walked carefully out of the bedroom, following the enticing coffee fragrance.

Morgan was in the kitchen, brewing what smelled like a rich gourmet blend. He had two slices of bread browning in the toaster oven, and he'd set a tub of butter and a jar of jam on the table. He turned at her entrance.

He looked...not quite grim. Not quite irritated. Not quite uneasy. A little of each, and very tired. Shadows circled his eyes, and his cheeks wore a stubble of beard. His hair was mussed, his T-shirt hanging untucked, his feet bare.

"Good morning," she said, though she suspected he wouldn't agree that it was particularly good. Knowing what could have happened last night, what had happened and what hadn't, she wasn't so sure it was a good morning, either.

"Morning." The coffee had finished running through the machine, and he pulled out the grounds. He emptied them into the trash, then rinsed the basket, then set it to dry. He seemed anxious to keep busy so he could avoid looking at her.

She scrutinized him as he moved about the kitchen. Even rumpled and fatigued, he looked gorgeous. She ached to race to him, give him a hug, tell him the real reason she couldn't make love with him. The ghost had something to do with it, but only because without the ghost Hope would have had no defense against him.

She loved him. She'd fallen in love with him before she'd been conscious of him—before she'd been conscious, period. But she couldn't make love with him, because he didn't love her. And like the ghost, her mirror image, Hope would be demolished if she gave her love to Morgan and he didn't return it.

She wished she could have told him the truth last night. But how could a woman tell a man she needed to hear him say he loved her, when the words wouldn't come from his heart? If he hadn't said it, he didn't feel it. Hope wouldn't beg for him to feel something he didn't feel.

So she'd hidden behind the ghost, instead. One way or another, the ghost was going to save her from her own unruly heart.

He spent an inordinate amount of time pulling the bread from the toaster oven and arranging it on a plate, continuing to elude her gaze. "I found something that might interest you," he said, although he might as well have been addressing the wall.

Without caffeine in her bloodstream, she wasn't sure she was in any condition to discuss something interesting. She moved to the table, lowered herself into a chair and waited for the Morgan who had just blurred into two overlapping Morgans to merge back into one again.

"I don't know if any of this still matters to you," he added. "Yesterday seems like a century ago."

That was the truth. Yesterday, Morgan had kept his distance from her for most of the day—and when finally he'd returned to her, all hell had broken loose, in the most incredible, regrettable way.

Curiosity nipped at her, but she was afraid to speak. If she opened her mouth, she might blurt out that she loved him, that even if they never made love, even if they never kissed each other again, or held each other through the night, or knew anything remotely like the intimacy they'd known once, her heart was his.

"Here," he said, lifting several sheets of paper, stapled together and folded, from the counter and passing them to her.

She spread the papers smooth and scanned the top page. It was Morgan's lease.

10

SHE STARED AT the document for a long minute, watching the tiny print swim before her eyes, multiply and then contract back into clear English letters. Morgan's Bachelor Arms lease. Why was he showing it to her now?

He wanted to get rid of her.

He knew she intended to learn whether Bachelor Arms was the estate her grandmother had told her about. Once Hope found out who legally owned the building, Morgan probably figured she would leave. By showing her the lease, he was speeding the process along.

Not that she blamed him. After last night, when she'd disintegrated emotionally while he lay beside her expecting a night of passionate sex, he must have decided his diagnosis was a bull's-eye. She was nuts. He wasn't going to get anything on with a lunatic, so he might as well move her out as quickly as he could.

She skimmed the first page of the lease. The neatly typed paragraphs ran one into the next, clause after clause of jargon. As she flipped to the second page, Morgan set a mug of coffee down in front of her. His nearness caused her to flinch.

She needed to consume the mug's contents, refill it, and slug down the refill. Then maybe she would be able to make sense of the lease—and maybe she would be able to utter a coherent sentence.

He remained at her chair, scanning the lease over her shoulder. "Does it answer your questions?" he asked.

"No." Only when she peered up at him did he circle the table and sit facing her, his own mug in one hand and the plate of toast in the other. He said nothing, just watched her with his cool, golden eyes. "Thanks for showing me this, though," she added, then bit her lip to keep from blurting out some personal sentiment that would only make them both feel awkward. "Wasn't I supposed to go through your contract—"

"Some other time, maybe." He jabbed his index finger at a clause in his lease. "The lessor, as they say in legalese, is a holding company. I have no idea who they are. I negotiated the lease with Ken Amberson."

She recalled the short, muttering man who'd argued with her over the Christmas decorations yesterday. "He might know something about the holding company."

"He might." Morgan lifted his mug and took a long sip.

"You want me to investigate this," she murmured.

"If it'll make you happy."

What would make her happy was hearing Morgan declare that he loved her, and that was out of the question. "Look, Morgan..." She dropped her gaze to the mist curling up from the black surface of her coffee. "If you want me to leave, I will. I'm feeling okay. And Peter can keep an eye on me back at my own place—"

"Who said anything about wanting you to leave?" For someone running on as little sleep as Morgan apparently was, he seemed extraordinarily alert, all of a sudden.

"Well, I assumed..." She searched his face but was unable to interpret his enigmatic half smile. "After last night..." She felt her cheeks grow warm and lowered her eyes once more.

"Sweetheart, the sooner you straighten out your thoughts on the subject of this house and the ghost and all that other claptrap you've got knocking around inside your skull, the sooner you and I can pick up where we left off. So there's the lease. Go to it, tiger. Work it out. I'll be here panting for you when you're done."

She saw the twinkle of humor in his sleepy eyes, and heard the tang of laughter in his husky drawl. He still desired her, at least. Even after she'd made such a hash of things last night, he still wanted her.

Which wasn't the same as love—but it also wasn't the same as a flat-out rejection.

Oh, for God's sake. She didn't want Morgan to tolerate her flights of fancy in the belief that he'd be rewarded with a roll in the hay once she came back to earth. What she wanted was to be as important to Morgan as he was to her, to be essential to him. To be his lifeline.

And that wasn't going to happen.

It was time to pull herself together, to resume the life she'd been living before the ghost of Bachelor Arms had hurled her into the path of Morgan's car. It was time to settle her alleged inheritance and fulfill her deathbed promise to her grandmother. Once she'd accomplished everything she had come to California to do, she could go back to Kansas and her old, stable existence.

Morgan was never going to be a part of that existence. Even if he was funny and sexy, more magical and magnificent than his creation, Mongo. Even if without him she would never have emerged from the darkness. Even if the thought of facing the rest of her life without him felt like a death in itself.

"I'll see what I can find out," she said, gesturing toward the lease. "Thank you, Morgan."

AN HOUR LATER, they reached the offices of Loomis, Metcalfe and Schwartz, Attorneys at Law, located in a skyscraper of steel and smoked glass in downtown Los Angeles.

Hope hadn't intended for Morgan to accompany her. For that matter, she hadn't intended to see a lawyer at all. But a lawyer seemed to offer her the best chance of finding out who, or what, Catalina Fidelity Trust was.

Ken Amberson had claimed to know as much about the holding company which paid his salary as he knew about the Christmas spirit—which was zilch. Hope had telephoned Catalina Fidelity, where a secretary had politely refused to answer any of her questions. Morgan had mentioned something about putting in some time at his studio, but instead of leaving, he'd hovered over her, suggesting she telephone this bank and that real estate broker and then abruptly pulling the phone out of her hands and making an appointment for her with his attorney.

"I can't afford your attorney," she muttered as he steered his car into the office tower's underground garage.

"I already told you, I pay him plenty. He'll do this as a favor for me."

"I don't want favors." Morgan's eagerness to help her was disconcerting. What if he was going through all this effort just to get her back into his bed?

She chided herself to stop thinking about Morgan in the context of his bed. She had to focus on the lease, the lawyer, the search for the truth about her grandmother's heritage. Morgan was right; she had to clear out the claptrap cluttering her brain. If she resolved the Bachelor Arms ownership issue, perhaps her dizziness and double vision would end. Perhaps she would even be cured of her love for Morgan.

They entered the building through the garage, and rode up the elevator to the sixteenth floor. The elevator let them off just outside the law firm's suite of offices. As soon as Morgan opened the glass door, the receptionist at the front desk beamed a megawatt smile at him. "Hi, Morgan! I'll tell Barry you're here." She immediately lifted the phone and punched a few buttons on her console. "Mr. Loomis? Morgan Delacourt is here."

Hope recalled Morgan's remark about paying his attorney plenty. Evidently he paid the man enough to warrant the royal treatment. Either that, or the receptionist had a crush on him.

"You can go right in," she informed them, hanging up the phone and sending another blinding smile Morgan's way. Morgan thanked her, then took Hope's elbow and ushered her through the maze of desks and recesses to an office at the end of a hall.

"They know you well here, don't they," Hope remarked, thinking that small talk might counteract her reaction to his touch. He hadn't meant it as an overture; she wished her body would accept what her mind knew to be nothing more than courtesy.

"Barry's saved my butt more than once since I arrived in L.A."

"Really? Have you had lots of run-ins with the law?"

Morgan grinned. "I've had lots of run-ins with complicated contracts. That's Barry's specialty."

"Contracts?" She frowned. "What do we need your lawyer for? Your lease wasn't terribly complicated."

"Then this'll be a piece of cake for him." He paused before a heavy oak door, rapped lightly on it, and then pushed it open.

An impeccably groomed man was seated at an arty desk, a flat-topped arch of solid teak outfitted with the requisite onyx pen stand, an elaborate telephone and a leaded-crystal ashtray filled with exotic-looking cigarette butts. He rose from his high-backed leather chair the instant Hope entered the spacious office. His suit was of designer quality, his hair styled by an artist, his fingernails buffed and his loafers constructed of soft leather—and his smile as phony as a two-headed penny. "Morgan, good to see you. And you must be Hope Henley," he greeted her, extending his right hand across the ornamental desk.

Hope shook his hand and returned a nervous smile. Why didn't this man like her?

"Hope," Morgan was saying, "this is Barry Loomis. He should be able to find out what you need to know."

"Please, sit down," Barry said, sending Morgan a quick, skeptical look before he waved at the chairs facing his desk. "Morgan explained your problem to me, Ms. Henley. Something to do with the holding company that owns Bachelor Arms."

"I appreciate your taking the time to see us," Hope said, wishing she could overcome his apparent animosity toward her. She glanced at Morgan, but he was lounging in his chair, his legs extended halfway under the lawyer's desk and a smug grin splitting his face. He tossed the folded lease across the desk to Barry, who smoothed it out and gave it a quick perusal.

"Catalina Fidelity Trust," he read. "It sounds like an entity set up to shelter investors. I'll have one of the associates run the outfit down, see what she can find out." He pressed a button on his phone console. "Arlene? I've got a project for you."

Before the silence became oppressive, Barry's associate arrived at his office. A brisk young woman, she skimmed the lease and shrugged. "Give me ten minutes," she said. "If I can't come up with anything on Catalina Fidelity by then, it might take a while."

"We can stick around for ten minutes," Morgan told the associate. Once she was gone, he relaxed back into his cocky grin. "Do you want us to clear out, Barry? We could go downstairs for a cup of coffee while we're waiting. Hope is addicted to coffee." He shot her a quick, conspiratorial smile.

Hope merely folded her hands in her lap and tried to look grateful. She sensed that Morgan was being extra cheerful to counteract the rays of hostility his lawyer was zapping her with. She appreciated Morgan's effort, but she still felt uncomfortable.

"Actually," Barry said to Morgan, "I'd like you to stay. We've got some things to talk about." He gave Hope a sidelong glance and added, "Perhaps Ms. Henley might like to get some coffee herself."

She could take a hint. "Why don't I do that," she said too brightly, shoving herself to her feet.

Of all the times to suffer an intense dizzy spell, this had to be the worst. She wavered, wobbled, closed her eyes and pleaded silently for the room to stop whirling around her. And then Morgan's hands were on her upper arms, holding her snugly yet gently, easing her back into her chair. "Ms. Henley isn't going anywhere," he told his lawyer.

"We have business to discuss."

"So we'll discuss business. Hope won't mind. Are you okay?" he murmured to her.

She nodded weakly. Her heart was pounding, her head spinning. She kept her eyes shut so she wouldn't have to see the room reeling around her.

"I take it she still hasn't recovered," said Barry.

"She's come a long way."

The lawyer snorted. "But the physical problems continue."

"It's not a problem, Barry. She's just a little dizzy, that's all."

"All that's missing is the removable neck brace. Morgan, I'm a lawyer. I've seen this sort of thing before. Let me guess—a generous settlement would really speed along the healing process."

She opened her eyes, annoyed that they were talking about her as if she couldn't speak for herself. "I'm much better," she told Barry, then added sarcastically, "Thank you for inquiring."

Barry caught her dig and nodded, a slight smile twisting his lips. "You probably think I'm a heartless thug."

"He's a lawyer," Morgan joked. "It's the same thing."

Barry scowled at Morgan, then turned back to Hope. His expression was stern. "Since Morgan is determined to have you present, I'll get down to the business at hand. The fact is, Ms. Henley, you've cost him a small fortune. The first bill arrived—"

"Morgan?" She stared at him in horror. "Oh, no—they didn't make you pay a fine, did they? I'll talk to the police, I'll tell them it wasn't your fault. And the damage to your car—"

"I'm talking about your hospital expenses, Ms. Henley," Barry interrupted. "Your sugar daddy here paid all your deductibles."

Her jaw dropped. "My deductibles?"

"A drop in the bucket," Morgan assured her, then winked at Barry. "She doesn't know how rich I am. Don't tell her."

Barry rolled his eyes heavenward and cursed. "I think you just did. You make my life very hard, Morgan. Very hard. How am I supposed to protect your best interests when you thwart me at every turn?"

Bewildered, Hope looked from Morgan to Barry and back again. "I'd like an itemized bill for my hospital expenses," she said quietly. "I'll pay them." It didn't matter how rich Morgan was. She couldn't stand being more indebted to him than she already was. It was bad enough that he'd taken care of her, opened his home to her, given her access to his lawyer. Bad enough that he'd been tormented by guilt over her, and that he'd made her fall in love with him.

But to have him paying her medical expenses . . . That was simply too much.

He dismissed her comment with a nonchalant grin. "Don't worry about Hope," he told his lawyer. "I trust her."

"You think I've got a screw loose," she reminded him.

"But you're getting better. You *will* get better, one way or another." He turned to his lawyer. "I'm planning to offer Hope a job as my marketing manager."

"What?" she blurted out. Even sitting, she felt dizzy.

He continued to address Barry. "She's got a business degree with a specialty in marketing, and she's got all kinds of cool licensing ideas for Mongo."

"The production company has a marketing department to take care of that," Barry reminded him.

"And they've got their best interests at heart. Hope will have *my* best interests at heart." He patted her hand and winked, as if to tell her, *Don't worry, I know what I'm doing.*

Hope wasn't reassured.

There was a light tap on the door, and then it opened. Barry's assistant stood in the doorway, holding a clipboard with a page of handwritten notes on it. "Here's the scoop," she reported. "Catalina Fidelity is a holding company that owns a fair amount of income-producing real estate throughout the county. As for the Wilshire Boulevard property in question..." She skimmed her notes. "The property was sold to Catalina by the Los Angeles National Bank, which obtained title in 1931 from a Mr. and Mrs. Stuart Blodgett, in settlement of a two hundred thousand dollar bank loan. The title on the house had passed from Stuart Blodgett to his daughter in 1929 in an effort to shelter the property from creditors. But the daughter died intestate a year later. Her parents being her only immediate family, they regained title to the house, and they sold it to the bank."

"She didn't die intestate," Hope argued. "There was a will."

"If there was, you're going to have to find it," Arlene said. "The bank has no record of it. Neither does Catalina Fidelity."

"Then I'll find it," Hope vowed. "Do you have any information on the daughter? What was her name?"

"Hope," Arlene reported. "Hope Blodgett."

"IT'S JUST A coincidence," Morgan observed. "Hope's a pretty name, that's all."

Hope stared at the row of numbers above the elevator doors, watching them blink on and off as the car descended to the basement garage. She was *not* going to give in to dizziness. She was *not* going to see double. She was going to hold herself together until she could assimilate everything that had taken place in Morgan's lawyer's office.

The facts surrounding the ownership of Bachelor Arms seemed to confirm what Hope had suspected. That she shared her ancestor's name had to be, as Morgan said, a coincidence.

But the other part, the spice he'd thrown into the stew—"Your marketing manager?" she asked, once she was sure her voice wouldn't betray how close she was to unraveling.

"That was just a thought," he said blithely. "It has a certain appeal, don't you think?"

"I don't know what I think," she muttered.

"The production company's giving me a lot of elbow room, plus they're paying me big bucks. You must have gathered that from the conversation upstairs."

"That you're rich? It's really none of my business. . . ."

"And of course you'd have to pass muster with Francine. She's my assistant, and she can be a serious bitch—which is generally what I need in an assistant. I think she'd be able to work with you, Hope. She basically keeps me organized, keeps the office running, makes sure I get everything done on time. Your responsibilities wouldn't overlap with hers."

The elevator glided to a halt, causing Hope's stomach to lurch. The doors slid open and they exited into the cool, gloomy garage. "I'm not sure what you're suggesting could work out," she said, her voice echoing eerily off the gray concrete walls.

He tossed her a quick, speculative glance, then shrugged. "It was just an idea."

"Quite an idea. Why did you even think of it?"

He eyed her again, this time looking thoughtful, and a bit disappointed. "You've got the education. You've got the college degree. You were the one who pointed out Mongo's licensing possibilities. I figure you know a hell of a lot more about this stuff than I do."

"Even so . . ." She shook her head, appalled by how beguiling she found the idea. She couldn't possibly work for Morgan. She couldn't even give his proposition a moment's thought. Surely if *he* gave it that much thought he'd retract the offer.

"Anyway," he concluded, "I had to say something to keep Barry from gunning for you."

"He hates me," she concluded.

"Not really. He just worries that you're going to sue the pants off me."

She wished Morgan would have chosen his words more carefully. Thinking of him with his pants off was much too risky. "Why on earth would I sue you?"

"I hit you with my car," he reminded her, then turned and focused on the car itself, several rows away. "Really, Hope, forget about the marketing thing. I'm sure that the minute you've found out what you need to know about your grandmother, you're going to go home to Kansas. You're not interested in hanging around here."

Yes I am, Hope wanted to argue. Kansas held nothing for her, except possibly her sanity. She had no family left there, and no job. Once she'd fulfilled her final promise to her grandmother, she could live wherever she wanted.

But she couldn't stay in L.A. if Morgan didn't love her—and obviously he didn't. If she'd entertained the slightest optimism that he might, it had been dashed by his offering her a job. A man didn't show his love for a woman by hiring her as his marketing manager.

With a mournful sigh, she waited as he unlocked the passenger door of his car, and then dropped onto the seat without taking his offered hand. The less contact they had, the easier it would be for her to get over him—or so she hoped.

He moved around the car to the driver's side and settled behind the wheel. "Where to?"

"I have to find Hope Blodgett's will."

"Where do you want to look? Probate court?"

"I'm sure there's no official record of her will. If there was, the bank couldn't have assumed title of the house." Hope turned away from him and closed her eyes. She felt overloaded, her head aching as badly as it had after the accident. Too much information was crammed into her brain. Too much emotion. She just wanted it all to be over.

"If the lady lived in Bachelor Arms—if she died there—maybe her will is there."

"It was more than sixty years ago, Morgan. Surely the place has been cleaned top to bottom more than once in that time. Why would her will be there?"

"I don't know where else you can look. Do you know the name of the lawyer who contacted your grandmother?"

She shook her head to indicate she didn't. "All right, I may as well look around the house. If Mr. Amberson lets me."

"The hell with him. We don't have to ask for his permission. We'll just poke around on our own."

"I thought you had work to do," Hope said. It would be easier to search the house with him; he knew his way around the building. But now was as good a time as any to get used to going it alone.

"My work can wait." He revved the engine, then gave her an impish smile. "I'm rich."

She fought unsuccessfully against a laugh. Anyone else would have sounded insufferably conceited saying such a thing, but not Morgan. He had such a quirky smile, such a playful drawl, his boast sounded more like a put-down of himself.

God help her, she didn't want to laugh with him. She didn't want to respond to anything about him. But as he navigated out of the garage and into the bright December sunshine, she glimpsed his profile, his smile undercut by a squint until he grabbed his sunglasses from the dashboard and donned them. She saw the rugged angle of his jaw, and the thin, sensual curve of his mouth, and his sunshine-filled eyes just before they vanished behind the dark glasses, and her heart turned over.

What had the ghost warned her? *This man has pledged nothing to you....* But he'd offered her a job.

Which wasn't even remotely what she wanted from him.

"Hope Blodgett," Morgan murmured.

It was Hope's turn to say, "Just a coincidence."

"What if the ghost somehow communicated down through the generations that your name was supposed to be the same as hers?"

"The ghost has been loitering in the mirror in apartment 1-G through the generations," Hope pointed out. "And anyway, Morgan, you don't believe she exists."

He glanced her way, then turned the corner and studied the road ahead. "You're right about that," he agreed, stretching his long legs beneath the steering wheel and maneuvering his car through the midday traffic. "I don't believe any of it."

LIKE HELL, YOU DON'T, an internal voice niggled at him.

He couldn't admit—to Hope or to himself—that her off-the-wall rantings were beginning to seem reasonable to him. But damn, weird things just kept popping out of him. Weird things kept happening, weird thoughts kept taking hold of him... and when they did, they made sense.

The job, for instance. He'd never given a thought to hiring Hope until he'd said it in Barry's office—but it was a great idea. She had the education, she had the savvy, and if she took the job, she wouldn't leave L.A.

The prospect of her staying put him in mind of those other weird thoughts that had invaded his brain last night—thoughts about how whatever he was feeling toward Hope Henley looked an awful lot like love.

But that went beyond weird. It was insane. He hardly knew her, and the way they'd met was abominably ghastly, and she wasn't his type. And last night, when he'd wanted nothing more than to make love to her until every cell in her body had experienced its own unique moment of bliss, she'd shut him down cold. Cripes. There had only been that one time, when they hadn't even gone the distance, and . . .

It had blown him away.

He could tell himself a million times he didn't believe in the ghost, but he *did* believe something was going on, something that involved him and Hope and God knew what else.

It was nearly lunchtime when they got back to Bachelor Arms, but he was too wired to be hungry. His answering machine was flashing—three messages from Francine, the first chewing him out for not showing his face at the studio, the second bragging about the alternate music festival her boyfriend had gotten tickets to, and the third telling him she thought the new plotline was pretty damned terrific. He ought to call her back and tell her what he'd accomplished last night at the drafting table in the spare bedroom. He'd worked like a fiend, and every drawing had been a keeper. He'd done incredible work. He'd been possessed.

Possessed. Another weird thought.

The rest of the messages were the usual tripe—someone was having a party in Laurel Canyon, someone wanted to sell him Colorado beef half a cow at a time—and he rewound the tape. "Are you hungry?" he asked Hope.

She shook her head. "Does the building have an attic? A basement? Someplace where things might be stored."

"If there's an attic, we'd have to get Amberson to let us in. I have no idea where it is. The basement is accessible, but I've been down there a bunch of times and I've never seen any wills lying around."

"It wouldn't just be lying around, Morgan. If it was, someone would have found it by now." She stuffed her hands into her pockets and smiled hesitantly. "How do we get to the basement?"

"We go down," he told her. The erotic connotation of his phrase overtook him, causing his blood to grow warm. The softness of her skin was still a vivid memory, as was the sound of her ecstatic cries when he'd taken her that way. If only they could forget about Hope Blodgett's will for a few X-rated minutes. If only Hope Henley's will resembled Morgan's.

He didn't dare speak—it was difficult enough to walk without giving himself away. Grabbing his keys from the table where he'd tossed them, he led the way out of his apartment, down the main stairs, past the Christmas tree to the cellar stairs.

The basement of Bachelor Arms was divided into utility rooms. One held the furnaces and hot water tanks; another held huge recycling bins; yet another was where Amberson stashed his maintenance supplies. The largest section of the basement was occupied by locked storage cages where tenants could keep bicycles, excess furniture, luggage, and other clutter they didn't want upstairs in their apartments. Each cage was labeled with a corresponding apartment number.

Hope slowed as they reached the cages. She peered through the mesh wire of the first one, assessing its contents: a drab lamp, an ironing board, an armoire and a hat tree draped with cobwebs. "You're not going to find a will here," he said.

Silent, she moved farther along the row of cages, surveying the skis, the surfboards, the rolled area rugs, the dusty hatboxes, the faded slipcovers and empty picture frames.

At the final cage, she halted. Like all the others, it contained old, dusty furniture: a listing chest of drawers, a freestanding hinged screen with flowers painted across its faded silk panels, a decrepit secretary desk, the glass in its upper doors cracked and one drawer hanging open and splintering. The cage was labeled 1-G.

"If the will is here, it would be in this storage area," Hope murmured, fingering the padlock that held the metal gate shut.

"What makes you think that?"

"She lives in a mirror in 1-G. That part of the house must have been special to her. Maybe that was where she spent most of her time when she was alive."

Morgan refused to laugh at Hope. Her words were braced by such a strong faith in their truth, he decided to accept her theory for the time being. "I wonder if Clint or Jessie is around. Since 1-G is their apartment, they'd have the key to this cage."

"Let's go find them."

"You wait here," Morgan urged her. In the uneven glare of the basement's naked ceiling bulbs, she looked as fragile as she had in the hospital. Her face was porcelain pale, her hair almost too black in contrast. "No sense in you running up and down the stairs. You just stay here and rest. I'll see if I can track them down."

Needless to say, he couldn't. They were both at work, and Hope's yearning to rummage around in their storage cage didn't seem like a crisis worthy of interrupting them at their desks. He might have asked them to give Ken Amberson permission to unlock the cage for Hope, but he really didn't want the crabby old guy to be a part of Hope's quest. The cage could wait until night, when Clint and Jessie got home.

Morgan went back downstairs and found Hope where he'd left her, her fingers curled through the wire mesh walls and her eyes wide. "Clint and Jessie aren't around," he said. "I guess you'll have to wait."

A shadow of frustration flickered across her face. Her eyes met Morgan's, and he felt his own brand of frustration as he absorbed the astonishing beauty in her dark, dark irises, her thick lashes, the unguarded emotion in her face.

God, she was beautiful. Even in the horrid lighting, surrounded by musty furniture and gray walls. She was the most beautiful woman he'd ever seen, the most desirable, the sexiest. He didn't know why, and he didn't care.

He was definitely possessed.

"We may as well go back upstairs," he said, wondering if she could hear the thick, hot lust charging his voice.

"I guess we may as well," she agreed. Perhaps it was wishful thinking, but she sounded a bit breathless, herself. Her eyes continued to glow, that strange, dark, passionate glow, and when she smiled, her lower lip lured him.

She took a step toward him, her smile growing, her face tilting to gaze up at him. He took a step toward her, and she extended her hand to take his. She probably was just feeling light-headed; she probably just wanted to lean on him as they climbed the steep stairs to the first floor, but...

Damn. He couldn't stop himself. She could stop him if she wanted, but he couldn't stop himself.

His arms closed around her, hauling her against him. His lips covered hers, crushed hers, nipped and probed and parted hers.

She didn't stop him. She lifted her hands to his waist and pulled him even closer. Her breath escaped in a sigh as her tongue beckoned his inside.

His restraint shattered. He pressed her back against the wire mesh of the cage and arched to her, his hips seeking hers. He hadn't been hungry for lunch, but he was starving for her, all of her, no more of that high school *almost* stuff, but the real thing, the home run, the all-the-way. He wanted to bury himself so deeply inside her that his soul was fused to hers. He wanted everything. He wanted Hope.

Judging by the way she rocked against him, the way her hands groped and clawed at his shirt, the way her head fell back and her mouth opened wide and her pulse pounded against his lips when he kissed her throat, she wanted him just as much.

Right here. He didn't care. On the cold, concrete floor. Or standing up. Anywhere, as long as he could have her around him, hot and seething. As long as they could go the distance together.

He wedged one hand between their bodies. She sucked her belly in as he reached for the button at the waistband of her jeans. A throaty moan escaped her, and she drew her hands lower, to his hips.

Abruptly, she started to fall.

He grabbed her, trying to hold her up, but she was tumbling backward, as if the chain-link cage wall had given way.

Not the wall, he realized, pulling her against him so she wouldn't collapse. The door. The lock hung open, hooked through a loop in the metal frame, and the mesh gate swung inward.

They stared at it for a minute, flustered, gasping for breath. He seemed to recover before she did. "What happened?" he asked.

"I don't know. It just seemed to give. Maybe the lock is rusted."

He gave the padlock a close look and found it not only clean but apparently recently oiled. "No rust. Maybe it wasn't shut all the way."

"Maybe—" Hope gazed up at him, her eyes round and bright "—the ghost opened it for us."

He couldn't come up with a better explanation. "Okay," he agreed cautiously. "The ghost opened it."

With a nervous, eager smile, she stepped into the cage. He took a moment to collect his wits and adjust his jeans, and then followed her in. She strode directly to the secretary desk. That would have been his destination, too.

The top drawer was too splintery to touch, and Morgan could see by peeking through the crack where the front panel had separated from the side that the drawer was empty. Hope pulled open the second drawer, releasing a cloud of dust. Then she opened the third, and the bottom.

Empty.

"Don't these kinds of desks have hidden compartments?" he asked.

This time when she smiled, it was for him. He saw gratitude in her smile, appreciation that he wasn't ridiculing her or calling her crazy or anything else, but was at least pretending he believed as firmly as she did that there was a will and a ghost. And maybe, at that moment, still caught in the spell of her kiss, he did.

She tugged at the hinged desk surface, and it moved. Morgan hurried to the other side of the secretary so they could lower the desk together, slowly so as not to damage it. Inside were a row of cubbies and several tiny drawers. They poked into all the cubbies and opened all the drawers.

Empty.

Morgan was bummed out. Of course there wasn't a will, of course he'd never really believed . . . And yet he'd had hope. Or Hope had had him. One way or the other, he'd wanted her to find what she was so desperately searching for.

She traced an ornamental wooden slat beneath one of the cubbies with her fingers. It seemed to be broken, because the carved scrollwork jiggled against her thumb. She pulled at it, and it slid out.

Her hidden compartment.

With an old, yellowed envelope inside.

Hope's breath caught. Morgan was afraid she'd really faint this time—or else maybe he gathered her in his arms simply because he had to hold her. He had to feel her, to make sure she was all right—to make sure *he* was all right.

She leaned into the curve of his arm, and he rubbed her shoulder gently. Her fingers trembled as she lifted the envelope's flap and pulled out the aged sheets of paper inside. Across the top of the first page, in a spidery fountain pen scrawl, was written, "The Last Will and Testament of Hope Elizabeth Blodgett."

11

FIVE DAYS HAD PASSED since Hope left. Five long, dreary, draining days.

He couldn't blame her for lying low. He, too, would have liked to escape from the media orgy brought on by her discovery of Hope Blodgett's missing will.

All it had taken was one phone call from Barry's associate, Arlene, to Catalina Fidelity, challenging the holding company's ownership of Bachelor Arms. In a fraction of a second, it seemed, reporters from all over southern California suddenly appeared at the grand pink mansion on Wilshire Boulevard, snaking cables across the front walk, shoving microphones into people's faces, rehashing ad nauseam the house's glamorous past—the three randy movie star bachelors who'd lived there in the thirties, the wild parties they'd hosted, the starlet who had drowned mysteriously in the swimming pool, the legend of the ghost in the mirror. It got so a guy couldn't even stroll next door to Flynn's for a beer without running a gauntlet of tabloid TV journalists shouting, "Did you ever see the ghost? Do you believe the legend? Is it true the house's real owner is a sales clerk in a souvenir shop?"

Most of Morgan's neighbors did their best to avoid the reporters, except for Ted Smith, who swore he'd seen the ghost dozens of times, thanks to which his greatest hope—to be universally admired by women—had come true. As far as Morgan knew, none of the reporters had come up with the scoop that Hope was a direct descendent of the alleged ghost. Clint McCreary—the one who had made the connection between the ghost and the woman who so resembled her—refused to speak to the reporters.

So did Morgan.

But it wasn't easy for Hope to hide. She, after all, had precipitated everything by claiming she owned the storied mansion. And when the reporters swooped down upon her like locusts, she ran.

He didn't blame her—but God, he missed her.

He had no idea where she was. She hadn't gone back to her efficiency apartment near the university. No doubt a battalion of reporters was camping out there, too. And when she'd left, she told him she herself didn't know where she was going.

"Arlene will take me someplace safe," she said.

Morgan wanted to argue that if anyone was going to take her anywhere, he ought to be the one. Yet he had no right to insist. Who was he, anyway? Just a guy who'd run her down with his car and was prepared to sacrifice his sanity to make it up to her.

"Will you let me know where you are once you get there?" he asked, deliberately erasing the plea from his voice. He wasn't going to beg. If she wanted to get away—from him as well as the reporters—that was her right.

"I don't know what's going on," she said vaguely, then lowered her eyes to her bags, packed and standing neatly by his door. "Once I figure things out, I'll try to get in touch."

She'd kissed him, a long, tremulous, sorrowful kiss that felt a lot like goodbye to him—and left the apartment. Morgan should have accompanied her downstairs to the entry, where Arlene was waiting for her, but he couldn't stand the thought of watching her walk out of his life.

He had spoken with Arlene a couple of times since, and Arlene had told him that it was best all around if Hope's whereabouts remained a secret for the time being. Morgan had pressed Barry, who'd scoffed and said, "You're better off with her gone, Morgan. At least this way she won't be suing you."

So he was alone, lonely, desolate. He vented his frustration by working with brutal intensity. It was easier to work all night than to retire to his bed—a bed where nothing had quite happened but so much had happened. His pillows still held her scent. The mattress stretched like a desert, too wide for him to sleep in alone.

He worked all day, too. He remained holed up in his apartment, screening calls on his answering machine in the gradually diminishing hope that one of the calls might be from her. Most were from the tabloid journalists, or from producers of TV shows about UFOs and the Bermuda Triangle, wanting to film a special on the ghost. He ignored them and kept on drawing.

Since Hope had vanished, he'd completed enough drawings for two entire books, written five plots for animated shows, and blocked out storyboards for three of the shows. Francine made daily pilgrimages to his apartment to pick up the results of his creative output, but even so, his floor was carpeted with drawings and his computer ran nonstop. He drank gallons of coffee, gorged on oranges and dry cereal, and worked. And waited for a call that never came.

How had he reached this point? Why couldn't he go back to dreaming his millionaire dreams and looking for the perfect 36-D blonde?

The clock next to his computer told him it was eight-thirty. The sun had set, leaving behind a fading residue of salmon-orange light. He stared at the drawing spread across his drafting table and frowned, wondering where all his recent creative energy had come from. Every drawing he'd done this week was great. Brilliant. Inspired. In the picture he'd just completed, Mongo looked almost alive. His eyes seemed to gaze from the paper, wistful and bemused, and his hand gripped his wand with an uncanny fervor.

Morgan decided not to analyze the symbolism of that.

His phone started to ring. He scratched his chin, listening to the sandpapery sound of his thumbnail against the stubble of beard that had sprouted since he'd last shaved, which was either yesterday morning or the day before—he'd lost track. The phone rang a second time, and then the machine clicked on.

"Morgan? It's Natasha. For pity's sake, answer your phone."

One disobeyed Natasha Kuryan at one's own peril. He lifted the receiver and said, "Hi, Natasha."

"Why haven't you been taking your calls?"

"Where's the law that says I've got to answer the phone every time it rings? I've been working."

"Have you been eating?"

He eyed the open box of Cheerios on the counter next to his computer. "Yeah, I've been eating."

"Well. You are to attend a party tonight."

A party. The absolute last thing he needed. "What party? It better not be hosted by any reporters."

"It's being hosted by Clint McCreary and Jessie Gale downstairs in 1-G, and no reporters have been invited. Clint and Jessie are celebrating their official engagement. They've set their wedding date for Valentine's Day, and they want to share their happiness with their friends."

Swell. One thing Morgan wasn't in the mood for was sharing someone else's happiness.

"I ran into Clint at the mail table a short while ago, and he said he'd left several messages on your machine, but he doesn't know if you received them. He would very much like for you to come."

Morgan groaned under his breath. He couldn't see a way out of it, not without alienating too many friends. "An engagement party, huh," he muttered. "Am I supposed to bring a present?"

"No presents. Jessie is accepting contributions for the shelter she operates for runaway teenagers, if you feel you must give something."

"Okay. I'll show my face. When do the festivities start?"

"They've already started. I'm on my way downstairs now. Do come, Morgan. I think it would be good for you."

"Okay, okay. I'll be there." He said goodbye, hung up, and cut loose with some exceedingly ripe language. Without Hope, he didn't feel like doing anything good for himself.

Without Hope. He was truly hopeless, in every sense of the word.

All right. He'd do the decent thing and attend the party. First, however, he'd have to make himself presentable.

Shoving away from the drafting table, he trudged out of the spare bedroom. He showered and washed his hair, trying to convince himself that socializing with people would be beneficial for him, that this wouldn't be the night Hope finally called—or that if she did call and connected with his machine, she would leave her number so he could call her back.

Who knew? Maybe his dream lover was at Clint and Jessie's party right now, and when he joined the party he would see her and instantaneously forget about Hope. Because the sorry truth was, if she hadn't contacted him by now, she wasn't going to. The next time he heard from her, it was probably going to be a "Dear tenant" form letter, evicting him so the building could be converted into high-priced condos.

He could afford a condo. In fact, once the money started pouring in from his Mongo the Magnificent cartoons, he could in all likelihood afford the whole damned house. He could buy her out, send her back to Kansas, and . . .

Spend the rest of his life haunted by her.

Jeez. He was in bad shape. He really did need to get out.

Emerging from the shower, he shaved, blow-dried his hair, and searched his closet for a fresh shirt and a pair of khakis. On his way out, he detoured back to the spare bedroom, located his checkbook beside a stack of bills and wrote a check for a hundred dollars for Jessie's shelter. Then he pocketed his keys and headed downstairs.

The party was going strong when he arrived. He recognized about half the guests—his neighbors, mostly. The other people crowding the cozy first-floor living room were no doubt professional colleagues of Clint's and Jessie's. The room was lit with candles and lamps set on low, and bluesy saxophone music wafted through the air. Potted poinsettias decorated the tabletops and a punch bowl of eggnog stood on the dining table, which was covered with a Christmassy red and green cloth. A sprig of mistletoe hung in the doorway between the kitchen and the dining area. Morgan noticed Ted Smith hanging around near the mistletoe like a spider in its web, waiting to snare a victim.

Natasha swept gracefully through the throng, a striking figure in a scarlet dress with a green scarf slung around her shoulders and a barrette shaped like a wreath holding her silver hair in an elaborate pile on top of her head. "Morgan. I'm so glad you came," she greeted him, as if she herself were the host.

"Where's the couple of the hour?" Morgan asked, trying not to sound glum.

Natasha gestured toward the mirror, near which Clint and Jessie stood, looking utterly smitten with each other as they conversed with their guests.

Morgan decided coming here had been a good idea, after all. Seeing two such perfectly matched lovers forced him to recognize how poorly matched he and Hope were. Clint and Jessie hadn't met through a near-fatal accident, had they? They hadn't tried to build a relationship on a foundation as absurd as the possible existence of a ghost, had they?

Actually, Morgan didn't know how they'd met or what they'd built their relationship on. It didn't matter, though. They were together. Morgan and Hope weren't, and they would never be.

"I guess I should go congratulate them," he murmured, patting Natasha on the shoulder and then working his way across the room.

As he neared Clint and Jessie, they spotted him, smiled and waved him over. "You made it!" Clint said, shaking Morgan's hand.

Morgan forced a smile and gave Jessie a peck on the cheek. "Way to go, guys," he said with as much spirit as he could muster. "Valentine's Day, huh. Pretty romantic."

"You think so?" Jessie asked, then tossed back her head and laughed. "My new project in life is turning Clint from a cynic into a romantic."

"You've succeeded beyond your wildest dreams," Clint complained, though he too was grinning. "You've succeeded beyond my wildest nightmares." His smile faded slightly. "Any word from Hope yet?"

Morgan shook his head. "Nothing."

"Has she been in touch with anyone?"

"An associate of my lawyer. Nobody will tell me where she is. I guess she doesn't want me to know."

Clint seemed about to say something, then thought better of it. Morgan silently thanked him. One thing he didn't want was sympathy.

"So," he said, handing Jessie the check, "here's an engagement present of sorts. Maybe it'll feed a few kids."

"More than a few," she said, then rose on tiptoe and returned Morgan's cheek kiss. "This is very generous, Morgan. Thank you."

"Yeah, whatever." He didn't want gratitude, either. He was too raw to accommodate other people's sentiments. Everyone was so warm, so full of love and holiday cheer. And none of the guests looked like his dream lover. He already knew what his dream lover looked like, and she wasn't present.

Bobbie-Sue and Brenda were approaching Clint and Jessie, and Morgan discreetly got out of their way so they could fuss over the lovebirds. The atmospheric lighting of the room, the clove scent of the candles, the muted wail of the sax... It was getting to him, big. He had to clear out before someone noticed what a foul mood he was in.

Turning away from Clint and Jessie, he hesitated. Something was glimmering in the mirror. The reflection of a few flickering candles, he realized. And yet...

The mirror grew hazy with smoke, not the waxy, fragrant smoke of the candles but a pale, silver-white smoke. And then he saw his dream lover.

No, it couldn't be. Hope wasn't there.

He glanced around, just in case a woman who looked like Hope happened to be behind him, her reflection caught in the glass.

Two men were standing where Hope should have been. They were fawning all over a blond, buxom woman who didn't attract Morgan in the least. He spun back to the mirror.

It *was* Hope. Not his Hope, the other one. The ghost.

She had to leave you, the ghost said.

"What?" he exclaimed, then clapped his hand over his mouth, mortified that anyone should see him talking to a mirror. Another quick glance behind him. No one seemed to have heard him. The revelers around him remained engrossed in discussions, sipping eggnog and nibbling on snacks, ignoring him and the misty vision in the mirror.

She had to leave you to protect her heart, the figure said. She was dressed in a flowing white robe, her hair a black cloak around her pale, narrow face. *She had to go so you wouldn't hurt her. You have the power to hurt her terribly.*

"Yeah, I know. I hit her with my car," he agreed, then looked around again. He was positive he was speaking out loud, but no one acknowledged that he'd said a word. His voice rang loud and clear inside him, and obviously the figure in the mirror heard him, too, because when he mentioned his car she nodded.

But no one else heard him. No one but the ghost. He might have been invisible, for all anyone noticed. Maybe he *was* invisible. His image didn't appear in the glass.

Only the woman who looked shockingly like Hope.

A shiver ran down his back.

You can break her heart, the ghost was saying. *My darling child has to protect herself. Men take a woman's body and then leave her.*

"Hey, now wait a minute! Don't go blaming me for what some creep did to you," he argued, refusing to think about this odd, soundless conversation, refusing to consider the implications that he was communicating with the infamous ghost of Bachelor Arms. He'd lived in the building for years and never once let himself believe any of the goofy myths about the place.

But here he was, making chitchat with the lady in the mirror. No, not chitchat—the ghost was accusing him of things he'd never done. And he resented the hell out of it.

She came to me, the ghost said. *My beloved daughter came back to me—*

"She's not your daughter," he snapped, still astonished that he could hear himself while the rest of the people in the room were deaf to him. "She's your great-granddaughter."

She came back to me. My greatest hope came true—my offspring returned to me. And now my greatest fear may come true. You may break her heart. You may destroy her.

"Come on! I want her back, too. I'm crazy about her! Those idiot reporters scared her off, and—"

You want her, but you do not speak of love. Like the man who destroyed me. He was an artist, too. He was hired to paint my portrait, and by the time he was done I had fallen in love with him. He stole my heart and my soul, and left me with child. Yet he never loved me. I lost him. I lost our baby. I lost everything worth living for, and I died here, mad with grief.

"But . . . but what does that have to do with Hope and me?" Morgan erupted. The room seemed to have grown darker, the voices around him blending into an indistinct hum. All the light in the room gathered in the mirror, in the potent, all-seeing eyes of the ghost, the Hope from another time, another world.

You do not speak of love, she accused. *You only want, you only long to take. If she gives you what you want, you will destroy her.*

"If I were as much of a louse as you seem to think I am, I wouldn't have held back when we were at her apartment. I wouldn't have stopped."

The specter in the mirror looked troubled. It dawned on Morgan that she hadn't known about the time he and Hope had done everything but the ultimate. *Did you leave her with child?*

Oh, for God's sake. "It would have been a miracle if I had."

The ghost let out a silent cry. *You have left her with child. She has gone to Monterey to have the child, as I did. She has gone in shame, and she will return broken and bereft. You have done this to her.*

Monterey?

His head steamed with the smoke from the mirror, from the candles and the haze of rapidly spinning thoughts. Monterey. The ghost had gone to Monterey when she'd been in trouble. Maybe Hope had gone there, too.

She was in Monterey. He was going to find her, and tell her...

He was already in his car, heading north up Route 101, before he had a chance to consider the sanity of what he was doing. He'd just had a dialogue with either a figment of his imagination or a creature from the afterlife, and said figment-creature had accused him of having knocked Hope up and broken her heart, and then implied that she'd fled to Monterey.

What was he thinking of, taking such crap seriously?

Traffic was heavy on the freeway. The sun had set hours ago, but people in L.A. liked to party half the night. For Morgan to be setting off on a three hundred fifty mile trip at nine-thirty made as much sense as...

As talking to a ghost in a mirror without saying a word.

But he kept driving, because he needed to see Hope. As wrong as the ghost in the mirror might be on some issues, she was right on one: Morgan had never mentioned the word love to Hope.

He hadn't even thought about love.

Yes, he had. Not consciously, not knowingly, but...yes. He loved Hope Henley. It didn't matter that she was crazy; he would match his craziness against hers any time. He had definitely lost his mind, and he didn't care.

All he cared about was driving to Monterey and finding her.

"You've seen the ghost, chump," he murmured to himself, relieved to hear his voice. "And what that means, old boy, is either your greatest hope or your greatest fear will come true."

His greatest hope was Hope herself, finding her, loving her.

His greatest fear was that he would drive all night long, all the way up the coast to Monterey, only to discover that she wasn't there—that wherever she was, he would never find her.

The second option seemed a whole lot more likely.

He kept going, anyway. As the dashboard clock ticked deeper and deeper into the night, and the mauve glow of Los Angeles after hours gave way to the gloom of the thinning communities north of the city, as the temperature dipped and the air vibrated with the silence of a world drifting off to sleep, Morgan kept going.

A GOSSAMER LIGHT was filtering through the fog as, seven hours later, he steered his car slowly past the state beach in the curve of the Monterey peninsula. He was beyond tired, beyond hungry. He had no idea why he hadn't nodded off behind the wheel hours ago, and driven into a ditch.

He hadn't. Fueled by adrenaline, by panic, by the same manic energy that had powered him through five phenomenally prolific days at his drafting table, he had driven through the cool, slumbering valleys and craggy hills on the inland side of the coastal range, choosing it over the more scenic coastal route because it was quicker and at that hour he wouldn't have seen much scenery, anyway. Besides, if he'd taken the twisting, twining two-lane road carved out of the steep palisades overhanging the ocean, he surely would have driven off the road—only not into a ditch, but into the drink.

Morgan squinted at the dashboard clock—five-forty-five—and then at his gas gauge, which showed him with more than half a tank. He'd filled up at an open-all-night rest stop just outside San Luis Obispo. He'd also filled his own personal tank with coffee. An empty jumbo-size foam cup rolled back and forth on the floor beneath the passenger seat.

Downtown Monterey obviously wasn't open all night. The quaint shops and tourist emporiums stood dark. Even the obligatory gourmet coffee boutique was shuttered.

What was he going to do? He had just driven hundreds of miles in the dead of night because of something a ghost had told him. If Hope Henley was in the vicinity, he had no way of locating her, short of knocking on doors and asking if anyone had seen a petite, black-haired woman with a slight bruise on her right cheek.

He sighed. He cursed. He veered off the main drag, cruising toward the outskirts of town. The road narrowed, inclining into the hills surrounding the bay. Dense redwood forests blocked out what little dawn light there was, and the fog hugged the pavement, blurring the beams of his headlights.

It wasn't the likeliest locale for a motel. But he had to find a bed, even though he doubted he'd be able to sleep if he did stumble upon a resting place. He was too keyed up, too hyper. Too crazy.

A car passed him in the other direction—the first sign of life, other than the sea gulls gliding in loops and figure eights above the beach, that he'd seen since he'd reached Monterey. The towering trees looked spooky, dressed in veils of gray mist.

He saw another sign of life—a jogger way up ahead on the road. Mid-December, before the crack of dawn, and sure enough some exercise freak had to be honing his cardiovascular system at this hour. It only proved that someone in the area was even loonier than Morgan.

He slowed as he neared the jogger, and then realized the person was walking, not jogging. He was dressed in white and carried a flashlight, neither of which did much to improve his visibility in the haze.

Closer yet, Morgan realized the walker was a woman. A woman in white slacks and a white sweater, with a face as pale as the morning light and hair as dark as a moonless sky. Morgan was so shocked he hit the brake. The car started skidding just as the woman turned to look at him. He thought of the proverbial doe caught in the headlights. He thought of the evening when he'd first seen her and nearly killed her. He thought of the horrific thud when he'd struck her, and he thought of the way he'd screamed.

Oh God, it was happening again. This time he *was* going to kill her. He couldn't be lucky twice.

Fighting for traction on the slick road, he heard the tires whine, heard his heart thump, heard every prayer he'd ever known slip past his lips in a jumble of desperate pleading.

The skid seemed to go on forever, but actually it lasted only a few seconds. The car rolled to a stop and he became aware of the stillness. The only sound was his pounding heart.

And then another pounding, a fist banging on glass. Slowly, cautiously, he opened his eyes and saw Hope through his side window. Alive. Shocked, angry, but very, very alive.

He rolled down the window. "What on earth are you doing here, Morgan?" she shrieked. "How did you get here? Why did you come? Why—"

"I love you," he said.

SHE GAPED AT HIM. Her pulse had been racing from the acute fear of reliving her ghastly accident, but now it was racing because she was facing another real danger, one that threatened not her life but her soul.

How could he love her? How had he found her? How could he have driven all this way to play games with her emotions?

She couldn't stand it. She was already too overwrought, trying to piece her life back together, trying to convince herself that she didn't—couldn't—mustn't love Morgan.

But he was here, undermining her best efforts.

"The ghost told me," he answered her unvoiced question.

She gripped the chrome door handle and took a steadying breath. Surely she'd heard him incorrectly. "*My* ghost?"

He chuckled, though his eyes were deadly serious. "Don't tell me there's more than one ghost. I saw the one in the mirror who looks like you. Your great-grandmother, or whatever. We—well, I can't rightly say we talked. I guess we kind of . . . *communed.* She hinted that I might find you here." Puzzled, he angled his head slightly. "What were you doing, taking a walk this early?"

"I couldn't sleep." In truth, she hadn't gotten a solid night's sleep since she'd found Hope Blodgett's will. Or maybe since she'd left Morgan.

"I couldn't sleep, either. Walking wouldn't have gotten me this far, though, so I drove."

"Morgan." Either he was making fun of her, or he'd somehow wheedled her location from Barry Loomis's law office and chased her up here for some nefarious purpose.

To get her into bed, no doubt. Why else would he appear out of the fog at daybreak and practically run her over? He'd gone to an awful lot of effort to get her into bed—and given her relative lack of experience, he would probably find her disappointing, anyway. But—

"This great-grandmother ghost of yours told me her lover was an artist like me," he went on. "He knocked her up and broke her heart, and she came to Monterey. I just thought—hell, if she went to Monterey, maybe you went to Monterey, too. So I came."

"Why?" she asked, unable to swallow the quaver in her voice.

"Because . . . because if I could see the ghost, I must be as crazy as you are. I don't know . . . It seems to me we might as well be crazy together."

"And do what? Open our own asylum?"

"Find asylum with each other?" he suggested. "I'm not going to break your heart like that man broke hers, Hope. I came here to swear to you that I'll never break your heart."

Heaven help her, she believed him. It was as reckless as running in front of a car, and yet . . .

Morgan had brought her to the edge of death, and then brought her back to life. He had laughed at her, but he had also trusted her. He had listened to her, talked to her, opened himself to her. And he had driven through hundreds of miles of darkness to arrive at the very place where she was. Just to tell her he wouldn't break her heart.

Of all the chances she had ever taken—believing her grandmother's bizarre stories, earning a business degree, quitting her job to nurse Gramma through her final months, moving halfway across the country to a strange city just to fulfill a deathbed promise—none was as great as getting into the car with Morgan right now, placing her faith in him, accepting his profession of love.

She got into the car.

"You'll have to make a U-turn," she told him, and then fell silent.

He looked drained, yet oddly energized. His eyes were the color of glowing embers. His outfit—khakis and a tailored shirt—was rumpled. His large hands ruled the steering wheel. His mouth cut a straight line above his rugged jaw. If he truly meant what he'd just said, well, he didn't exactly seem overjoyed about it.

Sighing, she watched the gauzy mist dance and scatter before his headlights. It held the scent of the woods and the scent of the sea. She'd been in this town for five days, aching to understand it, to feel some connection to it. It was the city where Hope Blodgett had come to give birth to Hope's grandmother. If there had been a home for wayward girls in town, or a midwife who specialized in delivering the babies of unwed mothers, Hope had found nothing in the town archives at the public library to enlighten her.

Still, Monterey offered her shelter from the brouhaha in Los Angeles. She'd left Arlene to negotiate with Catalina Fidelity over the value of Bachelor Arms. Every afternoon Arlene telephoned Hope with an update on the negotiations. Arlene's favorite word, when describing her discussions with the holding company, was "acrimonious." There were rancorous debates over the value of the house as a residence and as an income-producing property, disputes about how much the house had appreciated over the past sixty-odd years, charges and countercharges about whether there was a legal way to compensate Hope for her grandmother's loss of her estate.

Just a few weeks ago, such arcane financial issues would have fascinated Hope. Now, she didn't care. All she wanted was to feel she'd found her home, her history, her heritage.

She hadn't felt it until the moment she'd seen Morgan seated behind the wheel of his familiar red Escort, his eyes fierce and his chin defiant as he said, "I love you."

His silence now emphasized the words he'd spoken just minutes ago. She didn't dare to talk; she had no idea what to say. Instead, she indicated with a wave of her hand that he should turn right, and then left and down the winding road to the Victorian bed-and-breakfast where she'd found lodging five days ago.

He turned into the driveway, then eyed the gingerbread-trimmed clapboard house, with its broad veranda and its steep roof. "Is this where Hope Blodgett had her baby?" he asked.

"I don't know. I doubt it. It doesn't matter." The words spilled out in a nervous rush.

Morgan shut off the engine and turned to her. He must have sensed her anxiety, but he clearly didn't share it. As sure as his hands had been on the wheel, that was how sure he seemed of himself as he gazed at her, as he stroked her cheek with his fingertips and then cupped his palm under her chin, guiding her lips to his.

His kiss was slow, languorous, thorough. He wouldn't break from her until he had molded her mouth to his, until his lips and tongue had relearned hers, imprinted hers, conquered hers. Only when her breath was shallow, her eyes closed, her entire body seething in the aftermath of this one kiss did he draw back.

He climbed out of the car, helped her out and raced with her up the sloping lawn to the porch and inside. From the kitchen at the rear of the house came the sounds of dishes being stacked. But Hope wasn't interested in breakfast, not even a cup of coffee.

Morgan loved her. He had made his pledge, such as it was. He might still break her heart, but the ghost wasn't around to warn her, and Hope had no choice but to love him.

The room she'd rented was located on the second floor, overlooking a small pond and a dormant garden at the side of the house. The lace curtains let in pinpricks of dawn light that dotted the braided rugs and polished plank floors, the canopied bed and the solid maple chest of drawers. It was a charming room, but Hope had barely been able to tolerate it until this very instant. Now that Morgan was with her, it was the most beautiful room in the universe.

He followed her in, kicked the door shut and reached for her. And then they were kissing again, clinging to each other, moving in tandem toward the bed. Halfway there he had her sweater off. Two more steps and she'd succeeded in popping open the buttons of his shirt. Another step and she fell back against the mattress. Morgan descended into her arms.

The skin of his back was satin smooth against her palms. His shoulders were solid, his neck warm beneath his long, tawny hair. His mouth seduced her, coaxing and nibbling, roaming across her cheeks, her brow, the underside of her chin, her throat. She felt his breath, hot and damp, through the thin cups of her bra, and her breasts burned in anticipation of his touch.

The only sound in the room was the rustle of bed linens under their writhing bodies, and Morgan's sharp gasp as she slid her hands down along his spine to his hips, and her own faint sigh as he dispensed with her bra and closed his mouth tight around one nipple, sucking the hard bud until it was tingling and tender, and then moving his attention to the other breast and subjecting it to the same glorious torment. And her low moan as he worked free the button at the waistband of her slacks, slid down the zipper and stripped her naked. And his ragged groan as she undid the fly of his jeans and stroked him through his shorts.

He tore off what remained of his clothes, then lifted her higher on the mattress so her head nestled against the pillows. He remained above her, gazing down at her, his eyes burning through her with a turbulent mix of emotions, lust and need and—God, please make her be right about this—love. Love for her. A love deep enough to save her from the anguish her great-grandmother had known when her lover had betrayed her.

Still he said nothing. He brought his mouth to hers again, lowering himself slowly onto her, letting his chest rub against her breasts, letting his aroused flesh tease between her legs. His yearning ignited a matching yearning inside her, a low, throbbing heat that insinuated itself through her body, threatening to consume her.

He skimmed one hand down to touch her, to fuel the fire, stoke it, build it until she was caught within the sweetest pain, a pain that could be eased only one way, by one man. She opened to him and he took her, as slowly and deeply as he'd kissed her in the car, when she'd chosen to place her faith in him. This was not a wild, athletic coupling. It was something permanent, a fusion of not just bodies but hearts and minds and spirits.

He held his breath and then let it out, exerting control, holding himself still inside her until her body accepted him, shaped itself to him. Then he moved, and she felt the fire sear her, the flames growing hotter and brighter. He thrust again and she cried out, wanting more now, wanting him harder and faster until the blaze burned her soul to ashes. He thrust again and she arched to him, again and she clutched him, wanting him to stay merged with her, wanting him to become a part of her.

He brushed her lips with his as his body surged once more. The explosion came, her flesh convulsing in its radiant heat. He wrenched above her and she knew he was burning with her. His tremors echoed hers; his breath, his pulse, his ecstasy mirrored hers as she absorbed everything he could give her, everything.

Closing her eyes, she let the receding spasms lull her until she was inches from sleep. Morgan settled heavily on top of her, his bony frame digging into her soft flesh here and there, his hair tickling her nose. She had never felt so good in her life. She had never felt so . . . complete.

More than complete.

Everything happened in cycles. The name. The house. The artist lover. Her greatest hope—that Morgan would love her. Her greatest fear—that she would lose it all, as her namesake ancestor had. The other Hope, the first one, had lost her man, her pride and ultimately her life. She'd lost her baby.

No, Hope promised herself, her eyes widening as comprehension dawned. The cycle would be broken. Hope would *not* lose her baby. *She would not.*

"WE DIDN'T USE anything," he murmured.

"I know."

He let out a weary breath and rolled off her, leaving one hand to rest gently against her abdomen. Her heart drummed against her ribs as she waited for him to say something, something awful, something that would break her heart as completely as leaving her would.

After a timeless minute, he smiled. "So we'll get married."

"No." She wasn't going to let him marry her out of some empty chivalrous impulse. She appreciated his willingness to mouth the right words—but that was all they were. Words.

He had said he loved her only because the ghost had told him to, and his words had done the trick. He'd waved them over her like a magic wand—and he'd waved his magic wand, too, she thought with a wistful smile—and now good manners made him think he had to wave some more magic words around.

No, she would not marry him. Not when his love was such a tenuous thing. Not when they were both operating under the ghost's spell.

"I'm sure there's nothing to worry about," she fibbed. "I mean, the timing—"

"You're pregnant." He said it with such certainty she flinched.

"Of course not! I—"

"Hope. Don't you see?" He laughed, a soft, husky laugh of amazement. "You're like her. You share a name, you share a heritage, you both fall in love with an artist and get knocked up. Only I'm not the same man her artist was. I'll marry you."

"Don't do me any favors," she retorted.

"I was thinking it might be more of a favor to me," he argued, propping himself up on his elbow so he could gaze down at her. "I was thinking you and I belong together, and we love each other, and we're going to have a baby together. So I'd greatly appreciate it if you'd do me a favor and marry me."

"But..." She wanted to believe him so badly. She wanted to believe that somehow, even though the first Hope's legacy was now hers, she wouldn't have to relive the first Hope's sorrow. "But Morgan... We haven't known each other very long."

"We know each other very well," he countered. "We've taken a peek at mortality together, and we've each had our chats with the dead, and we're both very much alive. And I'll stake my Mongo the Magnificent contract against your Wilshire Boulevard mansion that we've just made ourselves a whole new life." He lifted his hand from her belly and bent to kiss her there, sending his love into her womb. When he lifted his face, she saw the shimmer of tears in his eyes. "So, Hope Henley—are you going to marry me?"

"Yes." Too much of what had happened to her lately had no answers. But Morgan, his love, his question—there was an answer to that. One answer. One perfect, timeless, death-defying answer. "Yes, Morgan. I'll marry you."

THREE HUNDRED FIFTY MILES south of Monterey, in the massive pink mansion on Wilshire Boulevard, Clint McCreary and Jessie Gale were jolted awake by a resounding crash. Racing from their bedroom, they discovered that the mirror which had hung in the living room of apartment 1-G for as long as anyone could remember, had fallen from the wall and lay shattered across the floor in a million glints of silver light.

Epilogue

THE SMALL CLAPBOARD chapel on the town green in Bailey Notch, West Virginia was crammed with people, nearly all of them Delacourt kin. Morgan had tried to identify everyone for Hope, but she'd been unable to keep track of all the first cousins, second cousins, in-laws of in-laws, great-aunts and grand-uncles.

Maybe she couldn't remember their names, but she adored them all.

They were loud. They were rowdy. One of Morgan's ushers, a strapping fellow introduced to her as Wynn Ewell, warned Morgan that if he didn't polish his shoes before the ceremony, Morgan's nose might somehow wind up fractured. While Hope didn't want Morgan's nose fractured, she did want his shoes shined. Wynn Ewell's threat won him a few points in her book.

One of Morgan's brothers was the best man. His sister Louise served as Hope's matron of honor, and her husband offered to give the bride away. What little family Hope had was gone: her estranged mother, her beloved grandmother, the great-grandmother she'd known only as a ghost. But marrying Morgan meant being adopted by his sprawling, drawling family. And they seemed just thrilled to accept her as one of their own.

"There, now, don't you look pretty," Louise murmured, crowning Hope with a wreath of ivy, red roses and baby's breath. She and Hope scrutinized Hope's reflection in the mirror in the church's basement powder room. "Real pretty. Who woulda thought Morgan would bring home such a winner?"

"Did he used to date losers?" Hope asked with a smile.

"Doesn't matter who he used to date. What's past is past," Louise said wisely.

Hope scrutinized her image with a critical eye. She wore a simple white winter dress that fell to midcalf, black suede pumps and the necklace—a diamond solitaire on a rope of gold—that Morgan had given her for Christmas. Other than buying the dress, a new suit for him, and a set of matching gold bands, they'd put forth little effort in planning this wedding. All Morgan had done was to telephone his parents and inform them that he was getting married and intended to bring his lady to meet the clan at Christmas, and his mother had taken over. "Don't elope," she'd commanded. "We'll get you hitched right here in town. How about New Year's Eve? That way you'll never forget your anniversary like your daddy always does."

Hope had assured Morgan that he would never forget their anniversary date—she'd kill him if he did—but she rather liked the idea of a family wedding. And since Morgan was the one with the family, she got on the phone with his mother and told her she'd love to get married in Bailey Notch on New Year's Eve.

"I think they're ready upstairs," Louise declared, handing Hope her bouquet of roses and steering her out of the powder room. The men's room door swung open, and Morgan emerged in his stylish charcoal gray suit, a red rose pinned to his lapel and his eyes luminous with flecks of gold.

"Oh, drat!" Louise howled. "You all are not supposed to see each other before the wedding! It's bad luck!"

Laughing, Morgan sidled over to Hope and gave her a perilously seductive kiss. "We've run through every kind of luck there is, Louise, and it only keeps coming out good." He grazed Hope's forehead with his lips. "How're you doing, darlin'?"

She gazed up into his beautiful eyes. "I'm fine."

"Feeling queasy?"

She grinned, aware that he was referring to more than just prenuptial jitters. "I've never felt better in my life."

"I've got a present for you."

"Honest to God," his sister groaned. "Morgan, I swear—"

"Get lost, would you?" he suggested, his smile tempering the rude words. "I need a minute alone with the woman I love."

"You're gonna have the rest of your life with her," Louise reminded him.

"And the rest of my life is starting right now. Scram, sister."

Grumbling melodramatically, Louise hiked up her long skirt and marched down the hall to the stairs.

Morgan enveloped Hope in his arms and gave her a steamy, nerve-rattling kiss. "Maybe we should just skip the wedding and get on with the honeymoon," she whispered hoarsely when he finally released her.

"And disappoint all those Delacourts upstairs? Forget it." He reached into a pocket of his jacket and pulled out a small, flat rectangle wrapped in white tissue paper. "Here, Hope. Open it."

She tore at the wrapping and pulled out a narrow box. Lifting the lid, she found a pocket mirror mounted on an intricate silver frame, a perfectly rendered version of the mirror that had once hung in apartment 1-G.

When Morgan and Hope had returned from Monterey, they had been greeted with Clint's apologetic report that, somehow, mysteriously, the mirror had fallen off the wall and shattered. "It was a terrible mess," he'd told them. "Ken Amberson, Jessie and I managed to vacuum up the splinters. There was nothing to save."

"That's all right," Hope had assured him. "It was meant to be."

"I'll bet you're going to want to evict me," he'd muttered. "Not that I'd blame you. At the very least, let me pay for it. Breaking a mirror—even if it *was* ugly—"

"Don't worry about it," Hope had assured him. "The ghost doesn't need it anymore. She's made her peace with the world. And I'm not evicting anyone for a long time. Especially you, Clint. You can live here as long as you want." If it hadn't been for Clint, after all, Hope would never have seen the mirror. She would never have confronted the ghost. She would never have run in front of Morgan's car.

She would never have been reborn.

Staring into the miniature mirror Morgan had given her, she let out a delighted laugh.

"Do you like it?"

"I love it! Look..." She held it higher, so that both their faces were captured in its small silver glass. "It's exactly like the one the ghost used to live in."

Morgan shook his head. "No, it's not. That mirror held the past. This one holds the future."

He was right. This mirror held Morgan and Hope, their smiles, their dreams, the joy of two people deeply in love. Like the last mirror, this one held magic. And like Mongo the Magnificent, Hope and Morgan hadn't known what the magic would create.

They knew now. They had seen the ghost, and as the legend promised, their greatest hope had come true.

From above, Hope heard the sonorous strains of the organ. Morgan kissed her one last time. "Let's get married," he whispered, then took her arm and escorted her up the stairs to the chapel.

MILLION DOLLAR SWEEPSTAKES (III)

No purchase necessary. To enter, follow the directions published. Method of entry may vary. For eligibility, entries must be received no later than March 31, 1996. No liability is assumed for printing errors, lost, late or misdirected entries. Odds of winning are determined by the number of eligible entries distributed and received. Prizewinners will be determined no later than June 30, 1996.

Sweepstakes open to residents of the U.S. (except Puerto Rico), Canada, Europe and Taiwan who are 18 years of age or older. All applicable laws and regulations apply. Sweepstakes offer void wherever prohibited by law. Values of all prizes are in U.S. currency. This sweepstakes is presented by Torstar Corp., its subsidiaries and affiliates, in conjunction with book, merchandise and/or product offerings. For a copy of the Official Rules send a self-addressed, stamped envelope (WA residents need not affix return postage) to: MILLION DOLLAR SWEEPSTAKES (III) Rules, P.O. Box 4573, Blair, NE 68009, USA.

EXTRA BONUS PRIZE DRAWING

No purchase necessary. The Extra Bonus Prize will be awarded in a random drawing to be conducted no later than 5/30/96 from among all entries received. To qualify, entries must be received by 3/31/96 and comply with published directions. Drawing open to residents of the U.S. (except Puerto Rico), Canada, Europe and Taiwan who are 18 years of age or older. All applicable laws and regulations apply; offer void wherever prohibited by law. Odds of winning are dependent upon number of eligibile entries received. Prize is valued in U.S. currency. The offer is presented by Torstar Corp., its subsidiaries and affiliates in conjunction with book, merchandise and/or product offering. For a copy of the Official Rules governing this sweepstakes, send a self-addressed, stamped envelope (WA residents need not affix return postage) to: Extra Bonus Prize Drawing Rules, P.O. Box 4590, Blair, NE 68009, USA.

SWP-H1295

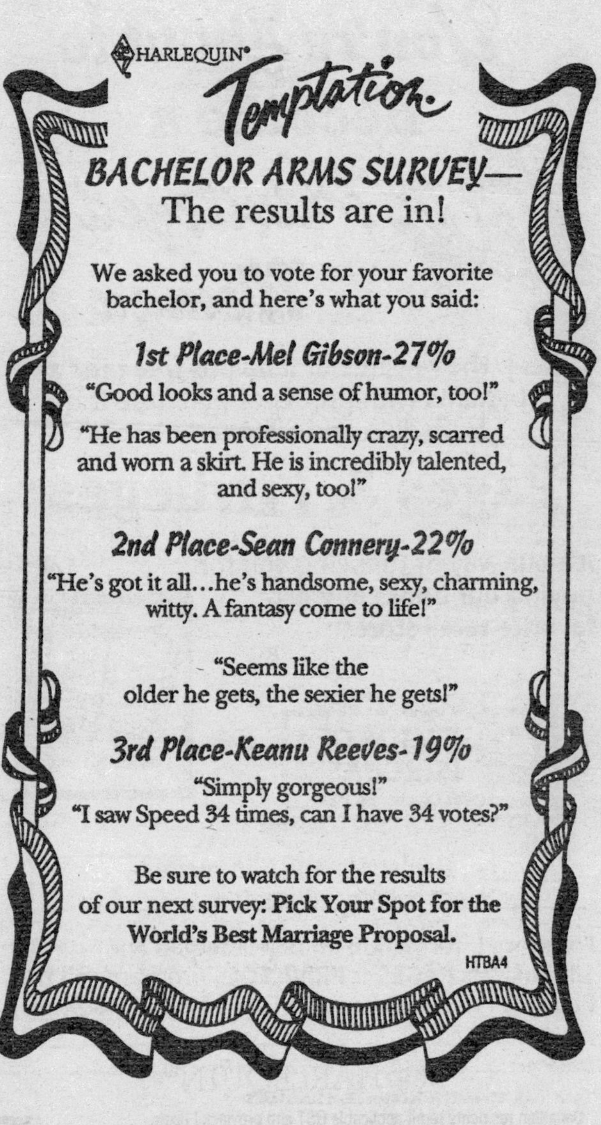
HARLEQUIN®
Temptation
BACHELOR ARMS SURVEY—
The results are in!
We asked you to vote for your favorite bachelor, and here's what you said:
1st Place-Mel Gibson-27%
"Good looks and a sense of humor, too!"
"He has been professionally crazy, scarred and worn a skirt. He is incredibly talented, and sexy, too!"
2nd Place-Sean Connery-22%
"He's got it all...he's handsome, sexy, charming, witty. A fantasy come to life!"
"Seems like the older he gets, the sexier he gets!"
3rd Place-Keanu Reeves-19%
"Simply gorgeous!"
"I saw Speed 34 times, can I have 34 votes?"
Be sure to watch for the results of our next survey: Pick Your Spot for the World's Best Marriage Proposal.
HTBA4